S.L. SCOTT

Paperback ISBN: 978-1-940071-40-4

Interior design: Angela McLaurin – Fictional Formats

Cover design: Kari March Designs

Front Cover Photographer: Samuel Ramirez

Cover Model: Charlie Matthews

Editing:
Marion Archer of Making Manuscripts
Marla Esposito of Proofing Style

To the love of my life who not only holds me each day,
but gives me the sun, moon, and stars each night.

You are and will always be my forever and a day.

A PERSONAL NOTE

We travel many journeys in our day-to-day lives. As a writer, each day offers a new adventure in real life and in the imaginary worlds that live inside our heads. I love doing what I do. I love daydreaming and then spinning those dreams into stories and sharing them. It's not an easy job, but it's a rewarding one.

Thank you for being a part of my dream come true.

There are amazing people who take this journey with me through their friendships and time, support, and kindness. Many work long hours to give feedback and some are there to listen when I need to talk.

Sending most heartfelt gratitude to the following for always believing in me and for being there when I needed you most: Adriana L., Amy B., Andrea J., Annette P., Cara A., Heather M., Jennifer S., Jessica H., Kellie R., Kerri Q., Kiersten H., Kirsten B., Laura E., Mary W., Ruth C., Serena M., Sonia D., The #Partywhores, and my awesome group – The Kiss & Tells/Sweet Talkers.

To my family, you are my heart and soul. I love you.
XOXOX

My editors are more than editors, they are friends and I adore them and their eagle eyes and amazing abilities. They are superheroes to me. Thank you, Marion and Marla.

Thank you to the uber talented Kari March Designs for the beautiful covers and to Angela of Fictional Formats for the amazing interior design. You both put the pretty in pretty awesome.

My sweet readers, you are everything to me. Thank you for reading my books and for your endless support. You amaze me and I'm so grateful for each and every one of you.

Dear Bloggers, I couldn't do this without you. You truly are amazing and inspire me every day. Thank you for your love and support.

Love,
Suzie

Jane Lewis

SQUEEZING THE STEERING wheel, I blow out the breath I was holding the last few seconds. My heart is racing almost as fast as my car.

This is it.

I'm ignoring my mind, flipping around my hurt feelings, and following my heart. Rolling my window down, I throw caution to the wind.

This feels right.

I've been apart from the other half of my heart for too long, and I'm going to reclaim him.

"I'm going to open your body, embrace your soul, and coax the moon and stars to shine inside."

Words whispered in my ear many years ago make my heart somersault in my chest. My long hair whips around my head, the wind heavy with anticipation as excitement builds deep within.

I park in front of the house he bought post-*us* and rush to the door. Knocking twice, I bounce on my heels waiting for him to answer while trying to peek in through the small side window to see if he's home. I hope he is. My feelings are about to burst free from excitement and I need to share them with him.

The connection we once had was derailed over misunderstandings and hurt feelings. Over the last year, wanting the life I had back, wanting him back, I've broken down and gone to see him. We haven't talked recently, but now is the time to come clean, to tell him how I feel, hoping he feels the same.

Luke Anders is my past, present, and soon to be future all wrapped in a sexy, hard body, and a lady-killer smile. I cannot wait to smother him with deep kisses and late-night snuggles, just like I used to do.

Lifting up, I peek in the window again and huff when I don't see any movement inside. I check the door and when the doorknob turns, I go in. "Luke?"

I get nothing in return, so I walk farther inside and call him again. "Luke?"

My happy bubble deflates as I try to figure out if I stay and wait or if I should go. The space draws me farther in, the calm of the environment, of Luke's life surrounding me, giving me peace. I smile, touching the bannister, running my fingers over the smooth railing.

"I know you."

I look up to find a bleach-blonde woman at the top of the stairs, holding the railing I was just touching like a barricade to the second floor. My heart suddenly feels heavy and blood rushes through my veins, loud in my ears. "I'm looking for Luke," I reply dumbly.

"He's upstairs." She points over her shoulder. "I can get him. He should be out of the shower by now."

The shirt... she's wearing *his* USC shirt. "Did you go to USC?"

"Huh?"

I point and she looks down and tugs on the hem that hits her upper thighs, and laughs. "Oh no. This is Luke's. I borrowed it."

My arm crosses over my stomach as I struggle to keep its contents down. I stare a moment longer before my eyes lower and I notice she has no pants on. Gulping down my hurt feelings, my disappointment, and replacing them with a false pride, I say, "Tell him I stopped by," then turn to leave.

"Jane?"

I freeze. After a deep breath, I turn just enough to look over my shoulder.

"He's happy."

Catching her drift, I ask, "Without me, you mean?"

She leans against the wall, his shirt sliding up her long legs as if she wants me to see just how model-esque she is compared to me. Her eyes stay fixed on me looking way too comfortable in his house. "With me."

My heart crashes and burns into the pit of my stomach and I lower my gaze. "I've changed my mind. You don't need to tell him I stopped by." I beeline for the door.

Just before it shuts, she says, "Tootle-loo," grinding the salt deeper into my open-heart wound.

Running to my car, I jump in and close the door fast, keeping the world and all its pain outside. I back out and when I'm driving away, I make sure not to look back.

My phone rings and I glance at the caller ID. It's not the person I want to hear from, but I answer it anyway, not wanting to feel so alone. "Hi."

"Please come home, Jane. I'm sorry I told people." Lawrence's voice fills the car as it comes out through the speakers.

"You lied to them. We're not engaged."

"You played along."

"I shouldn't have. I was put on the spot. You set me up to either play along or be embarrassed. I chose to play along to end it."

3

"I know you love me deep down."

"I care about you, Lawrence, but I'm not in love with you."

"Come home."

"It's not my home."

"It will be if you just give it a chance, if you give me a chance, a real chance this time."

My heart hurts as I enter the freeway. An hour later I'm sitting in front of Lawrence's house looking at the pink flowers he had planted for me.

I always wanted a white picket fence, a house full of kids, and an amazing husband I can't love enough. Two out of three isn't so bad.

Maybe I can be happy with Lawrence, happy like Luke is with that other woman. *"He's happy. With me."* Luke has moved on. He's really not mine anymore. *How could he move on without me? He promised me he'd love me forever.* He lied.

I'm not getting any younger and I want my dreams to come true. Lawrence... loves me. He says he'll give me everything I want and a comfortable life. *Comfortable.* Looks like that's all I will have now.

Luke is no longer mine. He's given his heart away and taken mine in the process.

Who needs a whole heart anyway?

CHAPTER 1

Luke Anders
Ten Months Later

"WHAT IF I touched you right where you want to be touched?" I slide my hand up her thigh, inching her skirt up slowly. Her breath catches, the quiet gasp making me smile. "What if I touched you right where you pretend to be so protective? I know you. I know you like it dirty... maybe even a little rough."

She finds her voice, though it's affected, sexy. "A lot."

"What is that?"

Clearing her throat, she says, "I like it rough. Really rough."

The right side of my mouth curves up, my hand stalling just below the apex of her thighs when my phone buzzes. I release a sigh. Grabbing the phone from my pocket, I sit up and read the text: ***Let's get the fuck out of here.*** I look back at the black-haired raven I've left squirming on the metal barstool next to me. *Pity.* I'd like to explore exactly how she likes it, but duty calls. Standing up suddenly, I grab my wallet and slap some bills down for the drinks.

"What are you doing?" she demands, desperation lacing her tone as her eyes go wide.

I tuck my wallet back into the inside pocket of my Vittori suit jacket and kiss her on the cheek. Since I'm there, I add with a wink, "I bet we'd be so fucking good together." Straightening upright, I smirk. "My apologies. I hate to run, but unfortunately, I have a prior engagement I can't get out of. Maybe we can pick this up another time. I'll see you around, sweetheart."

She huffs. "You're a playboy bastard, Luke Anders," rolls off her tongue in frustrated anger as she spins back to the bar.

I know. Not turning back, I nod. It's not the first time I've been called a playboy or a bastard. Name-calling doesn't bother me. Not getting laid tonight does.

Pushing open the exit door that leads to the alley, my asshole friends are waiting near the car they've pulled around.

The rusting red door slams shut, the click of the lock heard loudly behind me. The alley is quiet compared to the loud music that blares inside the club. "Fuckers." With my arms out wide, I yell, "What the fuck? Where's the fire? I was closing the deal."

"We were saving you, man. Trust me on that." My best friend is standing in front of the car with his arms crossed over his chest. Danny Weston is one of the best people I know, but right now, he's pissing me the fuck off.

"Saving me from what?"

"Ask Blaise. He has firsthand knowledge."

When I shoot an annoyed look in Blaise's direction, he clams up. With hands up in surrender, he backs away toward the driver's door. "I can't help that the ladies love me." Thus confirming he's already hit that pretty kitty.

I walk to the passenger's side of the car, punching Danny on the arm when I pass him. "Shit, man, just give me a heads-up next time. I wasted some of my best lines on her."

Danny claims the front seat, so I duck into the back seat of a restored 1969 black Gran Torino. Cocky behind the wheel, Blaise takes off before we even have our seatbelts on, and says, "Stop hitting on everyone that takes pity on you then."

"Fuck you. I can get any woman I want. No one's taking pity on me."

Danny breaks into the argument, "You guys really need to find a new hobby."

"One-night stands are plenty entertaining," Blaise retorts, smiling.

Danny puts his arm on the back of the seat and turns toward me. "I'm not going to lecture you—"

"Again," I add.

"Again," he repeats while rolling his eyes. "But we've talked about this a fuck ton of times. She's not Jane and until you figure out what the hell is going on there, or if anything is going on there, these women are all the same—just another disappointment you're going to have in the morning because they're not her."

Blaise verbally steps in, "Damn, dude, why so deep? You're bringing me down."

Danny laughs. I don't. We've been friends for many years now, so Danny knows my game. He knows me well enough to know what I'm doing. Until I sort out this mess with the first woman I ever loved, the rest are just regrets waiting to happen, along with the regrets I can't take back.

But I know him well too. We relate in a way that Blaise doesn't understand, on a level that one day he'd be lucky to experience. No matter what I've been through with Jane, I've loved, hard. I know what it means to love and to be loved. I have no regrets when it comes to Jane, except one: letting her go.

THE HOLLYWOOD HILLS holds many secrets. Behind the closed doors of the pristine homes belies a lifestyle of privilege and sacrifice. The residents may not realize what they've surrendered to be in the position to live in such a prestigious neighborhood, but it's always there lingering in the background—you're only as good as your last—film, hit song, series, novel, screenplay, production, last whatever it is that gained you entrance to LA's elite.

We walk up the driveway to the mansion atop the hill passing a woman who is vaping while on the phone arguing with what sounds like her boyfriend. Danny's over this scene, but he comes for us. I'm not sure if it's to keep us out of trouble or to watch us get shot down. Either way I'm glad he's here. Between his modeling schedule and his relationship, he's rarely in LA anymore or wanting to spend time out.

Blaise walks in first and we follow. The music is loud, and the crowd trendsetting in their attire. We find a bar full of booze before we find anyone we know. After mixing our drinks, we head outside to the pool area. I take the lead when I spot a group of women in short, very tight skirts and heels that make their legs look a mile long.

Actresses or wannabes. Either way, they're hot.

I stop and Blaise runs into my back. "What the hell, Anders? You just made me spill my drink down the front of my shirt."

When I see her, I'm suddenly frozen to the spot—stuck in a history I can't seem to forget.

Danny says, "I think you should talk to her."

I look back at Blaise. "Did you know she would be here?"

He's swiping his hands down his shirt. "Who?"

"Jane," Danny responds for me.

Blaise immediately looks up and over my shoulder. "Where?"

He signals toward the hot tub Jane is standing near, talking to people sitting inside it. "Over there."

His eyes dart from Jane back to me. "I thought it was kind of a given since she lives here."

"What?" I ask, scanning the room. "What do you mean? This is where she and her boyfuck live?"

"He's more than a fuck. He's her fiancé," he corrects. "Wasn't it understood when I invited you?"

What the fuck? Fiancé?

Surely I misheard him, but I'm too numb to voice my questions.

"You never said who the lawyer was." Danny pushes him enough so Blaise understands he just pissed off his friends. "You're an asshole, Blaise. You know that?"

I want to fucking pop Blaise. Before I can say, or do, anything more, I see *him. Him*—the man with the smug smile on his face when he sees me. I tell my friends, "I need to get out of here."

It's too late. I know it is. I would look like a pussy if I ran. So I stay. Lawrence Reinstardt—lawyer to the stars, LA bigwig, and fiancé to the one I once thought I was destined to be with. If he wasn't such an arrogant asshole, I might like the guy. But we remain at odds over a woman he takes for granted and one I can't forget.

Capped, bright white teeth. He's older than me by six to eight years maybe, easily mid-thirties or older. Tailored blue shirt with fitted slacks and designer loafers. Sure, he's well dressed, and most women might fall for his blond hair, dark eyes, fake tan, and fat wallet, but I fail to see what Jane sees in him. It's obviously something I can't. He smiles. "Anders. Surprised to see you here."

"I heard Jane was going to dump you publicly and wanted a front-row seat."

"Ha ha. You're a funny guy." He clicks his tongue and shoots me with his hands, as if they're guns, and we're five years old. "I can see why she chose me," he says with a snarl.

And there it is... the one thing he can hold over me. He has the one *person* he knows I can't have, and he taunts me, riles me, and makes me want to punch his fucking lights out. Just as I make a fast break forward to take him down, Danny throws his arms out to separate us. "Let's remember we're gentlemen here and not do this. It's a party, after all."

My breath isn't harsh. I'm the epitome of calm on the outside, my fury spinning like a tornado deep inside. He shouldn't fear the man that rages loudly. He should fear the one that rages quietly. It would be easy to knock that smug smirk off his face, but I don't need easy. I'm better than that. I'm better than him. I glare at him before backing down and straightening my expensive suit.

When Danny lowers his arms, Lawrence has the nerve to say, "Danny, my friend. So glad you could make it, but I think you should take your buddy and leave."

"First off," Danny starts, "you and I are not friends. Secondly, we're already leaving."

Just as I'm about to take a step, not wanting to be here another second longer, I hear, "Luke."

I know the voice. That same voice whispered my name in varying degrees of emotion from ecstasy to pain, the memories of her tone still emblazoned across my heart like a brand.

Why can't I just forget her and move on?

"Luke?"

When I finally look over my shoulder, my head drops after seeing her. I'm never prepared. Not ever. Her beauty never wanes in my eyes. Never. Maybe it's because of the memories attached to her, but I'm really thinking it's my heart that's still attached. "I don't want any trouble," I say, my voice sounding weaker than I like. "I was just leaving."

She stops a few feet behind me, and says quietly, "It's good to see you."

Lawrence snaps his fingers and when I look at him, his eyes are on my Jane, his tone harsh as he calls her to his side. "Come here, Jane."

I turn to look at her, insulted, offended, and infuriated he would treat her like a dog. Her eyes are on me but they aren't bright like when we were together. The soft smile she's wearing fades when she looks to him.

His demand is harsher this time when he snaps again and points to the ground. "Here. Now. Jane."

I want to fucking throttle him. But by the looks of it, Danny might beat me to the punch. Literally. The back of my hand hits his chest as I try to remain that calm I was bragging about a moment earlier. It's not my place to step in on her relationship, a relationship *she* chose over ours. "Let's go."

Danny acknowledges me, and silently, he takes a step back. Dropping my arm down, I turn to Jane. "It was good to see you." I head for the door, not rushing, though I want to. I walk, wondering where the hell the feisty girl I once knew was. When I look over my shoulder, she turns away from Lawrence and walks back outside, leaving him standing there with his finger still pointing toward the floor.

There she is.

My smile is wide as we leave a place I should have never come to in the first place. When we get back in the car, Blaise doesn't waste time getting us out of there, and I don't waste time telling him what I think about him bringing me here. "Don't ever set me up like that again."

"I didn't set you up. I told you we were going to a party."

"You didn't tell me *whose* party."

"I also didn't know it was Reinstardt who stole your girl."

"He didn't fucking steal her. I let her go." Stupidly.

Danny looks back at me. "You okay?"

"I'll be fine. I always am."

He won't accept that bullshit of an answer, but with Blaise here, he lets it slide. I appreciate not having an audience while my heart shatters, surprised I have enough of it left to be affected.

Danny asks, "Drinks or home?"

"Home for me. I'm done with today."

No one questions or argues. Thank God for one thing going my way.

Later, lying in my bed, the wind blows through the open door, the night getting colder by the hour. The room is dark, the lights out, and the moon hidden by a cloudy sky.

The day started on such a high. One email caused me to call my friends to go out and celebrate. The deal was closed. I'm a producer on a film I know will score on the indie circuit and I can sell to major distributers worldwide. Production begins next week, so work is good. Work is great, in fact. Normally my work takes my mind off everything, especially off *her*.

Not this time.

I'm about to be tested—heart and soul, mind and body. This will determine my future and I have no idea if that future holds the same ending the film does. Somehow I doubt it. Not everyone gets a second chance.

CHAPTER 2

Jane

WATCHING LUKE WALK away last week—walk away without me—was a shot to the heart. Lawrence Reinstardt turned that pain into anger quick enough, ruining the whole encounter. A relationship formed from loneliness has morphed into desperate actions. Lawrence was once appealing. I thought we had a real shot at love. I was wrong. *So wrong.* He approached me like he approaches his enemies in the courtroom. He analyzes the situation like a forensic scientist and then goes for the kill. He caught me off-guard, in a weakened state and made me feel good, wanted even. I hadn't felt wanted long before I left Luke, so this felt like the sun rising after a thunderous night. He offered me what Luke couldn't give me at the time, what I thought I wanted over all else—a commitment.

Lawrence made me feel special. He'd wined and dined me. Laid on the romance as thick as he could—gifts, flowers, expensive dinners, glamorous parties. Despite my entire world changing along with my social status, I still felt empty inside. That's when I realized it was never about the commitment that I thought would make me feel whole, it was about love.

I never loved Lawrence. I don't even know if I'm capable of loving another like I loved... *love* Luke.

Staring out at the ocean before me, I lean back not sure how my life ended up where it is. My career is finally taking off while my personal life is worse than ever. Maybe not worse. I think I got out of the worst. I'm just back to being lonely. Lonely is good right now. It means I'm feeling again. And maybe one day that feeling will be love instead, but for now I stand up and dust the sand from my jeans as I head back to my car. I'm not in a hurry to get home because I don't have a home to go to. The hotel where I'm staying is nice, but not a home.

With so many changes in the last two years you'd think I'd be used to it. I'm still resistant to my actual reality. Pushing that aside like I've become so adept at, I check my phone to find two missed calls and two text messages from my agent, Sarah Devers. The first message reads: **CALL ME!**

My agent gets demanding, but I have two screenplays out there so my heart leaps hoping for the best.

The second text from her: **CALL ME NOW!! <--- I used two exclamation points. You know what that means.**

My eyes squeeze tight and a smile erupts. I call her. As soon as she answers, I squeal. "I sold a screenplay?"

"The deal is closed. The papers have been signed. You gave me permission to negotiate and close it and we got our top offer, including moving you into script supervisor on set. You did it, Jane. *Until I Met You* is going into production next week."

"This is amazing. Thank you."

"Congratulations."

Deflating a bit when I look around at the empty parking lot, I ask, "Want to celebrate with me?"

"I'd love to join you but my boyfriend has threatened to leave me if I don't come home from the office before ten tonight. Too many late work nights have led to a lot of fights. I promised him tonight."

That pesky feeling of loneliness creeps in again. "Yes, you do work too hard. I'll let you go so you can get out of there. Thanks again for the great news."

"Congratulations and we'll touch base soon."

She hangs up and I start the car. I end up sitting in traffic. Typical LA. Doesn't matter the time of day or night. There's always traffic. In the distance the Hollywood sign isn't lit up, but I can still see it. The beacon that pulls me toward it has changed from when I first arrived in LA. I remember the first time I saw it after Luke and I moved here to attend school together. *We were young...*

Grabbing his pillow, I flop down on the bed in his dorm room and cuddle it while watching Luke organize his CD collection. I've watched him grow from a scrawny kid with charisma and a cute smile into a man with broad shoulders and confidence. The tank top he's wearing shows off the arms he's built over the summer, something he worked at six days a week.

Basically, he's hot.

And he's mine.

Leaning forward from a chair by the bed, his eyes meet mine. His comforting blues burst my daydream but the real thing is better than any fantasy anyway so I don't mind. He teases, "You didn't hear me, did you?"

I smile and roll onto my back. "No. Sorry. What did you say?"

A CD is held up, and he asks, "Is this your Foo Fighters? I have two."

Closing my eyes, I move the pillow off me. "Maybe. I'm not sure, but it doesn't matter. We share everything anyway."

"True. Should I toss it?"

"No, just put it next to yours and then come over here. I want you to lie on top of me."

I don't have to see him to know he's smiling. *"I'm going to write your name in this one, so we'll know whose is whose."* I hear the cap of the Sharpie and the light sound of the ink as he writes on the CD, then the click of the cases when he adds mine back into his collection.

The mattress lowers under his weight as he balances around me and then gently lies on top of me.

"I want to feel your weight, all of it."

He relaxes the rest of the way and my chest is heavy, my breath harder to release, but he feels so good. Too good to worry about simple things like breathing.

Dropping his head to the bed next to mine, he whispers, *"Are you okay? Am I too heavy?"* He starts to move, but I tighten my arms around him.

"I like you like this. Stay one more minute."

He does. But he also knows I'm struggling, so as soon as a minute passes he rolls off and looks at me. *"Why do you like that so much?"*

"I feel close. I feel surrounded by you. I feel connected to you."

His fingers weave into my hair and he leans closer to kiss me. *"I love you, Jane."*

My eyes remain closed as our cheeks press together, and I whisper, *"I love you, so much."*

...I take the next exit off the freeway before I can change my mind. Fifteen minutes later I'm parked in front of Luke's Hollywood Hills home. My lights are off, the engine idling, giving me an out if I want to take it.

The thing is, I don't want to take it. I turn off the car and get out. Nervously holding the keys after setting the alarm, I'm sure he's been tipped off to my presence as I debate one last time before approaching his door. I can still leave. I can still save myself the heartache of seeing him again—possibly with someone else—and not being his.

As soon as I knock, I turn to leave, but don't reach the corner of the house before he answers.

I lick my lips, push down my nerves, and turn back to face him. Why does he have to be so handsome, so everything I should have never walked away from? "Hi."

"Hi." He leans against the doorframe and smiles lightly. "Just in the neighborhood?"

"Something like that."

Silence spans the next minute that starts feeling like ten.

I finally admit, "I don't know why I came here." Hoping he doesn't think I'm crazy.

His smile grows and I can't help but return one. Righting his body, the door is opened wider. "Would you like to come in?"

Looking just beyond his shoulder, I worry he has company of the female persuasion. "Am I interrupting anything?"

"No. I was just cooking dinner. I have enough for two if you're hungry."

My stomach growls at the mention of food. I haven't eaten since breakfast and haven't had a home-cooked meal since I moved out on my own again. I don't tell him that though. "I am."

"Join me. I've got chicken in the oven."

My hand is flat on my belly in a ridiculous attempt to calm my nerves. *I used to be so comfortable with this man. Why am I so nervous now?* "I'd like that." I take a step toward the open door, toward him. Each one is heavy with our past and the many things we left unsaid, the things we should be saying even now. Maybe it's because of those things that I'm unsettled, restless, and aimless. Maybe beneath his put-together life, he's floundering from lost love like me. He looks too good in his low-hanging basketball shorts and T-shirt that seems to show off every one of the muscles across his chest, biceps, and shoulders. Broad shoulders I used to embrace when the whole world was lost to more blissful times.

I bite my lip as my gaze slides up to meet his eyes just before I pass him. His smile—that damn charming smile—tells me I didn't get away with that head-to-toe I gave him.

Turning my focus forward, the door shuts behind me and I stop to wait for him. The short sleeve of my shirt is tugged when he passes me. "The kitchen's this way." The smile remains in place and I look down as I follow him, smiling as well.

One hour.

Two.

It's been a few hours since I arrived and just after midnight when I realize it.

Easy.

He's so easy to be around. I had foolishly forgotten.

The TV is on and the movie is more than half over. We settled on the couch more than an hour ago, dinner long eaten and dishes cleaned. Not wanting the night to end, we opted for a movie. He watches the action flick and I watch him... well, when he's not watching me. "Do you want more wine?" he asks.

"No, I shouldn't. I have to drive."

"You don't have to."

The words are said so casually as he stares at the big screen in front of him. When he ventures to look my way, he catches my surprise. "I shouldn't have said that," he starts. "Reinstardt probably wouldn't appreciate another guy saying that to his fiancée."

My palms are flat to the cushion, ready to help me pounce and run. "I should go."

"Don't." A look of pain resides in his eyes. I remember that sadness so clearly from the last night we were a couple, the night I left. It has made itself at home in the dark blues of his eyes that used to look so happy.

I decide to stay a little longer, though I'm not sure if it's for him or me. Needing fresh air, I walk outside onto the back patio. The view is great from here. The silent night is broken when music wafts from inside, reaching me. *Foo Fighters*. I smile. Good to know some things don't change.

He comes outside and leans against the railing a few feet to my right. "How's work?"

Tentative to let him back in, I share my news shifting nearby. "I sold a screenplay today."

"You did?"

"I did."

"Congratulations."

"Thank you."

His gaze warms me. "You should be celebrating."

"I am," I confess. He smiles, that cocky one that makes all the girls go wild. Including me. "Settle down. Don't let it go to your head."

When he laughs, it's hearty and genuine. I love hearing it again. "I can pop open a bottle of champagne to celebrate your great news."

"I'd like that, but I shouldn't."

We've been dancing around real feelings all night. Until now, when he asks, "Tell me, Jane, why'd you come by tonight?"

Resisting him is still something I struggle with, and I don't have the energy to keep up appearances right now. I close the gap and lean my head against him. "There was no one else I'd rather celebrate with."

His arms come around me. And I never want them to leave. I never want him to let go again. No one will ever make me feel at home like he does. He could say so much about what I just confessed, so much about us, about Lawrence and how I should be celebrating with him. But he doesn't. I think he might want to forget all that and enjoy the right now too.

I leave the safety of his arms knowing the embrace can't last forever, just like we didn't. Inside, I look around. I feel lost here. Through the excuses I invented to see him since we broke up, I've been to his home several times. But I'm uncomfortable here—in *his* space. I've lost touch with who I am and where I belong.

There aren't traces of me to be found here, much to my disappointment. It makes me wonder if he got rid of everything I left behind or if he hides it not to be hurt by the sight of it anymore.

Does he still hurt like I do? Are we putting up fronts to protect ourselves or have we settled into an unwanted friendship? Is that what that embrace was? Two friends with no future of anything more? Or worse, was he taking pity on me for not having anyone else to celebrate with?

He follows me inside, not offering anything this time, not even a smile. I fill the void between us the only way I can. "Dinner was good. Thank you."

"The company was good. Thank you for stopping by."

I reach the door and with my hand on the knob, I stall, not wanting to leave... this time. I almost tell him about Lawrence, but I don't want to make this into a "thing." We can part and keep things easy, like they've been most of the night. Putting on my best Hollywood smile, I reply, "See you around."

"See you around."

As soon as my car door closes, I exhale a deep breath. The air is stale in here compared to the lightness of his house, but I start the engine and leave anyway.

In the quiet of my hotel room, I lie in bed with my hair twisted on top of my head and jammies on. I scroll through social media. Instagram first. My agent is celebrating the deal with a post and a pic of her drinking champagne. Since I'm tagged in it, I press the heart icon and then comment: *Next time we celebrate together. #Cheers*

I open Twitter, but I discover a message on the hotel phone flashing, so I set my phone down and call the front desk. Shortly after, they deliver a package to my room. The papers from Sarah can wait. My eyes too tired to read through them. I pick up my phone again and go to my Twitter notifications. There are three tweets. To my surprise, the most recent one is from Luke.

@RealLukeAnders: *@LAJane55 What if Chicken Thursday became a thing?*

Smiling, I type: *@RealLukeAnders That might lead to Pork Friday and then where does that leave us? #Trouble*

I haven't stopped laughing from the tweet conversation when another pops up.

@LAJane55 Pork Friday it is! Same time. Same place.

Wait. *What?* Did we just set a date on a very public social platform for everyone to see? He's lucky I like the flirting too much to stop, so I type: *@RealLukeAnders The pork was a bad joke that didn't land.*

@LAJane55 It landed exactly how it was double-entendred, and I am fully committed to making #PorkFriday a thing.

@RealLukeAnders What if I'm craving steak?

@LAJane55 We'll steak, then pork. Sound good? I'm starving all of a sudden.

I must be out of my mind to continue this, but like when we were together, I just fall into a rhythm that feels relaxed and fun with him. And I'm enjoying the flirting. *@RealLukeAnders Me too, but I'm not hungry.*

@LAJane55 I see what you did there... and I like it.

@BlaiseDaze tweetjacks our conversation: *@RealLukeAnders What is happening here? O.O @LAJane55*

Luke is quick to reply, washing away my frown: *@BlaiseDaze GTFO. I'm having a convo full of double entendres with @LAJane55 right now.*

His friend adds: *@RealLukeAnders @LAJane55 I'm outs. And congrats again on the deal.*

I respond before I realize what he is really saying. *@BlaiseDaze Thank you! @RealLukeAnders*

But my tweet is beat by Luke's: *@BlaiseDaze Thanks @LAJane55*

Wait. He wouldn't know about my deal yet. I guess he was congratulating Luke. Reading it again, I almost ask him what deal. Finding out he had something to celebrate too makes me feel bad. I tweet Luke: *@RealLukeAnders Congrats on your deal.*

@LAJane55 Thank you. We should celebrate, maybe on #PorkFriday?

Chuckling, I type: *@RealLukeAnders You really are trying to make this happen, aren't you?*

@LAJane55 More than you know.

CHAPTER 3

Jane

NO MATTER HOW long I stare at the papers in front of me, they don't change. I had ordered a bottle of white wine just as I finished flirting with Luke online. I opened the package and made it two sips and one paragraph in when I saw it.

Luke Anders.
Executive Producer - **Until I Met You.**

My wine spills when I accidentally knock the glass right off the nightstand in surprise. Rushing into the bathroom to grab towel, my mind is spinning. When I return, I keep peeking at the papers, trying to comprehend what is right in front of me as if it will change, as if all will be explained. I continue patting the floor, trying to soak up the wine. Fortunately the glass didn't break on the carpet. When I return to bed, I take the documents in hand, once again staring. The words make even less sense than before. Our history alone should have kept him away... our history should have kept me away as well, but there I was earlier tonight—knocking on his door, eating dinner, and flirting with him on Twitter.

This makes no sense. I just saw Luke and he didn't say a word. Why would he not tell me he's the executive producer of *my* movie? Why would he withhold something that big, something that important, something that will tie us together not only in the present, but in the future? This movie will put us in close working proximity. We'll both be on set.

Every. Day.

Together.

My heart beats heavily in my chest and I smile. Every day together. An opportunity.

Maybe.

But why would he not tell me? He obviously knew.

I sign the documents because no matter who is producing it, I can't pass up this deal. Personally, I admit I want this opportunity with him, this second chance. Professionally, this could be a nightmare. What's his vision for my movie? Is there a hidden agenda with him, a reason he didn't tell me tonight? We were together for almost three hours. The conversation was light, nothing that would lead into dangerous territory like our past. But why hide this? It affects both of our futures.

I stuff the papers back into the envelope and toss it on to the desk. I climb back into bed after filling a new glass with wine. Flicking on the TV, I try to get lost in late night shows. But even arguing housewives and drinking doesn't take my mind off him, or the fact that I'll be working so closely with him for a solid month, if not longer. Then there are promotions and potential film festivals...

He didn't want me before. He kept things light and cordial because he knew we would be working together. He did that to keep things professional. Should I be happy he opened the door tonight not only for dinner, but for our professional relationship to begin? I don't want to feel happy when it comes to him. Happiness with Luke Anders also means heartbreak. He rejected me, I remind myself.

He rejected me.

I sniffle.

And from what I hear, he has also happily slept around since our breakup. I'm sure it's been a field day for him with every night ending in victory in his bed.

Ick.

I turn off the lamp and snuggle down under the covers. I'm too restless to sleep well, but I need sleep to shut out the noise of my hurt heart pulsing in my ears. You would think almost two years later, I would be used to this feeling, to the pain, to the heartbreak.

The pain of the first night we spent apart still haunts me. The first two months after our breakup I held on to hope that he would come for me, that he missed me like I so desperately missed him.

But he didn't.

His texts were as if we were friends... as if we hadn't loved each other with every ounce of our beings. I wasn't his buddy. I was his soul mate.

How could he not feel half of his being missing? After all those years together, did he not miss me at all?

I thought I had resolved the fact that I would never recover from that relationship. His texts eventually stopped along with my hope. Floating through life had become automated. It was easy to ignore that life was moving, that it continued to go on without me. I pulled back from everyone, lost contact with friends, and poured myself into my work. I lost my life. I lost myself. I had become a master of pretending. I did it too well. No one believed that my heart could only belong to one man.

Even I fell for the lies.

But Luke, how could he not see it in my eyes? Every time I came over I was showing him I cared. Every time I cried in front of him, I cried that we weren't together. My heart struggled to voice my feelings, but he should have known.

He was the only one who really knew me and if he couldn't tell where did that leave me?

In my darkest hour, alone and with half a soul, I met Lawrence. He made me believe I could be whole again.

He was wrong.

THE ENVELOPE IS dropped on Sarah's desk. She eyes me as she wraps the call she's on. As soon as she says goodbye and hangs up, I ask, "Luke Anders? Why didn't you tell me?"

"Sit down, Jane, and relax. From my understanding he's happy with the script and not really wanting to make any changes."

Even though she wasn't my agent when I was with him, she's well aware of my personal history. "But Luke? What are you doing to me?"

"You told me to close the deal. I closed the deal and for more than a fair offer. I thought that extra zero on the deal would make you happy."

"It does. But..." I sit down in the leather chair across the desk from her and sink down while closing my eyes. "You don't understand, Sarah."

Leaning forward, she rests her chin on her hand. "Then tell me."

Closing my eyes to block out the world won't make the pain in my chest go away or soften the lump in my throat. "He broke my heart."

"This deal should heal it. You've done what you told me you wanted. You sold this story that you bled writing. You've sold something—"

"I've sold a piece of my soul and it was sold to the man who already owns the remainder." I open my eyes and look out the window.

Only a sigh is heard from the other side of the desk.

"Hypothetically... what if I still care about him, deep down and I can't handle seeing him all the time?"

Sarah comes around the desk and sits next to me. Covering my hand with hers, she says, "Let this process heal you, Jane. You need to heal so you can move on."

"I thought Lawrence would do that."

"He was a rebound. He wore you down when you were most vulnerable. That wasn't real love. Yes, you had feelings for him and he loved you, but he preyed on you when you were still hurt by Luke. It was never meant to be."

"What is?"

"What is what?" she asks, her eyebrows knitted together.

"What is meant to be?" I ask as if she can reveal the universe's grand plan to me.

"This moment in time. This deal. This—"

"Second chance."

A wide smile appears, and she says, "I was going to say opportunity, but second chance might be more fitting."

Embarrassed that I admitted something so personal, so emotional, I look down, my fingers weaving together.

She says, "This stays between us. You can trust me."

"I know. I do. I think I just surprised myself that I said that out loud when I hadn't even admitted it to myself. Not really."

"Take this second chance, or opportunity, or whatever else you want to call it and live in the moment. Live life, just live. Whatever is meant to be will be."

We stand and hug. "I know you're right, but I don't think I can face his rejection twice. I haven't recovered from the first time yet."

"It's going to be okay. I promise you. You're going to get an amazing movie from this partnership and I think you'll heal during the process."

"And if I don't?"

"Then I'll get you a bigger deal on the next movie."

"Wait. Shouldn't you be doing that anyway?"

"Busted." She laughs as she returns behind her desk and takes the signed contract in hand. "Okay, so either way, I'll be working on your other deal. You go make a great film and forget about that man. You do what's good for you and what you want to do. You owe him nothing, but a great movie once finished. That I know you can handle."

"I hope so."

"No hope," she responds, grabbing her phone to make another call. "This isn't by chance. This is your destiny."

"The movie or Luke?"

Her eyes flash up to mine. "That's for you to decide." Swatting away the invisible emotions in front of her, she adds, "Go and make movie magic. I have a call about your other screenplay in five minutes."

"I'm going. I'm going." I step out but poke my head back in. "Hey, and thanks."

"For hooking you up with your ex?"

"No, and I'm not hooked up with my ex. Thanks for listening."

"Eh, no problem. I'm like a bartender. I listen to the problems and keep my mouth shut... Okay, I won't go that far. I tell you how it is, but I do it with a little sugar on top to help ease the pain."

"I'll take any sugar I can get these days," I reply with a wave. "See you later."

Riding the elevator down, I find myself lost in the thoughts of what if:

What if Luke made a mistake two years ago?

What if he realizes it?

What if he realizes he still loves me?

What if...

What if I realize I still love him?

Or, what if I just miss the thought of us?

What if my memories are tricking me into believing I still love him?

And the one *how* that remains burrowed into my heart...

How could he not love me enough to stay together in the first place?

But that one is easy to answer. We were never meant to be or we would be.

"Miss?"

Looking up, I see an older man with kind lines running through his face waiting on me. With his hand holding the elevator door open, he asks, "Miss, is this your floor?"

L is displayed above the door, and I jump forward. "Yes, sorry." I hurry out and into the lobby. This whole Luke situation is distracting me from what I should be focused on—this movie and finding a new place to live. The hotel was only meant to be temporary.

Anyway, it's not good for me to spend my time wondering *what if* when *what is* matters more. While driving, I think about getting the answers I should have gotten last night. I could go to Luke's and ask him the questions I have rolling around inside my head. With mixed emotions from last night and today, I decide I need coffee to help clear my head first.

After ordering a half-caf macchiato with extra foam at one of my favorite coffee shops, I notice a worn brown leather chair available by the window.

I love this time of day—the work crowd has gone to work and it's too early for the afternoon crowd needing a pick-me-up. After setting up camp, I pull my laptop out of my bag and lean back to start my house search. The problem is, my desired neighborhood is the same one Luke lives in, bringing him right back to the forefront of my mind.

Luke Anders.

Memories may be fond but my body recalls his hard body against mine, his firm lips pressed to mine in desperation, and his passionate words whispered into my ear like a love song.

But...

I'm no longer that girl.

And...

He's no longer that boy.

Personally, I feel a little offended when I think of the man he's become. I remember the rumors I've heard over the years. Gossip travels fast in LA. Luke Anders is a playboy with a Hollywood Hills home and a penchant for dirty talk.

Maybe my fond memories have given him too much credit these past few years, my memories clouding over the bad, and highlighting the good. It couldn't have been all bliss even when we were together, but I've always struggled to hold on to the bad.

Staring out the window, my mind tenses as I search my thoughts for fights we had or times he hurt me. Nothing comes except the one that ended it all.

Surely there must be something. We were too young to know any better, much less each other. Even though I can't think of anything now, I know we were never meant to be, no matter what Sarah says.

Exhaling loudly with my fingers hovered over the keyboard, I acknowledge I'm not naïve like I once was. I know what I want. How hard can it be to find a man who can hold his own in business *and* in bed? Someone who is loyal. Dedicated. Someone who can love wholeheartedly. Someone who doesn't want to play the field when they can have something real and everlasting.

All the things I once offered Luke and he rejected. He hid behind youth and his rising reputation, deciding he wanted to pursue his career goals more than me. He no longer wanted what he had. I was old news once he got a taste of success. Offers for movies and from women go hand in hand in this town.

"I'm not bitter," I remark to myself. I see a couple on a nearby couch eyeing me and start wishing my coffee was vodka instead. Thoughts of an ex who broke my heart, and then moved on to a fabulous swinging single life has a way of doing that to a girl. Ten in the morning might be too soon for a cocktail though, so I continue drinking my coffee. Staring at the screen with a fancy zip code of houses for sale and a budget to match makes me feel better, stronger because I don't need anyone to take care of me anymore.

I'm an independent, self-sufficient woman. I don't need a man, and I certainly do not need a player using me and making me feel worthless. Nope, his charms won't work on me. Not again. He's proven he's more than moved on from me with a comfortable lifestyle and no trinkets of a past that he, at one time, claimed was his future. It's an insult to my heart that he's moved on so smoothly when I've been wallowing in memories that give him way too much credit. No matter how hurt I was, or still am, I believed deep down he still loved me. I never let Lawrence into my heart, not really. There was no room when Luke occupied the whole space. But Luke has built a life without me.

It's time I do the same.

So right here, right now, I'm choosing to believe the rumors. These I can hold on to in my weaker moments. Most rumors are based in fact anyway. It will be the only way to protect my heart against that sly-talking, easy-going, sexy heart swindler.

It's time I let him go and move on. I don't need a man. I don't need anyone. And I especially do not need Luke Anders.

Stupid memories.

Stupid broken heart.

CHAPTER 4

Luke

I SHOULD CALL her. I really should. I'm just not ready for the wrath.

The other night was good, the best three hours I've spent with a woman since... well, since spending it with her before we broke up. Even now, we're comfortable being around each other, the feeling of home still connecting us.

She felt it.

Just like me.

I could tell in the way she relaxed on the couch and laughed during dinner. I could see it in her eyes when she thought I didn't notice. But she still refuses to let me back in, fully. The wall she keeps around her, keeps me at a distance despite how at ease we may be. Jane's become more stubborn than she used to be. I think that's a good thing, but I'm not entirely sure yet. I have a feeling I'm going to find out during the film's production though.

Taking the phone in hand, I find her name in my contacts. I call her before I have a chance of chickening out. *Shit.* Why are my hands sweating? It's Jane. *My Jane.* The girl I've loved almost half my life. *The girl I've known since we were sixteen...*

"We're gonna be busted, Luke." She rubs her hand over my leg. She's nervous, which adds to her excitement. I've discovered she's very touchy feely when she's nervous—not like she can keep her hands off me normally, but more so when she's excited at the prospect of breaking the rules. "How can you be so calm right now?"

"Because I'm with you," I whisper, "and we've got nowhere else to go, so this is it or not at all." Please, Heaven above, let this be the night.

She looks around and smiles, the stress leaving her expression and her green eyes bright in the moonlight that slips in through the open window. "You did this for me? The flowers and blankets, the pillows?"

My dad, older brother, and I built this tree house when I was seven. It's as solid as our house across the yard from us. I spent the afternoon lugging stuff up here from the linen closet—pillows, blankets. I grabbed some vases and picked flowers from my mom's rose garden. There's even a small Igloo cooler with Snapple and soda in it. Now I'm nervous. "Do you like it?"

With a rose under her nose, she inhales and says, "It's so romantic like in the movies." The vase in her hands is replaced by a pillow she hugs to her chest.

"I would have had candles but I didn't want my parents to see the light."

She curls around the pillow, bending her knees and wrapping her arms around her legs.

I ask, "Are you cold?"

"A little."

Taking one of the blankets, I get up and wrap it around both of us. "I'll keep you warm." Touching her face, I run my thumb over her cheek and then into her hair and pull her closer. "I did

this for you. Only you. And I'll do more. I love you, Jane."
Hoping she feels the same about me, I kiss her.

...and the only girl to break my heart. "Fuck it." I call her. Each ring feels like a ping to my heart. Each heartbeat weighted equal with anticipation and dread. I have no idea how she'll react to the news of me producing her movie. When she answers on the fourth ring, it's too late to worry now.

"Hello?" Her greeting is curt.

"Jane." My voice trembles an octave too high. *Fuck.* I clear my throat and try again. "Jane, it's Luke."

"Yes, I know."

Not a great start. *Fuck, why am I so nervous?* "I want to talk to you about your movie, *Until I Met You.* I'm happy to be a part of the project."

"I was wondering if you were going to bother to mention that minor detail."

Shit. She sounds irritated. "I'm sorry I didn't tell you last night."

"Why didn't you?"

"Can we talk?"

"I thought we were."

"In person." I wait, the silence expanding across the miles that separate us.

Sounding as if she's been forced to give trade secrets, she relents and says, "I'm at Fair Trade Beanery down on Wilshire."

"I'll be there within the hour."

When I hang up, I set the phone down and release a huge breath of relief. Every step with her feels like a chess move. Professionally I need to get things on course. Personally... I wouldn't mind the same, but since she has a fiancé, I need to respect her boundaries like I did last night. I was the friend she obviously needed. I can play that role for her if she wants as long as it gets me more time with her. I can... yes, I can be her friend without our past being dragged to the forefront. We'll replace what feels like a lifetime of romantic memories with new ones—friendlier ones.

I grab my keys from the desk and leave to meet her.

When I walk into Fair Trade, I do a quick scan and find her in a leather chair facing away from the door. Her blond hair is in a messy bun on top of her head and I smile when I see her profile as she gazes out the window beside her.

She's heart-stoppingly gorgeous.

Friends, I remind myself.

I go over and sit down across from her in a matching leather chair. "Hi." My eyes are focused on hers, looking for a reaction to play off—anger, happiness, sadness, annoyed—anything that lets me into her world again, even if just for a moment. *Fuck, I obviously can't be just friends with her.* She means too much to me. Still.

"Hi."

My heart thunders in my chest. *Is my heart reminding me what I already know, answering my own question?* Probably. Be cool. Stay calm. Don't scare her with raging thoughts of how I want to tell her how stunningly beautiful she is. Or how I miss the way her body fit so perfectly, or she would say, "snugly" to mine. Nope, don't tell her I still relieve pressure with images of her on a weekly basis. Nope, don't tell her any of that and... *Shit.* I can't do this with her looking perfect in her cut-off jean shorts and plaid shirt tied at her waist. Her face fresh and almost makeup free apart from a little light pink lipstick that makes the light reflect drawing my attention right to them. Those lips... I miss them. So fucking much. Standing abruptly, I offer, "Can I get you anything?"

"No, thank you." A light smile appears as she reaches for her mug. "I've got a coffee."

"Banana bread?" *Shit, I sound like an insane person.*

"No, I'm fine. Thanks."

"Blueberry muffin?" *Shut the fuck up* runs through my head, scolding myself because I sound like an idiot, and for some reason cannot manage to keep my mouth closed.

She shoots me a look. "No, really. I'm fine. Get whatever you want. I'll be here."

I walk away, needing to before I make it worse. Not that it could get worse because that was pretty damn awful. This is Jane. I don't need to be like this. Who cares that at one point months ago I thought we had a chance to get back together. I hoped. Who cares that it fell through? I didn't tell Jenna to come over that night and Jane gave me no warning. Fucker Lawrence hopped on that fuck up fast and proposed.

None of that matters now. We're professionals and we can act accordingly. I walk back over and set a piece of lemon bread in front of her. "You always liked lemons."

She smiles and there's no irritation there, so I sit as she says, "Thank you. That's very nice you remembered."

"I could never forget."

Her lids drop down as if I've caused her pain. Her beauty still shines through the pain, making my heart ache. Leaning forward, I say, "I didn't mean to upset you."

She shakes her head and puts on a smile that feels more for appearance than felt from the inside. "It was very thoughtful. Thank you, Luke."

"You're welcome." After taking a sip of coffee, I get down to it. "I thought you knew that my name was attached to the project but didn't want to talk about work last night."

"I didn't know until I opened the papers after I saw you."

"I was never mentioned prior as a possibility?"

"Not to me." She tucks her legs under her and looks out the window again. "I'm not mad. I'm just shocked." When she turns back to me, she lowers her voice and asks, "Why do you want to work on my movie?"

Her hair is golden, looking even lighter next to the window. A few strands have come free, but I like the imperfection. *I like her.* Still. Too much. "Because it's a beautiful story and I want to make sure it gets told the way it was intended."

"Sometimes you say the most amazing things as if it is common, everyday small talk." With a sigh, she momentarily looks away and it kind of guts me not being able to really read her expression for those few seconds. "You have produced some beautiful films. I'm touched you want to produce mine." When her eyes meet mine, she asks, "Will we be able to do this?"

I think she's asking about of the film, but I'm not positive, so I answer both, "We will. We always did make a great team."

Jane

WHAT IS LUKE'S *endgame?* He sits there very unlike his usual confident self, distracted by something besides our discussion of the movie. Every time he glances toward another customer placing their order, the bell above the door chiming, or briefly, and uncharacteristically, lost in his own thoughts, I look at him.

Really look at him.

The muscle that highlights his defined jaw tenses and relaxes. Tenses and relaxes. I'm not sure if he's looked me in the eyes since he sat down and I don't like that. The tension is rolling off him, seeping under my skin, and my foot starts bouncing. "Luke?"

His eyes glance my way, but when they don't make it to mine, with a plea in my voice, I say, "Please look at me."

When we connect, my heart begins to race. His alluring eyes make it hard to remember we're here on business when I wish we were here together like we used to be. The feeling overwhelms me, tears suddenly filling my eyes. I stand up and grab my laptop and bag, knowing I need to get out of here. "I've gotta go."

He stands just as abruptly, his hand grabbing my forearm, keeping me from escaping. "Don't go, Jane."

Lowering my head, I shake it. "I can't stay."

"Why?"

Summoning the courage to look up and straight into his eyes, I say, "Because I'm weak."

"If you were weak, we'd still be together." Taking a step closer, he says, "You're strong. Too strong when you don't have to be."

"What are you saying?"

"I'm saying we're friends."

"We are?"

"We are. No matter what happens, I'm in your corner."

His hand drops down and I already miss the warmth. "Why are you telling me this?"

"Because we're going to be working together. I want you to know that no matter what happens, I will protect this movie, and I will support you."

My heart falls to the pit of my stomach as his words sink in wishing he had said, "I will protect you and I will support this movie" instead. I exhale softly. "Yes, of course, the movie." My breathing deepens as I build my walls back up, brick by heavy brick. I mistakenly thought he was talking about us when he so clearly wasn't. His priority is to protect his investment. I was foolish for thinking otherwise.

"I've got to go." I walk away before he can stop me again. I can't let him. Because if he stops me again I can't promise I won't tell him more than I should. I can't guarantee I won't tell him I left Lawrence. And I definitely won't be able to hold back and not tell him that I might still have feelings for him. No, I can't tell him any of that.

Not now.

As I leave, the bell above the door rings, ending the second round, and leaving me feeling worse for wear. Or maybe it's the third or fourth round for us? I'm losing track at this point. It's best I go and leave the memories of us behind as I prepare for the next round: a professional relationship as our future. Perhaps the only future I can survive in this battle of heart vs. head.

CHAPTER 5

Luke

JANE WALKS OUT of the coffeehouse and as much as I want to go after her, not only to spend more time with her but also to fix whatever made her expression fall, I don't. Instead, I sit where she was, the seat still warm, and watch her walk down the sidewalk.

There's something between us, so much unfinished business, making me wonder if it was a mistake taking on this project. I talked myself into going after this movie when I read the script as if that could justify the personal situation I've purposely put myself in.

This isn't going to be easy, not with all these feelings that aren't just lingering but strangling me.

Focus.

Perspective.

I need both right now. I need to do my job. Set personal feelings aside and concentrate on this film.

First or last resort, I'm not sure, but I know I'm owed a truckload of bro-favors, so I make the call.

"WHAT THE FUCK am I doing?"

"What the fuck *are* you doing?"

"Why can't I just let her go?"

"Why *can't* you just let her go?"

I send Danny a hard glare. "Why are you mimicking me?"

"Seemed about as helpful as what you were doing." He takes his glass and tops it off with beer from the pitcher.

"I have no idea what I'm doing. I need advice."

Danny pushes my beer closer. "Drink. That's the only advice you need right now."

I drink, but I don't feel better.

He refills my pint glass and then signals the bartender for another. Eyeing me cautiously, I think he can tell I'm on the brink of... of... What the fuck am I on the brink of? Fuck. Jane's got my mind all fucked up.

Danny takes another sip, and then sets his glass down loud enough to make me look up. He leans back, and smirks. "There's nothing I can say that you don't already know. Sure, I can tell you what you want me to tell you. Let's try that route first. Hey Luke," he starts, "stop fucking around and go after the woman. You can lie to yourself all you like, but your feelings for her run deep. They always have and they always will."

"I can't just go after her. She left me once. Why would I set myself up to let that happen twice?"

"But you just answered your own question. You didn't argue the fact of your feelings for her. You argued setting yourself up to be hurt again. No one wants to be hurt. It sucks. I get it. But," he says, "you don't get the good without working through the bad. So you have to decide if this is your shot at getting her back or if it's your chance to close that book and move on."

"I hate when you get all real and sensible on me. I was hoping you'd tell me to fuck her to get her out of my system," I deadpan.

"There's that option too." He laughs. "Do you know your shooting schedule?"

"The finances are basically in place since—"

"Since you got a loan to make it happen."

"It was worth it."

"Does she know?"

"It's only a small part."

"How much?"

"Two hundred K."

He whistles. "Will you see it back?"

"Definitely. It's a good film, which makes it a good investment. With the right cast in place, it will do well."

"When do you start?"

"I start working full-time this Monday and I told the other producers that we can start soon if they get us a director."

"That seems fast."

"Indies. We don't have the overhead like big studio movies."

"Where does it shoot?"

"Austin for the main shoot and New York if we get the financing for the exteriors."

"Ahh. At least it's a city where you only have to be as close as you want to be."

Close.

Very close.

"I'm fucked, right?"

He taps his pint against mine, and smiles. "Sounds like it."

We polish off two baskets of hot wings while watching the rest of the game. Just before the final two minutes on the clock, he says, "Let me ask you something."

"Okay."

"I know the basics of why you broke up, but what really caused the breakup with Jane? I mean, you guys didn't seem to fight much so I was surprised when she left."

Jane shouts from across the living room, "Ten years. I've wasted ten years of my life waiting on you. Are we not committed? We live together, Luke. We've been together since we were sixteen. You either see a future together or you don't."

"I do. I just—"

"You just what? What could possibly be holding you back at this point?"

"I'm not ready to start a new life. I finally feel like I'm in control of this life. What if we change and it changes us? After marriage, it's kids. I'm not ready for that."

"What are you talking about?"

"I don't want us to change. What we have is good."

With tears streaming down her face, she lowers her voice, the fight gone from her body as her shoulders slump. "That's where you're wrong. It's not been good for me for a while and you haven't even noticed."

"I was building a career," I tell Danny. "She was building a life. I used to think those were one in the same. That we were working toward the same goal." I turn my gaze to the pint, my life as murky as the beer. "Once she left, I realized how wrong I was. But by then it was too late."

Looking up, I see the sympathy in his eyes. He understands, which is why I called him. He also lets me sit in my own admission a bit longer, knowing I don't need the commentary.

He finally says, "All of that is in the past. It's the present and the future that matter. You have a choice to make."

"I have no more options. She's engaged."

"I think it's a ring of convenience, not one of love... you know that soul mate kind of love, and I'm pretty sure you guys qualify."

"Way too sappy, man."

"At least we don't have to hug it out again."

Standing up, I say, "Yet."

He pays for the food and drinks, and replies, "Don't threaten me."

"Ha! Like that one time wasn't for you."

Knocking my shoulder as he passes, he chuckles. "Me? That was all you, bro."

It's true. It was. But I can't let him know that. "Thanks for the brews."

I smile as he rubs his stomach. "I leave for a shoot in three days, so I had to squeeze in the good stuff before I have to show off these abs."

"You live a hard fucking life, my model friend."

"Eh." He shrugs. "Someone's got do it." Starting to walk backward, seriousness takes over his jovial nature. "And for the record, you don't need my advice or anyone else's. You know what you should do. You just need to let yourself do it."

"So I should break up an engagement?"

"I didn't say that, but you sure did." He gives me a small salute. "See ya when I'm back in town."

"See ya."

On the drive home I wonder if what I did was the right thing for me and for Jane. Going after this project means more time with Jane and I can't help but wonder if subconsciously, I planned it that way. The script is solid. Her best work yet. I know it will be a success, but deep down I start to think seeing her daily may be torture for the soul.

It's too late now to worry about that.

When I get home, I print out the manuscript. The best thing for a scattered brain is work. Pulling out my tabs and markers I start marking up the script. I have a method to my madness and color-coding is the glue to it.

THIRTY DAYS SLIP away with no personal contact with Jane. I'm sure she's had a million things to do like I have. My personal life has become non-existent. My sex life is the worst it's been in years. I'm edgy, but for some reason unable to make myself go out, and my little black book of numbers stored on my phone doesn't appeal. I did email her a few times with questions regarding the script, but we don't talk.

Professional.

We keep it professional.

I miss her.

Financing is secured and an up-and-coming director is brought onboard. I lose my salary in order pay for him. It's a gamble just like the loan, but I'm confident it will pay off in my favor.

Ian Burke is young and ambitious, a little cocky from what I've seen in interviews and at Sundance, so basically me a few years ago. His films are artistic in style—the magic caught in the details. As for lead actors, a couple names have been tossed around and two have already passed. I think I can get one actress. I know she would do a solid job, but she comes with personal entanglements that concern me.

"Jessica Pyles," Ian says. "We've got to have her."

"I'm still working on it."

"What does that mean? Where exactly are we in discussions with her?"

"She hasn't returned my calls."

He looks at me. "So nowhere?"

"I'll get her signed on."

Ian walks out of the office and I pick up my phone again to call her. This time she answers. "What do you want?"

"I want to talk."

"You didn't want to talk the last time I saw you. As a matter of fact, I think your words were 'Get out of my house before I call the cops.'"

Clingy is an understatement. She was ready to marry me after one night. I briefly feared for my life when I found out she had called my mother to tell her we were coming for a visit. It wasn't a pretty morning for either of us after that. "I thought it was a one-night stand, Jessica."

"What gave you the impression that I do one-night stands? I'm a celebrity, Luke."

Distinctly remembering how she grabbed me at the Vanity Fair Oscar after-party, telling me to take her home and fuck her might have given me that impression. However, right now I need her, so pissing her off might not be the best route to go. I suck up my pride. "I'm sorry."

"You are?" Her voice perks up.

"I am. I'm also happy to hear you and Ryan are so happy together. Actually that's what I'm calling about. You and Ryan."

ONE WEEK LATER, the deals are sealed. We have our stars signed on.

Ian tosses the script down on the conference table. We've been working on it for hours. He pushes it toward me, then leans back in his chair and rubs his eyes. "I'm wiped."

I drop my head into my hands, my eyes burning from the above fluorescents. "It's late. I'm tired. Let's pick up where we left off tomorrow."

A knock on the door draws our attention.

Jane.

Seeing her in the doorway, my body is on alert, my heart racing just from the sight of her. "Jane?"

"Sorry for interrupting." She shifts uncomfortably.

Ian pushes back from the table after spying her over his shoulder. When he gets a good look, he stands, his hand out as he moves closer. "Hi, I'm Ian Burke."

She smiles, the act itself reminding me of how much I missed her. "Hello. I'm Jane Lewis. You're the director."

"And you're the screenwriter," Ian replies, suddenly seeming wide-awake with his eyes locked on Jane. *My Jane.* "The pleasure is mine. We have a meeting this week, right?"

"Yes, we do." she says, glancing to me.

"Would you like to meet now?"

"I know it's late. I hate to bother you now. I actually stopped by to talk to Luke regarding a few scenes."

Not liking the direction of this, I walk over and direct her back to the door. "Why don't we go to my office to discuss those scenes? Ian was just about to leave."

He pipes up, "I'm good for a bit longer. I think I just got a second wind. Why don't we stay at the conference table to discuss them?"

Her eyes go from me to him and back again waiting for me to

respond. "It's fine."

"Thanks," she replies, taking a seat.

He takes his seat again as she settles in the chair across from him and I sit at the head of the table. Not liking his obvious attention to her, I change seats to sit next to her as she pulls the script from her bag. Only Jane Lewis has the power to make jealousy rear its ugly head in me. "What scenes do you want to go over?"

The script is tapped on the table and laid flat in front of us. She points to something on the page, but I'm still staring at her. Damn, she's beautiful. Is her hair lighter? She's wearing more makeup than she usually does and it makes me wonder where she's been today.

"Luke?" My eyes meet hers and a soft smile appears. "The script."

Caught. Her copy of the script is coded like mine, the same colorful tabs hanging out the sides and top. It makes me miss the nights we'd lain in bed, working alongside each other. We would stay up until all hours debating and working out scenes until they came together, until *we* came together.

God, I took everything for granted back then.

I took her for granted.

"What do you think?" she asks.

My eyes lift to hers again, responding to my name spoken from her mouth that sounds more like a melody than used in a professional meeting. "What?"

Ian cuts in, "There's this park in Austin that can double as an entrance to Central Park. We can keep the scene if you think it's vital."

She replies with conviction, "I think it matters to the story, to her character growth."

"Done. We'll keep it," he replies easily, as if budgets don't matter and he has the final say.

Thanks, Ian. Now I have to be the bad guy. "We can't guarantee that. It's not in our budget currently so I'll propose it to the other producers and let them go over the numbers. Are you willing to cut something else to make this scene happen?"

Holding the script to her chest, she shakes her head. "I don't want to if we can make it work."

I nod, not wanting to disappoint her. "We'll try. What other scenes?"

We spend the next forty-five minutes discussing tweaks and changes, little things that add to the visuals and setting of the scenes. I love that she dreams in such vivid color, her world and the sky always one in the same. She's enchanted me wholeheartedly as I see the woman I loved—*love*—so fiercely reemerge as if she's been asleep for years. She's animated, and playful, laughing, and smiling.

The problem is—Ian is enchanted too, hanging on to every word she speaks as if it's gospel sent to save his soul. When she stands to leave, he offers to walk her to her car, beating me to the punch.

Cocky asshole.

As we walk out of the building, I look across the parking lot and see her car next to mine, and I smirk. Right when I'm about to say something, Ian interrupts my reunion with Jane again, and says, "I'm starving. Want to grab some dinner and we can continue our chat?"

I'm left gobsmacked by his fucking nerve. Apparently Ian, who was tired earlier, has all the energy in the world now. *Because* of Jane.

And when I hear her say, "Yes," to him, I'm left with an overwhelming jealousy twisting in my chest causing it to puff. Fuck him and his private plans with my Jane. "I could use a drink," I interrupt like he has so much tonight.

Ian shoots me a look that lets me know I'm not welcome to join their little party of two. Fortunately Jane smiles and says, "Great. I can meet you both there." And just like that, all is right in the world again.

While Ian huffs toward his car nearby, I catch up to her. "I can walk you."

"I'm glad I caught you tonight. I feel a lot better about things."

Caught. Caught me lost in the sea green of her eyes, the petal pink of her lips... She caught me all right.

"I will support this project" *I will support you.* "I'll keep your vision as much as I can." When we reach her car, I stop a few steps back as she leans against the door of a new BMW. "Nice car."

Glancing back at it, her shoulders have eased, either from the late hour or because she's comfortable around me. I'm hoping for the latter. "Thanks." Her hair has fallen in front of one of her eyes. Instinctually, I reach out as if I have the right, and tuck it behind her ear. Her eyes don't leave mine, her hands don't protest, and she remains standing there, looking at me with eyes that if I didn't know better reflect my own feelings toward her.

But I do know better.

She's engaged.

She's not one I can have those feelings for any longer. When she sealed her future with Lawrence she sealed my fate as well. *Fuck.*

With our romantic fate determined, I blow a breath, and step back again. "I'll see you in a few."

"Hey, Luke, maybe we can ride together?"

She catches me again. This time I'm smiling ear to ear. I nod toward my car, hope returning too fast to be healthy. But I'd rather feel this than disappointment. "C'mon, you, I'll drive."

CHAPTER 6

Luke

I LIKE JANE in my car.

In my space.

In my life.

I like how close we are in proximity and how her elbow still hogs the console between us, just like old times. It's moments like these that give me hope when I shouldn't build up any expectation.

I can't.

Just enjoy the time we have together, I remind myself.

Jane reaches forward and changes the radio station. "Make yourself at home," I tease.

"I will. Thanks," she responds with a mischievous smile on her face as she presses another button. Keith Urban's latest comes roaring out the speakers and I immediately reach to turn it down, my hand covering Jane's.

An accident, a happy accident that wipes the smile right off my face. Our connection deeper than surface. I want to keep my hand there...

I shouldn't.

But she remains still, no smile on her face either. She gulps and though I hear it, I won't say anything because there's tension in my throat as well. Unsure what to do, I turn the music back up and put my hands at ten and two. Jane, maintaining the unspoken emotions between us, sits back and looks out the window.

Clearing my throat, I turn the music down again. "I didn't know you liked country music?"

"I do."

"Did you..." I don't finish the question, realizing if her answer is yes, it will only make me look bad for not knowing. I don't remember her liking country, like ever, but I won't call her out on it because I like when she's not defensive. This is about self-protection mode. I don't want to ruin what we are rebuilding. I don't want to ruin our friendship.

"I didn't when we were together. I've been trying new things in the last year or so. Country is easy to listen to, light for the most part. There are some real tearjerker songs out there, but I like the happier songs. Nothing sad for me these days."

"I guess when things are going great there's no reason to drag them down." I feel sick to my stomach for what I'm about to say, but I know it's only right. I take a deep breath and do it. "Congratulations on your engagement."

She looks at me bewildered. Her hand is holding the seatbelt away from her neck and she's staring at me. I glance back to the road and then to her again. "Thank you," she whispers as her eyes well with tears, an inner turmoil brewing in them. She turns away suddenly.

I have no idea why she looks so upset. "Did I say something wrong?"

"No." She pauses. "You're saying and doing everything right. Why is that?"

"Because I've already done everything wrong when it comes to us."

Her expression falls, her eyelids lower, and her hand momentarily blocks her face from my line of vision. I hear her sniffle, and then she asks, "Can we not talk about this right now?"

Pulling into the parking lot of the bar, I give her what she wants. "No need to revisit the past when you have your whole future planned out."

Jane's head snaps to look at me as quick as her tongue. "What does that mean?"

I cut the engine on my silver Porsche, and turn to her, surprised by her question. "What do you mean?"

"I don't have my whole future planned out. That would be... boring."

"I thought you wanted stability and predictability? The white picket fence and the two-point-five kids?"

"I don't." She's shaking her head as if that will offer a different meaning to the words.

Now I'm confused. By the way she's wrapping her arms over her chest, I can tell I've upset her and I don't want that. "Whatever I did to upset you, I didn't mean to. I'm sorry."

She struggles for a moment, her expression one of anguish. "No, you don't need to apologize. I just think you don't understand."

"According to you, I never did, so this should not come as a surprise," I joke to lighten the moment back up.

The door opens and she swings her legs out. "I think we should go inside. Ian will be waiting."

The door is slammed shut before I have a chance to respond. We were onto something, something real that needed to happen with us and she leaves, like she did before. Now I'm irritated. Stepping out quickly, I shut my door and call over the roof, "You don't get to control this anymore."

"Control what?" she asks defensively from the other side of the car. Exactly what I didn't want.

"Us, and how we in interact."

"There is no us," she clarifies quite concisely. "We're broken, remember?"

"Up," I correct.

"*Up* what?"

"You said we're broken. I said up. We're *broken up*."

"Yes, that's what I meant."

"But it's not what you said."

"God, Luke, don't be ridiculous." Jane starts for the bar, but I catch up.

"Ridiculous? Is that what you think of me now?"

Spinning on the balls of her feet, facing me, she positions herself higher, and says, "I don't think that at all, which is exactly the problem."

"How is that—" Realization dawns on me, and my mouth closes... *She still cares.*

She still cares more than she has let on.

With the seconds growing heavier, and our gazes locked in a standoff, I let her off the hook because I can see the toll it's taking on her. And I just don't want to see her cry. "Let's go inside. I'll buy you a beer."

Silently she turns away, and whispers, "I might need something stronger tonight."

"I'm great at something stronger. Come on." I wrap my arm over her shoulders and pull her to me, keeping her safe and squeezing her, trying to keep it platonic. I'm sure she's onto me. *But she feels so right tucked under my arm.* When she smiles, I release her. One of the hardest things I've done in a while, but I don't want to blow what we just healed. There's too much damage from the past to deal with to add more to it.

Inside, Ian is sitting at a booth near the back exit. I follow Jane through the crowd, wishing I could come up with something to keep us alone, but he's already seen us and is staring at her like something he wants to devour. I grab the back belt loop of her jeans and she jolts to a stop in front of me. Looking over her shoulder at me, she's shocked at first until our eyes meet. Then she smiles. "You used to always wrap your arm around my waist and hold me by the belt loop."

Yes, memories that make her smile are always good memories, and even better reminders. I acted on instinct with her alone, claiming her the only way I can. She asks, "Did you stop me for a reason?"

I have a million regrets and a thousand reasons, but I don't have the right to put my burdens on her. "No... well, maybe. I just wanted to say it's good to see you again."

Fuck. I sound like an idiot. It's good to see you again? What the hell?

She laughs lightly. "It's good to see you too, Luke."

When my fingers unwind, she goes to him as I stand and watch the only woman I will ever love walk away from me again.

This will never get easier.

Jane sits on the inside leaving a seat next to her open. I take it before Ian can because obviously I'm an asshole like that. Ian moves to the inside so he's across from her and they start talking. He uses the movie as an excuse to lean in as if it's top-secret stuff, as if it's the most important thing he's ever been a part of. Maybe it is. It's not for me because Jane was once my most important thing. Before I blew it.

Two rounds of drinks later and my mood is lighter despite Ian getting handsy. Jane has let him paw her wrist twice, her fingers once, and fix the chain on her necklace telling her to make a wish.

I almost had to excuse myself to puke. Instead, I roll my eyes. He's so fucking transparent and has no respect for her or her fiancé. I stand before I say something I shouldn't. "I'm gonna throw some darts."

Jane looks up. "I love darts. Can I join you?"

"Sure. My treat." Ha! *Take that, Ian!*

Ian's phone rings, and I smile. Perfect timing. He says, "I've got to take this. I'll be over after."

We don't wait. After getting the darts from the bartender, I head to the dartboard. "Ladies choice."

She chooses the red darts, leaving me the blue. "Can I go first?" she asks.

"Yep, you sure can."

Stepping up to the line, she squints one eye while holding the dart in front of her. I can already tell she's going to hit the backboard, but she's completely adorable trying so I let her do it her way. She throws and it bounces off the wood. "Damn it," she curses.

Two more darts are thrown and one sticks. That makes her happy, in turn, making me as well. She was always competitive and too hard on herself, but never a poor sport. "Your turn."

I step up and aim, throwing and hitting on the inside near the bull's-eye.

A little elbow nudge to my ribs gets my attention. She says, "You were always too good at everything. Not much has changed."

Not everything... Not the things that truly mattered. Still matter now. But I don't say that. "Nope," I reply. "Not much has changed."

The way she leans close to me, joy in her eyes as she looks up at me, sweet, pink lips, and matching cheeks. *Damn.* She's a dart to my heart, hitting bull's-eye every time.

It's her turn again. Her body is stiff and she's biting the inside of her cheek, taking it so seriously.

"Relax," I say. "Let your arm move naturally, but keep your wrist firm." I touch her at the shoulder and lift her elbow with the other hand. "Like this. Keep your wrist straight. Try that." She moves her forearm back and forth a few times, then peeks up at me. "That feels good."

I'm not sure if she's talking about the darts or the way I'm holding her. I'd love to stay just like this, but it's going to be bordering on awkward if I keep touching her, so I release her and she throws the dart. Laughter comes out in a wave of excitement when her dart lands near the center. Her hands on my shoulders and she's jumping up and down. "We did it! That's amazing."

My hands find her waist, supporting her small frame as she celebrates. Any other time...

"Amazing." If this was any other time and she wasn't engaged and we were together, I'd kiss her. Okay, fine, I'd kiss her if we weren't together too, but engaged, no, I won't cross that line.

She releases me, but I don't release her, not yet, our eyes steady on the other's. Her voice is calm and her smile engaging. "It's amazing how just one small change makes all the difference."

Again, I'm not sure if she's talking about darts, *or us*.

I say, "I'm sor—"

"I'm sorry for the delay. Who's winning?" Ian asks.

Jane holds our gaze a second longer then turns, my skin still alive though her hand has left me. Pushing a thumb my direction, she laughs. "Luke kicked my ass."

Ian steps up with a cocky grin. "C'mon, Luke. You and me for the championship."

"Sure."

When Jane returns with the darts from the board, she hands them over, and stretches to grab her purse. "I'm gonna take off."

Darts instantly forgotten, Ian says, "I'll drive you back to your car then."

"Thank you, but I can take a cab back." Her giggle expresses her mood. "Stay and show Luke who is boss."

My mood is of a different emotion now, turning on a dime as soon as she said she was leaving.

Ian jokes, "No problem there."

"Ha ha," I add, trying to play along when all I want to do is brood about our night coming to an end. When I turn, Ian is behind me, Jane in front, I whisper, "I'll drive you."

"That's okay. Finish the game. I still have some work to do when I get home."

I nod, and as she walks away, she says, "Goodnight, guys. Thanks for the drinks, Luke."

We both watch her go. She's not even out the door when Ian says, "That woman is too fine for her own good. She's going to be a *major* distraction on set."

I turn to him and break the news. "She's engaged."

"Really?" His brow knits. "That sucks."

"Yeah," I say, nodding. "It really does."

He grabs his pint glass and drinks not seeming to think twice about the woman he was hitting on all night. Just another asshole using women for only one thing. *I might resemble that remark.* But Jane's different. I won't let him use her. She's too good for him. Hell, she's too good for me. When he sets his drink down, he picks up the darts, and stands on the line. "After I warm up, we're on."

I go through the motions of the rest of the evening—kicking Ian's ass in darts, paying the tab, driving home. None of that takes my mind off Jane.

It starts to sink in, adrenaline coursing through my veins.

I want her.

I want her back more than ever. Tonight proved how good we can be together again. I've got one month with her to find out if I can stand by and let some other guy lock down the only woman I've ever loved. Or, use that one month to remind her how good we are together.

I've got one month, but that's all I'll need.

CHAPTER 7

Jane

IT WASN'T THE way Luke showed me how to throw darts or even the way he got jealous when Ian showed me too much attention. It wasn't the way I found him so endearing when he apologized thinking he had upset me. Nope. None of that, though I liked those things.

Lying in bed, starfished out and staring up at the ceiling in a dark hotel room with a big ole goofy grin on my face, I know it's not those sweet moments.

It was the way he looked at me.

Longing.

Sensual.

Sweet.

Caring.

Sexual.

Love.

I saw every one of his emotions, but even if I hadn't seen them weighing him down, I felt them through his heavy gaze. It seemed to pain him to look away... to let me walk away. My body was on fire in the car, and I restrained myself from running back inside and telling him every one of my deeply held secrets.

I'm weak to him, to his magnetic gazes, and handsome face, strong hands, and God, why does he have to look so good? It would be a challenge to not fall for him in any normal situation, but seeing the lust and the love in his eyes for me, I'm undone— unequivocally—ruined by that man.

My body burns for him. Our chemistry is electric. I see it in his eyes. I affect him like he does me. The current that runs between us is stronger than when we were together, if that's even possible.

Damn you, Luke!

Squeezing my eyes shut, I curse his name again and again until the tears fall from the corners of my eyes. I roll to the side and hold my arms around me while curling my legs to my body. So many wasted years. So many.

Too many.

And all because he couldn't make the verbal commitment he had already made in his heart.

Damn him.

My phone rings, startling me from my misery. I sniffle to gather myself together and answer the phone, hoping it's a friend I can talk to, someone like Sarah who will understand the emotional trauma I've gone through the last couple years with the mate to my soul.

"Hello?"

On the other end of the phone, I hear just a whisper in the dark and lonely room. "Jane."

No. *Not* who I wanted *or* needed. "Lawrence."

"I... I miss you, Jane." This is the man who treated me like a dog, expecting me to heel by his side on demand. *Asshole.* I leave his statement lingering between us, with nothing to say in response. "Jane, I want to see you. Will you come over?"

"Why?" I ask, not whispering.

"So we can talk."

"I don't have anything to talk about."

"I think we have a lot. I've given you space, time to find yourself, let you think about things like you wanted. I've done everything you said you needed, but now I want you to come home."

"What you forgot is that I didn't say I need time to figure out where I stand with us, Lawrence. I know where we stand and it's apart."

"No."

"Yes," I say, delicately. "I don't want to hurt you—"

"But I am hurting. Without you, I'm hurting."

"I'm sorry." I lie there with the phone to my ear, but a lone tear trails down my cheek for the man I lost, the man I love who will never love me back the same way—Luke. "We were convenient, Lawrence, nothing more."

"You were my life."

"I was an accessory to your life. I completed this picture you have in your head about how things should look for your career. I don't want to accessorize someone's life. I want to be someone's world."

"You can't find that here. This is LA. The land of narcissism. I can give you so much though—a good home and a comfortable life. You can open a spending account at Saks. Jane, I feel love for you."

I feel love for you replays in my head two more times. "I don't even shop at Saks."

"I'll buy you a new car—"

"I bought myself a car. Lawrence, this isn't about money. It's about love and although I care about your well-being, I'm in love with someone else."

"What does that even mean? You've been gone what, a month, and you've already met someone? Or, let me guess, you were screwing around behind my back? Fuck. I should have known. Wendy warned me about you and I defended—"

"Excuse me? How dare you! I never cheated on you. It's insulting you would even think that, much less say it. As for your sister, she's the slut sleeping with your best friend and business partner. Wise up, Larry."

"Goddamn it, it's your ex, right?" He sighs harshly into the phone. "Luke Anders? Really? I'm a lawyer to the stars. He's a D-level producer. He's not going anywhere in Hollywood."

"See, that's what you don't understand. My feelings for him have nothing to do with his career."

"Jane, listen to yourself. Are you insane? I know you like nice things. He can't give you those things. I can."

"Are you listening to yourself? You would settle for someone who looks good on your arm over someone who loves you? Why?"

"Because my career is my love. The rest are just pieces falling into place."

"I can't."

"You can't what?"

"I can't be with someone I don't love."

"We've been together for a while, Jane. There are no surprises with me. You know what you get with me, so what changed?"

"My heart."

"Damn, rein in the emotional crap and look at the big picture."

"I am looking at the big picture and it doesn't include you. Goodbye, Lawrence." I hang up the phone and drop it to the bed.

He's an emotional grand canyon: wide and expansive, picturesque even, but the faults are too deep to overcome.

Feeling a lot like I dodged a bullet, I do what I know I shouldn't. I play with fire, and text Luke. **Thanks for the drinks tonight.**

Luke: **Anytime. It was good to see you.**

I debate whether to text again or let him go to bed. Or maybe he's not even home yet. Or has company. Ugh! Lying in the dark, I light up my screen and stare at his last message. Then I dive back into this tumultuous pool and text again: **Yes, it was a fun night. Are you home or still out partying?**

Luke: **I'm home. Just walked in.**

Me: **Alone?**

Oh shoot! I shouldn't have typed that.

Me: **I'm sorry. That's none of my business.**

He doesn't text back right away and butterflies invade my belly.

Then he does, making them all go away.

Luke: **I'm alone, Jane. How about you?**

Me: **I'm alone too.**

Luke: **I meant your well being, but I like that answer better.**

Smiling, I type: **I'm grateful for more than just the drinks.**

Luke: **What are you grateful for?**

Me: **For the company.**

Luke: **Ian's ego can be a bit much, but he's a cool enough guy if you're into that GQ looking wealthy director type.**

Me: **O.o**

Me: **You, Luke. I meant you.**

Luke: **Me?**

Me: **Thank you for your company. The fun was needed more than you know.**

Luke: *I'm available for fun anytime. Like now, for instance.*

I hear a virtual knock and open the door of opportunity.

Me: *You're not tired?*

Luke: *Nope. You?*

Me: *I'm in bed already.*

Luke: *Wait, hold up. So you were just lying in bed thinking about me? I like where this is going. Continue...*

Giggling, I do continue, loving these lighthearted exchanges.

Me: *You have such a dirty mind.*

I roll onto my back again, holding the phone above me while I wait for a reply. When he does, I'm left debating again.

Luke: *Come over.*

Luke: *You're alone. I'm alone. Let's be alone together.*

Me: *How do you know I'm still alone?*

Luke: *Because I'm assuming you wouldn't be texting me from bed if you weren't.*

Me: *What if I actually said yes?*

Luke: *Yes, what if?*

Me: *Be careful what you wish for.*

Luke: *Or it might come true. *wishes harder**

My heart leaps from giddiness. He does want me. Just like I want him. I don't reply. I can't. I need to be with him now more than ever, so I grab my purse as I head for the door.

Even after midnight traffic sucks and it takes me longer than expected to get to his house. My headlights scan across the front of his house as I pull into his short driveway. When the lights settle on the garage door, Luke is leaning against the entrance, full-on panty-assaulting smirk on his face. The biceps are giving his smile a run for my money though. With his arms crossed, shadows detail the defined muscles—firm, carved from strength and creating pure sex appeal.

Sitting here, I'm faced with the possibility of what could happen if I get out of this car, so I stay inside, physical barriers in place. Our eyes stay steadily fastened.

Pushing off the wall, he comes to the driver's side window and knocks. His voice is muted through the glass when he says, "Hi." And though the window is electric, he makes a circular motion with his hand signaling me to roll it down.

I do, and then ask, "It's late. What are you doing out here?"

With his hands pressed to the top of the car, he leans down. "Wishing upon a star."

His voice is deep, seductive, fitting for the quiet of the hour. My grip on the steering wheel tightens. I try to keep up the conversation, knowing if I stop, it will only be because our lips will be too busy doing other things. "A lot of wishing going on tonight." I roll my eyes. I sound so ridiculous.

"I'm hedging my bet."

And yet, I continue to play along. "And what bet is that?"

"Come inside and find out." My door is opened and he steps back to let me out.

Seconds.

I only have seconds to figure out how this is going to play out, not just tonight, but what direction this relationship is going in.

"I missed you, Jane."

And I'm done for. It doesn't matter that he's the second one tonight who has said that to me. It only matters that *he's* the one I want to hear it from.

I get out of the car.

He shuts the door and offers me his hand, palm up. I want to convince myself that it's the stars reflecting in his eyes, but I know better. I've seen that emotion before. It's the same one he sees in mine, the same one I feel deep inside.

Taking his hand, he leads me into the house. The only light inside is the glow from the moon shining in. The only sound is my heart beating loudly in my chest, my soul wanting to reconnect with his against my head's better judgment. He exhales and I'm comforted by the sound, feeling less alone in this emotionally charged moment.

With the door locked behind me, I stand in the dark space. Our hands are still together when he starts to walk farther inside, stopping when I don't budge. Looking back at me, he whispers, "We don't have to do anything you don't want."

"I'm afraid of what I do want. What I shouldn't want."

I can see his own struggle in his actions. He shifts and as if he's that boy back in high school, he says, "I'll keep this a secret if we have to, Jane. I want to be with you so badly that it hurts to be this close."

Tears fill my eyes, and I drop my head down. "You'll be a dirty secret for me?"

"I'll be anything you'll let me be." Taking my other hand, he holds both between us. "Hey, look at me." When I do, he says, "And there's nothing dirty about this or us." The warmth of him calms me, my nerves subsiding. Our bodies inch closer on their own accord. *This* feels right. *This* is where I should be.

His scent.

His touch.

His lips.

They beckon me and I can't resist their enticing pull.

I may have been with Lawrence, but it never felt like this. Not real. Not deep and forever. Our feelings were superficial. The conversation with him earlier proves what my instincts told me a long time ago. Another downside of thinking of Lawrence while I'm with Luke is that I think of *her*, the blonde standing in Luke's shirt staking claims over his heart and home. And all the other *hers* Luke has been with during our breakup. I'm no longer his one and only. And he's no longer mine. The thought breaks my heart and another crack forms in the future I once dreamed of having.

Just before our eyes close and our lips meet, my head takes over my heart, the feelings of hurt smothering my desire. I say what I should have replied to his text. "I can't."

His hands leave my body, distance thrown between us, and a quiet "Fuck" is heard as he walks away. Standing in front of the windows, he stares ahead.

"Luke?"

The concern in my voice crackles and pops, the live wire energy between us breaks down. When he doesn't turn around, I go to him, touching his shoulder. "I'm sorry."

"No apologies. Okay?" Suddenly he turns and starts walking to the stairs. "It's late. You're welcome to stay here. I have a guest room or the couch," he offers. "Or you can go if you'll feel more comfortable not staying. I don't know what you need from me. I will do anything for you, but you have to tell me what it is, Jane."

"I don't need anything."

"You need something or you wouldn't be standing in my house right now." Taking three steps up, with his back to me, he adds, "For the record, I was hurt too."

"I'm sorry." He told me not to say it but I can't help it.

He hesitates, but then walks up the stairs. I watch him go. I'm left standing in his living room, alone with the darkness and silence of his surroundings and the reality of the life he built without me.

As I look around, I know what I'm doing before I do it. The answer is so obvious. His pull is too strong. My body acts on instinct. I'm not going anywhere, but up the stairs to join him.

CHAPTER 8

THE HOUSE IS unfamiliar, the layout foreign to me as I reach the top of the staircase. It's a lot like Luke is to me these days. Nothing is the same in his house or with us. I almost feel weird that I held on to things like photos and jewelry he gave me, and I still sleep in a few of his T-shirts sometimes.

There is no *me* in this house and I debate if I need to change that or let him continue to move on without me. *What is the right thing to do for both of us?* He didn't want a commitment. He made that clear. *Why would it be any different now? Why would he want to be with me years after he let me go?*

I'm different. *Is he?*

I've changed. *Has he?*

Maybe I need to be alone. I would say find myself, but I'm pretty sure the last few months I've been more sure of my decisions than I have been in years.

Maybe he's someone I can be alone with. No awkward *getting to know you* stage. No fumbling around in bed trying to figure out what turns someone on and what's a turn off. We know each other and we know each other's bodies.

Luke made it clear downstairs that he was willing to be a secret, for me. That goes to show he doesn't want to be the main attraction in my life. He's fine being the sideshow.

So we could keep this simple. Friends.

With benefits.

No harm.

No foul.

As I follow the sound of running water, the images that come with that sound flood my mind.

A shower.

Luke.

Naked.

Maybe this is exactly what I need to get over him. This *one last time*. Or maybe I just need sex, period. It's been a long time since I've been with anyone, even Lawrence—it must have been at least six months. I've lost track.

"Luke?" I call softly while pushing open the bedroom door. He doesn't answer, so I walk in. His bedroom is nice, just my style—warm, dark-wood furniture, fluffy duvet on the bed with pillows. I smile that he didn't make his bed this morning. I used to gripe so much about our messy bed. Somehow that small detail comforts me now when it used to drive me bonkers.

The water falls loudly and I go toward the bathroom. The door is wide open, so I walk in slowly. The mirror is steamed and a towel hangs from a hook nearby. My eyes drift to the figure behind the glass. The glass isn't clear, but not opaque enough to hide his body from view.

One hand supports him as he leans forward, the other moves up and down over his slick erection.

I was having carnal thoughts of Luke before, but now my body is on fire for him. A war rages inside me. I thought it was hard to figure out if I should come over. That was the easy part I've discovered.

This.

Here.

Now.

This is everything—where our minds and our bodies come back together. I take my shirt over my head, and then my jeans down. Stripping off my undergarments, I drop them to the floor and walk to the shower.

The door is opened and Luke's eyes go wide momentarily. Then he looks down my body, drinking me in, savoring me with his hand still on his hard cock.

Though his hand has slowed, he's still pumping. His voice is deeper, lust-filled breaths between the words. "Close the door."

Stepping inside, I swallow hard. Selfishly, I want him and like the way he looks at me, how he's looking at me now. With his hand on his body, his eyes are on me while ecstasy builds between us. I reach down and replace his hand with my own. His eyes flutter closed and the muscles in his jaw tense when I start moving.

The water rains over my shoulders and I move against his side, letting the spray soak the top of my head while pressing my cheek to his chest. His arm comes around me, holding me closer. My emotions take another hit to the heart.

This used to be us. We used to love so freely, so completely. Now we're a dirty little secret to lives that have gotten the better of us. All of it so much, too much. I try to move away before I fall under the darkness that shrouds my heart when it comes to the pain associated with Luke.

His grip tightens as his other hand takes mine away. He weaves his fingers with mine and holds them between us, between our divided and bruised hearts. He kisses the top my head and a tear falls from my eye, blending in with the water that runs down my body. "Don't cry," he whispers, his voice unsteady like my legs. "I'm not strong enough to survive your pain."

I'm not strong enough to survive your pain.

I know what he means. I don't think I'm strong enough either. I can't do friends with benefits with Luke. Not my Luke. He means too much. Always too much.

The faucet is shut off and I look up at him. Stroking my wet hair away from my face, he kisses my cheek, and says, "I never thought we'd end up like this. As broken together as we are apart."

Another tear falls and I whisper, "I'm sorry." I love that our cheeks are still pressed together. His scratchy to my soft. He pulls back to look at me, but I hold him in place this time, not ready for him to see my face, my tears, my heart exposed through my eyes.

Seconds lead to minutes as we stand there with our naked bodies, our broken souls pressed together. I'm not cold, but when I start to shiver, I turn my head and walk out, needing to put distance in our destructive path. I reach for a towel but his hand beats mine and he wraps the white terry cloth around me.

Drying himself, he glances to me, but doesn't let his gaze linger like usual. Maybe he's felt the same pain I have, the same one I'm feeling now. I ask, "Why would you want to be a secret?"

"I'd rather have you under those conditions than not at all."

He's willing to bear a scarlet letter to be with me.

And that's all it takes.

Dropping my towel, I turn to him, pressing my body to his, but this time in passion. I lift up and kiss him, kiss him with every *I love you* we ever shared, with every glimmer of hope bubbling to the surface.

Large hands find the small of my waist and he holds me to him. One hand slides up my back and then his fingers slip into my hair, the pressure of our lips intensifying. With our mouths accepting and open, our tongues are reunited for the first time in years. A moan slips out and my heartbeat settles into what it's missed for too long—the rhythm of his heart.

Another moan escapes me, then a squeal when I'm lifted quickly and carried over his shoulder. Laughing, this feels too good to protest. I've missed how easy it used to be with him. I'm tossed on the bed while he stands there with a smile that could electrify the LA skyline. The tenderness of his heart speaks through his soft expression as he looks down at me, and he says, "I can hold you. We don't have to do anything."

Moving higher on the bed, I rest my head on his pillow. His scent fills my chest, and I smile. Propping up on my elbows, I ask, "What if I want to do something with you?"

With no hesitation, he grabs his phone from the nightstand and turns on a song. A slow country song starts to play when the Bluetooth kicks in, playing it through the speakers. "I was hoping you'd say that."

"Keith Urban?"

He shrugs as he climbs on to the bed and over me. "I know you don't believe me, but I hear everything you say to me. You said you like him, so I bought a few songs."

"Because of me?"

"*For* you."

This is the Luke I know, the one I once knew more than myself. Oh how I've missed this incredible man.

It was never about money, gifts, or shopping in Beverly Hills. I never needed, nor wanted that. This is what my dreams are made of—kindness, thoughtfulness.

Luke.

Hovering over me, he breathes and I inhale, letting him fill my lungs. His hair is wet, but so is mine and I don't care if my makeup is running or if my face is clean because deep in the ocean of his eyes, his soul is revealed to mine. As if my heart wasn't already swimming in his heavy waters, he says, "You're more beautiful than the day I met you and the day I met you, you were the most beautiful girl I'd ever seen."

The tips of my fingers touch his temple, gently brushing back hair that has fallen. His hair is shorter these days, short enough to look professional in his field, but long enough to drive me crazy when I run my fingers through it. I love it. I always did. Stretching my neck up, I kiss him again. He leans down and I relax while he moves to my neck, his tongue swirling, and then he sucks lightly. "I missed the taste of your skin."

Curiosity killed the cat, so they say... "Do I taste different from the others you've been with?

Looking up, he gazes into my eyes confident as ever. "When we're together, Jane, it's you and me. Only the two of us. No one else. Okay?"

When his weight drops down slowly on top of me, the pressure of his frame on mine, I'm reminded of how much I loved being with him. "Okay."

A pact is made. A pact that doesn't require anything more than my soul signed over to his in a moment of passion, then returned gently with a little more wear and tear, but bettered through the process.

I sign my pact with a kiss to his lips and he signs in return.

The music switches to a ballad about being blue and not being treated right. I block out the words and my body moves to the mesmerizing melody. His body is hard. All over. My legs open wider as his fingers tap over my stomach. A slight pressure, one I love too much, is felt when he flattens his hand on my belly. He stills. Our mouths part as he lifts. His lids are heavy and I imagine mine are the same. "I've dreamed about you, touching you like this," he says, sliding his hand down until his fingers make me squirm, my body asking for more, begging if my body could speak.

Silently I reply, my head dropping back, my back arching toward him. His mouth covers one of my nipples, his teeth grazing lightly sending unabashed shivers down my spine. With his arm wrapped under me keeping me in that position, his whispers give me goose bumps. "Can you feel how much I want you?"

My fingers glide over the smooth skin of his length when he cradles my hand around his hard muscle. Unbreakable, but not insurmountable. Surmounting several times over is all part of the plans I have in mind. His lips are too far when I reach to kiss them. Instead they say, "Answer me, Jane."

With his caressing gaze locked on mine, my mind is loose while my body tightens. "Yes."

"Yes what, baby?"

Baby. Just like he used to call me so freely when I was his and he was mine. Another fiery-tipped arrow to the heart lands, relighting the torch I still carry for him.

"Say it. For me," he adds with his mouth on my chest, fingers working me.

"I feel..." My breath is harsh, but I catch it. "I feel how much you want me." Closing my eyes, my hands roll over the tense muscles in his shoulders. "Do you feel how much I want you?"

Circles.

One.

Then two.

Enter.

My moan comes out in a sigh of relief. His thumb returns to chase the elusive along with my mind, and he says, "I feel how much you want me."

Pushing up, he moves down my body until his eyes are

looking up at mine over my breasts. "I gave my soul to you when we were sixteen. Will you give me yours now?"

"You already have it."

"Only you, Jane. Only for you." With a cocky smile in place, he says, "I'm going to open your body, embrace your soul, and coax the moon and stars to shine inside."

My breathing deepens as he repeats the words I've held close for so long. Hearing those words again, after all these years, gives me goose bumps. *Because he had.* He had opened my body, embraced my soul, and coaxed the moon and stars to shine in my life. Each breath feels shorter than the previous as I begin to pant from his promise. I give in when his mouth covers me, my body his always as his tongue warms me.

The song changes. I barely notice except when the chorus kicks in and Aurora's "Conqueror" floats from the speaker. Conqueror. Conqueror. God, Luke can conquer me anytime he wants. His mouth twists, words mumbled against my sensitive skin, hot breath causing me to fist the sheets. Not three minutes. I'm falling apart and begging, "I want you inside me." He remains right where he is, placing my right leg over his shoulder, and burying deeper. When I touch his head, he stops. "Please."

He looks up. "No."

"No?"

"This time is about you." He licks his lips and I've never seen anything more fucking sexy than that right there. "I'll make love to you. I'll also fuck you. But not this time."

I fall back and huff unable to speak when his mouth takes me again.

And again.

And one more time before four a.m.

We fall asleep shortly after, but I'm restless.

I'm also hot and trapped under a large arm, nothing like the one that would try to cover me a few months ago. This one makes me smile, and for a moment in time, I allow myself to believe we're more than a dirty secret, that we're more than a one-time thing.

I allow myself to believe I can forgive and forget and that Luke Anders can love me so completely again like I love him.

CHAPTER 9

Luke

THE BED IS empty next to me where her body warmed me most of the night. I stretch my arm out, not liking the space. Looking over, the pillow shows where her head once lay. The sheets are wrinkled and bunched where her body was. I grab the pillow and throw it across the room. "Fuck!"

I sit up pissed for thinking we could be more than a fucking one-night stand. She's probably waking her fiancé up with a home-cooked breakfast, lying to his fucking face. I hate the thought as soon as I think it. Not because of the other guy, though I hate that, but she wouldn't do that to me. Would she? Has the Jane I've known so well, better than myself, changed that much? Could she have actually cheated on Lawrence? *With me?*

If she did cheat, could she return to him so easily as if last night didn't happen? I don't know what the fuck is going on with her, but the thought of her with him makes me angry. I need to shake out of it or I'll be knocking on Lawrence's front door and kicking his ass for stealing my girl. Fuck! How could she do this? *What the fuck?*

Getting out of bed, I go to the closet to grab a pair of

basketball shorts from the shelf and boxer briefs from the drawer. After slipping them on, I reach for a sleeveless Lakers jersey and socks as I head into the bathroom to brush my teeth. The mirror doesn't lie. I look like a fucking mess or maybe it's just how I'm viewing life this morning.

With a quick text to my buddy, I'm off to the courts to work these fucking emotions out of my system.

"SO YOU DIDN'T get laid?" Blaise asks in disbelief.

"We messed around some, but nope." I shoot and miss the basket.

Rebounding the ball, he says, "What happened?"

"Like literally what happened?"

"Fuck you. I don't want to know your gory sex deets. Why didn't you get laid?"

"First off," I say, jumping and blocking his shot. With the basketball swooped to the side, I *T* my hands and call a time out. "No one says deets anymore, so stop that. Secondly, I wanted to make it about her."

His face is twisted in horror. "What does that even mean?"

"Thought you didn't want the 'deets'?"

"I don't, but it sounds like you need help." He punches at the ball secured under my arm, but it doesn't move.

Faking him out, I step around him and shoot. This time I score. "You just gave me an idea."

"Drinks on you then." He rebounds again and this time shoots over my head.

Jumping up, the ball meets my hand. "You might be onto

something. I don't need your help, but I might need a detective."

He stops in the middle of the court. "Dude, what the hell are you talking about?"

Why didn't it dawn on me this morning? "I got distracted last night. Maybe it's not about what I'm being told, but what I'm seeing."

"Since we're not playing ball and standing around like two fucking girls gossiping, lay it on me. What the fuck are you talking about?"

Maybe what I think isn't what's real. Maybe seeing is believing. "Nothing," I mumble, my head still back in bed with Jane from last night.

"Fuck, man. Let's play ball then."

I throw the ball at him. "Game on."

SO WHAT SEEMED like a good idea in the middle of a half-assed game of basketball has now become complicated. Standing in the middle of my closet, I'm perplexed. What does one wear to spy on the love of his life? More importantly, what does one wear to spy on the love of his life in order to figure out if she's really going to marry someone else?

Because this is normal... not *in any way.*

I grab a black turtleneck, wondering when and why I bought a black turtleneck. Pulling it on over my head, I still have no idea where this came from or when I would have purchased it, but it works for my mission, even if it is a little snug. I swing my arms out several times to stretch it out, and then pick a pair of dark jeans and black sneaks. I add a charcoal beanie to complete the look and head out the door.

It's just gone nine when I park in front of Jane's house. I cut the engine and sit. And wait. I haven't heard from Jane today, despite a few texts and one call to her that she didn't pick up. I'm not sure what's going on, and on top of it, her sneaking out of my house in the middle of the night has not sat well with me. It's all wrong.

We're all wrong.

I wasn't lying when I told her we're broken. Are we too broken to fix? I hope not. Love will be the glue that holds us together again. I feel it deep inside. I'm meant to be with her. I wonder what she feels deep inside.

A car pulls up to the house and I duck down when they park in the driveway. I watch as Lawrence helps Jane out of the car. But when the woman stands up, her hair is dark, almost black, not like my Jane's.

I straighten up, hoping to get a better look at her.

Holy fuck! Is he cheating on Jane or are they actually not together anymore? Since she hooked up with me, my gut tells me they're broken up. But wouldn't she tell me if they weren't together when we spoke about being a secret?

They must be together. My ego is stroked thinking she just can't resist me.

Lawrence is a douche so her being with me comes as no surprise. But shit, if he's cheating on her and her on him, what kind of relationship is this? What we did was natural. We have a history. We have feelings that will always exist from a life spent together. Our attraction to each other was never the problem, so it remains just as strong. But Lawrence, he flat-out cheated. I start the car when the couple disappears inside. Driving away, I'm more confused than ever. Jane is a complete mystery to me.

I'm not sure how to process what I saw, or what to do with the information. I can't think clearly. My stomach growls. Food will help. I need to eat and then figure out if I keep this information from Jane or tell her what I know. I feel dirty with this knowledge.

Will telling her about her fiancé cleanse my soul or will the messenger be killed? Is this even my business?

Jane is always my business. The one thing I stuck to when we broke up was if I couldn't make her happy, I wanted her to be with someone who could. A cheating fiancé is one thing, but a *husband* is a whole other.

She has to know the truth, even at the expense of myself.

I place an order with an area restaurant and sit in the parking lot for a few minutes weighted down by the burden of being the bearer of bad news. I have no idea what I'll tell her or when. I don't even know how—phone, text, email, in person. Needing fresh air, I get out and go inside to wait, hoping the bustling restaurant will distract me for a few minutes at the least.

The restaurant is crowded, but my to-go order is ready and waiting for me when I walk in. I don't recognize this hostess from previous visits but she's more than happy to shoo the waiters away and help me. When she leaves to retrieve my order, I check my phone and scroll through emails with no interest to tackle them tonight.

"Luke?"

I look up, and with surprise in my voice that matches my eyes, I say, "Jane?"

"You still come here?"

Tucking my phone in my pocket, I shift, wanting to ask her why she left and a million other questions about last night. I don't because I don't want to bombard her right off the bat. With her looking so damn beautiful it's easy to forget everything but the good. "A few times a month if I'm in the area. What are you doing here?"

"Picking up food before I head home." She looks away when she speaks, but her gaze works its way back to me. She has a glass of wine in one hand and her purse in the other. Her eyes narrow in confusion. "Why are you wearing my sweater?"

"Yours?" I ask, tugging it away from my chest and looking down.

"I think so. I used to have one just like it. It was huge on me." Amusement dances in her eyes and I can tell she's poking fun when she says, "Looks good on you."

Rolling my eyes, I reply sheepishly, then chuckle. "It was in my closet. I had no idea where it was from."

She laughs lightly. "You can keep it."

"Yeah, thanks." I laugh too. "So ridiculous."

She takes a step back when the hostess returns with my order. The hostess hands me the bill. After glancing at Jane, her eyes make their way back to me, and she whispers, "If you're single, can I give you my number?"

Jane hears the posed question, which is not helping my case. She peeks back at me over her shoulder and a resolved smile is present on her sweet features. "I'm flattered, but I'm with someone."

"No harm in trying."

"Nope," I reply, reassuring her with a smile. "No harm done." I move off to the side so I'm standing face to face with my pretty green-eyed girl. Her cheating fiancé weighs on my mind though, so I lift the bag of food just a little. "Want to eat dinner together?"

Her smile lights up her entire face in response. "I'd like that." And once again I'm so confused to what is going on with this mysterious woman.

We go to the bar where her food is delivered and settle at a tall table near the window. We unpack our dishes and I notice her order is for one. For one, but she said she was heading home. Hmm? Sipping my beer, I watch her, trying to figure out what the real deal is. Her lashes shadow her pretty greens. There's a light pink to her cheeks as she looks up at me.

When I greet her with a grin that I've been struggling to control, she looks away, but a smile is followed by a giggle from her.

"What's so funny?" I ask.

"I got lost in the moment."

"What moment was that?"

"The one where I forgot about our breakup and all the water that's flowed under this bridge." She sighs, but she's not entirely sad. "I forgot about that and was simply enjoying the company."

"I did that last night."

"Me too." Setting her fork down, she spins the stem of her wine glass around watching the liquid coat the sides and slide back down. When her eyes meet mine, she confesses, "I shouldn't have left."

I set my fork down and lean my elbows on the table. Resting my chin on my knuckles, I ask, "Why did you?"

"Because I shouldn't have been there."

"There was nothing wrong with you being with me. That's in your head. Tell me, Jane. What's in your heart?"

Her eyes hold mine until the pressure builds and she looks away, adjusting the napkin in her lap. "You know we shouldn't talk about things like that."

"All I know is that I liked last night."

"You're not looking at the big picture. Last night was just another good time to you, so it's easy for you to see the silver lining whether it's right or wrong."

"I do see the silver lining when it comes to us and I don't

know why you're so resistant to this, *to me*, when we feel so right." I reach over and take her hand from the glass and hold it. "Tell me we're wrong and I won't push."

"We're wrong, Luke. We gave it a shot and it was a solid one. Ten years is a long time."

I take my hand back, but push even though I promised not to. "But?"

"But we didn't work out. That's the bottom line. We didn't work."

"Bullshit."

Her eyes go wide and she laughs. "Always the optimist, even on something as hopeless as we are."

"Until you say 'I do' to someone else, I'll hold out that hope."

A smile plays at the corners of her lips, but she refuses to give in to her own happiness. "What if it's not about me, but you?"

"What does that mean?"

"You're forgetting I came back once..." She looks away again, this time uncomfortable. Anger tinges her tone when she says, "Why do we have to do this every time?"

"We don't." She shuts it down anytime we get close to opening the wounds and digging deep to heal us. It's so damn frustrating. "That's the problem. It's always hot and cold with you." I should tell her what I saw earlier tonight, but how does what she did with me differ? The whole situation if fucked up and I don't know how to repair it.

"The problem is you see things your way and I see them mine and they're just two different ways." Taking her purse in hand and holding it tightly to her, she says, "I got the email about the production schedule changing. With filming in a month, I have another script I need to finish and stuff to take care of before I leave for Austin. Every time I see you, my mind gets muddled and I can't afford to lose sight of what's important to me, so I think it's best if we don't see each other before then."

"Because I'm so distracting?" I cock a smirk.

She's playing hardball and tilts her head not amused by my charms. "Because it's not good for me to spend time with you."

"For your heart or your head?"

"Both." She turns and walks out of the restaurant.

I have *sure things* giving me their numbers and I'm choosing the only woman who doesn't want me. She enjoyed last night but apparently spending time with me is a waste. I'm puzzled when it comes to understanding her. This whole mess is so fucking frustrating. I toss some money down to cover the clean-up of the table and head out. My appetite diminished the second she left.

While driving home, I recognize how much she's changed from the girl I once knew. She used to want to talk about everything the minute she was upset. She wanted to talk it out and resolve it, but she struggled to express her real feelings, hoping to spare mine. Apologies came fast and we never went to bed mad.

We rarely argued. It makes me wonder if that's why we fell apart. I wasn't aware of what was going on in her life while she was keenly aware of what was going on in mine. She tried to save us, to wake me up to the reality of what was happening. I wish I'd seen it, recognized I was losing her. We were growing apart and I let it happen. I was too caught up in stuff that didn't matter to see I was losing what did. I love my career, but I loved her more. And that hasn't changed.

These days, she speaks her mind and even comes around uninvited. That's not the actions of someone who doesn't want to see you, to spend time with you. That's the opposite, in fact.

I fucked up when I didn't give her the commitment she wanted, the commitment I had already made in my heart. I fucked up when I didn't see she was ready to come back to me. I missed the signal, didn't read between the lines of what she was really saying. Her actions were telling me, even if she wasn't.

If only I hadn't gone out that night last year to forget about the one girl I thought I'd lost forever. I fucked up my future with Jane on a one-night stand with Jeanette. *Fuck!* Ironically, now she's telling me everything I want to hear: I'm distracting, I'm affecting her, that it's about me holding us back now...

I'm pulling into the garage just as my phone lights up with a text message. I take the phone with me as I get out and look down in the dark of the garage.

Jane: *I'm sorry.*

It's good to see not everything has changed. I walk inside thinking about how I want to respond. She doesn't owe me an apology. If anything, I owe her ten. With the lights still off, I lean against the kitchen counter and type.

Me: *For what?*

Jane: *For leaving without saying goodbye.*

Me: *Would saying goodbye change the outcome?*

Jane: *Probably not.*

I didn't think so. I don't worry about the lack of goodbye tonight. I worry about a goodbye forever.

Me: *I liked last night.*

What I really want to text is that I loved seeing her body again, touching her body again, *loving* her body again. But I can't. Not yet.

Jane: *I liked last night too.*

Me: *I hated this morning.*

Jane: *I hated leaving that bed.*

Riddles. I want to know she hated leaving me. Not the damn bed. Me: *It's not "that" bed. It's MY bed.*

Jane: *I'm sorry.*

With the spy mission from earlier in the night still weighing on my mind, I debate if this is how I should tell her—through texts. Closing my eyes, I rub my forehead, debating if I should tell her or not. I know the right thing to do, but we're already so out of sync. Do I want to make it worse?

Lawrence Reinstardt was supposed to be a rebound. Nothing more. I wasn't going to hold him against her when we got back together. I was so fucking naïve. Together? I didn't imagine when she walked out that it was forever. He got to her. He wore her down. She's not weak, but I know she was broken. It was just like his style to prey on her and take advantage of a bad situation. Fucker. She was mine. She was always meant to be mine. Somehow things just got muddled between us along the way.

I don't want to break her heart even if she is breaking mine. This isn't how I want to win her back. I'm not Lawrence and I won't put her in a position to choose. That would be setting her up to hurt someone and it might just be me. I need to let her handle her business—personally and professionally—and then in Austin, we'll talk again.

Me: *I think you're right.*

Jane: *About?*

Me: *I think it's best if we take this time apart to take care of business before filming begins.*

She doesn't respond right away, but when she does, she sends: *I understand. Please know I really am sorry.*

Typing a final message, I pause before I push send: *Me too, Jane. Me too.*

She doesn't respond again. And I understand why. She has to fix this messy life she's leading. I add to her chaos and don't want her feeling divided. If we get a second... or third chance, I'm not going to ruin it by delivering bad news to her. We will be because we were meant to all along. I know that now.

If Jane Lewis just so happens to be single again soon, she won't be for long. *That is a promise.*

CHAPTER 10

Jane

TIME DOESN'T HEAL old wounds. It distorts them. Twists your memories so you forget the truth and see the extremes. *Love or hate.* Those are the only two emotions left to comfort me after all this time.

One or the other.

Changing, depending on the day. The hour. The minute.

Sitting on the floor of my hotel room, I rummage through my jewelry box looking for something very specific. It's been a week since I last saw Luke and I feel the need for a reminder of the good times. I find what I'm looking for underneath a light blue ribbon. Running the satin ribbon through my fingers, I remember when Luke gave me the corsage it once adorned for junior prom. With a lump in my throat, I set it aside and take the ring out, slipping it on my left hand ring finger.

I can't stop the smile that covers my face when I look down at my hand. The sapphire and diamond ring sparkles in the sunlight shining in from the window nearby. This ring comes with a broken promise, but I still love it, treasure it deeper than I should. Even now it's a symbol of us, of where we are in our relationship—broken cracks where promises slip through and love remains. I treasure him deeper than I should too.

It was all so simple back then. Our lives and the circumstances were easy with no real life problems or roadblocks, responsibilities, or regrets burdening us. If I were twenty again, I wouldn't change anything. I would go through the happy, the sad, the love, the fights, the growing up and growing together stages with Luke over again because even though we aren't together now and he couldn't give me the happily ever after I needed, loving him each day was worth it.

ANOTHER FEW WEEKS pass and I don't text Luke, or call. I should since he's on my mind all the time, like the ring has stayed on my finger. I like seeing it when I type, my heart swooning like the characters from the script. I respect his wishes. We take my suggestion to give it time. I thought it would fix me, allow me to forget the women he's been with. I should. I don't even have a right to be mad, but it's not mad I'm dealing with. It's hurt and I feel betrayed. I'm not fixed. That much is clear, so I must protect the rest of my heart that remains unclaimed.

What am I doing? Sighing, I should take the ring off, but I can't seem to part with it. Wiggling my finger, I hold it up in the air and continue admiring the pretty token of love. I'm tempted to keep wearing it. Just around the hotel room. Just for me.

So I do.

I pack my suitcases and close them. Carrying the jewelry box, I set it gently in one of two boxes that contains my whole life. Two suitcases and two boxes. It's not a lot to show for a life that feels lived in.

When I walked out on Luke, I left belongings we shared behind just like our lives. I thought I would be back. I couldn't bear to take *our* stuff and live with it elsewhere. *Could he? Did he?*

The rest was delivered to my mom's house—two boxes of stuff from photos to stuffed animals to yearbooks all carefully packed away that now lives in her attic.

I take the suitcases by the handles and load both into my car. When I return for the last box, I stop and look around. This suite, the size of my first apartment I shared with Luke, has been home for too long. It's time to move on. After one more look around, I leave this refuge, this place that gave me a new start, one last time. I stop by the front desk to say goodbye to the never-too-friendly clerk and set the key on the counter.

I have nothing holding me back. Only the future awaits. Driving to Texas is a good option for me. I never found an apartment or a house I wanted anyway. So I'm leaving nothing behind but a past it's time to move on from. As I pull away from the extended-stay hotel, I look in the rearview mirror, and then focus forward.

New adventures are on the horizon. Texas here I come.

An hour later, I'm still in LA.

Annoyed.

Stupid traffic.

I turn on the classical music station and try to relax. With a long twenty-four hours of driving ahead of me, I can't get upset before I've even left this smoggy city.

Three hours later, I dry my hands, leave the barely passable-as-clean bathroom, and go inside the mini-mart for road trip supplies. I walk the aisles twice before grabbing peanut butter

M&M's, a churro from the machine, a bottle of soda, a larger bottle of water, and sour cream and onion chips.

My passenger seat is littered with craptastic foods and I take off on my journey again.

Another hour passes and I've sung through the latest Keith Urban album including unwelcome squirming in my seat when certain songs played. The memories of the night with Luke affect my body as well as my mind. I think of him too often to be healthy. Even the manuscript I just submitted to my agent has a hero that he might have inspired.

...embrace your soul, and coax the moon and stars to shine inside.

My body clenches. *Who am I kidding?* All my heroes have pieces, lines, and inspirations from him. I grew up with Luke. He was my first kiss. My first date. My first dance with a boy. My first make-out session. The person I lost my virginity to, and coincidentally the last one I was with as well.

Lawrence was only meant to play a minor character in a subplot to my life's arc. I see that now. When did I lose the major plot?

How could I have been so blind to what Luke wanted and didn't want? I'm guilty of taking our relationship for granted. But it's not like he didn't participate in our daydreaming. We had talked about marriage and kids, rescuing a stray from the pound, and the home we'd all live together.

Time apart. I should have seen that one coming. Sure, I suggested it, but if he really wanted to be with me, he wouldn't have agreed.

He's sly with his smooth-talking and sexy self. He's well aware of how desirable he is and uses that against females. He's no more committed to a future with me than he was back then. So we fooled around. So what? He does that all the time, just scratch out my name and fill in the next.

He let that dream slip away years ago...

The scenery outside the car looks the same from Arizona into New Mexico. With the sun's brightness sending a prism of lights reflecting off the ring, the beauty reminds me of when he gave it to me...

The rain has soaked my clothes, but I still have two blocks to go before I'm home. I usually don't mind the walk to the stop where I catch the bus that takes me to school. I only have to take it on days Luke has his internship at Warner Brothers Studio. I get the car on other days for my shifts at the coffee shop. We're too broke for two cars and my mom helps with school as much as she can, but she can't afford to cover a car and insurance in addition to that. Luke's parents added me to their policy for his car. I'm part of their family as they are mine.

But the rain... it's not fun when I'm trying to protect my books in the backpack I'm carrying. My umbrella isn't big enough to cover both, so I sacrifice my hair and shirt to keep the pack dry.

I reach the apartment and shake out the umbrella leaving it to dry on the front porch. I slip off my wet lace-up boots and set them neatly in the corner next to the door. I'll bring them in later when they dry out.

The apartment is dark. We both left early this morning, making sure to turn out the lights so we don't waste electricity. I find the kitchen light switch and flick it on while heading to turn on the bathtub water. I'm shivering from the wet clothes and quickly discard them in the washer.

The bath water is warm and comforting, wiping away the chill from my bones. I sink deeper until my toes bob and my chin is resting on the surface. I dip all the way under, holding my breath. *Emerging when I need air, I gasp when I break the surface. My lids open and Luke is leaning against the bathroom door, smiling. "Hey."*

"Hey." Grinning, I ask, "How long have you been standing there?"

"Long enough. I thought I was gonna have to come in there and rescue you."

"You still can and then you can give me mouth to mouth."

Though we're flirting, his tone is more serious, his eyes fixed on me. "Would you like that?"

I nod as he comes closer to the tub. "I would."

He wastes no time. Luke steps in—socks and jeans, button-up shirt—right into the bathtub causing the water to slosh over the sides as he kneels down around me. I shout in excitement, "Luke!"

He laughs and takes my face in his hands, a huge grin on his that matches mine. "Let me love on you, baby." He kisses me.

Holding on to the edge of the tub for support, my grip keeps me grounded when he makes me want to soar. When our lips part, he says, "I got you something."

"What is it?"

He reaches into the pocket of his shirt and pulls out a ring. "It's more than a promise ring, Jane."

I gasp for the second time tonight when I see it. I'm in awe of how pretty it is as he slips it on my finger. "It's gorgeous. But why? And how? We can't afford this."

"Don't worry. I put enough down to make the monthly payments affordable until then."

"If we have to make payments, we can't afford it." I stare at it on my finger, growing attached to it already.

"Do you like it?"

I never want to give it up. "I love it." I wiggle my fingers and watch how it sparkles on my hand. I look up into his gleaming eyes and feel overwhelmed with thankfulness for the amazing man before me. I never want to give him up. "I love you. Thank you."

"We're going to get married one day. I promise you, Jane. I'll make all your dreams come true. The wedding, the kids, the house. All of it."

"Promise?"

"I promise and cross my heart." He leans down again and kisses me. With a simple twist, he's under me, my back to his chest, and we lie there in the water. His wet clothed arms wrap around my bare body, keeping me warm.

...I unload the last suitcase from the car, not wanting it to be stolen while I sleep in a motel in the middle of nowhere. The place is rundown and making me feel like I might be killed if I take a shower. No, I won't think of *Psycho*. I won't take a shower here or sleep with both eyes closed. Nope, not gonna do it.

I lie on the bed staring up at the swirly wallpaper they've hung. I've never seen wallpaper on a ceiling before, but I like getting distracted by the design. My eyelids grow heavy and my body starts relaxing. If only my mind would. Dreams weave throughout the night...

A car is in the driveway when I walk up. I recognize it. It's the same one he had in college. As I pass I remember all the times we had sex in that backseat. There's a large scratch over the right tire. He was so upset when I hit that guardrail, but he was more worried about my safety, and never said a word about the damage.

A cat jumps out from the bushes startling me. "Rascal," I say, kneeling down and petting him like I had when I was seven. He died when I was fifteen. Hit by a car. I never got to say a proper goodbye or even bury him.

Music comes from the house and Luke's friend, Blaise, walks by with a guy I once shared a table with in Chemistry lab. I'm so confused. They don't see me. I get up and walk to the door. It's been left open, the music louder, the notes a blur. I don't recognize the song.

"Luke?" I call out.

I walk inside when no one answers. The cat runs by me and I quickly move out of the way when it runs upstairs. "Luke?" I've not been here enough to feel comfortable in his space. Laughter draws my attention to the top of the stairs.

A woman with long blond hair is stroking my cat. My childhood cat. Traitor. When she sees me, her voice is muffled, but I understand exactly what she says, "He's happier without you. You left him and now he's mine."

"I didn't leave him forever," I protest. "It was never supposed to be forever. I love him."

"He doesn't love you anymore. You should leave before he sees you and you make him miserable all over again."

A tear falls down my cheek and hits the palm of my hand. When I touch my cheek it's dry. But my shirt over my heart is wet. I squeeze my eyes tightly closed.

My eyes flash open and I sit up, my heart pounding in my chest, my breath short. The dream was disjointed and chaotic, not making sense. What does it mean? I rub my eyes and roll onto my side. I've relived the time I caught him with that other woman many times, but I haven't had a nightmare over it in a while. I'll be seeing him soon and my anxiety over this reunion has seeped into my subconscious.

When will I finally heal? This time apart was supposed to

close those wounds, give us a fresh start as friends. Did I set myself up to be hurt all over again without even realizing it? I found myself in the cycle of wondering why he wasn't calling or texting. Was he dating or seeing someone else? I gave him no reason not to, but I hate it just the same. *Stupid dream.* My heart feels broken. Again.

It's six in the morning, and I throw the covers off me. I'm ready to leave this motel and this nightmare behind. Twenty minutes later, I'm pulling onto the highway.

I always hated that damn cat.

CHAPTER 11

Jane

HOTEL SAN JOSE'S TILED roof and green vine covered wall comes into view. The gray metallic sign is welcoming after the long journey. I park on the side and take one of my suitcases with me inside to check in. I'm given a room key and directions to one of the bungalows. The courtyard is quaint and quiet with posters on the fence advertising live music nights.

Compared to my car and the room last night, the room is a change that makes me smile. It's clean and spacious. This may be a temporary home, but it feels like just the new beginning I need.

When I head back through the courtyard to get the rest of my belongings from the car, I daydream of finally having some real food, not fast or junk food I had on the road. I'm lost in thoughts of a large salad and a glass of sauvignon blanc when I hear my name. I stop, my back to the familiar voice. I collect myself, brushing my hair back away from my face. Surely it's a mess. When I turn around, I smile. "Ian, wow, you're already here."

"Yeah, a few days now. We scouted a few of the locations and did some setups to make sure they'd work."

I forgot about that part of the process. That means Luke is

here. Somewhere. Looking around, I wonder if he's staying here or if he chose somewhere else.

Ian walks around the pool and greets me with a hug that I return. He's very attractive. Not my type, but very good-looking. With his dark eyes set on mine, he smiles too Hollywood—insincerely. I'm not a believer in the practice of the casting couch, but I have a feeling he might be. He raises his blue-lensed sunglasses and says, "I think you're going to like some of the locations we've chosen. They have a good vibe about them. You were concerned that setting wouldn't project the emotions of some of the scenes, but I think you'll approve."

"I'm looking forward to seeing them. Is it possible to have rehearsals there?"

He crosses his arms over his chest and nods thoughtfully. "We probably can with a few. The others we had to get city permits, so if they do it, it will be with an audience and on the crew clock."

"Of course, I wasn't thinking of that." I motion toward the exit, a subtle hint I'm ready to go. "Well, I'll see you soon."

"Yes, the schedule will be emailed later. We're tweaking the first three days, then it should smooth out. Glad you made it."

"Thanks. I am too." I rush to the car and grab a box before heading back to my room. My hotel room for the next month is situated in a row of three doors, with mine in the middle. Its design is sparse. Only the basics with concrete floors. I roll my case to the base of the bed and use the restroom. When I come back out into the main room, I hear the deep timbre of a voice.

A voice I'd know anywhere.

"I promise you, Jane. I'll make all your dreams come true. The wedding, the kids, the house."

I used to love hearing him dream along with me. But that dream turned into a nightmare. The nightmare from last night flashes back and I close my eyes, then shake my head to clear my thoughts.

From the one-sided conversation, it sounds like Luke is on the phone. I move closer to the wall where I hear his voice coming from—the space beneath the adjoining door. Pressing my ear against the wood, I listen. "I don't know," he says. "Today or tomorrow... A month... I'm not sure anymore... Of course I think about Jane. All the fucking time."

The door feels hot as if I've been burned and I jump back, realizing it's my ears that are burning. His voice lowers and I miss what he says next. Feeling guilty and a little dirty, I rush out of the room. The door slams behind me as I hurry through the courtyard. Smiling at Ian again, I don't stop. I don't stop until I reach my car and hide inside. Closing my eyes, I take a deep breath. When I exhale, I start the engine so I can turn on the air conditioning before I catch fire from this Texas heat.

The panic subsides and then reality hits me.

Luke Anders is right next door to me. For a month.

I've only been here for a minute or so and I'm sweltering. The air hasn't cooled me off so I pull my shirt away from my sticky skin. A knock on the window makes me jump; my hand instantly covers my heart.

Luke steps away from the car with his hands up in surrender. He mouths, "Sorry."

Shaking my head, I take another quick breath to calm myself, and push the button that slides the window down.

"Sorry about that. I didn't realize I was sneaking up on you."

"It's okay," I reassure him, my heart racing—from his close proximity or from being startled I'm not quite sure.

When I open the door, he opens it wider and I get out. I can't help but take him in, my breath escaping me just like the first time I ever saw him. He's stunningly handsome, maybe even more so. *Definitely more so.* One month without seeing him and now he's trying to kill me. His rugged good looks, the T-shirt stretching across his broad, hard body, and a week's worth of beard growth makes me want to rub my fingers and other things on it to see if it's rough or soft.

In a word?

Damn. Hot.

Fine, two words, but he's worth breaking the rules for.

And just like that, all my better senses fly out the window. "Have you been working out?" I regret saying it the second I do. I regret it doubly when that cocky smirk that made me fall in love with him appears, transforming his entire attitude.

He pops a bicep for me, and replies, "I've gotten in a little gym time recently."

"Well, it shows." *Shut up, Jane.* I wave my hand in the air, unable to control myself. "I've got a VIP ticket to the gun show. Any idea where I might redeem it?" *What the hell am I doing?* He drives me nuts and I fall for it every time.

Luke laughs. Pretending to take the imaginary ticket, he stashes it in his back pocket. One arm goes out and then the other. "Bam. Bam! Check these babies out."

Now I'm a giggling mess. Running my hand over one then the other, I smile. "It was worth every dime I spent on that ticket." I squeeze his muscle.

He laughs and drops his arm. "And how many dimes did you spend?"

"Ten shiny dimes for each." I walk around to the back of the car and open my trunk.

Luke chuckles even harder. "Glad you got your money's worth then." He comes around and grabs the large suitcase out, setting it on the sidewalk and pulling up the handle.

I reach in the backseat and pull out the last box, but he moves in and grabs it for me. "Take the suitcase. I'll carry this for you."

Rolling the suitcase behind me, we walk along the sidewalk back to the hotel as if we're friends, as if we haven't hurt each other's hearts. I ask, "What were you doing out here?"

"Getting coffee. I heard Jo's is great. It's next to the hotel."

"I could use one. The drive was exhausting."

He walks one step to the side and behind me. "Why did you drive?"

"I wanted to have a car." I hate lying, especially to him, but I'm not ready for him to know I don't have a place to call home anymore or a place to store my car in LA for a month. I'll have to face the fact of my reality once this film wraps, so I choose to hide my eyes and stick with the white lie.

A silence pervades the journey as we walk through the courtyard. I stop in front of my door. Looking to his, I wonder if he realizes the relation of the two. Turning back to him, his smile is much nicer, more the sweet boy I once knew. I still struggle with what to say, so I awkwardly shift, and signal to the door behind me. "This is me." I unlock the door, and step inside.

"Right next door." He follows me inside. After setting the box down on the table, he looks around the room. "Just like mine. It's nice we'll be neighbors."

"Quite the coincidence."

"Maybe. Maybe not."

"Maybe not?"

"Could be fate, Janie."

"You never believed in fate." I sit on the bed just as some of the old feelings come swirling back in the quiet of the room.

"I believe in destiny these days." He turns away from me and stares out the window.

Looking up at him, he's shadowed by the bright sun coming in through the window. His back is to me and I see those broad shoulders that used to eclipse me when he held me tight. So many hours and days spent in those arms that it makes me feel sad to see them without being able to touch him again. "How are we going to do this?"

Walking across the room with a polite smile in place, his thumb runs over his bottom lip. He stops and leans against the adjoining door. "You've made it more than clear that we won't be doing anything together."

"We shouldn't have done what we—"

"Don't say it, Jane. I don't need the reminder or the reprimand. I get it. It's all in the past. Just how you prefer." His tone is mean. His body language backs his words when he crosses his arms. Tense. Short-tempered.

I walk to the door and open it wide. I don't need to offer him a golden invitation to leave. He's clearly ready and walks out without being asked. He opens his and before I shut the door, I say, "I hate this."

"You and me both, honey." He goes inside his own room and the door closes to mine.

Shutting my door, it slams harder than intended. I stand with my back to it, wondering how we went from laughing to irritated so quickly and if the entire month of shooting is going to be like this.

I may have made a huge mistake closing this deal. But the deal is done, so I'm going to have to bend or he is. We can't continue with so much tension between us or we'll end up in a screaming match or worse... back in the sack like we were a month ago.

If there's one thing I've learned, it's that sleeping with Luke Anders doesn't solve problems. No matter how amazing the sex is.

Damn him.

"SO THIS IS what love looks like these days?"

"You don't know?" Scalia, the makeup artist, asks in between drags from her clove cigarette.

Fortunately she blows the smoke away from me. With my eyes still on the lead actors, we watch them rehearse. It's obvious their attraction is off, their hands awkwardly placed on each other—his on her shoulder, hers not able to stay still on his leg as if she's uncomfortable. "My love was different," I reply.

She laughs and holds her vodka martini straight up, ready to sip. "Oh darling woman, what was your love like?"

I've drunk too much. My tongue has become slippery with secrets. But I've had to watch Luke for the last two hours talking to the crew, greeting each one, getting to know them, being friendly and outgoing—ignoring me—and I've become irritated. I take another sip from my wine glass, but nothing reaches my mouth. I look down and it's empty. "Shit," I mumble.

Scalia offers me her glass but I shake my head. "I don't mix or I'll be a sloppy mess."

"I think you already are."

"I am not." I stand too fast for my body to keep up. I waver but am steadied just as fast.

"Careful there." Luke, looking like his gorgeous self, holds my upper arm.

"I'm fine," I snap, my happy-hour mood ruined long before by other insidious feelings like jealousy.

His hand disappears and I miss the feel of it along with everything else about him. I take a step, but by the third, I face plant into Luke's super soft burgundy shirt.

"You sure about that?" I hear a chuckle mixed in with his words.

Not wanting to give him the satisfaction, I pretend I'm sober. "Is this shirt made of cashmere? Very fancy, Mr. Schmancy Producer."

"It's called cotton." His smile is in place, but I can tell he doesn't find me as funny as I find myself. "Did you eat dinner?"

"Oh God, don't be the parent. I have a mom, thank you very much. Or maybe you've forgotten all about her by now." Looking up at him, I whisper, "She still asks me about you."

"And what do you tell her?" His fingers rub gracefully over the bare skin of my arm that he hasn't yet released, and I swallow hard, liking it so much more than I should.

"I don't talk to her much because I don't know what to tell her about my life."

"Tell me about your life then."

"I've nothing to tell that would matter to you."

"*You* matter to me." His hand drops to his side as he looks around, pretending this is a casual conversation when my heart would beg to differ.

"When we were together it was a mis—"

"Don't finish that sentence." He looks right into my eyes, making sure I see the emotion behind his words. "Don't ever think that again." He leans closer, and lowers his voice. "What do I have to do?"

"Don't waste your time."

We're momentarily distracted by the music when the band begins playing again after their short intermission. A few couples start to slow dance and when he looks back to me, he says, "Dance with me, Janie. Just like old times."

The sky is full of stars, the music slow and romantic, and the man before me my very own Kryptonite. Janie. Him calling me that with such affection to his tone causes me to move closer, wanting to feel secure in proximity alone if not in his arms. I take his hand and place my other on his shoulder. "We were a love story with an unhappy ending, but here we are two years later dancing in the moonlight in Texas. I couldn't predict this."

"Would you change it?"

"The ending. I'd change that." I don't look up, not able to look into his eyes that will match the night sky above and make my heart ache for an ending that will never be.

"Jane?"

"Hmm?"

An involuntary smile crosses my lips when warm hands touch my waist. I open my eyes to see his set on mine. We stop dancing. "Remember that bar we used to go to back in San Diego? Rocky's?"

I laugh, the good times unsuspectingly warming my insides. "They never carded us."

"One beer and you'd be done."

Sliding one of my hands up to his shoulder, I say, "I was done long before I ever tasted beer."

His lips part, but he holds back the words that seem to be teetering on the edge of his tongue.

"Some things are better left unsaid," I add.

He looks away, but I see him nod.

Laughter from a nearby table brings me out of the sadness that was starting to drag me under. "Luke?"

"Yeah?"

"I once had this cat named Rascal." He waits as I tell him the story that's been hanging over my head all day. I leave out a few details, thinking we probably shouldn't delve into those tonight. "It was a mean old cat. I hated it. It used to scratch me. But you know what it taught me?"

"What?"

"That damn cat taught me I could hate it for hurting me but still love the cat."

"Sometimes we're hurt unintentionally." His eyes harbor a darkness smothering the joy that usually resides there.

"That's what Rascal did. I just realized. I was the only one he let pet him."

"But you got scratched."

"Yes." I pause then look into my soul mate's eyes. "He broke my heart." The music stops, and Luke's hold of me tightens just enough to keep me. Unwanted attention from the crew and cast is not welcome, so I step back. "I think I should go to bed."

"Probably. I'll walk you back."

Just as we leave the dance floor, I catch eyes with Ian who has a slew of women around him as he holds court. He tips his imaginary hat to me before I turn back to Luke. I hand him the key, feeling unsteady, and when we reach my door, he unlocks it.

I walk inside, but he remains at the doorstep. Leaning my shoulder against the doorframe, I think about asking him in. I don't do it. *But I think about it.* Instead, I start to close the door. "Good night, Luke."

Right before it closes, he says, "Janie?"

"Yes?" I open the door wider again.

His body is angled away, his hands in his pockets, his beautiful eyes full of sadness. "Even though he hurt you, do you think you could ever love him again?"

We're not talking about Rascal anymore. That much is clear, even in my tipsy brain.

"I never stopped."

CHAPTER 12

Jane

DESPITE MY LINGERING hangover, I arrive early to the meeting and choose a seat by the window. Staring out at the trees with leaves blowing in the breeze, I think about how I never sleep well anymore, not like I used to when I was younger. Or maybe it's that I don't sleep well without Luke. Just another thing I seem to blame him for regardless of his innocence in the matter. It's easier to keep my distance when I can keep a few key issues on hand. And I should definitely be keeping my distance. Everything about him is dangerous not just for my heart, but also for my libido.

Good Lord, when did I start using that word?

Libido. It's such an icky word.

I know when. It was when that sexy bastard came blazing back into my life changing my narrative. Resting my chin on my hand, I purse my lips and ponder last night. It was the most honest without being direct we've been with each other. It makes me wonder if we can get back to that place again sometime soon. It was nice.

Ian is the next to arrive. "I'm impressed, Jane. I like timeliness."

"I've dreamed about this project for years. I can't wait to get started."

He sits across from me, leaving the rest of the long conference table available. "I want to talk to you about something."

Dread fills my chest like I've been called into the principal's office. "Okay."

Leaning closer, he says, "I'm not sure it's a good idea for you and Luke—"

"Good morning."

We both turn to find Luke standing at the head of the table. A few others walk in behind him, including our two stars—Jessica Pyles and Ryan Kantz.

The room is filled with chatter and Ian leans back in his chair, not finishing what he began with me, leaving me curious as to what he wanted to say. He doesn't think Luke and I... *what?* Instead of answering me, he speaks to the group, "Let's get started."

Damn it.

Hours later, I stare at the schedule in front of me in wonderment of how we're going to fit in everything we need to do to make this movie. Rehearsals start tomorrow, a new script has been handed out, and lunch is served. I avoid looking at Luke at the other end of the table, but it seems as much as I avoid the eye contact, the connection is still there. My body shifts under the weight of his gaze and when I finally dare a peek over the apple I'm biting into, my suspicions are confirmed. He glances from me to Ian and then down at his food that's barely been touched. His jaw tightens and then he stands. I watch as he says something that must be very charming to Jessica by her giggly reaction before he scoops up his food, drops it in a nearby trash can, and walks out.

Others start to follow since the meeting has wrapped. I follow suit, quick-stepping out of the boardroom. Luke isn't too far ahead on the sidewalk and I hurry to catch up. "Hey," I say right behind him.

He turns, an eyebrow raised. "Hey there, yourself."

I try for casual, but professional. "So the schedule is pretty intense."

"It is."

"You think we'll fit it all in?"

"We'll try our damnedest."

His pace doesn't slow and he has almost a foot in height on me, so I double time to keep up with his long strides. "Are you okay?"

"Fine and dandy."

"You don't sound fine *or* dandy."

He comes to an abrupt halt and looks down at me. "How am I supposed to sound?"

"I don't know. Cordial?"

That makes him laugh, but it's not the amused or entertained kind. It's filled with sarcasm, maybe even a little anger. "I got the hint. Sorry for bothering you."

"Actually, you haven't gotten the hint."

My mouth drops open as I stare at him in disbelief. Then I close it and start walking up the sidewalk. There are too many people around for us to discuss whatever he's referring to.

"Yeah, walk away, Jane. It's what you do best."

I spin around, my finger already pointing, ready to unleash a whole lot of my reality on him when I see Jessica, Ryan, and Ian heading our way. I swallow the rapture of my words, exhale loudly, and lower my hand. Turning around, I do leave. Yes, I leave him standing there in all his aggression to be dealt with another day and when we're alone, in private.

Too angry to return to a hotel room to sit and stew, I keeping walking right past the entrance. There are shops—a costume store, kitchen shop, restaurants, and more. I walk into a candy store.

"Yeah, walk away, Jane. It's what you do best." His words cut deep because I don't usually walk away, but he's right. I did when it mattered. He knows me though, so he should have known I never meant to walk away forever. In my anger, I accidently knock a small display over, and as I am righting it, I hear the bell above the door rattle. *Great.* Hopefully it's no one from the movie. It's too much work to pretend to be happy right now. My mind is rattled. *"Yeah, walk away, Jane. It's what you do best."*

Shit. I need to move on. *I am so confused.* He held me in his arms. We danced. I told him I never stopped loving him. And he's barely acknowledged me today.

Guessing that's a pretty big hint. He's moved on.

As I turn to see who came in, my face is grabbed, and all-too familiar lips are pressing against mine. My eyes are wide open, my mouth unmoving, my hands pushing against strength and passion. But then I'm released just as hastily. Luke's breathing is harsh, a fire in his eyes. "I loved you. I know you don't believe that, but I did. With everything I had."

I find my breath stuck somewhere in my chest as I watch this man that is always a pillar of confidence, break. His truths come spilling out, filling the candy store and my heart.

He looks at me and takes a step back as if I've hit him with a fresh rejection. "You were everything and you walked out as a test, as a threat, wanting me to chase you, to beg you to stay."

"You didn't though. You let me go knowing how hurt I was."

"You walking away hurt me. I just wasn't willing to play your game."

"It wasn't a game, Luke. It was my life."

"It was my life too. It was *our* life, one we shared together."

"Years had passed since you promised me the moon and stars, but every time I looked up, there they were exactly where they had always been, a constant reminder that you didn't want that same commitment."

"I never promised the moon or the stars. I only promised my heart and you already had that."

"Semantics."

"Truths, Jane. *My* truth." He releases a deep breath, the fire inside him dwindling down in the dark depths of his stare. "What about last night?"

"My body may be easily swayed by your flirtatious ways, but my head can't forget the past." I hate that I'm the one that extinguishes his fire, the passion that fuels him. Even his anger comes from something deeper. But I still struggle to get past what happened. "I can still see *that* woman in my head. So vividly." My voice cracks, the image springing tears to my eyes.

Coming closer again, his shoulders start to sag. "I read everything wrong. I'm sorry. You don't know how sorry I am. You didn't tell me."

"I was telling you the only way I knew how."

"Not with words."

"No, actions."

"Jane," he says, shaking his head, "when you came over last July, you were still with *him*. How is it fair that you could be with someone and I couldn't? I thought you were over me, that we were done."

"That's where you were wrong. I was living in *his* house because I had nowhere else to go."

"But I didn't know that." His hand touches my arm and electric currents shoot straight to my heart. "We're a house of cards. The slightest movement brings us crashing down."

"When did we become such a mess?"

"We never fought."

"We never talked either."

He smiles. "We made love."

My own smile forms from the memories. "We sure did. A lot."

Another giggle comes, but this time not from me. I turn around to see the clerk smiling. "I hope you guys make up because it will be a real shame to let a love like that go."

I look down, a smile on my face. Luke's hand falls away and when I turn to him, he's not smiling at all, so mine disappears. "Luke?"

He takes two steps away from me. When I reach out, I struggle to touch him. Confusion sets in as I search his eyes for answers that he's burying deep inside. "Luke?" This time it comes out in fear of losing him.

Again.

"I've gotta go," he says, a silent plea lost in translation runs through his gaze. He turns and walks out of the store and this time it's me watching him go.

I hate it.

What just happened? When I look over my shoulder, the clerk lowers her head and looks away, pretending she didn't witness my heartbreak. Forgetting about the candy and the clerk, I rush for the door. I look down the sidewalk toward our hotel, then turn and look in the opposite direction. Where could he be? How did he disappear so quickly?

Good or bad, my heart and my head finally agree and insist on more, so I start running.

I reach the entrance and hurry through the courtyard where an early happy hour has begun. The crew says hi as I rush through the tables straight to Luke's door and knock.

Fine, I bang on it. *Whatever.*

The door swings open and he's standing there, not saying

anything. Just staring, waiting for me to speak, or act. I choose the latter and push him inside, two hands firmly pressed to his chest. The door closes behind me and he has a hold of my wrists, questioning me with his eyes. "What are you doing?"

"I'm not fighting with you anymore."

He almost looks nervous, but his usual bravado quickly replaces the previous. When he releases me, he crosses his arms, and asks, "What do you suggest we do instead?"

My bottom lip is scraped under my teeth. I look down, the light making the ring shine even brighter. The ring...

I close the gap, fisting his shirt, and pull him closer. Staring up at him, his eyes lock on mine. He whispers, "What now, Jane?"

"This." I lift up and kiss *him*. Large hands cover my shoulders and we're spun around slowly, our bodies gravitating even closer until there's no space keeping us apart.

Our lips part and I lower my head, resting my forehead against his chest. His breath warms me, the scruff of his beard catching strands of my hair as he lowers. With his mouth to my ear, he whispers, "What are we doing?"

"Not letting us go."

"You're engaged. I thought I could be the other man for you, but I can't. I want all of you."

The statement sobers me and the magic is lost. I turn my back to him, not wanting to lie to him any longer. Will the truth set my heart free or set it up to be broken all over again? He touches my shoulder. "Don't turn away from me. I need to see your eyes."

"What's so great about seeing my eyes?" I try for levity, but even I know it's not funny.

"They tell me the truth, even when you don't."

Slowly, I turn back. With my heart thudding in my chest, I find the strength to look up at him. "I'm not."

"You're not what?" he asks.

"I'm not engaged, Luke."

His confusion registers through the crease in his brow. "You're not engaged?"

"No. I'm not."

Backing away from me, his eyes stay on me as he sits down on the bed. "Since when?"

I don't want to fight and I know the truth could lead to a major blowout, but I don't want to lie either. "A couple of months, maybe never."

"What does that mean? A couple of months? Maybe never?"

The scrutiny of his gaze causes my honesty to sink to my stomach. I walk to the window, wrapping my arms around myself, needing the comfort. "Please don't be mad at me."

"Tell me, Jane."

"I was never engaged."

"You told me you were. Others told me you were."

"Lawrence told everyone we were before he asked me. I was embarrassed so I never denied it."

"But you let me believe... You made me your dirty secret, then left as if it was true."

Turning around, I plead my case. I need him to understand. I don't want a lie to destroy either of us anymore. "No, you were never that to me. You were so much more. You were everything to me, Luke."

He cocks his head to the side. "How's that if you were lying to me?"

"I lied because you hurt me."

"So you lied to get me back?"

My arms fly up defensively. "Why did you have to fuck half of LA?"

"Because you were fucking engaged to that asshole lawyer. Why didn't you just tell me? You were coming over to my house, showing up unannounced as if I should leave my arms and door wide open for you to come and go as you fucking pleased. From me, back to that asshole, and then back to me again like a fucking yo-yo."

I gasp. "Fuck you."

"Fuck me? Fuck you, Jane."

Staring at him, I realize I don't know him at all anymore. With a lump in my throat and anger filling the void my love for him once occupied, I say, "I told you the truth because I knew I owed you that much, but you owe me something too."

"What is that?"

"My heart. It's been a long damn time since I felt whole and I'm tired of feeling empty." I walk to the door. I knew better and yet, here I am arguing with him over the past. There's no going back for us and moving forward will never be anything more than working acquaintances. That much is clear to me now.

To my back, he says, "You've had your heart all along. You packed it up along with the rest of your shit the day you decided you needed to test how true my love was for you."

My eyes trace the subtle grays in the cement floor. I wasn't paying attention before, but now, they're obvious and feeling very much a metaphor for our relationship. We were never black and white. We've been lost in the subtly of our lives, not living in full color for years. I stop, slip the ring off my finger, and wordlessly return it to him.

With the ring in the palm of his hand, he sighs. "What are you doing?"

"Protecting my heart."

"You don't have to protect it from me."

"You're the only one I have to protect it from."

"I don't want the ring back."

"I can't hold on to it any longer. It's like holding on to a dream that will never come true." I drop my head down. "It hurts too much."

His arms are around me just as the first tear falls. "Don't cry." His tone is softer. His body is warm and comforting as if we can carry on like this despite this unsettled life solidly dividing us.

"I'm sorry for lying to you," I reply to his chest. "I hated it, but I had to. I've been hur—"

"*Shhh.* It's okay."

Loving the feel of him, this closeness, I inhale his scent deep into my lungs to soothe my soul one last time. Pushing gently off him, I turn quickly and open the door, this time before he can stop me. "It's not okay. *I'm* not okay—"

"Then let me help you."

I didn't run from Luke into the arms of another. I didn't sleep with Lawrence for months after we started dating. I was lost and vulnerable to a drowning heartbreak. I gave in to him when I gave up on the hope that Luke wanted me. I stupidly thought time apart would make Luke realize he couldn't live without me. My heart had been so bruised and battered, feeling as though our lives weren't moving in the right direction. *I missed him. Missed us.* Even though physically we were still together.

This last two months on my own have been good for me. I have survived. But I have been living in a state of limbo. There was no way I was going back to Lawrence. That had been a mistake from the beginning. I think I was still waiting for Luke to chase me, even though we agreed to keep our distance. That wasn't fair to any of us. But that distance didn't provide healing. It only caused more hurt.

"You've had your heart all along. You packed it up along with the rest of your shit the day you decided you needed to test my love for you." He's wrong. I haven't had my heart. But I need

it now. It's time to move past my state of displacement and be whole again.

I open the door determined to walk out of his life one final time. To never again experience his arms around me. To never hear his heart beat when my cheek rests on his chest. To no longer love the man who has owned my heart for almost twelve years. He can help me. He can help me by allowing me to leave, knowing I'm not expecting him to chase me this time. Allowing me to go.

If this is the right decision, why does it hurt so much?

CHAPTER 13

Luke

WHAT THE FUCK just happened? I'm holding the ring I gave Jane years ago while standing in the middle of my hotel room completely dumbfounded.

She wasn't engaged.

My fingers close around the ring and I punch the fucking air, fury in my fists. "Fuck!" Years wasted. We should be together, not lost to fucking misunderstandings and lies. She lied to protect herself against me. *Fuck.* How did we get so fucking lost?

When I open my hand again, impressions from the ring mark my skin. This is wrong, all wrong. I shouldn't have this. Seeing it on her finger in the candy store, seeing it on her left hand ring finger has hit me hard. Every mistake I ever made when it came to her, to us, comes rushing back hitting me like a Mack truck.

Why was she was wearing it? To taunt me? To show me she had it? I think back to the coffee shop in LA last month. Was she wearing it then? Did she wear it around Lawrence? They were never engaged. Not officially, but are they together? Are they not? He was with that other woman... I need answers to fill in the gaps she's left behind in her destruction of my heart. I march to the

127

door and open it.

Ian jumps. "Holy shit, you scared me."

I stop, not sure what to say to him. The door next to mine opens and Jane's eyes go wide for a split second before she recovers. "Um. Hi."

Ian smiles at her.

Fuck him. Fucker.

Then he has the fucking nerve to ask her, "You're coming on the bat cruise tonight, right? I wanted to see if you want to come with?" He rocks back on his heels like he's a nervous teen.

Come with? Like he can't fucking finish the question. Adding the word "me" is apparently much too tasking for him. *Fuck him.*

And now I'm stuck in purgatory watching this play out before my very eyes.

Her eyes are red. It's obvious to anyone who's paying attention she's been crying. Everyone but Ian. Jane glances to me, but looks away just as quickly. "When is everyone leaving?" She looks back into her room. "I have a few things I need to do first."

"Two hours or so. We have the boat reserved. It has a bar."

She sniffles and Ian's still oblivious. I shake my head, disgusted by this whole scene. My disgust might be jealousy but I won't give them that much pleasure. She finally says, "Sure." But then she shocks me. Looking straight at me, she asks, "Are you going?"

The sharp edges of the stones dig into my skin again, not easing my anger that this joker is banging on her door wanting to bang my Jane. *Mine.*

It doesn't matter that we just argued, hurt each other deeper than before—

Fuck yes, I want to go. Someone's got to keep him off her.

"I wouldn't miss it."

Ian does not look happy, and turns back to Jane. "I'll come by and get you when we're leaving."

"I'll be ready." Suddenly she seems to struggle to make eye contact with me, so when Ian walks away, she whispers, "I'll come get you, Luke." Her door is shut, my initial plan ruined by Ian.

But *I* have another. I go back inside my room. As soon as my door is shut, I'm knocking on the door that adjoins our rooms. "Jane, open up." The double meaning is *not* lost on me. I know she's pressed against the other side. I heard her, the cement floors giving every click of her shoes away. "Please."

One latch and then another unlocks before the door cracks open, her face peering back at me. I don't waste time because I don't know how much she'll give me. "I want you to have the ring." With an open palm, I wait.

"I can't, Luke."

Her lack of deliberation makes me think it's an automated response, not one from the heart. Reaching to touch her, my hand comes to rest on her cheek. I rub my thumb gently across her wet skin, wiping away her tears. "Open the door." She steps back and allows me to enter. I move into her space and take her in my arms. I expect a fight, but she doesn't give me one. "The ring is yours, Jane, just like I am, just like I've always been."

Her shoulders shake with a quiet sob. "Don't say such things. I don't deserve either."

Lifting her chin up, I make sure her eyes are on me. When her tear-filled eyes meet my confident ones, I say, "I've never loved anyone like I love you."

"I thought you would come after me."

"I know. I should have, but I never was very good at tests."

The softest of laughs is heard and a small smile appears. I adore the sound, wishing I could hear it all the time. "What are we going to do?"

Knowing exactly what we're going to do, I reply, "We're going to go and watch millions of bats fly out from under a bridge."

She laughs again, this time leaning back so I can see her full face. There are pink trails running down her cheeks where tears once traveled. I kiss each one, hoping to make it better, to make *her* feel better. Turning her head just a bit, my mouth covers the corner of hers and I kiss her again. Another shift on her part and our lips meet. The sweetest taste of heaven warms me.

"What about in the meantime?" she asks with our mouths a breath apart.

Taking her in my arms, I sway slowly to music that only exists in my head. "I was hoping we could get reacquainted."

She moves on her own accord, matching my rhythm, dancing with me to music that is ours alone.

I spin her around and pull her in fast before dipping her. With her head tilted back, I lean down and kiss then lick the exposed skin of her neck. She looks up at me with the prettiest smile of any woman I've ever seen. "I never could resist you, my love." When I right her, her arms remain securely around my neck. I continue to dance where we left off, my hands lowering to her waist. "I want to kiss you again."

She's nodding, green eyes beneath dark lashes bright with anticipation. "Kiss me again."

My feet stop, my whole body knowing what it would rather be doing with this woman other than dancing. I cup her face and lean down. When my mouth covers hers, her body leans into mine. Bending quickly, I pick her up and walk to the bed. With one more kiss to her lips, I set her down. I have no game, even when I try. The woman still makes me nervous, just like she did in high school. With a unsure voice, I ask, "What do you want, Janie?"

"You. I want to be with you." Lying back, she stretches out with her arms above her head and turns her knees to the side.

"Let's make up and make love, Luke."

"You sure about that?"

"Positive."

"On one condition. You stay this time."

"I can do that. *I want to do that.*" She lies back and starts to take her jeans down.

While watching her, I smile while taking my shirt over my head. "Fuck, I've missed your sexy-as-fuck body, Janie." I undo my belt and jeans. I let them drop and start on my socks. "I'm gonna lick you, suck you, then fuck you. Not a day has gone by when I don't think about you. One month has been too long, baby, since I last had the taste of you on my tongue."

Unbuttoning the top two buttons of her shirt, her chest is rising and falling deeper than before, the perfect shade of rose coloring her skin. With her chest exposed she lies down on the bed, her hair fanning across the pillow. She's gorgeous. She whispers almost breathless, "I've heard about your dirty talking skills, but oh my God, Luke."

"Where did you hear such rumors?" I take down my boxers.

"Hollywood parties." Her eyes skim my body as she removes her shirt, leaving her only in her bra and undies, and way too clothed. "Your dirty talking reputation precedes you these days."

Climbing down over her, my torso rests on my elbows above her. Sneaking a quick kiss to her neck in, I say, "I'd rather be known for my skills."

She laughs, spreading her legs and letting me settle between them. "Oh I bet you would."

Waggling my eyebrows, I clarify, "I meant my producing skills."

"I thought they were one in the same."

"Guess it depends on what I'm producing."

"Movies or orgasms."

I chuckle again, kind of joking, but not. I know about the rumors. Most are true. Who knew speaking sexually to a woman was the best foreplay? It's my forte, but I didn't know Jane knew. I would have thought she'd be mad. Her curiosity is foreplay for my ego, my cock hardening at the thought. "Yes, those are my skills. I should add them to my résumé."

"You should. I heard you're the best."

I kiss her neck slowly this time, inch by inch. "As I said, it's all rumors." I lick and then nip under her jaw, trying not to fuck her through her panties.

Her arms come around me and she leans her head back, giving me more access. "So very disappointing. And here I thought there were secrets that you'd reveal to me, skills you'd learned in our time apart."

"Let me make love to you, beautiful."

Fingers slide through the back of my hair. Fisting it, she tugs my head back. When our eyes meet, she asks, "Is that the best you can do, lover?"

The way she commands turns me on. I find the spot between her legs that turns her on, my fingers slipping under the lace that covers her. "I'll be the best you ever had."

"You always were." Her breath comes out harsh as the top of her head digs into the pillow beneath her.

I kiss her. *Hard.* My fingers caress other parts of her body while I nuzzle her ear. I trace the shell with my tongue, then whisper, "I want to fuck you all night, then eat your pussy for breakfast."

Her body stills, mine stopping in reaction. Worried I said too much, that my words were too vulgar, I lift up and look at her.

Something wild appears in the darkness of her pupils, something unfamiliar, but lustful, carnal at a base level. "Yes, I want that. Fuck me, Luke."

Sliding down her body, I keep my eyes on her while my mouth warms the apex of her thighs. "Show me your tits."

Her bra comes off within seconds just as I rip her panties on one side, and then the other to sounds of gasps. Watching her breath escape as her back arches, her tits glorious and full as they bounce from the sudden movement, I keep my eyes steady on her. I run the flat of my tongue over her, soothing the red marks on her hips from the material burn.

And then I go lower.

She's wet. So wet between her legs. I keep my voice firm, clear, directed right at her pussy while I tease her mind. "I'm going to taste you. Savor every fucking ounce of you."

Her fingers tighten, the sheets strangled in her hold.

My mouth takes possession of her clit and she moans, free by the lack of her body's good-girl restraint.

I fucking love it.

I fucking love her body.

I fucking love her.

Kissing her, making love to her with my mouth, her orgasm comes quick and hard, her hands scrambling to pull me to the top until I'm there and she's kissing me. I'm hard. So hard. I want to fuck her. I want to fuck her right now, but I can't just yet. I push off. "Fuck. I forgot a condom." I run into my room and rummage through my suitcase.

Calling from where I left her, she says, "It's almost like we're back in high school." Laughter follows, making me smile and glad she's not mad for me not being more prepared.

Rushing back, I tease, "Back then, you used to beg for sex."

"What's your point?" With a *cat ate the canary* grin, she laughs lightheartedly.

I'm back in position on top of her, my cock right where I want to be. "I'm about to drive my point home. Are you ready for me, beautiful?"

"Not much has changed from then to now. Give it to me, big boy."

Any other time I might thrust as hard as I can, but looking at her now, despite the dirty talk and teasing, I worry I'll hurt her. And that's the last thing I want. We should build to that level, not start with it.

I push slowly forward, inch-by-inch, as her body welcomes me. Being with her in any way is ecstasy, but this is the most unforgettable sensation—awareness and every emotion I've ever felt gathers and disperses, then builds again. *It brings home just how much I have missed her. Sex with her... so real.*

Our bodies move, an insistence to every motion. An unspoken language is shared with every dip, curve, push, pull, our bodies becoming fluent in each other. I love her. I love everything about her and it's killing me to hold back.

But as I make love to her, I do.

I have to. For her. And for me.

She's not ready to hear my soul confessions. So I thrust harder and harder, attaching my body to hers, to drown out the future and grabbing hold of the present. Taking her wrists, I stretch her arms above her head and use the leverage against her.

"Luke," falls from her lips and I kiss the letters away, inhaling her breath.

Finding her most wanton spot, I touch her softness and am rewarded with moans. "God, you're so fucking sexy."

A small smile dances across her lips. "More, Luke."

A cocky grin pops into place. "Turn over."

Limber and purring each precious breath she releases, she turns without breaking our connection. Taking her by the hips, I lean over, take a handful of her hair, and pull her back until her ear reaches my lips. "You're mine, Janie. You always were and you always will be."

Her breath catches, her mouth wide open, as her eyes steady on the bed before her. Commanding, I tell her, "Say it."

She readily obliges, satisfying a sexual desire held deep inside like the torch I carry for her alone. "I always have and I always will be."

Pulling back, I slam into her, forcing her breath and a lustful moan. Two more times and I stop. Holding back to gain control again. For me, and her, to give her what she wants.

"Every time I fuck you, you say my name. Do you understand?" When I release her hair, she turns to look back at me. Her green eyes are emeralds on fire. She nods, and I repeat, "Say it."

"Yes, I understand. God, Luke, please. I'm so close."

I give her everything I can until she's calling my name so loudly that I cup my hand over her mouth, and whisper, "*Shh. The walls are thin.*"

Dropping down, she hides her face in a pillow and I continue to rage in sexual ways until we're both covered in sweat with lascivious words tumbling out. Rolling to the side, overly heated and exhausted, I poured every ounce of my soul into her, to please her, to make her believe that we can be one again because this is what I missed. This feeling that I couldn't capture with other women. Only Jane makes me feel this amazing. She is and will always be my one and only.

Our breathing hasn't evened when my sweet angel makes her second request. "Will you lie on top of me?"

I smile. I don't think she sees since embarrassment has taken over and she holds her eyes closed tight. I rid myself of the condom, move closer, and maneuver slowly on top of her. Dropping my weight down, I do what we both want, finding the connection that binds us forever—my heart beating against hers until they find their rhythm, in sync how they were always meant to be.

CHAPTER 14

Luke

"YOU DIDN'T CALL me any names," Jane remarks casually before sipping her coffee.

"Do you want me to call you names?"

"I thought name calling was a part of dirty talking." Big eyes peek up at me over the to-go cup.

"I think it depends on the people involved."

"And the names."

Nodding, I watch her leaning against the green wall, "I love you so much" spray-painted in red over her shoulder. The sight makes me smile, feelings reignited inside, not from the sex, but from the woman. I take the photo on my phone and save it for later. I join her, standing next to her, trying to pretend I don't feel those red painted words for this woman. I do. More deeply than I ever did before. Maybe it's the sex I just had with her fogging my brain. "Yes, I guess what names are being called matter too." After taking a drink of coffee, I ask, "If I were to call you a name while we are intimate, what name do you think you'd like to hear?"

We made love and while dirty talk has its place, it doesn't feel dirty when it's with someone you love. It's fun to see she doesn't get embarrassed as easily as she used to. I'm liking this new Jane mixed with the old. I'm liking me with her.

"I'm not sure. I've not thought about it before." As if a light bulb goes off, she turns to me. "I wouldn't like slut."

"Okay. So slut is out. Anything else?"

"Bitch. I hate that word." She settles her back to the wall again, watching a group of teenagers walk by. As soon as they pass, she makes a disgusted face. "No body parts or bodily functions. That would be a turn off."

"Like shit or fart—"

"Or moist or dick."

Turning to her, feeling a little disgusted myself, I ask, "Who the fuck is calling someone they're attracted to those names?"

"I don't know," she replies with relaxed shoulders and a frown on her face. "I just know I don't want to be called those."

"No worries there."

"You're the expert. What do you suggest?"

"I don't know about expert." I eye her, testing the waters. "How do you feel about pretty?"

"Pretty is great, but it's not enough."

"Whore?"

"Whoa. Whoa. Whoa. Slow up. How'd we jump from pretty to whore in one name?"

This time I shrug. "I don't know. Just figured I'd throw it out there."

She elbows me and nods her head toward the sidewalk to follow her. "We should head back."

"Okay," I reply, the disappointment too hard to hide. I'll still try to appreciate these last few minutes we have alone while we walk back to the hotel.

Right before we enter the courtyard, she bumps me. "Would you like to call me a whore?"

Our coffees remain an endless source of distraction during this fascinating and equally awkward conversation. "I don't want to call you a whore unless you want me to call you a whore." She remains quiet in thought as I take a long drink of the soothing liquid, so I'm more direct. "Do you want me to?"

After a thoughtful pause, she says, "Whore might be okay."

I smile, but I don't laugh, not wanting her to feel self-conscious. I like that she wants to experiment too much to tease her.

Ian is knocking on her door when we return. When he spots us, his eyes dart between us, but land on her. "I was just coming to get you."

Holding her coffee up, Jane says, "We went for an energy boost."

"That's a good idea. I wish I would have known. I could have gone with you and kept you company."

Because I'm chopped liver...

"Luke kept me company."

He eyes me. "Yes, of course, I meant extra company. Are we ready to go?"

She asks, "Do I have time to change clothes?"

"Yes, if you're quick," he replies. "The cabs have already been called."

"I'll be quick."

As she unlocks her door, Ian says, "You might want to wear something a little cooler. You look a little heated. Your cheeks are flushed."

She turns back, her gaze hitting me, then eyes him. "I think you're right. It's been a hot afternoon."

I add to the inside joke, "A scorcher."

Ian cuts in, "Meet us out front, Jane," ignoring me.

Not even fifteen minutes later, he fucks me on the cab

situation. Ian is so quick with the placements of who rides in which cab that I'm still standing on the sidewalk when the first cab drives away carrying Jane. The assistant director is nice enough, but I'd rather be with the woman I just made love to.

By the time our cab arrives at the drop off point, Jane, Ian, Jessica, and Ryan are already on the boat with a cocktail in hand.

Other crew members are talking, their backs to us as they point at the Austin skyline. Not Jane. She steps away from them, smiling right at me. The skirt of her white sundress is blowing in the wind along with her hair.

She's just so damn beautiful that my heart momentarily stops as I take her in, reminding me so much of the first time I ever saw her...

"Who's that?"

When Ricky doesn't answer, I turn and see him gawking at the same girl I just asked about. "Shut your trap. You're embarrassing yourself, Rick."

"Dude, who is that?"

Rolling my eyes, I say, "I just asked that."

He's on the move, but there's no way I'm giving him a shot before I get mine. As junior varsity football captain, fucker gets enough girls. Now that I have my license, I need to put it to use. This hottie might just be the first girl to get a ride—pun intended.

Like in every cheesy high school movie and some porns, the beauty takes her hair from this knot on top of her head. Ricky and I stop at the same time, gobsmacked, as her hair comes tumbling down past her shoulders. She slips her Raybans to the top of her head and I whack Ricky in the chest with the back of my hand, stopping him. "Holy shit!"

"What?" he asks, his eyes still glued to her like every other guy in the vicinity.

I know her—blond hair, even lighter from the summer, long tan legs that must have grown since I saw her last. "That's Jane Lewis."

"What?" His face crumples. When he looks back at her, his eyes go wide. "No way!"

"Way."

"How that fuck did that happen in three months?"

Shaking my head, I correct him, "She was always cute."

Now he's shaking his head. "Yes, cute. Now she's fucking hot." With a devious grin growing, he says, "I think I need to reintroduce myself."

"You've known her since sixth grade."

"No, I knew cute Jane Lewis. I want to get to know spank-bank material Jane Lewis."

"Dude, do not put your dirty details in my head."

"Like you're not going to be jacking off to her later, Anders."

"I'm not." He looks at me in disbelief, and I smirk. "While you're jacking to the memory of her, I'm going to be with her."

When he bursts out laughing, like gut-chuckling until tears-start-forming laughter, he steps back and waves forward, rolling out the imaginary red carpet that leads right to her. "You know you have no chance once I start talking to her, so how about I be kind and give you a head start. Once she rejects you, she'll be primed for me."

"Fuck you. I can get a girl."

"You're sixteen and still a virgin, man. We're buddies, but let's not kid ourselves here. You have no chance in hell against me."

"You're such an asshole."

"Still your friend."

I have shitty taste in friends. One day I'm gonna find friends who have my back instead of ones who stab me in the front over a girl. I walk away from him and it's starting to feel like I'm walking away from a friendship.

I should.

According to him, I'm a total geek. Trying to shrug off his insults, I remind myself I've chosen not to get laid. Marie Luppino begged me to pop her cherry last year. With her brother at the bonfire twenty feet away, it was hard to get hard behind a tree, even with her groping me. She had no skills in that area either so that didn't help. I never told Ricky that story because he would have made fun of me. He has no shame in his game. He would have fucked her in front of her parents so her brother would have only been seen as a speed bump.

His true colors are showing. He likes me driving him around and using me for burgers and fries then sticking me with the bill. Fuck him.

Forgetting about him, I look ahead. Jane Lewis sits on top of a picnic table laughing with her friends, two girls I know from classes over the years. We've always hung out in different groups, but we still go to the same school and know about each other.

Twenty feet until contact...

My steps slow, nerves starting to creep in as I get closer. Her smile is beautiful. Her lips are a shiny deep shade of pink. She's always had the prettiest green eyes. I told her that once when we were in sixth grade English class, just after the bell rang for dismissal. But her friend, Caroline Stacie, dragged her away before she could reply. I always wondered what she was going to say. I remember her mouthing sorry before she caved to her friend's peer pressure and left the classroom.

Fifteen feet until contact...

I get it. I've been a wingman to Ricky for years, caved to him staking claims from girls to video games. His arrogant attitude is annoying on many levels. I think it's time for me to step up and go after what I want for once. A wingman no more.

Ten feet until contact...

She sees me. So do her friends. Like gatekeepers to a great treasure, they sit up straighter and angle protectively in front of Jane. Caroline Stacie smiles as if she can't wait for me to be shot down.

That doesn't help my nerves. I think she's just bitter I shot her down in the fifth grade when I told her I'd rather surf than ride bikes with her after school. We've never spoken again and I've been on the receiving end of many dirty looks since.

The one I'm getting now might top them all. Caroline leans over and whispers to Jane. Jane's eyes go from her back to me, but her expression remains neutral.

Shit. Like Ricky said, I have no chance in hell.

Five feet...

Shoving my hands into my front pockets, it's not too late to turn around and serve her up on a silver platter for Ricky to come in and hook up with her. It's not too late to make up some excuse like I'm selling chocolate bars for the football team to help them get to the State championship even though I don't play football. I can come up with a million excuses.

But I don't.

Contact.

"Hi." *My hand comes out and I do this stupid little wave thing with the other. Fuck. I shove it back into my front pocket, trying to hide my nerves. I hear Ricky laughing in the distance behind me.*

Her smile is shy, but it's there, just for me. "Hi," *she replies, her eyes looking up into mine.*

"Do you have plans this Friday?"

"I'm free."

Caroline interrupts, "Heard you got a car, Luke."

"I did," *I reply, fully focused on the beautiful girl who seems fully focused on me.* "Maybe I can drive you home sometime, Jane?"

"Maybe today," *she replies.*

"Today's good."

She nods, and then says, "You look like you've been working out."

I shrug. "Yeah, I started lifting over the summer."

"Oh yeah? I can tell."

"Thanks. You look—"

An arm drapes around my shoulders. Ricky is leaning against me and pats my chest. "Thanks, Anders, I'll take it from here." *Walking around me, he sticks his hand out to shake Jane's. When she accepts it, he turns it over and kisses the top. Smooth.* "You look hot in that skirt, Jane. You coming to watch me play this Friday? I'm starting quarterback."

Standing up on the bench, her smile is gone. Her friends stand up in unison. Jane steps down, and says, "I'm not that into football, so I think I'll pa—"

"Maybe we can hook up afterwards and go to Eli's party? His parents will be out of town. We can celebrate my victory on the field and I can show you my moves off the field." Ricky waggles his eyebrows as if the come-on wasn't straightforward enough.

She looks to me anxiously, her eyes sending a silent plea. I move closer and help her out, which means helping me out too. "We already made plans for Friday night."

"Really?" he asks shocked, and then appears confused.

"Yes." I nod confidently, though I'm sweating inside. "I'm taking Jane to, ummm—"

"The new Ridley Scott movie. It starts on Friday."

My heart might have just skipped a beat listening to a girl, who visually could give a Sports Illustrated model a run for the swimsuit cover, mentioning Ridley Scott like that's normal. That she even knows who he is blows my mind. Jane was hot before. Now she's downright dream-girl material. And yes, definitely spank-bank material.

"Yes," I say, adding to her answer, "I'll pick you up at seven."

Jane touches the short sleeve of my shirt. "You're still taking me for a ride in your car after school, right?"

Caroline gets impatient, rolling her eyes. "We're going to be late, Jane."

Jane continues to look at me, ignoring her friend.

I respond with a smile, "Yes, I'll see you after school."

When Caroline tugs her by the elbow, I have flashbacks of sixth grade. Jane frees herself from the confines of her friend's grip, and steps closer to me, the gap almost closed. "What were you going to say, Luke? Earlier. I look what?"

Pretty eyes. Great smile. The world shifts beneath my feet, my heart growing for this wide-eyed beauty. "Lovely. You look lovely today."

Her smile spreads, then she lifts up on her toes and kisses my *cheek. "Thank you. I'll see you later, okay?"*

"Okay."

...I'm walking the plank, falling into the deep end of the feelings I've always had for this woman.

Ian comes up to her and takes her by the elbow. I'm really starting to dislike that fucker. Jane makes a wonky face he doesn't see. Then she rolls her eyes, which makes me laugh and reassures me at the same time.

As soon as I board the boat, I don't hover around them. I don't need to stake a claim or anything else Ian is so blatantly attempting to do. I know whom she chose more than a decade ago. It's the same guy she chose this afternoon. And, if I have my way, she'll choose to be with again tonight.

CHAPTER 15

Luke

LEANING AGAINST THE railing of the boat, I look up at the sky while millions of Mexican free-tailed bats swarm above. A dark mass stream, floating with the winds keeps all eyes on the boat facing up. "Amazing, right?"

I'd know that voice anywhere. Her arm presses to mine. The boat is crowded along the railing, the act not so obvious, except to us. I steal a glance down at her. "Amazing is right." The sun is setting, but the blush that colors her cheeks from the compliment is prettier. She looks down and then peeks up at me, pretending to be looking at the bats. But I see those bewitching eyes and ask, "What are you doing later?"

Turning around and leaning her elbows on the wood, she arches her back and it reminds me of earlier. My attention turns to the bats so I don't get an erection... or should I say become harder than I already am. Images of her naked body beneath mine floating through my head don't help the situation. She's got great tits and that dress is highlighting them perfectly—low-cut, thin material showing off her nipples. When the wind blows just right, I see the top of her breasts and I want to cover them with my mouth again.

She replies, "Hopefully you."

"You're tempting, Ms. Lewis. Very fucking tempting."

"I'm hoping to pick up where we left off."

"Today or years ago?"

Bumping my hip with hers, she says, "That's for you to find out. See you later." She smiles as she shakes her ass for me.

"I'll hold you to that."

"I hope you hold me to many things, like beds and windows, maybe even bathroom counters."

"I'm liking this pervy side of you."

"I hope you like all my sides. Start with my backside." She taps my nose.

"It's not about the start, but the finish, baby."

Her smile falls and I see her swallow. "That right there. Talk to me like that, Luke."

I laugh. "I can't turn it on and off. It comes with the situation, and territory. But if you want, we can flirt and tease, make love and fuck because if it turns you on, it gets me off." Looking around to make sure no one is watching, I lick my lips and run my hand down her hip giving it a squeeze. "I'm going to make you come harder than you've ever come before."

"I've never done anything on a boat before." Her right eyebrow rises in challenge as she stares up at me.

"That can be arranged."

"Arrange it then," she replies as if I won't.

"Meet me downstairs in the bathroom in ten minutes."

"What if—"

"No, Jane. No what ifs. Only *yes* will do. Yes, sir is even better." She glances around nervously, so I offer her an out, just in case, "We don't have to do anything. I thought you wanted—"

"I do."

"Then what do you say?"

Her fiery eyes meet mine, and she whispers, "Yes."

"You don't sound sure."

After clearing her throat, more confidently she says, "Yes, sir."

"Ten minutes. Don't keep me waiting."

She walks away without saying another word. Her shoulders are tense, her eyes searching the boat as if everyone is aware of our planned rendezvous. No one cares. No one is even paying attention to us. But I like her tense. I like her nervous and excited. I'll make her come and forget her worries and everything that lies on the other side of that bathroom door. I'll be the only thing she feels, touches, thinks of while I take her against the wall, making her mine all over again.

Watching her over my shoulder, she's chatting with Ryan and they go to the bar together. I could let my jealousy get the best of me like earlier, but I know where she'll be in a few minutes. Catching her eye, I look down at my wrist to check the time, tapping it. When I look up, Jessica is standing before me. The sun blocked by her presence. She sits on the bench next to me and acts like we're old friends. "Hi."

I'm in no mood for her. She was a huge, drunken mistake, but I'll be cordial in public until all patience is lost. "Hi," I say, and sigh. I'm not a great actor though.

"I agreed to do your little movie. You can give me the courtesy of being civil."

A pain in my right temple flares so I rub it. She's right, but I need to remind her of our agreement. "You needed this 'little movie' as well, so let's recognize that it's to our mutual benefit to work together." I glance at her. "And be civil."

The last part makes her smile. She clears her throat and perks up. "A few of us are going out after we dock. Do you want to join us?"

My eyes find Jane across the crowded boat. Almost every man on it is aware of her presence and has gravitated closer, warming in her sunshine. *Fuckers.* She was always the center of attention and never realized it. *Still doesn't.* "Who's going?"

Jessica follows my gaze so I turn my attention on her so she doesn't find my weakness. She looks at me, and smiles. "Me."

"Your boyfriend might not appreciate you asking me to join you."

"Things with Ryan are," she starts, but pauses, searching for the right words as if they're written in the sky, "open."

That's quite the unexpected finish to that sentence.

The label of my beer bottle is torn, so I help it along. When I look up at her, the sun has almost set and in this light I see the pretty woman that Jessica can be. I just wish her insides matched the exterior.

Looking back to where Jane was, she's gone. Checking the time, I have three minutes. "I'm not sure what to say to that, Jessica."

"Say yes."

I exhale louder than intended. "You know I can't—"

"Don't say it. It took a lot for me to ask you. I'm not sure hearing a rejection will be good for me tonight." She stands, but stays a moment longer. "I don't want to keep dragging this up—"

"Then don't. Now is not the time nor the place."

"Are you seeing someone?"

The beautiful blonde I've dated almost half my life and known longer is waiting for me. I stand. "It's complicated."

"It always is with you," she says hopelessly and walks away.

I work my way toward the stairs and see Jessica at Ryan's side, her arm possessively around his, but her eyes on me. It doesn't matter. All that matters is the woman waiting for me downstairs. I take the stairs and find the bathroom. Knocking lightly, I wait. The door is unlocked and opened. I'm grabbed by the shirt and pulled inside, the door closed and locked quickly behind me. "You're just in time, Mr. Anders."

Turning the tables on her, I trap her, leaning forward until her body is pressed firmly between the hardness of the wall and my hardness. "I always come... on time."

She smiles—devilishly parting her lips and licking them. "And what about me?"

Sliding to my knees before her, I lift the skirt of her dress and see my good girl is bad this evening. "No underwear?"

"Guess I forgot," she replies, feigning the innocence of a vixen.

"Did you do this for me?" *Please say yes.*

Her fingers run through my hair and she tilts me until I look up at her. "Only for you."

Placing one of her knees on my shoulder, I say, "I fucking love it when you get down and dirty."

"Speaking of down." Her hands encourage me forward until I slip my tongue out for a taste of her more adventurous side. One taste is all it takes and I'm lost in paradise.

My beauty forgot about the people on the upper deck, *and* the thin bathroom walls. When her body became jelly, her tension released, I wanted so badly to fuck her... so I did.

Fifteen minutes later, we're back on deck. With a glass of champagne almost to her lips, her cheeks the perfect shade of rose pink, she says, "I feel incredible."

"You are incredible." I straighten my cuffs.

"I haven't felt like this in forever." She tugs playfully at my shirtsleeve. The gesture would look normal to anyone watching. I don't think anyone is, but I look around to make sure.

"I'm happy to oblige anytime you like."

"Doing that, does that turn you on too?"

The right side of my mouth goes up. "Making you feel good

turns me on if that's what you're asking."

"Yes." She doesn't look convinced.

Who knew she'd be shy about dirty talk? She's just too sweet. "It was amazing watching you come, Jane, feeling your body contracting around my tongue, my fingers, my cock."

"Shhhhh." She holds a finger to her mouth. "People will hear, Luke."

"And if they do?"

Jane looks away. When she turns back, she asks, "What was Jessica talking to you about? You looked upset."

"I wasn't upset," I lie, to keep her from worrying. "She was asking if I was going out with them tonight."

"Oh." She glances at Jessica who is with Ryan at the other end of the bar. "She didn't invite me."

"Everyone's invited."

"Well I wasn't specifically invited like you."

"Do you want to go?"

"I want to know why she's personally inviting you when she has a boyfriend."

No creeping of smiles. It just pops right onto my lips. "Are you jealous, Ms. Lewis?"

Jane tilts her head, her hair sweeping to one side. "Only when it comes to you."

"So for the last two years when you were in a relationship—"

"I stayed in it because of you."

Now I look away, not wanting to hear that answer. "I had a feeling you might say that." When I turn back, she looks reflective, staring off into the distance. It won't solve anything, but I say it anyway, "I'm sorry."

"You have nothing to be sorry for." She finishes the last of her champagne and sets the glass down. Facing me, she smiles as she reaches for my hand, her fingertips making my skin spark to life.

She pulls back and looks around to make sure we don't have an audience. "I want to touch you, to feel you, for you to hold me like you do when we're alone, but we have to keep our distance."

"Why?"

"Because I don't want people to think I slept my way into this movie deal."

"You earned it. No one will think otherwise."

"You're a man, Luke, so no one will question how you got where you are in your career. But for a woman, every move is scrutinized and even more so in Hollywood. You know that."

I do know. It sucks but it's true. And for her to get any respect in this industry, Hollywood has to feel she earned it. "How long do we have to keep this act up?"

She looks torn. "I need this movie to be made. I need to build my career and neither one of us needs a scandal. I just wish we had figured out everything with us before production started. Then we could be open like Jessica and Ryan and not hide our..." She doesn't say relationship but I know she was thinking it.

"They're *open* all right," I say sarcastically. If Jane only knew that Jessica was hitting on me, she wouldn't use them as an example, that's for sure.

Jane is unsure about what I mean by my tone and it's probably best I keep her in the dark about Jessica, at least for now. She murmurs, "I live in an ocean of regret when it comes to us."

"I want to kiss each and every one of them away." I want to clear the worry lines from her face. But she's right. It's unprofessional to hook up with co-workers on set.

Her hand disappears just as I hear Ian behind me. "What are you two talking about?"

She puts on a good show—chipper, smiling, pointing up at the night sky. "The bats were so cool, but we have a starry night too."

Touching her arm, he says, "I'm glad you came, Jane."

Oh, she came all right. Twice, in fact. I don't say that though I'd love to brag out loud. "I'm standing right here," I say instead, not joking despite the smile I've put on. "Just in case you forgot."

Ian pats my back. "Nope, it's hard to forget you're here. Impossible almost." He looks to Jane. "You ready to go? We're almost docked."

"Actually, I talked Luke into taking the scenic route and walking back. It's such a beautiful night."

With a scrunched brow, he tries to downplay his desperation, and remarks, "That's a *really* long walk. Are you sure?"

"Positive," she replies just as the boat bumps the dock and the boat crew sprints into action. "We'll see you back at the hotel or in the morning if we get back late. You ready, Luke?"

It's impossible not to feel smug and even harder not to show it as I pass him. *Fuck it.* I don't give a shit if he's upset or not. His assumptions when it comes to Jane are annoying. He reminds me a lot of that fucker in high school—Ricky. Jane's given him no encouragement that she's even remotely interested in him, yet he keeps on trying. "I sure am."

"IT'S LESS THAN a mile to the hotel. You know that, right?" I ask her as we leave the group behind and start back on the trail that leads to the bridge.

"I know."

"Just making sure."

Without remorse, she says, "I didn't want him to come."

"He's going to figure it out." I wait to hear how she feels about that.

"Coming here, we rode in a cab that took less than three minutes. He should have already figured out that it's not far to walk."

"And what about us?"

"What about us?" she asks, knocking into me.

I think she did it on purpose, and I like it. "What if he figures *us* out?"

"If he couldn't tell earlier, I think we're in the clear."

"I like the confidence."

"With you, there's no other way to be." She winks, and I chuckle.

"I have no idea how to take that so I'm just gonna take it as a compliment."

"Will it make a difference if I confess that I have no idea how I meant it? So I guess it's up to you on how you take it."

"You've gotten sassier. You know that?"

"I do."

Her fingers rub against my hand. We pretend this is not a big deal, that we can touch and the world doesn't seem a little brighter for it. Even at night. We're great at pretending. Until we can't any longer.

I turn to her and she to me. Our expressions are on the edge of asking questions and answering them simultaneously, resting in a place of certainty instead of where we existed for years now. "I want to hold your hand," I state clearly, so there's no room for misinterpreting how I feel about her.

"I would like that too."

Her hand fits in my hand like her body fits to mine—perfectly. *I've missed this.*

Holding hands is intimate and tells of connection, so I've not held any other woman's hand in the last two years. But here we are fitting again.

"What ever happened to Caroline Stacie?" I ask as we walk across an intersection.

"Wow," she says, her eyes lighting up. "I haven't thought about her in years."

"So you're not friends again? I thought for sure you would be. She was the head of the *I hate Luke Anders club* so it seemed natural for you to become a member."

Her hand tightens to mine. "I couldn't afford the dues." A sparkle gleams in her eyes as a small smile plays at the corner of her lips.

"You could have billed me," making a pun right back.

"The rules are very strict. All of them said I must hate Luke Anders, and I just never got around to it." Bumping against me again, she laughs.

I don't want to push her for more, but I definitely *want* more. Right now, especially. Her hand is freed and I wrap my arm around her shoulders, holding her as close as I can. I can tell by the feel of her body that she's happy to stay awhile. Her head dips to the side resting on my arm. We stay like this, quietly content, until we get within a few blocks of the hotel.

Then we part.

Begrudgingly.

And for all sake and appearances, we're just friends again, friends working together on a project.

We pass a restaurant and see the camera crew in there, laughing, having a good time. It makes me wonder if they would actually care if Jane and I were together or not. I know the answer, but all it takes is one person to sell information to the tabloids and Jane's career is marred forever. I won't do that to her.

Before we enter the courtyard, both of us expecting to see the others we left at the boat, I ask, "What do you think about staying in my room tonight?"

Her bottom lip is tugged under her teeth, but the smile can't be held back. "I'd like that."

"Come over when you're ready. You know where I'm staying."

"I think I'm going to like that adjoining door." She winks.

I hold the door open and follow her inside the courtyard.

From Ian to Jessica, all eyes are instantly on us. I purposely drop my shoulders to come off as casual. "Can I get you something to drink?"

"Water would be great."

Nodding, I go to the bar inside as she works her way to an already crowded table. I order and while waiting, I watch the scene outside. Jane is sitting with Ryan and Jessica, Ian standing behind her chair, hand resting on the back too content for my liking. We were lucky to score him to direct the movie, but I'm really starting to fucking dislike him.

I'm not going to let him upset me. I've got the girl. Anyway, I have no doubt she can handle him, and will. I've also got enough work to keep me busy, so maybe it's best if I go do that instead of watching him and letting my irritation grow by the minute. The upside to working now is more time with Jane later.

After changing my order to match Jane's, I walk back out and set her water down on the table in front her. When I keep walking, Ian asks, "Where you going, Anders?"

"I've got some work to do. I'm gonna call it a night. See you guys tomorrow."

I catch Jane's eyes on me, but I keep my expression neutral just as she does. Turning around, I leave and go back to my room.

Over an hour later, it's just gone eleven when I hear the room next to mine come to life. A certain dream-girl fumbling around brings my attention from the laptop screen in front of me to the wall that we share. Then a light knock is heard, and again before I have a chance to open it.

I stop typing and go to answer my door that adjoins hers. When the door is opened, I'm greeted with the best sight ever. Yes, this would be where I should say the most beautiful woman I've ever laid eyes on, but we already know that. As I skim down her naked body, I realize just how damn lucky I am. Pulling her to me, she gasps, then giggles, and I say, "I've been waiting for you."

"I was letting your anticipation build so you'd appreciate this even more," she replies assertively.

I want to stay in this moment forever, loving how easily we've returned to our previous selves as if time never separated us. "I don't need time to appreciate you. The anticipation has been building for years, pretty woman. Now get your ass on that bed and let me appreciate you up close and personal."

CHAPTER 16

Jane

HE OWNS ME.

More than I ever knew. More than I ever thought possible. He does. Luke's lips could whisper a sonata across my back and it would be no less permanent than a tattoo.

Luke Anders owns me.

My soul.

My heart.

My love.

My body.

My—"Oh my God, yes. Yes!"

Every one of my orgasms is his and his alone. I never have to fake anything with him like I did Lawrence. I shudder from the thought of the latter. There's no place for him to exist in my life any longer, in any way. He was filler, until my soul, my whole love, came back to me.

Just when I think I can't physically handle another one of his amazing orgasms, my body tremors from ecstasy. The fullness of Luke lingers long after he's gone and I realize it's not just the connection with his body that makes me feel whole.

I turn to look at him on the bed next to me. His eyes are closed, but a big grin is present making me roll my eyes because he's just so damn cute, just like he always was...

"Luke Anders is over there," Caroline Stacie says under her breath, keeping the scowl squarely on her face. "I can't stand him. What do you think he wants?"

My head jerks around until I see him. After a too quick once-over I look away before he sees me staring at him. In that glimpse, I catch:

He's gotten even better looking. He's easily the most handsome boy in school. Though the term is definitely not fitting for how much he's matured over the summer.

He's growing into that tall frame of his very nicely. Broader shoulders even. He looks like he's bigger, like he's been working out.

I like the way he's styling his hair. It's a bit longer than he used to wear it.

Nice clothes.

He is still oblivious to the attention he gets from all the girls.

Looking around the quad, students are gathered in their cliques. But at least three groups of girls have their eyes on Ricky Shallard and Luke Anders. I never understood their friendship. Ricky is such a douche and has been since middle school.

Luke must have the patience of a saint to put up with his crap. Ricky always thought he was God's gift to women, but once he was announced as J.V. Captain at the end of last year for this football season, he's become an asshole. Luckily I prefer surfers.

I saw Luke surf a few times over the summer—unbeknownst to him, of course. Other girls were there as well to watch him.

The boy is blind sometimes, but I find his humble nature charming.

Caroline interrupts my analysis of Luke with a pointy elbow to my upper arm. "Oh my God, he's coming over here. Turn your backs to shut down whatever idea he's gotten in his head."

Oh my God, is right. My palms start to sweat, so I shift on the picnic table. My skirt leaves me feeling vulnerable. Damn, I need lip gloss. I knew I should have reapplied.

"Jane?"

"Huh?"

Caroline asks, "What are you doing?"

"What do you mean?"

She glares at me. "It's Luke Anders."

"I know." I smile. Wrong move apparently.

"He's enemy number one, Jane. Have you forgotten?"

Sighing, I say, "I remember you telling me but it was the fifth grade, Caroline. Just because you were all over him doesn't mean he had to be all about you. I think it's time to let it go."

She scoffs. "I was ten, Jane. I wasn't all over him. Secondly, no one turns me down, especially not Luke Anders."

I look up again. Seeing a shy smile on his face, his chin tilted down, his eyes up and straight on me, makes my cheeks heat. "I'm going to talk to him, Caroline. It's a new year. This is our chance for new beginnings. He's always seemed nice to me."

"Jane, we hold all the power this year. Don't give it away to the first guy that comes along. At least hold out for Ricky. I'm predicting king of junior prom this year. Look at you. You finally got some boobs. You might be his queen..."

Her voice trails off as I tune her out. Luke tucks his hands in his pockets, his pace slowing. The longer it takes the more my heart races. I bite my bottom lip and angle my body to face him, still unsure why he's coming over here. Caroline has never hidden her feelings for him and our other friend, Tara, is more interested in the jock types like Ricky. That leaves me. I want to stand up, to stand on unsteady feet, which seems more stable than staying here like a sitting duck. I take a quick glance around to see if he could be coming to see anyone else, but no one else is close enough.

Our eyes meet, and then he's standing right in front of me. "Hi," he says, waving at me awkwardly, then looking down again and shaking his hand.

Did I do something wrong already? I've never been that girl—the one who uses her looks in trade for another rung higher up the social-climbing ladder. These boobs are new. Over the summer they burst out of that size-A bra without my permission. Suddenly I was shopping with my friends for more than new miniskirts. My hips widened just enough for my mom to note my figure is no longer one of a tomboy's. She called it hourglass. I like this new me, but today, on the first day of my junior year I'm worried how others will judge me—changes for the better or for the worse?

Looking up at Luke, and seeing his sweet smile, I realize it doesn't matter what everyone else thinks. I've had a crush on Luke Anders since I was eleven years old. As he sticks his hand out for me to shake, I smile because whether my boobs are in training or have become fodder for the locker room, he only looks into my eyes.

"Hi," I reply, noticing how the blue of his eyes reminds me of the ocean he loves to surf.

...Rolling to my side, I run my fingers through the hair covering his temple. "I used to get my mom to drop me off at the beach in hopes you'd be there," I confess. When his eyes open, he's sleepy but his happiness is evident. "I would watch you surf.

And sometimes, I'd bring binoculars."

Luke smiles. It's lazy from exhaustion, and utterly sexy. "I know."

"You do?" I ask in surprise.

"I would spy on you too. I'd wipe out and hope you didn't see. I felt so lame. A couple times I paddled in to talk to you. It took me like an hour to convince myself to do it. Every time I did, your mom would show up and you'd leave."

"My mom had a knack at keeping the boys away."

"She was smart."

"She failed when it came to you."

"Thank God." His hand slips under the sheets until it's flat on my stomach. "How tired are you?"

Looking at the clock, I say, "It's almost one in the morning. Should we get some sleep?"

"No." He lifts up on his forearms, shaking his head. "I want to tell you something and I want you to listen."

"Okay."

"I'm sorry you didn't know from my words that you were the only one I ever wanted. When you came over last year and we talked, I knew you cared, but I didn't realize you couldn't say it because you didn't want to get hurt. I thought you were being selfish—leading me on while staying with Lawrence. I just wish we had talked about everything then." When a tear appears and slides down my cheek, he whispers, "No more tears. I don't want to be the cause of anymore of your tears."

"They're happy tears."

His thumb wipes it away anyway. He comes closer and rests his chest on mine before kissing me. Then he says, "I want to feel your heartbeat next to mine."

When he whispers such romantic words, I fall even deeper in love with him. I don't use that word, careful not to rush into something I can't control, something that could not just hurt but devastate me again. He used to tell me he'd love me forever, but I stop remembering the past and feel the present, letting our bodies speak to each other instead.

We don't bother with foreplay, both needing the physical connection more right now. He's inside me, moving slowly, purposefully, engulfing me back into an emotional space where our problems don't exist, no pain exists, a place where our pleasure intensifies drowning out the rest of the world. We're sweating and sated, our breaths uneven, and our pulses are currents, every nerve ending electrified until our hearts give in and I kiss the top of his head as it rests on my chest.

He kisses my breast, his arm wrapping around me tighter. I'm not sure what time I fall asleep, but I'm well aware when I'm woken up. My heart stops when someone bangs on the door. I'd jump, but the weight of Luke holds me in place. But the moonlight coming in allows me to see the panic in his eyes. His voice is low but firm, "Go to your room and lock the door." He stands up and grabs some boxers from the floor. "Go, Jane."

I scurry to my feet and hurry back to my room. I shut the door and lock it like he said. I hear the lock bolt into place on the other side. Though I'm naked and cold, I press my ear to the door, needing to know who would bang on Luke's door at this hour. Glancing over my shoulder to the clock, I see a three from across the room. *Three a.m.? Who is coming to see him now and why?*

The voices next door are muffled but I can tell it's a woman. I try to peek out my peephole but can't see far enough to the right to see who it is, so I run on tiptoes grabbing my robe from the bed and hurry back to the shared door to listen again.

Luke's voice is similar to the one he just used on me—strong, mindful, terse. I can't tell whom the female voice belongs to but I'm starting to get pissed when they lower theirs and are talking.

Why is she not leaving? Why is he letting her in? What the hell?

Through the volume of their voices, I track their movement around the room to the point when it seems she is now where the bed is located, the bed I just crawled out of. I back up, staring at the door in offense. If looks could burn holes through wood that door would be incinerated.

Luke's voice is close all of the sudden, which means Luke is— just on the other side of our shared door. "We'll talk about this later. You should get some rest, Jessica."

Jessica!

My fists ball at my sides and I silently scream. *What the hell is she doing in my boyfriend's hotel room at 3:23 in the morning?* I move away from the door before I explode through it. When I sit on the edge of the bed, I lie back, fuming in anger.

A light knock causes me to sit up and I go to unlock the door and head right back to my bed. As Luke opens it, I crawl under the covers, pulling them up to my neck.

He stops at the end of the bed, a sexy smirk on his face that makes it hard to stay mad. "Can I join you?"

But somehow I manage to. "I don't think so."

His head tilts as his eyes level on mine. "Janie, what's wrong?"

We seem to be locked in a standoff. Like in the past, even though thoughts are running furiously through my mind, I can't vocalize them. *Is that what went wrong for us? I didn't communicate what was really on my heart? I couldn't tell him?*

I don't want to consider why another woman is coming to his room in the middle of the night. Or worse, why she thinks it's okay to do so. He's the producer, not the director. Surely if she had issues with anything to do with the movie or her role, she should have gone to Ian. But, I'm angry and tired, and don't want this right now. I give in and speak just to end it. "Nothing's wrong, *Luke*." The K in his name is hit hard, just to prove how pissed I am. "Go back to your room." I pull the blanket even tighter to my neck, cocooning myself in its comfort, and turn onto my side, away from him.

He doesn't go though.

He stays, standing there for at least one long awkward minute or two until I look back over my shoulder. Luke doesn't say anything or make any excuses, so I turn to face him, my breathing harder as anger continues to course through me.

Then he has the nerve to climb into bed with me. Irate, I glare at him, shocked by his gall. "What are you doing?"

"I'm going to sleep."

"Go back to your room to sleep."

"No," he says, getting too comfortable for my liking.

I push him, but he doesn't budge. "Yes. I mean it."

Grabbing my wrists, he holds me still. "I mean it too. I'm not leaving. I know what you're thinking, but what you're thinking is wrong."

"Why would she think she can come to your room at this hour?"

"Because she's used to getting her way."

I squirm, trying to free my wrists. Our knees bump together, but I'm determined to get away from him. "Luke," I whisper yell through gritted teeth, "let me go. I'm not playing around."

Turning me around in one swift move, his arms are around me as his body cradles mine from behind. With his lips to my ear, he says, "I'm not playing around either, Jane. You are not going to do this. Whatever crazy is going on in your head right now, clear it out." His arms tighten when I continue to squirm.

"I don't want to talk about this. Just go."

"I didn't give her any reason to assume it was okay for her to come to my room."

"Then why would she?"

"Because she's spoiled."

"What does that have to do with anything?" *Does she want him? Isn't she with Ryan?* I roll my eyes. "Just go. I'm not in the mood to play your games."

"My games? You've got a starring role in the game we play, the game you started." He moves on top of me, trapping my legs beneath him while holding my arms to the bed. "So I'll say it again. Look at me."

"No."

"Jane? Please look at me."

When I do, he says, "I did not invite her. I have no control over her decisions, but I do over mine and I choose you. I always have." He leans down and kisses me.

I don't care how much I like his defense of us, and his kiss. I hang on to the anger a bit longer. "How dare you kiss me when I'm mad."

"You have no reason to be mad." His voice is calm, no anger found in his tone. "So if you are, I'll kiss you until you aren't anymore."

I scoff and free my arms, immediately pushing against him. He's quick and stills me again. "Oh no, you won't."

"Prepare yourself, Jane Lewis, because I'm going to kiss you and you're going to kiss me back." This time he frees my arms, so confident and cocky, testing me.

With both hands pressing up against him, I warn, "Like hell I will. Get off me."

"Yes, you are, because you know I'm telling you the truth. You know I wouldn't betray you."

"You did. You betrayed me before," I let it come out, tears filling my eyes.

His stare is hard. I turn away, not able to face him when he asks, "When? You say that but I still have no idea what you mean.

Was I fucking other women? Yes. There. There's the truth you've wanted me to confirm for you. But you were fucking your so-called fiancé, so tell me why your situation is more acceptable than mine."

"Because I never stopped loving you, but you stopped loving me." My confession halts us. I close my eyes so I can hide my pain from him.

His tone is composed, sweet even, causing me to soften my stronghold on this issue. He whispers, "See, baby, that's where you're wrong." He kisses me gently.

This time I don't struggle. I don't want to keep falling into this pattern of pushing him away. I want to forget about our time apart and feel this, feel everything again with him. As much as I want to hate him for moving on, he thought I had already. For a short time, I thought I had as well. But there's no getting over losing part of your soul.

Disappointed in myself, I confess my sin, "I called you my boyfriend."

He smiles.

"Don't. Please."

"I like being your boyfriend. So what's so wrong with you calling me that?"

"Everything, because if I called you my boyfriend that means you're in here," I say, tapping my chest. "And that leads to heartbreak."

"Not if I can help it." And then he smiles. It's not cocky. It reminds me of the timid boy who approached me that first day at school. *Genuine.*

I can't hold on to this anger anymore. He doesn't deserve it no matter how much it hurt me to find that woman at his house. *He* thought I was over him. I'm so stupid to let pride and hurt feelings destroy what we once had. I let him kiss me again because I want his love so desperately. I want him. All of him to be mine. We need to try to wipe the slate clean, overlook each other's... indiscretions. And he can help me do that.

"Kiss me and make it all go away."

CHAPTER 17

Jane

"I'VE BEEN HEARING rumors," Scalia singsongs, sidling up to me.

I keep my eyes on the actors as they rehearse. "What rumors might those be?"

"That you're fucking a few of the crew members."

My mouth drops open and I lurch my attention in her direction from shock. "A few? I am not!" Luke is not considered part of the crew. *Is he?*

We're shot a dirty glare from the assistant director since the actors are rehearsing, but Ian's expression is more on the side of curiosity.

Scalia taps my shoulder, and whispers, "Well, you're fucking somebody because your skin looks amazing, all dewy and you're happy, like annoyingly so. Did you even realize you were whistling earlier?"

"I was not. Was I?"

"Well, it might have been more of a hum, but it sounded chipper. Are you going to spill or do I need to ask the gaffer?"

I smile, but hold back the laugh I want to let out, whispering instead, "I am not having sex with the Gaffer, the Grip, Craft

Services, or any other crew member. Can't a girl just be happy?"

"No. I'm going to get to the bottom of this, missy. In the meantime, I'm heading to Continental Club tonight. Wanna come?

"Text me later with details. I might stay in tonight. I have some work to do on a different script as well as a few rewrites I might need to do on this one."

"'Kay. Have a good one. I'm off to shop."

Rehearsals aren't going well. Jessica and Ryan are fighting on and off set. No surprise since she's showing up at hotel rooms other than her boyfriend's in the middle of the night. She's gone to Ian more than three times to complain. He finally, on her demand, comes to me. "She's not connecting with the character."

"And?"

"And she's the star, so we need to appease her."

I just look at him, cross that I'm expected to change the character to suit her whims and moods.

When I don't respond, he says, "I think we need to look at this scene and see how we can fix it."

"Fix it? The scene is not the problem. They are. *They* are not connecting. I think they either broke up or are on the verge of it."

He looks over at them. "Really? Why do you say that?"

"Just a hunch." I want to tell him because she's slinking around my boyfriend in the middle of the night, but I don't. "Watch their body language." We watch as they interact. Jessica's closed off to Ryan with her arms crossed over her chest, completely unreceptive as he tries to get her to interact with him.

"Huh? Shit. This is why we never should have cast them. Relationships that form on set like theirs did on the last film never last and now we're paying the price." He taps the script in my lap. "What can we do?"

"It's not the script, so maybe close the set down to give it a

more intimate feel. Right now they're 'acting' instead of feeling."
Luke walks in and like my heart, my gaze drifts to him. His eyes
meet mine, but we both promptly look away. I gulp, trying to coat
my throat that has suddenly gone dry.

"I'll get Anders on it." Ian walks off.

Exhaling loud enough to let Luke know he has me in a
complete tizzy mess over him, I sit back and watch as Ian starts
talking to Luke. They both watch the actors, nodding, and then
Ian walks on set while Luke comes toward me.

Though I'm looking away, I feel our connection even at a
distance. So much of this reminds me of high school. We were a
couple from that moment the first day of our junior year. The
pain was lessened last night, but didn't go away entirely, making
me wonder what we are now.

"Hi."

"Hi," I reply.

His hands are shoved into his pockets and he rocks back on
his heels. "So last night..." He looks over his shoulder at the set.
Ian is leaning in, talking to Jessica and Ryan, distracted from us.

I repeat, "So last night..."

"What happened?"

"We made up and made love."

"We did, but I don't want that to happen again. I've been
thinking about things." My heart falls to the pit of my stomach
listening to him. "That wasn't us. That wasn't you. I understand
you've been hurt, but I didn't like that. I didn't like that when
someone else did something, you lost trust in me."

It rushes out, but I still feel both words immensely. "I'm
sorry."

His hand reaches for me, but then he remembers where he is
and shoves it back in his pocket. "I don't want you to be sorry. I
want you to believe in me again. I've not lied to you, not about our

past or the past few years apart. I understand you were hurt. I understand that more than anything, but if you want us to be together again, you need to trust me. Or we'll need to take this slower."

"Is that what you want?"

"No. I would have you moved in tonight if we were in LA. But we're not. We're on location and there are a lot of reasons to keep things professional until we're home again. While we're here, no one can control what we do after hours. So if I have my way, that door that connects my room to yours will remain wide open, just like my heart. If you want to keep that door wide open too, then we will."

Ian calls out, "Luke?"

Luke looks behind him, but says to me, "I told him if they can't work it out we'd look at the scene again, but I need to go." His expression is one of kindness and patience when he looks to me. "I don't want you to rush an answer or feel pressured. Now you know where my head's at. I'm not leaving anything off the table. I'm all in. Think about where you are with us and let's talk tonight." He walks away after a quiet goodbye.

He did it. He has laid it all out for me, been so open, which he wasn't before. Has a few years apart made him realize he can't hold back when it comes to love or did being back with me do that? Whichever it is, I'll take it. He's giving me what I want, making his intentions along with his future direction crystal clear. The ball is in my court and I'm either going to accept our past and move forward or walk away so I don't destroy what we have rebuilt.

When I look over at him again, talking to the stars, why does it feel like I'm opening myself up for the pain I thought I had gotten over?

He's told me everything I need to hear, everything I dreamed of hearing for years, but I can't seem to hold on to the words, my heart is still too damaged. A quiet ticking is felt inside my chest, awakened for the first time since the day I left. I watch him speaking, listening when others talk. His body language reveals he cares for them and their needs. And I know he cares about mine. But he has needs too. I get up, my heart beating in double time—along with my biological clock, is his now ticking in sync with mine?

I need to clear my head and think about the scene and a potential rewrite as well as figure out what I'm doing with Luke. Last night I was running off emotion, hurt feelings that he wasn't responsible for. Today, I have to think clearly. If I get back with Luke, there's no back and forth with him. I love him too much to date him casually. Like him, I need to be all in or let him go.

Thirty minutes later I'm out of the hotel and jogging down to the trail along the water. It's misting, but the rain feels good on my hot skin as I push myself physically. Everything with Luke needs to make sense for who we are now, the people we became when the other wasn't looking.

Mist turns to rain, but I keep running, keep pushing until I only know the gravel beneath my feet and the gray skies above. I don't know how much time has passed or how many miles I cover, but when I come back to Congress where the street meets the trail I stop in my tracks.

Luke.

Not thirty feet in front of me with an umbrella in hand, he stands, waiting.

For me.

Offering protection from the rain.

The metaphor is not lost on me. This man who offered me comfort for every formative year of my life is now here ready to weather the storm with me.

My heart is pumping but I'm not sure if it's from the long jog or from the sight of him. When he comes closer, my knees weaken and I know it's definitely from him. He holds the umbrella over my head though I'm drenched already. Through rain-covered lashes, I look up at him, and ask, "What are you doing here?"

"I'll always be here when you need me."

The sentiment hits me straight in the heart. I'm not sure if it's rain or tears that fall down my cheeks until I remember the umbrella shielding us from the rain. But he sees them. Just like he sees the real me through every wall I've built to harbor myself in safety. "How did you know I needed you?"

"Because I need you, Jane. I want you, but I need you too."

I can tell he wants to kiss me, to make this better, but he holds back and just that little hesitation breaks my heart enough to put me in motion. My wet body clings to his dry chest. "I don't want to be without you anymore."

Dry arms hug me, the umbrella shifting. When I tilt my head up, the rain is pouring down over his. He opens his eyes, and with a small smile he says, "I don't want to be without you either. Can we leave everything in the past?"

"I'll try. For you, I will." I nod against him. Righting myself, I tilt the umbrella to cover his head. Then I take his face in my hands and look at him. The shadow of the beard growing across his jaw is prickly, but it doesn't dissuade me. I go all in.

Our lips meet and my world spins around as rain comes down, falling on us. The umbrella is dropped to the side and his hand covers my neck as I tilt in for more.

I've dreamed of kisses in the rain, but they fail in comparison to this. Not wanting to stop, I persevere by stepping forward, even when he takes a step back. With a laugh, he says, "Let's go back to the hotel. I don't want you to get sick."

Giddy.

I feel positively giddy right now. This is what happens when you let love in. You get drunk on it. "Don't you see, Mr. Anders? I'm already sick. *Love* sick over you. No one makes me feel like you do." I turn in a circle, looking up at the sky, then twirl into his arms and wrap my mine around his neck. His smile infiltrates my heart completely, happiness spreading through my veins. "Please stay with me here in the rain along the river, and kiss me until we can't kiss any longer."

Lightning strikes.

The sky lights up across the bridge and we jump. As if he needs to talk some reason into me, Luke leans down until he's eye level with me. Holding my hands, he pleads, "We're standing in the middle of a lightning storm, Janie. I'll kiss you the rest of the day and all night. I'll cover your body with mine and with hickeys if you want, but don't put your life at risk for mine or anyone else's. I can't survive without you. I've already learned that the hard way." I'm grabbed and pulled close to him, tucked neatly under his arm. "I have a cab waiting for us. Let's go back and I'll kiss you in the shower. I'll recreate this whole scene for you if you like, but I want you safe."

"We can go back." A wide smile covers my face, my chest bursting with sunshine and glee for this man. "But I'm holding you to that shower."

"You can hold me however you want as long as I get to return the favor."

A quick kiss to his lips, then we walk toward a taxi parked in the distance. I ask, "And how would you like to hold me?"

"I've got a few very dirty ideas."

"I bet you do. Sir."

A wry grin covers his irresistible lips and he asks, "What are you willing to bet?"

"My whole heart."

"I'll take that bet, and raise you mine."

Standing at the car, I ask, "How did you know when I'd be here? Your timing is perfect."

"I didn't. I waited over an hour. I think my fare is over two hundred dollars." Luke holds the door open for me. "Pray for my wallet."

"Pray for my heart," I add with a wink before slipping inside the dry cab.

"No need for that." He slides in after me. After kissing my cheek, he says, "I'm in just as deep, my dear Janie."

CHAPTER 18

Luke

THE HOTEL ROOM is quiet. The thunderstorms continue outside the window, setting the scene as we work through the script. I sit on the bed with my legs stretched out, watching Jane a few feet away.

She's poised at the window, just how I always saw this scene play out in my head. The lines from *Until I Met You* are spoken from somewhere deep inside, somewhere real and raw, as if she's one of the characters we're rehearsing. "You're pistachio and I'm rocky road. They just don't mix."

"I could argue that, but I have a feeling anything I say wouldn't matter."

"That's where you'd be wrong," she says. "How long have we known each other?"

"We don't know each other at all."

"Ah," she replies as Jude would, nailing the lines. "Yes, that's right. You're a Barrett."

I read from the page in front of me, hoping I don't break the magic. "And what are you again?"

"Hopeless. So very hopeless."

"And here I thought I was the impossible one."

Jane laughs. "Clever." Standing up, she pretends to get dressed. "I called it the minute I saw it."

"Saw what exactly? My eye color?"

"No. Your soul."

I wait for her to say her next line, the line that I know means as much to us as it does to Hazel and Jude.

"I knew we'd be put in an impossible situation, a love affair that would mean more than it should, more than either of us could endure once it was over." She looks away just as I see the pain in her eyes.

"Jane?"

She stays focused on the outside, droplets hitting the window in large splats, keeping the room inside gray to match the weather. "Yes?"

"We're not Hazel and Jude. I'm Luke. You're Jane. There's nothing keeping us apart."

When she turns to look at me, she asks, "Together. Is that what we get to be now?"

"We do."

Her smile blooms and the room suddenly feels brighter because of it. "We should be together without rubbing it in everyone's face."

"I agree." I kid, "No one should have to watch how I'm going to maul you."

"For sure, and add to it that we're reunited lovers on top of being hot for each other. No one wants to watch PDA between two reunited lovers. That's the kind that turns X-rated and quick."

Hearing her joke eases me. This movie is emotionally heavy. For a split second I was convinced she was speaking from the heart instead of from the script. I'm glad we've moved passed it. "Do you want to order food?"

"They don't have room service here. Can we order delivery?"

"Anything you want."

"Pizza. The answer is always pizza."

"Then pizza it is." I grab my phone and start searching for the name of the place across the street.

Fifteen minutes later, I walk out of my room to the Congress Street sidewalk. The storm has given us a slight reprieve from the rain. The streets are wet, the lights reflecting off them when cars drive by. Not even a minute later, she's next to me smiling. So contagiously big. "You're not very good at hiding this secret affair you just said we need to hide."

Pointing at my ridiculously big grin, she remarks, "You aren't either."

"Then let's not."

While we walk to the corner to cross the street, she appears to ponder this option. "Is there anything contractually saying we can't? I don't want to ask my agent or she'll tease me endlessly."

I reach for her hand, my fingertips touching her palm before I remember to pull my hand back. "We can check when we get back, but I doubt it. I've never noticed any clauses like that. With that said, I've never had a reason to research it either, so there is that."

"I like that."

"You like that I've never researched it?"

"No." She hip bumps me just as we reach the other side of the street. "I like that you've never had a *reason* to research it."

I grab her playfully around the shoulders and pull her to me, giving her a light noogie without messing her hair up completely.

Pushing off me, she laughs and my breath stops, her beauty overwhelming me. I look away, not wanting her to see how much and how easily she affects me.

This woman could destroy me in the blink of an eye. What if

she changes her mind about us, about me? All this happiness could be gone in an instant. The security I was giving her earlier has been lost on me.

I want to touch her.

I want to hold her hand.

I want to kiss her.

I want her…

"Paybacks are hell, Anders. Remember that."

I chuckle, playing along to hide my feelings on the inside. "I will. I might even remind you."

"Did you call in the order?" she asks, eyeing the long line out the door.

"I did. When you were getting dressed. It should be ready. We can pick it up and walk somewhere or return to eat in the room?" I look up at the stormy sky. "The rain has let up, but it doesn't look like for long."

"Let's be rebellious and eat in bed." When we reach the pick-up line, she says, "This must be some damn good pizza. Is it wrong to be so excited about pizza?"

"If it's wrong I don't want to be right." I hold the door open for her and we go to the counter.

When we return to the courtyard with our box of goodness, Scalia is out vaping. Jessica next to her, and some guy I don't recognize. Several bottles of wine are open on their table. Scalia raises her arms and waves us over. "Jane. Join us."

Guess it's a private party. I stop anyway, and wait, only *sort of* worried about Jessica and Jane talking. I don't think Jessica would say anything to her, but I can't guarantee it either. With all Jane and I have been through lately, I don't want us screwed up again.

Jane keeps things light, friendly, when she says, "We got a pizza. We're gonna eat and go over some scenes."

Scalia coos, "I'm starved."

Jessica adds, "So am I." Her eyes are on me.

Somehow we end up hosting a pizza and beer party in my room. Jane is patient but antsy. She gets up frequently and paces a bit. We play cards—blackjack, poker, Go Fish, Memory. It's fun, but not as much fun as I originally had intended for tonight. The rain stopped for the night and moods are lighter, the beer also playing a part in that.

By midnight, Jane yawns. It's the third in a row. She casually looks around the room and leans back, settling in even more than she has. Resting her head on her hand, her eyes start to close. Jessica, who seems more awake than anyone, laughs loudly. Jane's eyes flash open and she sighs. Standing up, Jane looks at me, and says, "I'm gonna go to bed."

Jessica smiles. If I had drank less I might have picked up on the clues. Too eagerly, she says, "Goodnight, Jane. See you tomorrow."

Scalia asks, "You sure you don't want in on the next round?"

Jane eyes me as she passes by. She makes a sad face that the others can't see. "I'm good. Too tired. Have fun."

The one person I want to spend time with is leaving, and there's another round? *Fuck.* "I think I'm calling it a night." *Hint. Hint.*

Scalia gets to her knees, reaching to gather the cards. "We can keep going in my room if you guys are up for it?"

Jessica's mind does a one-eighty. "Actually, I'm super tired. I'm going to stay and help Luke clean up then go to bed." She looks back at me and winks, then puts on her charade for Scalia, helping her get the cards in order.

The door closes harder than expected and we all turn to see Jane has left. *Shit.*

Scalia stands, beer in one hand, cards in the other. "It was fun.

We should do it again." She heads to the door with a guy named Joe without being asked.

"It was," I say, following behind her. "Don't worry about the mess, Jessica. I've got it."

"No worries at all. I hate leaving you with a mess."

Scalia laughs. "I have no problem leaving you with it. Next time I'll host and let you leave your bottles for me to clean up. Night."

"Ha! Thanks. Night." She walks out and I stand there with the door open, being more than obvious. "It's like ten bottles, Jessica. I've got it."

It's apparent she's not giving up the excuse to stay, so I let the door close, and go to help. That way she'll leave sooner and I can get over to Jane's. I'm not sure if it's the door clicking closed or the beer she's drunk, but as soon as we're alone, she's on me.

Before I can stop her, her lips are on my neck, her arms wrapped around me, fingers in my hair. *Shit*. She whispers, "Finally alone."

Pushing her back, I say, "We've talked about this. I'm not available."

"You said it was complicated. Now you're not available?" I'd say she looks disappointed but she's too determined to let the reality of the words deter her.

With my hands firmly in place between us, I'm steady when I say, "It's not happening. You need to go."

Feigning offense, she starts blinking rapidly. Her bottom lip sticks out and she actually manages tears. She's quite the award-winning actress. "But Luke, I'm lonely."

"Unfortunately, I'm not." Next door the TV starts blaring... *Shit*. "You need to go."

The tears are gone. Just like that, and anger replaces them. "What is wrong with you? Do you know how many people would kill to sleep with me?"

"It doesn't matter. I'm not one of them. Anymore. I've tried to be polite, but you refuse to listen."

She pouts and crosses her arms over her chest. "Because it's one night. No one will know."

Crash.

A loud noise comes from next door. *Fuck.* I need to get her out of here. "I'll know."

When her tears return for their second audition, my words start rushing out. "I'm sorry if I've hurt your feelings."

Her eyes go wide. "You're for real, aren't you?"

I nod, then walk to the door. When I open it, I say, "I'm sorry, Jessica."

As if she refuses to comprehend what's happening, she walks toward me in a daze. "I thought your complication was just that."

"I'm sorry," I repeat, this time looking her straight in the eyes so there is no misunderstanding. "My complication is not as complicated as I once thought."

"But..." She shakes her head, staring at me in disbelief. Her eyes narrow as her temperament suddenly changes. "You'll pay for this. I've never been so insulted in my life. I swear to God." She walks past me without any other acknowledgement. "I will make you pay."

I feel bad for hurting her feelings at first because I know she's not a horrible person, until the threats come flying out. She's like most stars in Hollywood. They're crazy, that world eating away a little more of their souls with each year they live in the limelight. Her threats mean nothing. It's just an actress having a diva moment. She has them more often than most. There's nothing she can do to me.

The TV next door is still on—loud and clear. I lock the front door and go to the other. After knocking lightly, I turn the handle and it opens without resistance.

Jane is leaning against the wall three feet in front of me, her eyes set, freezing me to the spot. I know she heard what happened with Jessica, and I'm about to speak but she puts her finger to her mouth, and says, "Shh."

I expect to get reamed, but anger isn't the winning emotion on her beautiful face. Lust is. "You kept me waiting. I almost went to bed. *Alone.* Do you know how disappointed I would have been if I'd gone to bed alone?" Still standing there stunned, I watch in complete fascination as she takes her shirt over her head. "I like you in my bed. I want you there every night. I've become spoiled." Her jeans come down. Then her undergarments are gone and she's before me completely naked.

The TV drowns out my hard swallows, fortunately. I watch as her hands run the length of her torso and over her beautiful tits. "Difficult indeed," I mumble, following her hands until she stops one between her legs while one remains on her breast.

I only look up when she says, "I'm yours. *This* is all yours, Luke. But never forget, you're mine, too. You'll always be mine."

Panting, I mutter, "I won't. I never have." My cock is straining against the denim that's become too tight in the inseam.

"Do you see this wall?"

"Yes."

"I want you to fuck me against it. Will you do that for me?"

"Yes," I respond again, feeling a lot like that's the only word I'm currently capable of.

"Come here."

When I do, the palms of her hands run over my chest before tugging at my shirt. I take it off, and then watch as she kisses where her hands were. She works on undoing my jeans. I step out of them and watch as she slides lower, taking my boxers with her. My hands tangle into her hair as her tongue tangles with my cock.

When she takes me in her mouth, my back hits the doorframe. "Fuck."

Cold air swallows me instead when she stands up and nips my jaw. Pulling my hair, she's up on her tiptoes, my head jerked to the side, my ear to her mouth. "Talk to me."

Taking hold of the hair at the nape of her neck, I pull her head back until she releases mine and our eyes meet. "Get back on your knees."

"Say my name."

"Get on your fucking knees, Jane."

The smallest of grins passes quickly across her lips before it's gone and she's on her knees again, taking me wholly between those sweet pink lips. With one hand at the base of my cock, her other hand finds mine woven into her hair. She adds her own pressure, so I do as she requests and add mine to the back of her head, pulling and pushing likes she wants.

She moans, the vibration and the tightness of her hold around me, causing me to react. My head hits the wall as she fucks me with her mouth.

I'm close. Too close. Too soon.

My thoughts go fuzzy as my body reacts, fisting her hair, and thrusting. "Fuck. Fuck. Fuck." Breathing comes hard after and I open my eyes. Leaning back, Jane looks up at me. Our eyes are on each other until I say, "Get on the bed."

And she does.

I never thought the girl I once knew—her body, her mind, her everything—would ever like being commanded. But maybe like me, she's changed and more open to what we like now instead of what we were then. Maybe we needed the time away to allow us to change things up. *Had we fallen into habits in our sex life?* I don't think so. But this? This is hot, and well worth the wait.

She is every fantasy I've ever had rolled into one. She always was, and remains the center of every fucking sexual thought I have. No other woman stood a chance against her memory. No matter if their name started with J or any other letter of the alphabet. No one was ever going to replace Jane.

I walk to the bed, her naked body lying in the middle. Her face set on mine, waiting for the next command. With the real thing before me, I waste no time. "Spread your legs for me, baby."

Her knees butterfly open and I lick my lips when I spy her pink pussy. A fucking flower with the sweetest of scents, I debate if I want to fuck her, inhale her, or eat her.

"Luke?"

Looking back up at her, I ask, "What?"

She takes a deep breath, and says, "I missed you. More than you'll ever know. More than you'll ever believe. I did."

Kneeling before her, I breathe out my own deep breath. "I know, baby. I know." I make love to her with my mouth, and then fuck her into ecstasy.

Time has passed, but I have no idea how much. I watch Jane with her eyes closed, the moonlight falling beside the bed. I know she's not asleep by her breathing and reach my hand over, holding hers. "I thought you'd be mad at me," I whisper in the dark.

She rolls onto her side, resting her head on my chest while her hand runs over my stomach. "Why would I be mad?"

"Because of what she said."

"I'm not mad because of what you said." Looking up at me, she smiles lightly, thoroughly worn out, and I mentally high-five myself, pride from putting that relaxed and happy expression on her pretty face. "You told me to trust you. I do."

"Thank you."

"Let's go to sleep before I say something I shouldn't."

"So you are mad?" I ask surprised.

"No, quite the opposite, in fact. And we shouldn't be going to *that* opposite yet. It's too soon."

Now I'm smiling but it's not small. It's big because I'm wide-awake and happily in opposite for her. I'll take it slow because slow with her is better than fast with anyone else.

I kiss her forehead, and then she slides her head back down. I kiss the top of it, right in the middle of her gorgeously messed-up hair, and whisper, "I feel the opposite of mad for you too."

CHAPTER 19

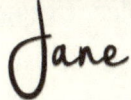

LYING IN THE dark I stare at him. With the curtains open, I see every little freckle, scar, line of his body, remembering each as if I never left. The outline of his muscles has changed some. They are more defined, more solid, but I guess that's what happens when you're playing the field. All the love pounds you once had, all the softness that came with romance hardens, building solid walls of muscle to protect a heart once broken.

That happened to me. I know it well. I've never been in better shape. I've also only loved, truly loved, once. I had fooled my heart into believing it could replace that four-letter word with someone else's name. It couldn't. I still can't. I owe Lawrence an apology just like I owe Luke a lifetime of them.

Leaning forward, I kiss Luke on the cheek. I love him. So much. So much it makes my heart hurt sometimes. Actually all the time. I continue with a kiss to his shoulder, then his chest. Soon he's waking to kisses elsewhere, receiving instead of controlling. His confidence in giving and taking power is attractive. I can dwell on how many women he was with to pick up such tricks, but I don't want to think about that.

None of *them* matter.

I see how he looks at me. I know his heart. He's not shy about reminding me who he was always meant to be with, who owns the heart that the hard muscle stands in guard.

His large hand covers my cheek and slides to my neck. "Why aren't you sleeping?" His voice is groggy. Four a.m. will do that to you.

Moving closer, he holds me to his chest as I snuggle against him. Tucked beneath his chin, I whisper, "I'm happy."

"I am too." He kisses my head. "Get some rest. We have a long day tomorrow."

"I'm not mad at you anymore," I say, meaning so much more than I can express in those six words.

He lets me off easy and makes me smile when he says, "I'm not mad at you anymore either."

I kiss his neck, and then cuddle back down, and close my eyes.

"JANE?" I LOOK over my shoulder, adjusting my glasses to the top of my head. Ian comes toward me from the shadows of the set, smiling too confidently to be trusted. "Wow, I've never seen you in glasses?"

He poses it as a question, making me feel self-conscious. "My eyes were tired today, so I didn't put my contacts in." Trying to move him along to whatever he originally wanted, I ask, "What can I help you with?"

"Let's have lunch together. There's something I want to discuss with you."

I look at my watch, and then glance around looking for Luke. I haven't seen him in a few hours. Wishing I knew what his plans were, I hesitate. "What about?"

"Privately. We'll talk privately," Ian insists. "Okay?"

Now he's got me worried. "Um. Sure."

"Meet me outside in fifteen. I rented a car. I'll drive."

"All right."

As soon as he leaves, I get up and start searching for Luke. Unfortunately, I find Ian waiting by his rental before I find the man I'm looking for. He holds the door open. I get in and buckle up. "Where are we going?"

"A taco place I keep hearing about. Are tacos good with you?"

"Yep. So what did you want to talk about?"

"Let's just enjoy the ride and we can talk over lunch."

"You make it sound serious. Is it?"

He laughs. "No. I'd just rather not talk while driving since I don't know the streets here and need to listen to the GPS directions."

I don't say anything more, and watch the world go by outside, wondering what I've gotten myself into.

When we walk into Torchy's Tacos, we order and find a table. I'm even more nervous about this conversation by the way it's been built up. I get right back to it. "So what's up?"

"I was part of a meeting this morning and it was decided we have to cut two scenes."

"What? No." I wasn't physically slapped but it feels like it from the emotional hit.

"I didn't want to. I fought for them. I need you to know that."

"What's happened?"

"Money and time. Isn't that always the problem?"

"Luke promised all the scenes were safe."

"Well I can't speak for Luke, but it was a producer decision."

"A producer decision or a decision a producer had to deliver?" I try to clarify before jumping to conclusions. It would be easy to make Luke the bad guy before having the facts, but I don't want to do that. I trust him.

"It's circles. At the end of the day, it came down to them. I'm sorry, Jane."

Silent while the tacos are delivered, my leg begins to bounce. As soon as the waitress leaves, I ask, "Which scenes?"

"Luke has a list of potentials. We'll be deciding tonight."

I feel sick, not hungry at all, so I push the basket away.

"I'm sorry, Jane. It guts me too, but this is how the business works. Two is better than five. I've been on movies that had fifty percent of their budget cut after it started filming. Sometimes money falls through, but we're ahead of the game here. We just need to find two scenes that fix the budget issue and don't change the integrity of the project."

"You make it sound so easy when deleting more scenes at this stage will change the final movie. It might not even make sense once completed. This story builds. Each scene matters because each is a piece fitting together for the final puzzle. If we start tossing out the pieces, what will be left will be a story full of plot holes."

"You're emotionally attached. I understand how you feel, but it will be okay."

"You aren't emotionally attached?"

"I am, but like I said, it's just two scenes. I'm going to—"

My anger and hurt get the best of me. "You are or you and Luke are?"

"Luke and I will find the scenes and cut them. Hopefully we'll be in the clear the rest of the shoot."

I want to call Luke, but I'm still in shock that he didn't tell me first. Feeling trapped, I look across the table at Ian while he eats, suddenly suspicious. "Why did you tell me if it was a producer decision?"

"And not Luke?"

"Yes."

"I don't know why he didn't tell you. I only knew that you weren't aware and thought you should know. We need to get ahead of these changes so they don't affect the shooting schedule." He starts eating his taco as if we're talking about the weather. With a bothersome tiny piece of lettuce hanging from his lip, he adds, "The movie is still going to be amazing." He swallows the food in his mouth, then wipes it with a napkin, but the lettuce is still there. I've officially lost my appetite. "My name's attached, so I'll make sure of it."

Eventually I give in and eat the damn tempting taco in front of me. It looks too good not to and it tastes even better, but my mind is a lost cause to the disappointment I feel inside from the news.

As soon as we arrive back on the lot, I look for Luke again. I'm not sure what to think about what Ian said at lunch, but I don't want to jump to conclusions. I find him sitting on set with Ryan. It doesn't look to be a rehearsal, so I go over and tap him on the shoulder lightly. "Hey."

They both look up, and say in unison, "Hey."

Luke adds, "I looked for you before lunch."

"I went with Ian." He stops blinking at the mention of Ian and I nod my head to the side, I ask, "Can I talk to you real quick?"

"Sure," he replies, standing up and following me outside. "What's up?"

I'm not sure if I feel hurt that he made the decision without telling me or upset that they're cut without giving me a chance to fight for them. Since this is the first time I've had a movie made from a script I'm not sure if this is the norm. I tamp my emotions to give him the benefit of the doubt and hear his side first. At the corner of the building, I stop and turn around, trying to steady my voice. "Two scenes need to go?"

He sighs, and crosses his arms defensively. "There is no other way around it."

"Why didn't *you* tell me?"

"I tried. I looked for you as soon as I left the conference call. I see Ian beat me to the punch."

"Because he cares about the film."

His jaw tenses, then he asks, "And I don't?"

"I didn't say that."

"No, you inferred it instead." As if he's trying to solve a riddle, his eyes narrow. "What I find interesting is why Ian rushed to tell you before I could. Look at his motives, Jane."

"What are yours?"

His eyes go wide in disbelief. "What's really going on here?"

"I don't know," I answer honestly. "It just hurt to hear it from him."

Leaning against the building, he shadows me. His voice softens, matching his expression. "This is business. Whether I tell you or he does, it is what it is, but I'm sorry I didn't tell you first. Didn't seem I was given the chance."

"You promised back in that conference room in LA that there would be no more cuts."

"That was based on the financing *at the time.* One investor pulled fifty percent of his funding this morning. I wasn't hiding this from you. I was dealing with it, hoping to get it back."

"Ian said it was a producer decision."

I watch his Adam's apple bob, then look back at his eyes as he tries to find the words he's looking for. His arms relax to his side, and he reaches for me. Taking my hand in his, he says, "It was, but there was no good choice. We either lost a whole storyline or cut a few scenes. I made the content decision, so if you're looking for someone to blame, you're looking at him."

"You tried?"

"I tried my best to save them." When I rest my forehead on his chest, he moves us around the corner and wraps his arms around me. "If I could pay the difference, I would. For you, I would."

"I would too."

"Are you still mad at me?"

I back up, but still struggle to smile. "I wasn't mad. I just didn't like hearing it from Ian."

"He's the director. A lot of money is resting on his shoulders. But I have no doubt that he had ulterior motives."

Hitting him on the arm, I tease, "Then don't give him a reason next time."

"Lesson learned." He takes a step back, and says, "I need to get back. We still have to cut those scenes. I'd like your input if you want to be a part of the meeting. I'll understand if you don't."

"I'll go."

Before he walks away, his eyes fix on mine. "I can't make anymore promises regarding the movie, Jane. Our investors are looking for gains, not losses. Things are tentative."

"Could more be cut?"

"I don't think so and I will fight for every penny and scene. I promise you, but next time I ask that you please hear all the arguments before waging a war. I have a feeling Ian made his move today, but don't think for a second it was professionally motivated. I'm usually the one who talk to the screenwriter." He looks over my shoulder, then back. "Okay?"

"I promise."

"We should get back." While walking, he nudges me with his elbow. "See? We don't have to fight as long as we talk."

"Maturity looks good on us," I reply proudly.

He eyes my breasts, waggling his eyebrows. "It does indeed."

I roll my eyes, and laugh. "Ignore that maturity comment."

IT'S AS IF I accepted a prom date from Ian. He's been walking around all afternoon with some pep to his step and talking about how we went to lunch together. I have no idea what that's about, but it's becoming obvious that people are seeing us more as a couple now... to Luke's *and* my dismay.

Luke's chest presses to my back, and while we pretend to watch them rehearse in front of us, he whispers, "I'm going to fucking punch him."

I smile, and then whisper, "Let's finish filming first."

"Only a few weeks to go."

A laugh bubbles out. "Yep, two to be precise."

Hands grip my waist and I'm pulled back to close the small space, my ass against his—I cough. "Why are you hard?"

"Because you look so damn sexy right now in those glasses. You're giving off sexy librarian fantasy vibes."

"Oh good Lord. I was too tired to mess with my contacts this morning. Who knew glasses would garner so much attention?"

"Me, and every other guy in the place. You're gonna have to wear them later."

"Later?" I ask, raising an eyebrow.

"Yes, I've got big plans." He rubs against my ass again. "Big—"

"Huge, in fact."

"Plans." I can tell he's smirking just from his voice. "What time are we wrapping today?"

Air invades between us again, distance adding to my disappointment. "Six," I reply. "If we stay on schedule."

"I'll see you at seven."

Before he walks away, I ask, "Your place or mine?"

"I thought it was *our* place?" he asks rhetorically with a wink and a smirk.

"I like that."

"I *love* that. I'll see you later, Janie."

Not sure how long I stand there with a goofy grin on my face, but apparently long enough to be noticed. Scalia comes over, and says, "So in addition to the crew—Gaffer, Grip, and all of Craft Services—and now the director if he has or has had his way already, you're doing the producer? Busy girl. Where do you find the time?"

"What? Me?" I feign innocence. The rumors are already out there so why not stir the gossip pot.

"Don't even try to lie. He's hot, smart, and loaded. You've hit the jackpot, but you might want to keep that to yourself. Jessica Pyles can be quite the volatile actress from what I read." She walks away, but turns back and nods with a thumbs up, giving me her approval.

I don't mind her knowing about Luke and me. I actually don't mind anyone knowing that Luke and I are together, even Jessica Pyles. *Especially her.* Luke and I are in too good of a place to let her taint what we've fought to find—love—again.

CHAPTER 20

Luke

JANE IS TRULY breathtaking.

I wake up to the most beautiful woman in the world. She stretches before she even opens her eyes. A smile firmly on her lips as she turns and kisses me. "Good morning," she says, softly, her greens bright in the early morning light sneaking in between the curtains.

"Good morning, beautiful. How are you today?"

Resting her chin on my chest, she looks up. "Better than I've been in years."

"Well, that's saying something."

"That's saying everything." With her ear over my heart, she says, "I could listen to the sound of your heart all day."

Rubbing her arm gently, I keep her in place, liking her just where she is. "Let's skip work today and play hooky."

"You think they'll miss us?" There's a mischievous lilt to her question.

"Nah," I joke, wishing I wasn't.

Rolling onto her back, her arms go wide, her breasts exposed. "Good, because I want to spend the day in bed with you."

"Fine, if you insist," I reply as if kissing her breasts is a burden when it's all I want to do all day, every day. My résumé would be simple: *Professional Jane Lewis Breast Appreciator.*

But then again there are other things I want to do to her. Her legs part just as her lips do for me. I almost kiss her, but don't. Inhaling her, my body hardens as I press my erection against her. "I want you. Just like this. Open for me, giving me access to all your vulnerabilities. To all of you. Do you want me, Jane?"

"So much," she replies, her eyes fluttering closed. "So much."

I reach for a condom, because I want to fuck, not have a conversation about it. I'm quick with it, and back on top, the tip of my dick against her wet pussy. "Tell me how much you want me. Tell me how much you want my cock inside you, filling you over and over until you come so hard you'll be thinking about this all day long and dreaming about it all night." I tempt because I can. Squirming beneath me, she angles to get me inside. "Eh. Eh. Eh. Not until you tell me."

Exasperated, she releases a hard breath. "I want you, so much."

"You can do better." I withdraw just enough to tease. "I want you to ache for me, the pain inside so unbearable that you beg me to fuck you."

Frustration and lust comingle on her tongue when she says, "I want to feel your hard cock inside me, *Sir.*"

Fuck me! My hips jerk forward in reaction to her calling me that.

"Make me come so you're the only one I think about and the only one I dream about. Please, Luke. Fuck me and make me yours forever."

Fuck me. That's hot. I thrust, her body jolting as her hands go to my shoulders, nails cutting my skin as they dig deeper. A playful, self-satisfied smile appears when she doesn't bother quieting her tone and moans as I fuck her into oblivion.

"Turn over," I demand, manners forgotten. I grip her hair and tighten my hold as she moves to her hands and knees before me. Her back is slick, her neck sweating. I pull her golden strands just as my tongue glides up her glistening skin until I'm positioned again. With my free hand, I rub the head of my cock against her, down the center, and farther to where I love to be most. Pushing in, my head drops back. "You're so fucking tight for me. So fucking good."

We fuck until every last moan is freed from our bodies.

After working up a sexual sweat, we lie in the peace of the room, only our breathing heard. Her eyes are closed, her chest rising and falling, her body splayed next to me. Sitting up, I lean over and kiss her swollen lips. When her eyes open, she smiles. I don't. "I want you to listen to me, to hear what I'm saying because I need to be very clear about something."

Her smile slips away, a look of worry creasing between her eyes. "Okay. I'm listening."

I place my hand over her pounding heart. "I own this." I run my hand down her stomach and between her legs. Burying two fingers deep inside, her eyes strain to stay open, and her body tenses for more as she arches up just enough for me to control her desire. "And owning your heart means I own this. I don't have to fuck you to make you mine. *You are mine.* You always were and you always will be. Do you understand, Jane?"

Her blinks lengthen as her body reawakens from my touch. *My touch.* Only my touch. "I do."

"Save that for the ceremony." I get out of bed and walk to the bathroom. "I'm going to take a shower."

"Wait! You can't just walk away like that, leaving me like this." She sits up just before I start the shower. "Luke, please."

Chuckling, I turn the water on. "Remember that while

thinking about me all day. I just bought my insurance policy. Now to that begging for more part."

"Bastard."

"You're not the first woman to call me that."

She grabs a pillow and throws it, and then flops back on the bed groaning in irritation. "Yeah, yeah, yeah, ya big player. Rub it in. Rub it in... Hey!" She sits up excitedly. "You can rub. It. In."

I love that dirty girl. The water is finally warm though. "Come on, sunshine. We have work today."

A smile plays on her lips. I can tell she wants to be mad, but is fighting to hang on to the emotion. I cup her face and kiss her. "What? Three orgasms weren't enough?"

"Call me greedy."

"I like you greedy."

Perking up, her hands run over my chest as she bites my chin. "In that case, finish what you started, you big tease."

She's got a head full of suds, exhilaration in her eyes, and she's beyond beautiful. I bring her under the water and hold her tight. As her bubbles wash over us, I readily admit, "Those feelings that are *opposite of mad* are getting stronger."

When she looks up, she says, "Mine too. Is it awful that I wish we could freeze time and just live in this bliss a little longer?"

The death of me.

This woman is going to do me in once and for all with her sweetness. "If I could freeze time, I would have done it two years ago and not let you go."

"When you say stuff like that I have a hard time calling my feelings *opposite of mad*."

"Good." I kiss her nose and then the apple of her cheeks.

WE DON'T GET to play hooky, and the rest of the morning flies by. A few weeks to finish a movie, a passion project at that, doesn't allow for skipping work.

But I see her. Always. When she thinks I don't, I do. I love that she keeps tabs on me too, and that she always seems to be aware when I return to the set. I wonder if she notices when I'm gone as well.

I wonder if she notices I do the same, my eyes on her, looking for her when she's gone and when she returns. Now that I have her back in my life, I want to keep her in it. Call me greedy this time, or even selfish, but I want her back in all ways, including when we go back to LA. I just need to keep the project on track. A few more phone calls and hopefully it will settle down so we can finish this film as planned.

If I can't.... I won't be the one to destroy this dream of Jane's. I'll do whatever it takes to make it come true, despite the threats against the project. For her, *anything*. I screwed up once when it came to her dreams of marriage. I had no idea she needed the reassurance of our future together, a verbal promise. I thought we just knew it would always be us. So, I'll show her that I won't screw up when it comes to her professional aspirations either.

The problem is, when I see Jessica talking to Jane, I start to sweat. Jessica cannot be trusted. After her theatrics, I don't want her saying things that aren't true, let alone telling Jane that we once hooked up.

Tugging at my collar, I keep the phone to my ear in a bad attempt to listen to Robert, one of the investors, but my eyes stay on the two women. "Yeah, I'm here. I'm managing," I speak into the phone when asked about my contributions. "The hotel is paid for. I've got five of the rooms covered. We still have funds to cover the other four and the crew is doubled up."

Robert asks, "How far are you willing to go, Luke?"

"Whatever it takes."

"The movie is good, but is it worth going bankrupt over?"

"The movie and script are solid. I know we can sell this. I'm thinking Sundance, TIFF, and South by Southwest. The acting is solid and the cinematographer is nailing the visuals. It's looking good in playbacks."

He sighs. "Look, I'll give you the extra fifty thousand, but that's it. I'm tapped for this project. Can you finish it?"

"I'll find the rest and make it work. I promise. Thanks."

"You're welcome. This is a risk, but I'm willing to take it based on your endorsement. Screw me on this and we're done."

"I know. I appreciate the faith."

"I don't give money based on faith. I give it on results. You've never failed me. Don't start. I've got another call to take. Make it happen, Luke."

"I will."

Jane and Jessica are laughing. *Thank fuck.* I hang up the phone and start in their direction. Jessica's eyes are instantly on me. Jane steals a glance but then looks down at the script. She's not a good liar, and her acting skills could use some polishing. I like that she can't hide her feelings from me. She's damn cute.

Jessica jumps at the opportunity. "Hey there, handsome. How's your day going?"

I catch a glimpse of Jane when I'm called handsome. "Hey," I reply flatly. Moving around her, I tap Jane on the hand. "Do you have a minute?"

She seems surprised. Her eyes go wide before her expression settles into restrained joy. "Sure." Looking to Jessica, she says,

"Excuse me."

We walk in silence toward the table set up for craft services. "What are you guys talking about?"

Her head tilts. "The script. Why?"

"I was just surprised after what happened the other night." I move closer and lower my voice. "You know she can't be trusted."

Relaxing in her stance, she smiles. "Don't worry. I've got her number when it comes to you, but I also have to work with her so I'm trying to keep the two separate."

"I'm surprised you're overlooking her actions."

Popping an imaginary collar, she says, "I'm not in competition with her, so I don't have to play any games. I'm secure in our relationship."

I step closer, and whisper, "I want us to together, Jane. I don't want any confusion to how I feel about you."

"I wish..." She looks around. "I wish I could kiss you right now. I feel so much for you too. I'm glad this movie happened. It's like destiny bringing us back together."

"Yes, destiny." I step away from her. *Now* is not the time to tell her I had sex with Jessica. She'll hate me. I'll tell her. I'd just prefer to do it when we're not filming and keep the peace on set. "I need to go. Duty calls. Are you going out with everyone tonight or do you want to stay in?"

"I always love staying in with you, but Scalia made me promise I'd go to Continental Club tonight. Everyone's going. Will you?"

"I might try to get some work in. I'm still on West Coast time, which gives me two extra hours."

"Come. For me."

"I'll try. As for Jessica, it's best if you keep your distance from her."

"I'll be fine. Don't worry about me." Everyone is called for the next scene when Ian returns to the set. "Gotta go. Later, handsome." I prefer the name from her mouth. Her grin is sassy, a lot like her. I'm glad she's unburdened. This feels right.

When my phone rings, and I see it's the call I've anxiously waited for all morning, I head outside, not wanting to risk Jane hearing.

Forty-five minutes later, the deal is done. The finances are secure. I lean against the wall near the door, staying out of the way as progress is made. Ian comes over to stand next to me, crossing his arms, and watching the crew in action, preparing for the next setup. "Update?"

"Fifty K from Robert."

Eyeing me cynically, his mouth drops open enough for me to know he's not impressed. "That's not going to wrap this film. I already cut my pay by twenty K to help get it done. What are you going to do, Anders?"

What have I done? I've wagered my house on this project, but this douche doesn't get to know that.

"You knew this was a risky project when you were brought on, but it's even riskier when you pose threats in the form of loaded questions. I've taken care of it. I've played my part. Now play yours and make a fan-fucking-tastic movie."

He pats me and nods before walking away. My house and future rely on his shoulders. I hope he can pull this off.

10 P.M.

Rubbing my eyes with the palms of my hands, I need to wake up. I'm exhausted. Three intense calls and a shitload of emails later, I want to be done with work and see my girl. I close my laptop and change clothes, pulling on a T-shirt and jeans. With my wallet and the room key in hand, I head across South Congress and inside the iconic Continental Club.

The bar is smaller than I imagined, which makes it easy find our group. They would be the noisy ones taking up residence along the bar. I laugh because they're louder than the live band on stage.

As I cruise over, I say hi to everyone, secretly scanning a few barstools ahead for the one I most want to see. I'm grabbed and spun around, a big smile taking over until I come face to face with Jessica, which instantly eliminates it.

Her finger goes to my lips. "Looking for someone?"

I move away from her hand, not liking her touching me where I last touched Jane. "I'm not in the mood for this." I turn to go, but she clings to my arm.

"Don't make me look bad."

"I don't have to. That's something you're quite good doing all by yourself."

"Screw you, Luke."

I shake my head and walk away, like I should have done when we were first introduced. Other words come to mind thinking about her, but I settle on unpredictable to be courteous. The problem though, is that her hot and cold impulsive side is about to cross a line with me that I won't be able to sit idly by and ignore. How can a single mistake with her last year become a nuisance in veiled threats?

Before I have time to track down Jane, Scalia calls me, "Luke? Come over here. You look like you could use a drink."

I take the shot she's offering, and smell it. "Tequila?"

"Of course."

We clink our drinks together and both polish off the clear

liquid. Afterward, we slam our glasses on the bar top. "Have you seen Jane?" I ask, trying not to seem too anxious.

She laughs, making me wonder if she knows more than Jane and I have revealed. Leaning closer to me, I follow the direction of her gaze and see the one I'm looking for, just as Scalia points her out standing on the edge of the dance floor. My instinct tells me to go to her. My mind tells me to stay. Professionally, she'd want me to stay. Not taking any chances, I do because I know if I go over there, I'm gonna need to kiss those ruby-red lips right here in front of everyone. Choosing instead to stand here watching her smile, laugh, *and* watch Ian touch her arm like they're familiar and he has rights to do such.

They aren't alone, but the conversation looks intimate. I've had a shitty night and this makes it worse. Turning to Scalia, I say, "I'm going to call it a night."

"You just got here. Stay."

I glance back to Jane. She's not seen me. If she does, she'll come over and I'll be taking my bad mood out on her, so I make the tough decision. "Maybe another night."

"I'll let Jane know you stopped by."

My eyes meet Scalia's all-knowing ones. I nod, an understanding exchanged before I leave.

Out on the sidewalk, I hear my name uttered from the only lips I ever care to hear it from again. When I turn around, Jane is rushing toward me. She practically collides into my chest, but I catch her, as she anxiously asks, "Where are you going?"

"I'm tired. I'm gonna get some sleep."

"I want you to stay." She grabs my arms, hanging on to me. "Please."

"I'm not in a good mood. I've had a rough night. I need sleep, but I'll leave the door open for you."

Her body moves fluidly as she shifts, a telltale sign she's tipsy, or maybe drunk. "We're having so much fun. I want you to stay. Please."

"Another night."

"Why do you seem mad?"

"I'm fine." I can hear the edge to my tone, so I know she can.

She wobbles back, but catches herself. "Fine," she replies tersely.

Sighing, I look down, frustrated that I'm letting a conversation between co-workers get to me. When I look back at her, I say, "My bad mood will only ruin your good one. You stay and party as late as you want and I'll be back in the room waiting for you." She looks up at me, but doesn't reply. "Goodnight." I turn and leave, hearing the crosswalk light beep, signaling me to cross. Once I'm on the other side of the street, I look back. *She's gone. Shit.*

Disappointment settles into impatience. I want to spend time with her, but I can't do that with everyone around because I don't think I can hide how I feel for her any longer. Just as I reach the hotel, I hear quick-approaching footsteps from behind. Jane stops where she is on the sidewalk. Even the dark skies can't stop her beaming smile, her hopefulness displayed in her eyes. I ask, "What are you doing here?"

"I only went back to get my purse," she replies, holding it up.

"I mean, why are you here when everyone else is there and having a good time?"

She comes to me. Standing toe to toe, she says, "I was only there waiting for you, so if you don't want to be there, I don't either."

"My night will be boring in comparison. I'm just going to bed."

"I can't think of anything I'd rather do than go to bed with you, Luke."

Knowing everyone is back at the bar, I wrap my arm around

her freely, renewed from her enthusiasm. "Replace 'go to bed' with 'have sex' and I'm happy."

My ribs get an elbow needled in just enough to make me flinch, but only slightly. She's laughing, and that in and of itself is a beautiful thing. With the business deals falling together behind the scenes, I want us staying on track.

I repeat what's become my mantra: there is no way I'm losing her again. I refuse to let that happen and will do everything I can to protect her and keep what we've got going again.

CHAPTER 21

Jane

LIFE SHOULDN'T BE this good.

I almost feel guilty feeling this happy.

We're surrounded by thousands of people, but we blend in like any other couple there to see the band at Auditorium Shores. Just the two of us here, able to act how we want, is a nice reprieve from all of the group events we've been attending over the last few weeks. Keeping things professional takes a toll on me some days. I just want to enjoy every minute I get to see Luke, knowing how special this time together on the set is in the scheme of life. This is what we had dreamed about all those years ago now that I think about it. Being involved in the same project, creating together.

An afternoon off is just what we need. The wine bottle is half-full, and most of the food has been eaten. I crawl around the picnic basket and kiss his cheek.

"What's that for?" he asks, a smirk in place on his face.

"Just because I can."

I've seen other women checking him out, some extremely pretty, but he seems almost oblivious to the attention.

Almost.

He's not blind.

At six foot two with dark hair, blue eyes, a chiseled jaw that makes me want to bite it, sculpted ass that could put a Roman statue to shame, and another part of his body that makes me want to do naughty things to him, Luke is the full package and has got an even bigger one—literally.

He's well endowed. Beyond knowing from first-hand knowledge, but I'm also a writer. I've looked up the topic on Google... for research, I convince myself.

Fine. I'll admit that the man knows he's attractive. He's just not an arrogant ass about it. Luke has a knack for putting everyone at ease, his charms work on women and men alike.

Don't even get me started on how hot he looks in those Wayfarers. Damn him and his naturally sexy self.

He interrupts the naughty thoughts I'm having and says, "The band's good."

Settling down onto my back, I rest my head on his lap. Clear blue skies for as far as the eye can see. I take it as a good sign for where we are in our relationship as well. His fingertips tickle as they pull the straps down from my shoulders one at a time. My breasts are covered, but the top of my chest is exposed to the sunshine. He leans forward, his shadow covering my face and upper body, and asks, "You ready to go back to LA? Only one week left."

"I'm not ready for reality."

He chuckles. "I don't know about you, but this movie has been a heavy dose of reality for me."

"What do you mean?"

Lifting his head, he watches concert goers roam around, hopping over towels and blankets that are spread over the grassy field. He looks back down at me, takes his sunglasses off, and rubs the bridge of his nose. "Just work stuff."

"Everything okay?"

"Everything's fine."

He's had a lot on his mind lately, made a lot of calls, and been stressed. Trusting that it's behind him, I say, "That's good, but you know you can talk to me if you—"

"I don't want to talk about work. I want to enjoy this date. I like that it's finally just us alone."

"Me too." I give him a reassuring smile. He always did try to protect me from the stresses of life. If he only knew I would take the weight of the world on my shoulders for him if he needed. I decide to push the heavy away. Enjoying the indie rock, I close my eyes remembering how we used to be together like this all the time...

A picnic, beers, and beach volleyball make a perfect Sunday.

Except this day was organized by Danny. We've been friends with him for years now, and he's been Luke's best friend for a while. In the time we've known him he's become famous. With that fame, we've been privy to a lot of uncomfortable situations like paparazzi hounding us outside restaurants, nightclubs, and when I look over my shoulder, I see a guy with a long lens hanging out of his car in the parking lot.

I know Danny means well. He hates living under the microscope as much as we do, but when you add in a bunch of mostly naked swimsuit models, we get more attention than normal. They've been prancing around on the sand for the camera that they're more than aware of, and love.

While I sit on the doublewide towel spread over the sand somewhat hiding, Luke's been playing volleyball. He goes to retrieve the ball when it is hit out of bounds by one of the girls. She's wearing a suit that would only be considered a swimsuit next to a birthday suit. He retrieves it and tosses it to her and one of her nips slips out. She acts shy, slightly embarrassed, but her acting skills are lacking.

My boyfriend is a saint.

He covers his eyes, but she insists that he help her tighten the top. At least Danny notices, winks at me, and goes to her rescue, sending Luke out of the game.

Luke lands next to me on the towel. He lies back and pulls me to him. I go willingly, lying on top, and ask, "You weren't much of a knight in shining armor to that damsel in distress."

Laughing, he replies, "Distress is not the word I would have chosen for her."

"What word would you choose?"

"Since we're at the beach, shark comes to mind."

Now I laugh, and roll off to his side, tucking my head in the shadow of his arm. After a quick peck to his bicep, I maneuver into one of my favorite positions with him. He sits up, resting on his elbows while I rest my head on his lap. He takes the baseball cap from his head and rests it on mine to block the sun from my face. "Don't get burned," he says casually, watching the game continue.

I smile from his thoughtfulness. "What's the game plan for tonight?"

The cap is tilted and he looks down into my eyes, his practically twinkling with insinuation. "You're the only thing on my agenda."

"Oh really? Go on..."

"First," he says, dragging his finger under the hem of my tankini top, then skips up to my lips, running over them gently. "I'm going to ravage this mouth."

I smile. "And then?"

"Then," he starts, his fingertips grazing lightly down my neck to the top of my cleavage. "I'm going cover you with kisses, *maybe even hickeys."*

"No hickeys."

"Hickeys, but no one else will see them except for me. All right?"

"Okay." I continue waiting with bated breath to hear what else he has planned.

"You know those freckles on your hip?"

"Yes."

"Those are mine. I'm going to mark each one, then move to your puss—"

"Ugh. You know I hate that word."

His roguish smile promptly reminds my body how much I crave his. "I know you hate it, but I'm going to use it anyway because that sweet pussy of yours tastes like heaven and feels like hell, torturing my soul until I'm so far in there that our—"

"Our bodies are one again?"

"Our souls, baby. So our souls are one again." His smile isn't mischievous this time, but completely swoon-worthy.

I sit up and spin around so I'm facing him. Letting my hand run the course of his hard and sweaty abs, I find him utterly intoxicating in ways I never knew possible. "I love you."

Leaning forward, he cups my face. "I love you." The kiss leaves no room for mistaking who he loves.

It's a kiss that I feel deep inside, causing my tummy to tingle. When we part, I open my eyes, my breath coming in pants. "What do you think about starting that game plan sooner than later?"

"Let's go."

...I finish another glass of wine and tuck the glass back into the basket. "Where'd you get this?"

Delight tantalizes in his eyes. "I have my ways. If you're ready to go, our chariot awaits."

"Chariot? Now I'm feeling spoiled."

Luke tilts his head and kisses my neck. "Is it wrong that I love to spoil you?"

I giggle. "Do you want me to answer that honestly? Because the answer will always be it's not wrong. It's soooo right."

Leaning his forehead against mine, he whispers, "I want to be with you."

"You are with me," I reply, stroking his cheek.

"Back in LA."

My heart leaps to life, racing from his words. With amaze and elation in my voice, I ask, "Luke?"

"Janie?"

"What are you saying?"

"I'm saying that I want us together in LA."

My lips part as I go through all the meanings of such a simple phrase, making sure this is real, that he is real, the words he speaks from the heart are real and I'm not dreaming. When I don't speak, he adds, "I don't even know where you live. Did you know that? You've never told me."

"You've never asked."

"I should have. We've been so caught up here that it was easy to forget about life there."

"With one week left it's good we talk about it, for you to know the truth." I lie back on the blanket. "I don't currently have a home." When silence creeps between us, I dare to glance his way. "You wanted honesty."

"Of course I want honesty. I just don't understand what you mean by you don't have a home. You literally don't live anywhere?"

"No. I put my stuff in my car and drove here."

By the changing expressions on his face, he still doesn't seem to comprehend what I'm saying. "You had some boxes and two suitcases?"

The upturn at the end is heard and I see the question in his eyes. Discomfort starts rumbling through my chest, walls wanting to rebuild are held in place while I debate what to say. When I take too long to answer, he asks, "What's going on?"

No sense in hiding the ugly truth from him. I have nothing to be ashamed of and I don't want to lie to him anyway. "I had nowhere to go, so I lived in one of those extended-stay hotels."

"For how long?"

"Months."

"It had been months when we went into preproduction and probably two since I saw you at the party. With Lawrence."

"Why do you sound mad?"

His frustration is evident as he looks away from me while running his hand through his hair. "I'm not mad. I'm confused as to why you were living in a hotel."

"Hotel is putting it nicely. It was kind of between a hotel and a motel," I say, trying to lighten up the situation.

Standing up, he starts throwing our trash into the basket. "Stop joking around."

"Why are you so upset?" I reach out to touch him, to get him to look my way, but when he doesn't, I say, "Look at me, Luke. Why are you upset?"

"I'm upset because you chose to live in a hotel instead of coming to me." He tugs the blanket, giving me more than a healthy hint of his intentions. I stand and he gathers our stuff and starts back in the direction we came.

When I catch up to him, I have to move twice as fast to stay caught up. "How could I come to you? You had women in and out of your house quicker than I could find your number in my contacts."

"Fuck that. You left me."

Staring at this man who is usually a vision of strength now doused in pain, I stop. My shoulders sag under the weight of the grief he still bears years later. His pain is fully exposed for the first time. Through his sorrow, he would have still protected me, taken care of me at the expense of his own heart. Even though he feels as if I gave up on him and walked away from our relationship with the intent of never coming back, he would have helped me.

I hurt him.

In my anger and pain I never saw the damage I did or the pain I was causing him.

Spending time with him, I have forgiven *him*, because I realized I didn't have a right to hold to a grudge any longer. But I don't think he's forgiven me. I think he wants to, but underneath that confident, cocky façade, is the geeky boy I said yes to back in high school. I gave him my heart and he gave me his. But when I told him I wasted years of my life waiting on him, I damaged his heart. *How could I have said that to him?* It was what I felt at the time, in the heat of the moment, my rage determining my words.

While trying to make him see how hurt I was I never meant to cause him pain. I can't go back in time, but I can reassure him that I want us back, that I had never intended to leave permanently. *My broken, beautiful man.*

He doesn't notice I'm not next to him for a good thirty feet or so. When he does, he looks over his shoulder and around as if he's lost something...

Our gazes connect. Even from a distance, we're both drowning in the heartache I caused, one I've tried so hard to replace with a better emotions. The basket and blanket are dropped and he jogs back, taking my face in his hands. His touch is too light, too careful as his eyes search mine. "Hey," he says, "I'm sorry."

"I'm starting to hate those words. We say them too much and they don't heal like they used to."

"Then let's not say them anymore."

"How do we repair the damage I've done?"

"I should have come after you."

"You were right not to. I was petulant—"

"You were frustrated." A slight smile takes hold of him. "We were both wrong and lost sight of who we were."

"I lost sight of us. I'm sor—"

"Nope. We just agreed not to say it." I nod and he adds, "We have a second chance to right this, and I'm not willing to give that up." His lips meet mine and in it the apologies are caressed away. "With love."

"With love?" I ask.

"The only way we can repair the damage we've done is by staying present and loving each other through it."

"You make it sound so simple."

Another kiss.

"It's only as hard as we make it."

"Let's not make it any harder. Okay?" I slide my arms around him.

Looking at me with the most devilish grin I've seen in forever, he says, "Speaking of hard."

"Oh good Lord, Luke." I head for our stuff with a smile on my face that I refuse to let him see because if I do, he'll know he won me over. Just like he always does. And right now, I like the way he's chasing, racing me to the stuff. He picks me up and swings me around.

As soon as my feet land on the ground again and the laughter dies down, I grab him and hold him still long enough to admit, "I was scared."

"Of me?"

I nod. "You're the only one I ever gave my heart to, Luke Anders. You're also the only one who ever broke it. So yes, I was scared to come to you in such a *transitional* time in my life."

"We've wasted a lot of time protecting ourselves from the only thing that ever really mattered." Right there in the middle of thousands of people, he kisses me like we're back in the hotel room alone.

He kisses me, claiming me in ways that make me feel beautiful on the inside.

I feel his love for me.

He kisses me, the embrace of our tongues confessing every sin I've ever wanted to commit with him.

I feel his desire for me.

He kisses me, and then says, "Let's not waste any more." And he doesn't, sweeping my heart up with his and kissing me again.

I feel whole.

CHAPTER 22

Luke

"SIX DAYS. THAT'S all we need."

"I'll be a nice guy and give you seven. If it's not wrapped in seven, I own whatever is done with the film and your house. By the way, I had my agent drive by it yesterday. It's prime real estate, two to three mil when it's listed. I'm going high since it will be all profit for me," Robert says.

"Don't be an asshole unless I don't deliver."

"Just preparing."

"I've got to go. Seven days." When I hang up, I rub my temples trying to ease the headache I've had for days. I know it won't go away anytime soon though. How did I not see this coming? I reached out to him as a friend, but I got the shrewd businessman for my effort. I've watched him pull the plug on projects before. I've also seen him win awards for movies he believed in. His unreliability is starting to remind me of a certain actress. This is what I get for making a deal with the devil disguised as a friend.

I need fresh air. Closing my laptop, I walk outside the building where we're shooting and squat down. The cream-colored stone is cracked at the seams, but I lean against it anyway.

I've two to three million thoughts running through my head, each one representing a dollar I'm about to lose if I don't get this project wrapped on time. I will lose my house if Ian screws this movie up.

"Hi, stranger. Fancy meeting you out here."

Looking up, Jessica stands a few feet away, signature smile in place. It may work on millions of moviegoers but does nothing for me. Our one night was nothing more than a drunken shitshow. The morning after was made worse when she didn't want to leave.

When she asked to move in, it became embarrassing all around. I was thrilled when I heard she had latched onto Ryan Kantz on a film set. Currently, he's one of the hottest properties in Hollywood. I knew she wouldn't try to see me after that, not at the risk of losing him and his rising star power.

"It's official," she trills. "Ryan and I are over."

Shit! "What?" I'm upright in an instant. "Why? What happened?"

She waves her hand flagrantly around. "Like you didn't know it was coming. We haven't shared a bed since we got here." Though she speaks in a hushed tone, she clearly doesn't mind sharing all the dirty details. "I don't feel anything for him and haven't in a long time."

"You've only been together for six months." He was my insurance policy. No wonder she's been hanging around me.

"And five of those have been a waste of time and energy. That man doesn't know how to treat a woman in the slightest."

"You've got to make this work. Can you get along for the sake of the movie?"

Leaning against the building, she replies, "Maybe."

I begin to pace. "*Maybe* doesn't work. I need a definitive like 'I will for the sake of the movie and crew and all involved.'" Her mouth opens, and then closes again. She always appears to be one syllable away from drudging up the one night she believes is the same as sharing a real past. "We have six days left of filming and then it's goodbye for good. You'll be ready each day, right?"

Rolling her eyes, she says, "That's all you care about. People don't matter to you. We're disposable."

Sigh. "No. That's not true. You okay?" I hate opening this can of worms with her, but originally we both needed a favor, so I'll play nice despite what I feel.

A smile that she uses on the red carpet—superficial, hiding her real smiles behind it—appears. "You hate me."

"I don't hate you."

"You act like you do."

"I don't mean to." *I'm just protecting the one thing I love more than anything else in this world* from *you.* "Sometimes life is difficult. I've been stressed."

"I know. I've seen it. I wish I could help you, but you won't let me."

"Things are complicated, but we're so close to things working how they're supposed to."

"Can I ask you something, Luke?"

"Sure." I brace myself.

"Why do you love her?"

Jane. Protect Jane at all costs. "What are you talking about?"

"You and Jane Lewis—you're in love with her. I can see it so clearly in the way you look at her, the way you talk to her, the way you touch her then play it off as platonic. It's not platonic. You love her."

I remain quiet, not wanting to talk about Jane with Jessica.

"I see the way she looks at you. She loves you too." A sly smile appears. "It would be easy for you to break her heart." Her eyes find mine locked on hers. "Are you going to break her heart like you did mine, Luke?"

I shake my head before I realize I've admitted more than I want, and to someone who, if given the chance, will abuse the knowledge. *Fuck.* Turning away, I avoid eye contact and any more admissions. Why can't she just leave the past in the fucking past and move on? Why does she keep coming after me?

Jessica laughs, like we've shared an inside joke, then says, "Her naivety is almost charming. *Almost.* Is that what you like? Is that what turns you on? I remember very distinctly that my prowess was something you once enjoyed."

"Once."

"Well, it was one hell of a night. At least for me."

I'm thinking now is not a good time to tell her I barely remember that night after the fourth tequila shot. Moving forward, I stop, our eyes challenging each other's. "Don't go near her."

"Or what?"

"Why does there have to be an *or what*?"

"Because I don't take orders. I give them. And I most certainly do not take lightly to threats."

"I'm not threatening you, Jessica. It's best for the movie that people don't know our private business."

"You mean it's best for you and Jane?"

I don't take lightly to threats either, but this secret could ruin everything if revealed. "Yes."

"Yes, what, Luke? Yes, you have fallen for her?"

"Yes."

"See? Wasn't that easy? Now we can go about the remainder of filming knowing where we stand on this."

"If you knew, why'd you insist on me confirming it?"

"Because I need you to understand that you are not in control of this situation. I am."

Mistake after mistake. I keep making them with her. "I'm sure they're looking for you on set."

"I'm sure they are," she says without a care. "Did you ever care about me?"

Impasse.

We've come to an impasse of the heart.

Hearing she even has the ability to conjure feelings is new. I've debated many times over the last year if she had the skills to care about anyone other than herself. I can't say I believe the ingénue act she's got going now either. Unlike what she thinks of Jane, I'm not naïve. Do I lie to make her feel better or tell the truth and put this to rest once and for all?

She speaks again before I do, need filling the gaps between the pleading. "Tell me you did. Please." This is the most vulnerable I've ever heard her.

I lie to spare her the pain of rejection. "I did. Once."

"Thank you," she whispers. "That's all I needed to hear."

When I turn away, I debate if I should stay or leave her be. Dread fills each step as I walk away. Is Jessica as fragile as she wants me to believe? What is her endgame here? Why me? Why the hell did I trust her with something so important? *Fuck.*

When I walk into the apartment building, I head up to where they're filming in the space we've rented. The lights are off, the crew crowded into the living room where Ryan lies on the couch, shades pulled as he tries to fall asleep like the character he's portraying.

The first face I see is Jane's. She smiles quickly, but turns back to watch her movie come alive.

"Action," is called, and silence on the set is achieved.

I stay by the door while they film for a few minutes. When "Cut" is called, I move around the kitchen island and wait for everyone to disperse for the next scene. Jane comes over, and stands too far for my liking, but acting professionally will do that.

She asks, "Where have you been?"

"Calls and other boring stuff."

"The life of a producer."

"Not quite the part I signed up for, but yeah, a part of the job."

"Are you coming to happy hour? We're going down to Guero's. I'm dying for a margarita."

She's gotten some sun, her cheeks a soft pink. "Texas suits you."

Her gaze lowers, and when she peeks back up, she glances around, then says, "So do you."

"You suit me too." I return her genuine smile. "Fine. You twisted my arm. I'll meet you, but I have another call in two hours so I'll be late."

"That's fine. We have one more scene we're trying to squeeze in first."

Sliding my hand over the cold concrete countertop, I let the tips of my fingers rub the top of her hand, needing to feel her any way I can. She turns her back to me to watch the crew move the equipment, but keeps her hand in place. When Jessica enters the apartment, I remove my hand and tuck it in my pocket. "I'll see you later. Okay?"

Jane nods as I pass and I pretend I'm not completely in love with her. Like a hawk, Jessica eyes us. But unlike her, I'm not trained in the art of acting and know she sees right through me.

THE STRESS OF getting this film in the can is taking its toll. Six days. I can survive six more days. I glance at the clock. I'm tired, but I promised her I'd meet them, so I will.

Get in. Get a drink. Get her out. Get inside her. This is my much-needed game plan.

I'm getting tired of this room though. I can't wait to sleep in my own bed again. I can't wait to sleep with Jane in my own bed again... in *our* bed again. Thinking about pulling those boxes out of the spare room makes me smile. I haven't seen that stuff since I moved and had to pack it away. Storing it in that closet kept it out of sight and out of mind, though Jane never left my thoughts.

There's no way to get the stuff out before she arrives because I'm sure as hell not letting her drive back to Los Angeles on her own. No way. No how. Maybe she'll let me ship her car back on a truck. Guess this is something we need to discuss, and soon.

Still stunned by the fact that she has no place she calls her own, I remember that time I spied on Lawrence. I feel so dumb, so blind to what was right in front of my face. She wasn't with him then. I saw her that night and she left the restaurant to go where? Why didn't she come to me? Why didn't she tell me?

I destroyed her trust by not pursuing her. Not going after her *and then* tapping anything that showed interest. I just hadn't seen it coming. I had thought we were okay. I can't undo what I did, but I still wish I never hurt her in the first place.

I need to talk to her, tell her everything I haven't, making sure she hears it from me first.

Grabbing my phone, I take off for the restaurant. I'm walking into Guero's ten minutes later. The place is packed, our group the rowdiest in the bar area making me proud, and making me laugh. We've become a family. Dysfunctional, but what family isn't.

Jane is easy to find, her mere existence draws me in. I probably look stupid with this grin on my face, but even after a twelve-hour day and with little makeup on, she's the prettiest girl in the place. I can't hide the pride that she chose me.

Scalia grabs my arm, tugging me closer. "You made it. Do a

shot with me."

"Sorry, I need to work later."

"Oh c'mon, everyone's done one, except Jane who I suspect was waiting on you. But some," she says, nodding to Jessica and Ian, "have done more."

"Not sure how this fits into her rehab situation," I remark.

"Eh, pills are a hard habit to kick, but she did it."

"After her manager threatened every doctor in Hollywood to stop hooking her up with prescriptions."

"Don't be a downer, Luke. Look at Jane. That should perk you up."

She's right. I'm being mean. My conversation with Jessica earlier has put me back on edge. I glance over and see Jane, her sweet smile washing away the bad feelings I had building. "I've been meaning to ask you, Scalia, what do you know about Jane and—"

"You?"

I nod.

"I know that you can't fake the chemistry you two have together. You also can't hide it."

Nodding again, I rub my thumb over my bottom lip. "I care about her."

"I'd say you more than care about her."

"I love her."

Sober.

I'm completely sober.

Yet, I just admitted I love Jane to someone else again. I should feel bad for letting it slip, but I don't. It didn't slip. I wanted to tell Scalia. I wanted to tell someone who's on our side. I want to tell the whole world. I'm tired of secrets and lies, hidden mistakes. I want to tell everyone about me and Jane and I want to tell Jane everything else. It's time. "If you'll excuse me."

JUST WHEN I thought we were moving in the right direction, that my relationship with Jane could pick up where it left off years earlier, my fear plays out as if in slow motion.

Underestimating Jessica Pyles was my first mistake.

My second—not safeguarding Jane against her. Or for that matter, against Ian.

The crowd inside this restaurant is loud. Above it all, I hear Jessica's gravelly voice, "It was an incredible night. One of the most sexually expressive I've ever had."

I push past a gaffer to see Jessica's animated eyes land on me and a devious fucking smile on her face. "There he is. Luke," she says, waving me over, "join us. I was just telling Jane and Ian about our time together in LA."

My gaze sweeps to her left landing on Jane, who's gone pale. I struggle to swallow much less speak as my heart collapses to the pit of my stomach.

"Tell them, Luke," she insists as she comes closer, swaying on her heels, and latching on to my shoulder.

My skin crawls beneath the cotton separating us. I'm trapped between the truth and the love of my life. When I fail to address Jessica's whim, she declares, "I slept with Lawrence too."

What the fuck? Why is she doing this to Jane? To me, whatever. I'm fair game, but to Jane?

Jane's mouth drops open.

Ian smirks. "Who was better?"

Jessica laughs, completely entertained in Jane's devastation. Just as Jane turns to leave, Jessica adds, "Luke is the best sex I ever had. Wouldn't you agree, *Janie*?"

Before my very eyes, with no chance to intervene, much less stop it, I see my life destroyed in mere seconds.

Jane's small frame withers under the humiliation, but she manages to start walking toward the exit.

With his face twisted in a fucking *I told you so* expression, Ian stops me when I try to reach her. "I warned you not to get involved with someone on set."

"Fuck you." I yank my arm away. "And fuck off."

A hard poke to my chest is followed by a threat, "You've embarrassed me, Anders. You'll pay for that."

I take a step backward in the direction of the exit, but scowl at him. "You embarrassed yourself. Jane's never given you any reason to continue pursuing her, but you did it to your own detriment anyway." I redirect my attention to Jessica since I'm here, and say, "You might want to get back on that wagon. Alcoholic actress is just as unattractive as pill-addicted socialite."

"You didn't think so."

"Fuck this. The one time was a huge fucking mistake that I'm still paying for apparently."

By the time I get out to the sidewalk, Jane is gone.

I punch the air, and yell, "Fuck."

CHAPTER 23

Jane

I WANT TO run, to hide, to be anywhere but here. As soon as I get in my car, I start the engine ready to drive away from this nightmare.

But I can't.

I can't leave. I'm trapped here for six more days...

Luke runs across the street in front of me, not seeing me hiding inside. I'm sure he's going to the hotel. That's where I would look first too, which is why I didn't go there. I'm so relieved he doesn't see me hiding in the darkness of the interior. Relief comes as the tears are swallowed, knowing I don't have to look in his eyes as he tries to defend the life he created after me and the lies he's told me since.

Trust—he has no concept of what that means. He used to, but once he got a taste of Hollywood, he wanted more even at the expense of us. I pull at the promise ring, but it's stuck. Stupid margaritas and Texas heat making my fingers swell.

I finally give up and hit the steering wheel out of frustration. Damn him! *Why wouldn't he tell me? Why did he lie?* When she came to his room that first time, I asked him. I asked him twice why she would think she could come to his room. What were his answers? *Because she's used to getting her way. Because she's spoiled.* No. She came to his room, *and* then propositioned him after the pizza night because *she'd already been with him before.* I barely registered her words after she dropped that bombshell, but I did hear her sing his praises. *It was an incredible night. One of the most* sexually expressive *I've ever had.*

Backing out of the parking spot, I need to get out of this place and away from him. *Why did he lie to me? Would I have hated knowing they'd been together? Yes, of course.* But going in blind... that was cruel. *He said he wants to be all in. Wants my heart.*

While I'm waiting for the light to turn green, my phone rings, startling me. Just after I see his name on the screen, I see him. He's standing on the sidewalk, holding the phone to his ear, frantic as he searches the area. The light changes just as our eyes meet.

Like an Olympic sprinter, he runs toward my car. I make the turn and head north, putting distance between us. My eyes dart between the rearview mirror and the street ahead. He's running as fast as he can. His speed and the red light ahead makes me fear he'll catch me. *And then what?* What happens? I can't deal with that confrontation, praying to the saint who presides over streetlights, "Turn green. Please. Turn green. Come on."

Glancing quickly over my shoulder, Luke is running down the middle of the street, coming straight for me. My heart races as my foot becomes impatient on the brake, slowly lifting just in case.

Twenty feet...

Ten feet...

Five feet...

Green.

I punch the gas. Up ahead, green lights pave my way as he's

left behind in the midst of honking cars.

Right then, as if cued, the sky opens and rain pours down. When I glance in the mirror one last time, he's bent over out of breath with his eyes fastened to the tail end of my car as I drive away.

And then I exhale, able to breathe again.

Once I leave downtown, I drive faster, in a hurry to get nowhere fast, but out of here even faster. My phone keeps ringing, so I turn it off knowing who the calls are from without looking.

Not recognizing where I am, I realize that over the last month I've learned certain parts of Austin—downtown, South Congress, Lamar, and the Triangle. I don't know this part, so I pull into a supermarket lot and park.

Just breathe. I remind myself over and over again.

Each one comes heavier than the last until they alter and turn into sobs. I lean my head against the steering wheel and let it come like the rain, an unstoppable force from within.

When I look up, my vision is blurred and I focus on breathing again, willing my thoughts to clear and imagine nothingness. It doesn't work for long before the highlights reel from Luke and my relationship starts playing on a loop.

Soon the all the parking spots around me are empty and I look at the time. With the rain and clouds, I hadn't noticed the evening disappear and the night's arrival. I was distracted by Jessica's words cutting into the insecurities I still cling to. While I felt terrible for being with Lawrence, Luke was with many women. With that kind of track record can I ever be enough for him? Will I ever be "sexually expressive" enough? I don't even know what that means, so how can I be that for him if he needs it? He says he wants to move forward, wants to leave the past in the past, but how will I do that if the past keeps finding us

I've been here for over an hour with my thoughts whirling in a history that will only ever be just that at best. I can't live a life where the past is constantly haunting our present. The humiliation alone will do me in, much less the heartbreak. I can't go there. Don't think about how it aches in my chest. Don't think about the dullness that follows, the one that became too familiar after the last time. Don't think...

It's past nine o'clock and I know I'm not returning to my hotel room. I can't be that close to him. Not tonight. I'll find a hotel in this area for tonight.

The rain has stopped and I get out and check my trunk, hoping I still have my gym bag back in there. A pair of yoga pants, a tank top, a hoodie, socks, and sneakers inside. Good. One full outfit I can wear to work tomorrow. That means I'm safe to stay away like I want, like I need.

I go inside the store and buy some essentials like a toothbrush and paste, a comb, and rubber bands for my hair. Yogurt and string cheese get tossed into my basket, along with Fiery Hot Cheetos, two large bottles of Smart Water, and some grapes. I'm careful as I walk around, paranoid that the sunglasses I'm wearing inside a grocery store at nine at night draw too much attention. Does it matter?

Nothing does right now.

I purchase my goods and go. I don't have to drive far. The cashier pointed me in the direction of several hotels all situated next to each other. I have my pick.

After checking into a chain hotel, I set my gym bag down on the dresser and my food on the bed. Creature comforts are what I'm calling them.

I flop down on the bed and check my phone messages out of habit. I've missed a dozen calls from Luke, and one from Scalia. That's the one I return.

I'm greeted with panic, "Where are you, Jane?"

"Hi."

"Are you okay?"

"I will be. I just needed space." *Space that he'll not invade. Space that is free from actresses and their bragging egos.* "Just some breathing room."

"Jane, I'm sorry."

"Don't be," I reply, opening my string cheese. "He should have told me before now."

"Yes, he should have, but maybe he didn't feel he could."

"He slept with an actress who spends more time headlining tabloids than movies these days. How that story never broke, I don't know. But I've been naïve to think I could let his past go without it affecting me."

"Where are you? Do you want some company? We can talk about it or talk about other things or whatever you want? I hate the thought of you alone."

Lying back, I ask, "You'd do that for me?"

"Hell yeah, I would. I can even bring some booze."

"I don't want to get drunk. I don't want to wallow, but I could use the company."

"I'm on my way."

SCALIA ARRIVES WELL after I devoured the cheese, yogurt, and half the grapes. She's excited to see the Cheetos have made it this long untouched. After busting the bag open, we climb in bed, and turn on Jeopardy.

She answers a trivia question, *"What is Sacramento?"* and without skipping a beat says, "Jessica's a cunt. Sorry for the harsh language but it's true. She is."

"You don't have to apologize to me." We toast with our Cheetos. "I couldn't agree more. She was on a mission and she succeeded. I blame myself. I should have seen it coming long before now."

"You are not to blame for her actions, so why do you say that?"

"She hasn't exactly been subtle in her attention to Luke."

"What is Legends of the Fall?"

When the correct answer is revealed on the game show, I say, "You're really good at this game."

"I'm good with useless trivia, which means I'm great at Trivial Pursuit. *What are Ray-Ban sunglasses?"*

I glance back at the TV. Yep, she nailed the sunglass question. Russian literature is the category and she turns to me, ignoring the answers. "Do you want to talk about Luke?"

"Kind of. Kind of not." I feel shy, somewhat embarrassed about it all. She doesn't say anything, so I do, "I feel betrayed. Do I have a right to be upset? *What is The Brothers Karamazov?"*

"Good grief, you know Russian literature?"

"I had to read it in college as a requirement."

"Impressive. As for the betrayal, did he betray you? This was before you and he were even an item. You didn't even know each other then, so think of it in that light. It was before he found someone he really cared about."

"It's not that simple." *Do I tell her about our history?* My eyes stick to the game show. It's easier than looking her in the questioning eyes. *"What is Doctor Zhivago?"*

"Damn, girl, you are owning this category. As for Luke, maybe you're making it complicated when it's not."

"Whose side are you on anyway?" I grab the bag of Cheetos

and get a handful, not even caring about my orange-coated fingers.

"Yours, but I should clarify that I think all of his sides are good."

Well, she isn't wrong about that. "Then what does that make me? *What is War and Peace?*"

"Dang, girl. Remind me never to go against you in trivia."

"Lucky guesses," I remark as if they really are. This category is doing my heart in, remembering how Luke used to read books and poems to me...

"That has got to be one of the most romantic things I've ever heard."

The touch of his fingers as they run up and down my arm sends goose bumps pebbling across my skin. "No normal man can compete with these fictional characters. I bet they even pee with the seat down." He rolls his eyes.

I sit up and angle toward him. "You're better than any fictional characters. Just sayin'."

"I can read you this stuff, but I don't think I can ever live up to the expectations that women have of guys now."

Leaning forward on my knees, I kiss him. And then again. "You're doing just fine."

"Thanks for the vote." He sits all the way up. "Do you want me to read more of the poetic doctor or can we go see the new Dwayne Johnson movie?"

"Hot yes, but there is nothing romantic about The Rock, the wrestler slash actor, so I might have to take back what I just said to you."

"Might?"

"Depends on if you force me to the theater."

"I'm forcing you, but after..." He kisses my collarbone and

pulls the straps of my dress down over my shoulders.

"After?"

I'm scooped up and taken to the bedroom. The door is kicked closed, and I'm set down on the bed. "How about we skip the movie and the book tonight?"

"Don't skip the book. It's so romantic."

"I can be romantic."

"Yes," I reply, sweeping his hair from in front of his eyes, "you can be. Tell me something romantic."

Turning the ring around my finger once, he says, "One day I'm going to replace this with a forever ring."

"Is this not a forever ring?"

Looking back at me, he eases my legs apart with his hand. Pressing with just enough pressure to entice, but not enough to satisfy, his usual smile is not visible. "This is the ring that reminds you I love you when I'm not around. This is the ring that shows every other fucker out there that you're taken." The pressure increases, and I wiggle, wanting more. "This is the ring I worked three summers and two Christmas breaks to show you that you already own my heart, but I'm willing to give you each and every minute of my days as well. I love you, Janie."

"You're so much swoonier than any hero in a book."

"You know what else I am? In love."

"I thought you were going to say horny."

The zipper of my dress is sliding down. "That too. It's a dangerous combination—in love and horny."

"Dangerous for whom?"

Sitting up, he pulls the dress over my head. "For you. Get naked."

"So demanding."

"I think you like it."

"Only in the bedroom."

He smirks. "That works for me."

...Scalia rolls her eyes. "Sure they are."

"Sure they are what?" I ask, not hearing what she was talking about.

"Your guesses. I don't believe for one minute that your answers to the Jeopardy questions are guesses."

"Don't you mean questions to the answers?"

She laughs, grabbing the bag back. With a mouthful of Cheetos, she says, "Yes, whatever. And for the record, holding a grudge just makes you a lonely girl at the end of the day."

"If he's lied about this—"

"He didn't lie."

"He didn't tell me either."

"Why would he? Did you tell him about every guy you've ever slept with? Name, social security number, mother's maiden and all that?"

She has no idea that he knows about both men already considering he's one-half of them especially. "I said it was complicated."

The bag is discarded and she wipes her hands on a tissue. Rolling to face me, she says, "Jane, I don't know you all that well, but I am pretty certain I saw love in his eyes when he looked at you, and love in your eyes when you looked at him. Do you think you should allow his past to determine your future? I know that sounds harsh, but we all carry baggage. That's the nature of being humans." She swings her legs off the bed. "Come on. We have an early call time. Maybe rest on this tonight. But no matter what you decide, you have five days left to figure it out. Then it's poof, back to our own worlds again." She gets out of bed and walks to the bathroom. I can hear her brushing her teeth and running water before she returns. "Let's get some rest. It's the best medicine for tonight. Good night."

I know she's right. "Good night." I get up and go to the bathroom to wash my hands clean of the junk food too. When I brush my teeth, I look in the mirror and see pink eyes and puffy lids.

With watery eyes, I'm almost surprised I have any tears left to cry. Scalia makes many good points, but I'm still stumped why Luke would ensure Jessica was cast on this project. Ian told me Luke had made that decision and brought her in. There are other actresses that could have played Jude. Sure, he didn't know we would rekindle things, but *he slept with her.* As we were getting closer, why not just confess that? What was his motivation? And why didn't he tell me. What was his intention?

After turning off the TV, I lay my head on the pillow, but my mind is still spinning through a million questions, trying to figure out what Luke was thinking when he requested Jessica for the lead role on *my* movie. Is this revenge for hurting him? Does he hate me? Deep down, does he despise me so much that he would do this just to get back at me? I can't believe that about Luke. No. He has never been someone to play games with people's emotions. That was one of the things he never liked about Caroline or Ricky. He's not a liar. *But then why didn't he tell me about Jessica.* Was he trying to protect me or deceive me? He told me several times to stay away from her, but never why.

I think about the times we've spent together and how he seemed confident we shouldn't hide ourselves away from others. *He* was happy if others knew about us. Scalia is partly correct though. It is Luke's past, and not his present. *But I'm still gutted.* She deliberately blindsided me tonight, intentionally ensuring I was there when she told the room about her and Luke. I feel as though I've fallen into a mess smack dab in the middle of heartbreak. *Again.*

CHAPTER 24

Luke

STARING AT THE door has had absolutely no effect in bringing her back to me. It's been six hours since Jane left. I've left close to two dozen messages and texts with no reply in return. The door that adjoins her room to mine is wide open, so I've waited in hers. *For hours.*

I lie back and smell the faintest of rose scents, her signature fragrance perfuming her pillow. I gave her the first bottle of the French perfume for her seventeenth birthday, and she's worn it since. She's received other bottles, different perfumes over the years, but they remained unused and were eventually thrown out.

The one I gave her was the only one she ever wanted. She told me she wanted only me, that I was it for her. Another one of the hints, the little things I wasn't paying attention to because I was caught up in the big picture instead. It was a mistake, another one I can recognize to add to the list of many.

Lawrence was with that dark-haired woman and I thought he was cheating. I assumed he was a scumbag... well, he is an asshole, but it never occurred to me that he and Jane weren't together.

She wasn't wearing a ring any of the times I saw her.

She came over and we had dinner together. I never even asked why she was there. Something was going on, something heavy, and I didn't ask in fear that she'd leave if I were too intrusive.

The ring. She was wearing the ring I gave her and I thought it was for kicks. It wasn't. Jane was trying to tell me in the only terms she knew how—from her heart to mine. *Actions.* Why wasn't I seeing? Why was I so blinded by the past that I couldn't see what was right in front of me? How did I manage to fall in love with the only woman who doesn't use a ton of words to express herself? She was showing me and I failed to notice.

I'm so fucking stupid.

Sitting up, I lean my elbows on my knees and drop my head down. I'm not sure I'm going to get any sleep, though I need it desperately. I pick up my phone and stare at the time. No missed calls. No new messages. I text one last time: *I love you.*

I set it down, and get up to take a piss when it buzzes across the wood surface. Grabbing the phone, it fumbles in my hands before I catch it and read the message.

Jane: *I can't get past this. I'm sorry.*

Me: *Please talk to me.*

Jane: *I can't talk about it anymore. I just thought you should know where* my *head is at.*

Me: *Where's your heart?*

My eyes stay fixed on the screen for another hour, but she doesn't reply.

THE SUN HITS the back of my lids, waking me up. I pull the pillow over my head and yawn, trying for more sleep. Then it hits me.

Shit.

I'm late.

Throwing the covers and pillow off me, I grab my phone. 9:16 a.m. I don't remember falling asleep but I guess I did during my bleary-eyed exhaustion. I run into my room and grab a clean button-up from the hanger and jeans from the bed. I brush my teeth and try to tame my hair, but it's unruly and I don't have time to fuck with it. I'm out the door in five minutes. I run two blocks and up another to the building where we're shooting today. When I arrive, Scalia and the assistant director are standing on the sidewalk out front.

"Hey, sorry. I overslept."

Scalia vapes, and then says, "It's crazy town in there."

"What's going on?" I ask.

The AD looks worried. "Jessica."

Thank God he didn't say Jane... *Wait, what?* "What's going on with Jessica?"

"She's refusing to work. Since she locked him out of the bedroom, Ian's been on the phone with her manager all morning."

Fuck.

I rush inside and up the stairs. When I barge in the front door, the first person I see is Jane. Her mouth opens to say something, but then she closes it and turns to Ian who is in the next chair.

What I want to do and what I should do wages war between my head and heart. Ian stands and comes toward me taking away my choices. He says, "Follow me." He keeps the phone to his ear, and nods, then speaks into it, "We'll talk to her again and see. I'll call you back." Shaking his head, he sighs. "She's a fucking mess. You need to talk some sense into her."

"I doubt I can do anything."

"You're the only one she's asked for. Repeatedly. You need to get this project back on track or we're wrapping today with an unfinished film. No actress. No movie."

"I'll talk to her." I avoid looking in Jane's direction. I can't bear to see her pain. I need to save this movie for her. I feel like a traitor when I open the door and look inside. Jessica is sitting by the window, smoking. When the door is closed, I move to the corner of the bed. She's well aware I'm here, but she continues her self-indulgent game by blowing smoke into the air. It slips through the open window just as she speaks, "I relate to the role I'm playing, I relate to Jude."

"How so?" I keep the anger I feel toward her at bay, hoping to turn this nightmare around.

"She's a dynamic character. The world is conspiring against her and the odds are insurmountable."

"She surmounts them."

"With her true love."

"You have a life full of people who care about you."

She turns to me, finally looking me in the eyes. I can tell she's been crying, but the tears stopped a while ago. "I don't have anyone in my life that's not on my payroll."

It's a sad statement about the life she's created, so I try to redirect. "We only have five days left of shooting. We can wrap this film and all go home."

"I have no real home."

"You have a beautiful home in Los Feliz, Jessica. In five days, we can return to our homes, to our friends, and teams."

"Something's been bothering me since we last spoke."

"And that is?"

"Tell me, Luke. What does she have that I don't?"

I sit, but turn my gaze up and stare at the ceiling. She's exasperating and obviously not going to do this film without a fight. "Who?" I ask, knowing full well who she's referring to. I turn back to her keenly aware of her eyes on me.

"Jane Lewis, the one you can't take your eyes or hands off." She rolls her eyes to emphasize her annoyance.

This is a no-win for me. I won't leave this room unscathed, but I'll do whatever I need to make sure Jane's reputation does. Stepping away from the comparison she wants me to make, I simply tell her the truth, "My heart."

Forced tears trickle down her cheeks. I can remain here heartless or give in to what she needs right now—a friend. I move to the chair next to her because she needs someone to show they care, someone not on her personal payroll. I like to think beneath the heavy makeup and the diva attitude is a woman with a heart and soul who cares for others and not only herself.

In a broken tone, she says, "I'm leaving for LA in an hour."

Bolting to my feet, I reply, "You can't. You can't leave this project."

"I'm already out the door."

"No, you're right here. You just said you relate to the character. Be the character and bring Jude to life. Only you can do this, Jessica."

"Spoken like a true producer. You only care about the movie. And to think I thought you were different."

"I care about this project and everyone attached. They'll lose their final paychecks. The movie can't find a distributor if it's not finished."

"I have to put my mental well-being first."

"No," I demand. "You need to think of everyone else. They have families they need to feed, careers are on the line."

"And what about you, Luke? What have you sacrificed?"

"Everything."

"My car will be arriving in ten minutes. That's ten minutes to change my mind."

Pointing to the door, I say, "Those people are relying on you. You have a contract in place. Stay and see this through."

"This is not a good environment for me."

"Fine. Let's make it good. Whatever you need, I'll get it for you."

"Promise?"

Third mistake—I fail to catch the devious glint in her eyes. "I promise. Just name it."

"I'm tired of being alone." All traces of tears gone, a wicked grin moves in.

I get up and walk to the window, praying she's not saying what I think she is. "I know some great guys who would love to take you out. We'll get back to LA and I can set you up."

"I don't want other guys. Don't you see, Luke? I only want you."

"Me? That makes no sense. What are you saying?"

"I want you to give me your heart like you gave it to Jane."

"Jessica..." I sigh. "Don't do this."

"I have nothing to lose anymore and everything to gain."

"Why do you want it? My heart is bruised and battered, completely broken."

"It's more whole than mine. Please, Luke, stay with me. I know I can finish this movie with you by my side, with you holding me at night so I can finally sleep."

Jane. "You're asking me to hurt someone on purpose. That's the kind of man you want to be with?"

"I haven't thought this through or planned this out. I just know I want to spend time with you."

"What you're asking is too much."

"I have some events to attend when we return to LA and I'd rather not go alone. Simple appearances. Surely, you can do that for me after the favor I've done for you?"

"You needed this movie too, don't forget. And I see through you. This is not about the movie. It's about revenge and I refuse to hurt her because of some fantasy you're holding on to."

"Not even to save the movie?"

Fucking fuckity fuck fuck fuuuuuccck!

Thinking of Jane losing this movie, her future, her salary when she has nothing but a few boxes and two suitcases... If I lose my home, I have nothing to give her, she'll have nowhere to go. I have to fight this. "I'm pleading with you. Please don't do this, Jessica. It's only five more days."

"My mind is made up."

"What does that mean?"

"It means if you want this project finished, we'll finish it together or not at all."

"You're blackmailing me, threatening the future of this project, all because you want to spend time with me? That makes no sense."

"I want more than time. I want something solid, something reliable. At least for a few weeks. It will help get the press and my father off my back. We'll date and do those couple-y things real couples do, like go to dinner and the movies, dancing. We'll be seen by the paparazzi and all will be good again for me." Her gaze drops. When she looks back up, coy, the most foreign of emotions on her face next to innocence appears. "And if you want, we can make love again."

After my eyebrows shoot straight up, I say, "Clearly it's not *love* you're wanting."

"Fake it. You work in Hollywood. *Fake it 'til you make it* is our motto. You can do this."

"And what if I refuse?"

"Goodbye, movie. Hello, rehab. I'm thinking I'll stay in rehab for a longer stint this time. Maybe six months to a year." She stands, light on her feet, her blackmailing scheme giving her confidence. "That means I can't revisit the film until after and if I have other projects lined up... we just may never finish this movie."

"We'll sue."

"Sue all you want. I'm well aware that my contract says I only have to pay twice my salary if I pull out during production." She laughs. "I took a pay cut to be with you. Do you really think I don't have half a million in the bank? I've been working since I was four, Luke. I could spend that in a day shopping on Rodeo Drive."

A rotting sensation fills my stomach. She's got me cornered. A woman with nothing to lose has everything to gain. I actually don't think she hates Jane. She hates me, but will hurt Jane to make me pay. Turning my back to her, my thoughts scatter, searching for any out, anything I can think of, anything left that can give me a different outcome. But I'm not dealing with someone in her right mind, so nothing comes to mind. Except one...

I'm fucked.

It's Jane or the movie.

From every angle, I'm fucked.

Jane doesn't have to be. I can protect her. I can save her. Even at the expense of us. *She'll hate me.* But, I can give her a future, solid footing in Hollywood that can lead to more work. She can buy a house, a condo, a place to call home. She can settle down with the dream I thought—*hoped*—I could give her.

Cold hands slide over my shoulders, thin arms wrap around my neck like a noose. A bony cheek is rested on my back. I have no idea why Jessica is doing this. Just to be manipulative? Some form of fucked-up control? Just for hateful kicks? Whatever the reason, Jane has to come first.

Jane. She'll never forgive me.

The pain will engulf her, like it's consuming me. But from the destruction of us, she can rise.

She will.

She has to.

I will do anything I have to so she does. *I will do this.* I will sell my soul to the devil, but I will never give her my heart. Jane will always own that. Reaching up, I cover Jessica's hand with mine. The only choice I have.

The deal is done.

Fuck.

My.

Life.

CHAPTER 25

Luke

MY HANDS ARE sweating.

It's hot in here, or it's the fire flaming from the devil beside me, melting me from the inside out. I swipe the back of my arm across my forehead. I race through any other scenario, but there's not enough time to map one out. There has to be other options. But I can't seem to land on one that doesn't destroy this project, thus destroying Jane's future.

With her hand on the doorknob and a big grin on her face, Jessica turns and asks, "Are you ready?"

"It's unprofessional to make a production of our personal lives."

"Don't try to get out of this. You agreed to three weeks." She turns around and straightens my shirt like we're a married couple. "Make it good, Luke, or I'm out of here."

Five days of filming. Editing and voiceover work. Three weeks. "My word is good."

"You haven't given me your word."

"And I won't. But I want this movie made."

She's about to enter the living room, but stops to add, "If

anyone, including your *Janie*, doesn't believe we're a couple, I will destroy you and this movie. It will never see the light of day, much less the inside of a theater. Are we clear?"

I nod, but that's all I'll give her. She's stolen enough from me for a lifetime. "Before we go out there, tell me how this will ever make up for the real thing? It won't. You know that, right? You're acting like you believe we're real, that an emotion other than hate can exist between us."

"Hate is a strong word."

"It's the only thing I feel for you. You're destroying lives, and for what? Gossip fodder? Hoping not to look half as desperate as everyone knows you are?"

"Don't be cruel, Luke, or I'll walk. Now put on a smile and make them believe." She grits her teeth. "Better yet, make *me* believe."

The door is opened and she walks out. "I'm ready, Ian. Let's shoot this movie."

Ian smiles, happier than I've ever seen him, and claps his hands together. "Good. Places, people. We're in the home stretch. Let's get this movie wrapped."

I can't even muster a fake smile. I feel sick as panic courses through my veins. Am I doing the right thing? Should her career highs come at the expense of Jane's heart? Should, could, would doesn't matter now. Jessica's vengeance won't be satiated until the spoiled princess gets what she wants. Of all the regrets I have—and I can count them on two fingers—sleeping with her is the biggest. I'd let Jane walk away a thousand times to find happiness without me if I could take back that one drunken night, not attend that party, to have stayed home and watched football instead.

But I had something to prove. I had to network and mingle with Hollywood's elite. I had to schmooze with studio big wigs. I had to wine and dine the brightest stars in the film industry. *I had...*

I had...

I had...

I had to fill a void that the love of my life left inside me a year earlier...

The green eyes I thought I'd be waking up to for the rest of my life are braced on mine. We didn't have a good night. We never got to talk, not like we should have. Today will be worse.

Stepping over large black cables and walking around the camera, I go to her hesitantly. I can't manage to say anything, not sure where to start. We stand awkwardly next to each other for a few seconds until we blend in with the commotion of setting up for the next scene. When no one is watching, I turn to her, my knuckles brushing against the back of her hand, and savoring this lightest of touches while knowing it will be my last.

Her eyes are glassy, the lids swollen from a hard night. I briefly close mine to block out her pain. I have to do this. I have to turn off my heart and use my head. This is the only thing I can do—for her, for me, for this project and everyone working on it. She won't understand now, but maybe one day. Maybe in three weeks. That's not a long time. Maybe she'll take me back...

No. There will be no maybe. She already struggled to trust me. With this, I'm done.

There won't be any more chances.

I keep my tone steady, level, like my eyes are on her. Instead of looking at her, I try to see through her. I don't want to see the soul that fills her eyes when she sees me, *the me* who can't lie to her. She'll see through me, through this story I'm about to tell. "We need to talk."

After holding my stare, she blinks. "Okay."

She knows what comes next. I can hear it in her voice—the

soft quiver of an aching heart mixed with the tears I promised never to cause her caught in her throat. I don't have to say the words for her to know. I'm sure she can hear it in mine—emotion kept at bay. My eyes are vacant without the beat of a pulsing heart to make them come alive.

The tension between us is palpable as we walk out of the apartment. The door is closed. She's behind me, my strides longer than hers, but she's there, keeping up. In the silence of the hallway, I hear each step we take, and her breath. The words float in my head forming into coherent lies to convince her that I no longer love her.

Three weeks will ruin the possibility of a lifetime. My house is meaningless without the prospect of her laughter to fill it, so I'll do this for her, for her alone. We reach a corner near the stairwell and stop. I thought I could do this by sticking to a mental script, but her hair is messy in the most natural flattering way as if this goddess just wakes up this beautiful. I know firsthand she does, and I know this will be just as painful for me to do as it is for her to hear.

Standing in front of her, in front of the woman I love, I already feel empty.

There are moments that define who we are as people.

When I look down into her mournful eyes, I know this is the right thing to do. For her, this is it. For me, this is one of those moments.

My gulp is followed by one of hers. I open the stairwell door and she enters, passing without so much as a glance my way.

She knows.

The first few stitches used to heal my heart rip back open.

Act One.

She needs to believe the lie.

The metal door closes and we're sealed inside, just like my

fate. Jane sits on the top stair with her back to me, and says, "This is it."

Her long hair trails down her back. It's untamed and loose. Reaching out, I almost touch it, but I retreat to the corner holding myself to the white painted brick. My heart weakens as I gain momentum, reminding myself I must do this. I'll do this for her. Anything to protect her. Anything. "Yes."

The word vibrates, bouncing around the echoing chamber, and I start silently praying: *Please don't believe me, Jane. Please. You know you own my heart. You always have and always will.*

Her shoulders shake, the smallest of movements, but I catch it. Her voice trembles. "I loved you."

"I know."

I'm determined for her to walk away hating me, hating us. I need her to move on from this stronger than when she came back into my life. It's the only way I'll know she believes me. *Anything to protect her.* All for her. I stare at her, wishing I could see her face.

Act Two.

Keeping her back to me, she stands, gripping the railing tightly with her right hand. "I hate you, Luke Anders." She turns and when her eyes pierce mine, she repeats, "I hate you."

One lie down, and I hate myself more.

"I know."

This is all for you. All for you, Jane. I love you. I love you with every part of me, every part of my soul, and with my whole heart. When she leaves this place, she'll take the best of me, and all my love with her. And I'll let her.

Her gaze falls, as do her shoulders, her hope crushed just like my heart. The job I came to do is done in two acts. Her future secured. She takes one step down, and then two more. Moving on shaky legs, she stops on the lower level and looks back up at me.

"You're not the man I used to know. Nothing about you is the same."

She's right. I'm nothing without her. I never was. As I stare into her eyes that used to see the good in me, I know she's it. There will never be another for me. Against everything I believe, everything I love, I repeat, "I know."

She walks down the next set of stairs. I hear the door two floors below open and then close loudly. I sink to the concrete, my knees wavering under my own heartbreak. I haven't cried... I don't even know when I last cried, but my eyes sting, burning like my soul.

I'm gone long enough for Jessica to be searching for me. The door to the apartment opens just as I arrive. "There you are. I need you."

"For what?" I snap.

"To help me get into this scene."

"Find Ryan." I sidestep around her.

She stamps her foot. "Luke!"

"Don't you ever say my name like that again." My teeth clench.

"Don't threaten me. We're only fifteen minutes into our agreement. The hard part is done. You've handled it, now it's time to move on with me."

It? It... her... *Jane.* I think I'm going to be sick. "You know nothing about genuine feelings. The last time you felt anything in that black soul of yours is before your rich daddy bought you your first role to get you out of his hair." I turn around to leave, but she grabs my arm. Leaning in, she says, "That's strike one. Two more and I'm out of here."

I want to tell her to fuck off, but I can't. I can't do that to Jane. She needs this movie. Pulling my arm away, I glare, and then leave.

Outside, I look in both directions before walking toward the river downtown. It's humid, undecided if it wants to be hot or rain. Like me, the weather is caught up in its own turmoil.

Once I reach the bridge, I stand there lost—my soul feeling detached and aimless. I start walking again, wanting to find something that will guide me. I don't find what I'm looking for, but I find a large Oak tree to lie under on the lawn of the Capital building.

The tree's shadow moves and stretches with the sun's positioning. I'm tempted to stay here well into the night. It's peaceful in a world that's gotten out of hand.

How could I hurt her?

How could I break her heart even when it's for her own good?

I'm unsure what hurt more—her telling me she hates me, or the lack of tears in her eyes when she said it. Either way, I'll never forget either.

Despite my tired legs, my weary mind, and my soulless body, I walk back. When I get closer to the hotel, I look around for Jane, a small seed of hope planted that I might find her on the street and we can talk. Will I tell her the truth? Will I be able to crush her dreams instead of her heart? What's worse?

Pulling my phone from my pocket, I call the only person I can tell anything to, that I can tell how I've fucked up, and gotten fucked.

Two rings and the call is answered, "What up?"

"I've screwed up, Danny."

"I leave the country for a few weeks and you manage to fuck up your entire life?" There's lightness to his voice.

Heaviness coats mine. "So much shit has gone down."

"With Jane?"

"I've lost her."

We talk for a few minutes before he has me going back to the hotel room to talk to her, remembering I can talk to her in private there. I can fix this. She can pretend... maybe she'll play along if I can make amends.

I open the adjoining door, but Jane's door is locked, so I knock, but there's no response. I press my ear to the door and listen to hear if she's there. It's quiet next door—no TV, no music, no voices speaking on phones.

Nothing.

While I'm in the privacy of my room, I call Jane, willing her to answer her phone. She doesn't. I call again, this time going to voicemail. "Please call me."

Like I'm willing to sacrifice everything for her, I'm also willing to risk telling her the truth in private. There's a knock. I shut the adjoining door quietly and when I open the front one, Jane stands there. A smile I can't stop floods my face... until I see Ian behind her. "We need to talk," he says. *Jerk.*

Jane looks away and I open the door wider. "Come in." When they're standing in the middle of the room, I remark, "Shouldn't you be on set? We have limited hours to finish the film."

"We got the last scene, so I, I mean *we*," he says, with his hand on Jane's shoulder, and a shit-eating grin on his face, "wanted to share the good news while the crew changes locations."

Jane won't look at me. But I can't take my eyes off her.

Ian begins rambling again, "Jane and I are dating."

My gaze shifts to him just as Jane scolds him, "Ian!"

He keeps talking, ignoring her reprimand. "We wanted to let you know we support your relationship with Jessica. She's happier than I've seen her since we've been here. I know at one point you were developing feelings for Jane, so we also wanted to share with you first and would appreciate your support."

Developing...

That never happened with her. She owned my every emotion from the first time I saw her in the sixth grade.

He's not a threat to me. I've already taken myself out of the running. He's posturing. Peacocking, and pissing on what he thinks is his territory.

Jane doesn't care about him. It's written all over her body language, her impatient expression, and her tone when she corrects him. "Oh for goodness sake, Ian. We aren't dating. I only agreed to dinner to discuss the New York locations the scout sent us, but that's not why we came here."

We stand in front of each other, as if we never knew each other at all, as if we've never loved each other. "Why did you come here?"

He answers before she has a chance, "We're wrapping sooner than we thought."

"What?" I ask, shocked by the news. "The schedule is in place."

"We don't need five more days in Austin," Ian says. "We'll be finished tomorrow at the rate we knocked out the scenes today. So Manhattan is up to bat next."

With her gaze landing hard on me, Jane crosses her arms over her chest. "Whatever has come over Jessica has changed her. She nailed her scenes. Not one retake was needed." Her glare scorches my empty chest, my body acutely aware of the lack of heartbeats.

She moves to leave while saying with more resigned apathy than I've ever seen, "So whatever you did for her is working. Seems we'll be done in two days and can leave."

Ian touches her lower back as they move and I want to rip his fucking arm out of the socket. He opens the door for her and then like the true gentleman he is, he walks out first. *Bastard.*

I ask, "Do you?"

She looks at me for the first time since she walked in. "Do I what?"

"Do you leave in two days?"

Her honesty is revealed, and with Ian out of earshot, she shrugs. "I don't know anything anymore." The door closes and I'm left staring at the back of it.

"IF YOU WERE looking for Jane at the bottom of a bottle of Jack Daniels, I can confirm you won't find her there." I can already imagine the cocky grin on his face before I even see it. Danny sits down across from me and rests his arms on the table. "Trust me, man, I've searched there myself and nothing ever good came of it."

"Did you try Crown? Or Patron? Maybe I should switch liquors."

He chuckles and sits back. Scanning the courtyard, he smiles at a few gawkers before turning back to me. "The only thing I found at the bottom of Patron was an almost arrest down on the border past San Diego. Oh right, you were there and the one buying."

"You were cuffed. Not arrested. I should call you the Great Embellisher."

"Let's get to it. I have to be in Miami tomorrow."

"What do you want to know?" I ask, and then finish my drink.

"Do we want to pretend this isn't about Jane, and oh, I don't know, sightsee? I heard the Duck Tour is fun. Or how about we cut to the chase and you give me the lowdown. I didn't fly to Texas for the humidity."

"Why did you fly here?"

He shakes his head and takes the bottle in hand. "Got another glass?"

"Nope." A glass suddenly appears, a woman to the side of him stands there offering. Danny gives her the smile that made him famous—the one I tease him over—and he accepts it. The waitress then asks if we need anything else. "No. Thank you."

He pours a shot and downs it before responding, "You're being dumb as fuck, not thinking clearly. You know what I've been through and yet you learned nothing from it. It's time to step up to the plate and go for the homer. The house is a possession. Nothing more. Shit, I sold it to you a few years ago and I could care less about it. Jane on the other hand—"

"She is not a possession I can control."

"You wouldn't want her if you could."

"I can't have her if I wanted."

"Bullshit." He pours us both another shot.

"For someone who just lectured me on the loneliness of a full bottle of liquor, I'll take this shot as a sign you've reconsidered your stance."

"It's called truth serum."

"I don't have a problem with the truth. I have a problem with a five-foot-eight actress who thinks the world owes her when her privileged life falls apart."

"What upsets you more—the fact that you made a deal against your conscience or that you made a deal with Jessica?"

"They're one in the same and have the same outcome—I lose Jane."

"You didn't fight for Jane. Again." Danny sits forward, no smugness, no joy, just irritation singeing his words. "You gave her up and then sit here as if you did it all for her. Don't call me all crying that you're being "blackmailed" by the shallow actress who can't find her car at the end of the night, much less plot out a huge master plan just because she thinks you're the cherry on top of a mountainous sundae. You give yourself too much credit."

"Speaking of shallow, how's the modeling world?"

He smiles. "About the same as Hollywood these days, and nice try. I wouldn't be a good friend if I didn't try to set you straight. So here it is. Listen up, brother. You're fucking up. Big time. I can't save you. No one can, except you. Fix this, Luke, before it's too late."

"It's already too late. She told me she hates me."

"If she spoke to you at all, it's not too late." Danny stands after setting his empty glass down. Scanning the crew, he asks, "Where's Jane?"

I set my glass down. "I would assume on her date with Ian."

Danny's face crinkles. Not good for a model who makes his money off his face. "The director? What the fuck?"

"Fuck if I know," I reply, shaking my head.

"Where are they?"

"They didn't bother to fill me in on that detail before they left. Scalia might know." I get up and cross the courtyard. Ryan, Scalia, and a few others are sitting together drinking wine.

Ryan stands when he sees Danny. His hand is out before I can even make the introduction. "You're Danny Weston."

Danny shakes his hand. "Yep."

"I'm a big fan."

Danny looks down at their still-joined hands and pulls his back. "Thanks."

I interrupt because this is just awkward on many levels. "Have you guys seen Ian?"

Scalia looks sympathetic the way her brow creases and her eyes go down. "He and Jane went to dinner just a little while ago."

Danny asks, "Do you know where?"

She smiles—like everyone does when he speaks to him—and says, "I think to this Italian restaurant a few blocks down from here. Take a right on the sidewalk. I know they walked."

"Thank you."

We leave the group and walk outside the hotel grounds. I'm about to head south on Congress, but the back of his hand hits my chest. "You stay here. I've got some business to take care of. I'll meet you later."

"What business?" I ask skeptically.

"Nothing important," he replies sarcastically, "just your entire future."

Right there.

That's what friends are for.

CHAPTER 26

Jane

MY THIRD YAWN triggers Ian to ask, "Are you okay?"

"Just tired. I didn't sleep well last night."

"I can imagine. Finding out the person you were mildly interested in is sleeping... I mean *dating* someone else can take a toll. Maybe tonight, we can have an early night and go back to my room to relax. I've got a great bottle of Beaujolais we can try."

I thought my frown would be a big enough hint, but apparently not since hope sits firmly in place on his face. "I think you're jumping ahead a few steps."

"I know what I want and you are lovely."

"We should get back on topic. New York."

But he carries on as if I didn't speak at all, lost in himself. He reminds me of Lawrence. "I think we make a great couple and we're old enough to not waste time searching for something that's right in front of us."

"Ummm..." Both hands go up. "We need to take some major jumps back, Ian. I just got out of a relationship with a foundation of business. That's not what I'm looking for. I'm not trying to hurt your feelings, but your sudden determination to have me in your life makes no sense. You barely know me and I don't know you at all."

"There's an electricity between us, from the first time we met back in LA. Don't you feel it?"

Over Ian's shoulder I see him. "Shit." *Danny Weston.*

"What?"

"No," I say. "I'm not talking to you." I have a strong suspicion him being in Austin and walking into the same restaurant where I'm dining isn't a coincidence. I stand. "I'll be right back."

"Where are you going?"

"A friend of mine just walked in." I move around the table. Danny sees me and his grin is friendly, looking innocent enough, but I still keep my guard up when I approach. "Luke's not here."

"I'm not looking for Luke."

Yikes. "I was worried about that."

"No need to worry." He moves forward. "It's good to see you, Jane."

"You too." I step into his embrace, briefly closing my eyes, feeling closer to a life I used to love. When we part, I ask, "What are you doing here?"

"I'm here to see you."

My voice going up an octave reveals my surprise. "Me?"

"Do you have a minute?" he asks, seeing Ian watching us with a frown on his face.

"Okay. I'll be right back and meet you outside." When I return to the table, I tell Ian, "I hate cutting tonight short." I don't at all. I need to thank Danny for saving me. "My friend flew out here. I need to speak to him about a few things. Thank you for dinner."

"We didn't even order."

"Oh. Well, thanks for the glass of wine. I'll see you tomorrow on set."

"Jane?" While I pull my purse around my shoulder, angling it at my hip, Ian stands. "What about New York? I was thinking a suite at the Plaza."

Turning to him, I touch his arm. "Ian, we're not going to happen. You're a nice enough guy and an amazing director, but there's no chemistry."

"Chemistry is overrated. We can be great together. This movie is going to be huge and we can be the power couple behind it."

"I love your optimism, but I want to be part of a couple because of love, not a movie. Goodnight." I give him a friendly pat on the arm and leave.

Out on the sidewalk, Danny pushes off the wall. "Where are we going?"

"There's a place up here with cheap beers, an old jukebox, and ripped vinyl barstools. When was the last time you went to a dive bar, Mr. Suave?"

"My tastes aren't against dive bars, just against bad beer."

"Good to hear your ego is being kept in check." We cross the street and walk in the door that's propped open with a cinderblock. I turn back, and say, "Welcome to Austin."

He grabs a pitcher of beer and two glasses, then joins me at a table near a large window that's open to the street. It doesn't take him long to get down to business. "You two were a package deal when I met you. You still are if you ask me."

I'm open to hearing him out. "I'm asking."

"I want to hear your side of the story."

"I never took sides. I never knew I had to. I just trusted that he was the same Luke I've always known, but he's not. He's changed. LA has changed him. *She's* changed him."

"Don't give up on him. He loves you."

"He has a funny way of showing it." I feel my eyes start to well, so I tip my head back and blink a few times hoping to stave off the tears. "And when I say funny it wasn't funny at all."

"He can be an ass sometimes, but you know his heart is in the right place." He shakes his head. "Most of the time. I'm not sure what the fuck is going on with the actress, but it's not real. You and I both know it's not."

"Does *he*? Because he stopped being with *me* to date *her*."

Danny watches people walk by outside and says, "I just saw him. He's a mess, so if she's making him happy, she's doing a shitty job of it." When he looks back at me, he searches my face before settling on my eyes. "You know when you start dating someone new and everything is exciting, everything they do is cute or funny?"

"Yeah."

"He's not in that stage. He's drowning in a bottle of whiskey. Would someone buy a bottle of whiskey and be drinking alone if they were happy?"

"I don't know what you want from me, or what you want me to do. *He* made the decision to end us, not me."

"You were fighting—"

"Over her. He fucked her. Did he tell you that? He fucked her back in LA and then lied to me about it."

"You guys were broken up. He never saw her twice."

I scoff. "So Ross and Rachel of you. But tell me this. Why did he insist she had to be a part of this project if it was over between them?"

"Because this movie needed a name and she needed a new start. Everyone in Hollywood knows her history. She's fucked over most of the major studios, but she can still get an indie movie financed. He's a producer, Jane. His job is to get movies made. He got your movie made using whatever connections he has."

Crossing my arms defensively over my chest, I think about what he's saying. It makes sense business-wise, but on a personal level, it makes none. One of those annoying tears falls down my cheek landing on the bar napkin. I look up into his caring brown eyes when he reaches across the table and covers my hand with his. Through a stifled breath, I finally say what has hurt me the most about the time Luke and I spent apart. "Why did he have to sleep with so many women? I wasn't enough to make him commit to a lifetime, but knowing what he's done since makes me believe I was never enough and never will be."

"Don't say that. You were. You still are."

"He hates me and wants to see me in pain like I caused him."

"I understand why you left, but the consequences of that decision is that you broke him. He can't commit to a pizza topping without second-guessing himself. So when he was sleeping with those women it was never to commit to one. It was to erase the one he lost."

"So I'm to blame for him being a manwhore?"

"Yes." He shrugs. "He didn't need them when he had you." My mouth drops open as the sting of his words backhand my heart. "Luke is the only guy I know who never cheated. That's the harsh truth you need to hear."

While I sit there in shock, staring at Luke's best friend as he doles out the medicine he feels needs to be given, the truth sinks in. "I am to blame." Acknowledging that causes more tears to fall. Danny leans over and pulls me into his arms. "I'm to blame. I loved him. I still love him. I think I always will." I cry on his shoulder, not caring that I'm in public, but grateful it's not crowded in here. "He was the first man I ever loved. My father left us when I was two. I swore I would never fall in love and go through what my mom did and then Luke showed up. He showed up and showed me how love worked, how it felt, and he loved me."

"He still does, Jane. He still does."

He hands me a napkin and I dry my eyes, hoping I don't look like a raccoon.

Leaning on the table in front of us, Danny asks, "Can I tell you a secret?"

I nod.

"It's a secret about Luke."

A smile involuntarily arises. "Do I want to know?"

"It's just something I've noticed over the last two years."

I sit back and dab a napkin under my eyes.

"Every woman he's been with since you... are you ready for this?"

"I don't know. Am I?" I brace myself, not normally wanting to know about Luke's sex life.

He smiles. "I find it ironic. Maybe you'll give me your thoughts on it."

"Just say it, Danny."

Chuckling, he says, "Every one of their names started with J."

Narrowing my eyes, I process what he's saying. "Like Jennifer?"

"And Janet."

"Jenna."

"Jackie."

"Jada."

"There wasn't a Jada, but there was a Jacinda."

"What's your point?"

"Jane..."

My gaze locks on his. "Oh my God! You're kidding me, right?"

After taking a swig of beer, he sits back pretty damn satisfied with himself. "Not kidding at all. Coincidence? I think not."

Glaring at the blinking beer sign above the bar, I say, "Jessica."

"Ding. Ding. Ding."

"He slept with J-named girls because of me? That makes no sense whatsoever."

"The weird part is I once brought it up and he had never connected the dots. It's like his subconscious is telling him what his heart wants. He's just not listening."

I finish my beer, and glance outside. "I don't know if I should laugh or cry about that."

"I'm not sure either, but I felt you should know." After chuckling to himself, he adds, "I could point out the L thing with you."

I pop him on the shoulder. "Don't even try it. Trust me, there's nothing those two have in common."

"You're right." He stands. "I should go. I'm hungry and I need to talk some sense into that boy."

"I don't want you to guilt him into wanting to be with me. I want him to want me because he can't live without me."

"He can't. Trust me on that." Danny smiles. With two fingers tapping on the table, he asks, "But can you live without him?"

"I've not lived since I walked out that day."

"Don't assume he has either." I stand, and we hug tightly, like old friends do, friends who don't see each other often. "Take care of yourself."

"You too."

"I will."

"I know you're Luke's friend, but thank you for being mine too."

"We'll always be friends, Jane. You have my number if you ever need anything. Don't be afraid to use it."

"Thanks. And hey, maybe I'll see you around again soon."

"I look forward to it."

"Goodbye, Danny."

He waves and walks out. I watch as he crosses the street,

heading back to the hotel. I stay seated, liking the view of the cars passing, liking the beer, feeling good about the conversation and the company I just had.

I pour myself another beer, emptying the pitcher, and think about everything Danny said and the way Luke has acted. So much has happened in such a short time, and then he immediately turned. Danny just might be right. Something might be going on that he can't control because deep down, deep inside my heart, I still don't believe that Luke would hurt me on purpose.

Revenge is an easy excuse to jump to, but that's not the man I know. Is it the man in the stairwell though? Is that version of Luke the real one? Or is the one I've loved for what feels like my whole life still inside him?

Is it possible I'm buried deep inside his heart like he's buried deep inside mine?

All the J names just might be the answer to a question he wasn't even aware he was asking. The biggest question I have is one I've never been brave enough to ask.

Until now.

Am I willing to put myself, my love, on the line again for someone who can break my heart again?

Despite all the pain he's caused me, I will always answer yes when it comes to Luke Anders.

CHAPTER 27

Luke

"WE ONLY AGREED to three weeks because it covered the time we knew we needed to wrap this project. If it takes less time—"

"This wasn't just about time, Luke." Jessica stands near my bed and whines, "I need you. I need to be touched. I need to feel loved again. It's been too long."

"You'll never get that from me. There is no love between us." Just as she's about to make herself more comfortable and sit, I say, "No. You're not staying."

"Do not test me!" Her voice rises with her temper.

I keep mine calmer. "Don't test me."

"I hold the cards. You knew what I wanted when we made this agreement."

"Sex? Fuck, Jessica, you can find a million guys to fuck out there. You're a celebrity. Why do you want me?"

"It's not just about sex. It's about companionship."

I laugh *at* her. "You do realize even the original agreement was only for three weeks, right?"

"I'm hoping we can get to know each other—"

"And what? I'll change my mind and fall in love with you?" I laugh harder this time, and then end it with anger just as quickly.

"For something that you mock as insignificant, you wasted no time in breaking little Janie's heart."

I shoot her a look, wishing she'd burn in hell for what she's made me do. "You said I had to, that it would prove that I want this movie made, so I did. But don't ever confuse what I did for anything more than a means to an end. There'll be no love lost on you, sweetheart."

"I like when you call me endearing names."

Bitch comes to mind, but a knock on the door saves her from hearing my real thoughts regarding her. Turning my back, I go to answer it, smiling when I do. "Perfect timing."

Danny comes in, but stops when he sees Jessica. "I, uh, didn't know you had company."

Jessica shuffles quickly toward him the second she lays eyes on him.

I nod my head toward the door. "She's leaving."

"So nice to finally meet you. I'm Jessica Pyles. Enchanted."

She holds out her hand as if she expects him to kiss the top. When he glances my way, I just shake my head. She thinks she's Hollywood royalty. The thing is, Danny isn't pretentious. He forgoes her hand and walks past her. "I've heard a lot about you, too."

"I hope all good."

Neither of us says anything.

Jessica decides to leave on her own accord. Miracles do exist. "So I'll see you later, Lu—"

I shut the door and bolt it. Just in case.

Danny flops on the bed. I lean against the desk, and ask, "Do I even want to know what happened with Jane?"

"How do you know I was with Jane?"

"It might be from that goofy grin on your face."

"I'm paid a lot of money for this goofy grin, and yes, I had a good chat with Jane. She really is a great girl."

"I can agree with you on that."

"So while I was with her I realized something."

He takes a moment to ponder, so I ask, "And what might that be?"

"You two have it bad for each other."

"We do?"

"Yup," he says, emphasizing the p, and smirking.

"What did you find out?"

"I found out that the director is a little weasel of a man."

"And what do you expect me to do with that?"

"Do what you want with that information. Simply making an observation."

"Get to the point, Danny. What did you find out?"

"First of all, I wasn't on a recognizance mission. I was visiting a friend and talking. That's it."

"Don't play games, man. Just tell me what she said about me."

"You fucked up by fucking every J in LA."

I sit in the chair and lean forward, resting my forearms on my legs. "I didn't fuck every J in LA. Would you stop saying that?"

"She thinks you did." He sits up. "Got anything to drink?"

"No. Now tell me more."

"She blames you, but she understands her choice to leave also contributed to your choices." He laughs. "She even threw out the *Friends* breakup."

"Shit. She's not going to forgive me."

"Hey. The breakup sex is one thing. That's all meaningless at the end of the day. But Jessica is a whole other ballgame. What are you doing?"

"Saving the movie."

Asking me more directly, his tone gets firm. "No, Luke. Listen very carefully. What. Are. You. Doing?"

I almost repeat my answer, but I realize that's not what he's referring to. He's referring to Jane. I drop my head down in shame. "Losing the only thing I ever loved."

"Don't."

When I look back up, I ask, "How do I make things right when I've screwed them up so badly?"

"I don't have all the answers. You have to figure it out on your own, but you will."

"What if I'm too late?"

"There's never too late. There's only not trying that you'll regret."

I regret not pursuing her last night and simply letting her go. "You should consider a career change from modeling to a relationship counselor. You're pretty good at it."

"I'm pretty damn good at modeling too and it pays better."

"True."

He stands, and says, "This went better than I thought it would. I think I'm going to head out tonight."

"Such a jet-setting show-off."

"Life is good. What can I say?" After picking up his suitcase, he shakes my hand. I pull him into a man-hug and we pat each other on the back. "I'll see you back in LA."

"Thanks for coming." I walk him out.

When the cab arrives, he says, "Don't let your head sidetrack your heart. You'll be the one paying the price if it does." He ducks inside the car and shuts the door.

Patting the top twice, the car drives away, leaving me with lots to think about, as if I didn't have a ton already.

I DON'T SPECIFICALLY listen for when Jane comes back to her hotel room, but I hear signs of life next door around ten. I set the eavesdropping glass down on the nightstand, comforted knowing she's still there, but curious where she's been.

The volume of my TV is turned up, the baseball game loud enough to let her know I'm right next door if she's curious. I want to set her mind at ease that Jessica isn't here with me. I get ready for bed and climb under the covers, restraining myself from knocking on her door. She deserves the peace after the hell I've put her through.

The next morning I walk onto the set with two coffees in hand. Jessica smiles on camera when she sees me, so Ian yells, "Cut. Take five."

Just as my eyes meet the prettiest greens I've ever seen, Jessica intrudes, bouncing my way and cutting off the view of Jane. "You are so sweet," she says, reaching for the other coffee in my hand. "I'm dying for caffeine. Thank you, honey."

Holding it just out of reach above her head, I whisper, "It's not for you."

Offense immediately strikes her symmetrical features. "Who's it for then?"

I know I shouldn't have. I know this. I'm not dense, but when I was standing in line at Starbucks, Jane's order just came out. Oops. I guess I suck at pretending to like Jessica when all I think about is Jane.

Jessica's hair is flipped when I don't answer, and she turns on her heel, returning to set. Without the barrier between us, I catch Jane watching the whole thing play out. The most fascinating part is that she doesn't seem angry. She might actually even be intrigued. I close the distance quietly as the set settles back in to shoot the scene. Sitting down next to her, I offer the coffee wordlessly, and receive in return, "Thank you."

"You're welcome," I whisper just as Ian calls, "Action." Maybe Danny's right. Maybe this gap with Jane can be bridged.

Everyone skips a lunch break in lieu of wrapping another scene. Snack trash litters the place—candy bars, chips, pretzels, whatever else could be found in the vending machine. The facility is standing in as an asylum today and it feels fitting.

I clean up, then head down the hall to see if anything is left to buy. When I round the corner, Jane stands in front of the machine debating between a Mars Bar and Corn Nuts.

She's not much taller than back when we started dating, but her body has a woman's curve to it now. She stays in shape, but I like that she's not hard. I miss her softness at night. I miss her. "Go for the Corn Nuts."

"You always did like candy bars best." When she does look my way, a smile enters around her eyes. "You just want me to get the Corn Nuts so you can have the Mars Bar, right?"

"You always did see right through me." *Please try now.*

The smile softens, the thought of our predicament weighing on her expression. "I used to. I don't think I can anymore." Danny was right. I need to fight for her, show her I want her to see right through me.

I take two steps closer. "Try."

"Why?"

"Because I need you to. I need you to see through me more than ever, Jane."

I watch as she closes her eyes, takes a deep breath, and then bites her bottom lip. *Something she does when she's stressed.* I still remember it so clearly. She's stressed. She should be telling me to fuck off and to leave her alone. *What did Danny say to her last night? Did he tell her that we're made for each other, that I'm lost without her, and there's a reason for what I've done?*

"I'm not sure I can keep looking for more, Luke, because it feels as though each time I do, I get scratched."

Scratched? Oh fuck. Rascal. That damn cat.

That horrible cat taught me I could hate it for hurting me but still love the cat. What did I say to her that night? What can I say to her now to help her see what I'm doing? "Sometimes we're hurt unintentionally, Jane."

She shakes her head and starts to turn away. *Shit.* Quickly I ask, "How about we split the two?"

"What?"

"The Corn Nuts and the Mars Bar?"

As her eyes search mine, she appears more confused than ever. "What are you doing, Luke?"

"I'm starving but I want to make you happy."

"No," she says, shaking her head, her shoulders dropping a bit. "I mean with your life."

"Trying to save yours."

"What does that mean?" she pleads.

"Please trust m—"

"Luke, don't. I can't. I'm sorry, but I'm not sure I'll ever trust you again." Brushing past me, she adds, "Please just stop."

Standing there alone, I drop my head back and close my eyes. I blow out a heavy breath and rub my temples. "That didn't go well."

"What didn't?"

Shit. Turning to see Ryan in the doorway, I cover, "There's only a Mars Bar and Corn Nuts left."

"Corn Nuts."

"They're all yours, man."

"Nothing for you?" he asks just before I'm out the door.

"No, I've lost my appetite."

"Hey, you haven't seen a phone around, have you? I can't find mine."

"No, but I'll keep a look out."

"Thanks."

When I go back to the set, I find a chair by the window and sit, leaning my arms on my knees. I've spent more time than I usually do on this set making sure everything goes off without a hitch, but mentally I'm done. I'm exhausted. I'm ready to be back home. I'm ready... I catch a glimpse of Jane standing behind the camera watching a playback.

She comes toward me and I sit up. But she detours to her purse one seat over and drops her wallet inside before returning back to the group. Her phone is lying on the seat between us, so I pick it up to drop in her purse. When I do, the background image lights up. I do a double take before bringing it closer and tapping the screen.

"What are you doing?" Jane stands in front of me with her hands on her hips.

I stand up, pissed, and flash the phone at her. "What are you doing with a picture of my friend on your phone as your fucking background image?"

"Your friend?"

"Yeah, my friend."

She laughs when she sees it. "What of it?"

Leaning closer, I lower my voice, but my tone remains rough with anger. "Danny?"

"Settle down." Crossing her arms, she admits, "I like Danny, but not like how you're so rudely insinuating."

"Then why do you have an image of him in his underwear on your phone?"

"It's not my phone. I thought it was from over there. I thought you were digging in my purse." She reaches inside her black bag and reveals her phone, an identical white and gold phone, waving it in front of me. "This one is mine." She presses the button, but I see regret color her expression as soon as she does.

A photo of us from college fills the screen, but is instantly gone. The front of her phone black again as she drops it in her purse."

I comment, "I always liked that picture."

She hesitates, but finally gives in as her shoulders relax. "Me too. It was a happier time."

Just as she starts walking away, I say, "We can have that again."

Turning back, she says, "Can we? Maybe I'm blind to what's happening, but I'm not seeing a way back from this. You've pretty much made sure of that."

"I'm not giving up yet."

"You gave up already."

"You'll see."

"Is that a threat or a promise?" She huffs in frustration. "Never mind. It doesn't matter just like I don't to you. The saddest part is that I'd rather have a threat full of passion than an empty promise. What does that say about me? What have I become?"

She's got this all wrong. It's not what she's become. It's what I've become. Disgust with myself sinks in and I have a feeling it's one that will live here for a while, if not forever. The only way to redeem myself is to prove her wrong. But for now, I have a phone to return. I track Ryan down in the corridor and hold the phone up. "Found your phone."

Relief washes over him. "Thank God."

While it's in the air, my thumb presses the button and the

screen lights up. A look of horror crosses his face, his eyes going wide, his mouth dropping open. "Noooooo!" He lunges for it.

"Calm down. Your secret's safe with me."

Snatching the phone away from me, he says, "I don't have a secret to hide." He takes a step forward to leave, but I block his path, and then step to the right to block him again.

Left.

Right.

"We can do this dance all day, Ryan. Or we can talk about this in private."

"There's nothing to talk about, Luke."

"You've got a picture of my best friend on your phone as the screensaver. First off, yuck for making me see him like that."

"That campaign is beautiful," he defends. "He's a stunning ma—Crap! I like pussy."

I just stare at him while he unravels before me. He clears his throat and says that again, "I like chicks, pussy, and all that jizz. I mean jazz."

"All that jazz?"

"You know, girls."

Chuckling, I try not to draw attention by laughing too hard. "You do not like girls. At least not sexually or you would never say 'All that jazz.' But why'd you hide it?"

He leans against the wall, defeat in his slouching shoulders. "I'm supposed to be a heartthrob. My manager told me I need broad appeal to make it in Hollywood."

"Who says you can't appeal to a large audience? You're in the business of acting. You'll be judged on acting."

"It doesn't work like that unfortunately." Pushing off the wall, he says, "I should get back, but I need to know that you won't sell me out."

"I won't. But I think you should live the life you were meant to live, not one anybody else wants you to live."

"Good advice. You following it?"

Busted. "It's easier to dole out than take, if you know what I mean."

"I know exactly what you mean."

Holding up the phone, his smile slides into place. "By the way, your best friend is hot and thanks for finding my phone. And, Luke? You should definitely take your own advice and steer clear of Jessica."

Reality dawns on me. "She knew, didn't she?"

"She wasn't happy about it. I'm sorry, man, but there's nothing worse than a woman scorned I've learned."

"You broke it off?"

He looks down at his phone, then to me. "It was easier to let her replace me. She felt better and I wasn't outed to the media."

Staring at him, I realize my role in their disaster of a relationship. "Easier on you."

"Like I said," Ryan says, "I'm sorry." An apologetic look is exchanged before he walks away.

Two lives—mine and Jane's—destroyed over *their* lies. *Fuck.*

Welcome to Hollywood.

CHAPTER 28

Jane

THE LAST SCENE of the movie is wrapped at two in the morning. Ian, the cinematographer, and the cameraman were on a flight to New York for exterior shots by five. The budget is so tight at this stage that everyone else was booked on flights back to LA instead.

I can't say I minded not getting the chance to say goodbye to Ian. That just relieved one burden. I still had twenty hanging over my head with Luke.

After checking out at eleven, I load my suitcases into the trunk. Two boxes are in the backseat, and I'm ready to go. Go where remains to be seen. Maybe I should go back to San Diego and visit my mom. Whether I do or not, either way, Southern California, here I come.

I start the engine just as Luke and Jessica exit the hotel lobby *together* and feed out onto the sidewalk ahead. His words, *"I need you to see through me more than ever,"* have played on rotation since he insisted yesterday. I don't see him clearly though. I don't see my Luke at all, in fact.

Even now, the Luke standing on the sidewalk is too slick, too put together, too Hollywood compared to the one in the photo on my phone. I miss that one, the one I fell so easily in love with. Jessica can have this Luke and he can have her. He can have fame, gossip rags, and limos. I never needed any of that. I'll just dream of a white picket fence and a husband who loves me endlessly instead.

Stealing one last glimpse of him before I drive away, my car idles at the stop sign. Jessica goes back inside and a whirl of commotion captivates me as Luke comes running down the street as fast as he can. My car door is opened, his bag thrown to the backseat, and he's hopping in before I have a chance to lock him out. "What are you doing? Get out of my car!"

"Go, Jane. Drive!" He pushes the button to lock the doors.

I press unlock, and demand, "No! Get. Out."

"Drive. Please, Jane." The locks go down again. "I'll fill you in, but you have to save me. She's crazy."

Unlock. I lean over to open the door and push him out. "And you're just now figuring that out?"

Looking back at the hotel, Jessica steps out and his seat leverages back as far as it will go. Slightly blocked by the box, he maneuvers lower toward the floorboard. That can't be comfortable for someone of his stature. The doors are locked again and now he begs with my face a mere inch from his most prized possession. "Please. Just get me out of here. I'll owe a forever."

...A forever.

A forever?

I sit straight up and clarify, "Forever?"

"Yes, that's what I said. I'll owe you forever."

"No, you said, I'll owe you *A* forever."

"What?"

"Huh?"

"Jane, drive."

Without thinking, I gun the gas and pull out between two cars that have left the perfect amount of space between them for me. When I drive past the front entrance of the Hotel San Jose, I wave to Jessica right over Luke's hidden head—with my middle finger. She returns the favor. *Whatever.*

Looking in my rearview mirror, I see her searching everywhere for Luke and the whole situation does kind of make me laugh. We're well out of her sight when he asks, "Can I sit up now?"

I make a wonky face. "Not yet. She still might be able to see you."

He nods, and I laugh on the inside. Mr. Gullible. It's kind of fun messing with him.

Finally, he peeks up, and looks around. While adjusting his seat upright and clicking his seatbelt into place, he says, "We're long gone."

I burst out laughing. "I got you good, sucker."

"I'll get you back."

"You owe me *A* forever already."

He rolls his eyes. "I didn't say *A* forever."

"You did too."

"That makes no sense. I said I'll owe you forever."

"You sure about that?" I ask, teasingly.

"Which part?"

"Forget it." I turn on my maps app and ask him, "Where am I dropping you off?"

"LA."

"Ohhhh, no. No." I shake my head. "You're not riding with me back to California."

"Why not?"

"Because *we* are not a couple. *We* are not even friends. Just a few days ago you had me crying in a corridor, so no. You are not riding with me. I'll drop you off at the airport."

"I'm sorry." The sincerity in his voice causes me to look over. His voice matches his expression. "If you only knew my reasons, you would understand."

"But I don't, so I don't understand how you can look at the person you claim you love and shatter their soul for entertainment. You've become a monster." I press a button on the maps app. "Take me to the nearest airport."

The car guides, "Austin Bergstrom Airport – Take the first left onto Highway 71."

"Come on, Janie."

"Don't call me that."

"Let's talk about this."

"There is nothing more to talk about. You're lucky I didn't kick your ass out of the car at your girlfriend's feet."

"She's not my girlfriend and you know it."

"I don't know anything about you or her and I don't want to. Thank God you kept the game on and turned up the other night so I didn't have to suffer through listening to you have, ick, sex with her."

"What are you talking about? I didn't have sex with anybody but you while in Austin."

I clap. "Bravo! What a guy you are. How'd you manage that?"

"I'm lost, Jane."

"Obviously."

"On the other night. I don't know what you're referring to."

"I heard you turn up the TV. I should thank you for not torturing me. It was actually considerate of you."

"*Shit.*" He drops his head into his hands. "You couldn't be more wrong."

Taking offense, I say, "*Me?* Wrong? You're in the wrong."

"Jane, please listen to me. I turned up the TV so you would

know I was there."

"Yes, I know. So I would know you were there with her."

"No, so you would know I was there if you wanted to talk."

Gripping the steering wheel, I ask, "Why would I want to do that?"

"It was wishful thinking on my part. Jessica wasn't with me. I was alone. I turned up the game so you would know I was there and not with her."

"I thought..." I pause to collect my thoughts, so many suddenly rampant.

"And I didn't think. I'm sorry."

Running my hands over the wheel nervously, I debate between what I should do and what I *kind of* want to do.

Luke leans his elbow on the door. "Let's take this road trip together, Jane."

"Why?"

"Two days. We can say everything we ever wanted to say or nothing at all. You have complete control. And I can make sure you're safe."

"I can take care of myself. I've done it for a long time now."

"Okay, you're right. You can take care of me then." He laughs lightly.

I don't. I roll my eyes instead. I'm crazy for even considering this, but I do consider it because I saw the way they interacted. There was no love shown between them and I didn't get a chance to see through him. Maybe this is my chance. "What if I want silence?"

"You got it. I'll sit here as quiet as a mouse."

"This is crazy. It's stupid on my part to even think we can be in the same car together, much less for two days."

"You always were an optimist."

I nod. "Stupidly so." Danny is right. I need to take responsibility for my part in our breakup. We *were* always a package deal. Is it truly too late for us? "That I just helped you escape proves I've lost my mind."

"You were always too good for me."

"You're not a bad person. I know you're not, Luke. I just don't understand what is going on with you, with us, or what happened."

"Give me this chance and I'll never ask for another. Let's take this road trip together and talk, really talk. I promise to tell you everything."

I care about him too much to let him go and not get any answers. I lay down my verbal weapons and set my anger aside because I need this just as much as he does. "You've got your ride home."

"But?"

"But it's my car, so it's my rules. My tunes. My route."

"Deal," he replies with a big ole grin that makes me want to punch him... or cuddle with him.

Damn him.

He rubs his hands together, and asks, "So when's the first stop?"

Feeling lighter already, I waggle my eyebrows, and smile. "Have you ever been to a Buc-ee's?"

NOT EVEN AN hour later, we reach the Beaver mecca in New Braunfels, Texas.

Luke comes around the aisle and is rubbing his temple. "I

don't understand what beaver nuggets are. Are they really beaver?"

I lean in for a closer look. "They look like a pancake of some sort. Maybe chicken? They're just keeping with their theme with that name. Surely they're not made of beaver?"

"Are you sure?"

"No, and I'm not going to test them either."

He follows me as I walk away. "Me neither. What are you going to eat?"

"I don't know. Maybe some chips? Though I'd kill for a salad right now. After all the junk I've eaten lately I really need a vegetable in my life."

"They had salads over there." We make a U-turn and go back, each grabbing one. "Are we eating here or on the road?"

"Road. It's only been an hour."

"Good point."

TWO STOPS FOR more food, coffee, gas, and over eight hours later, we're in El Paso. The sun set a while ago and it's dark outside. There aren't many buildings around, but I find a hotel that looks nice enough and pull into the parking lot. "Maybe we should get a room for the night, unless you want to take the wheel for a while." The minute I offer I realize it will be too tempting for him to resist. Cocky might be an understatement in describing the grin he's wearing. "Two rooms."

Disappointment befalls him, but he quickly recovers and wraps his arm around my shoulders. "We'll see about that." When he releases me, he opens the door to get out.

When I get out, I lean on the top of the car and say, "Luke, I need you to listen to me. We've been getting along so far, but I've not forgiven you. You are not forgiven—"

"Yet."

"Not ever. I've laughed with you a few times. That doesn't mean I've forgotten what happened. One moment you were saying you wish everyone knew about us and that when we get back to LA, you wanted me to move in with you. The next, you were telling me we're done. So, I can't just sweep that under the carpet. I really don't understand what is happening right now between us. All I can do is live in the here and now. If I deviate and let my mind wander back to how you gave me up, how you threw me away, for a fling with Jessica Pyles, my heart will break all over again. So I don't want to think about it. I don't want to feel anything deeper than surface." I walk toward reception, avoiding eye contact with him before my emotions get the better of me. The door is opened and I walk to the front desk with him close behind.

His sadness covers me, but I remain strong as I speak with the clerk. When the desk clerk is ready to charge for the rooms and incidentals, a black credit card slaps against the counter. "I'll get this and we'll only be needing one room. Thank you," Luke says, rocking back on his heels and eyeing me.

I don't want to make a scene, so I sigh. "Two beds."

Luke agrees. "Fine. Two beds."

The clerk looks like she's about to go grab popcorn to watch this play out. He really is too cute for his own good. I lean against the counter and say, "One room. Two beds please." I don't have to turn around to know he's gloating behind me. But I do because yeah, cuteness. He winks when I look back and I roll my eyes and laugh. "Happy?"

He confirms, "Very happy."

Once we're in the room, I open my suitcase and start reorganizing it.

Luke is on one of the beds with the remote in hand flicking through the limited TV stations. "What are you doing?" he asks.

I'm bent over straightening my shirts pile. "Folding my clothes. I was in a hurry and I hate a messy suitcase. It's been bugging me since we left Austin." I glance over at his duffle bag. "How do you squeeze everything in there?"

"I don't. I ship a lot of my stuff."

Sitting up, I look at him. "You do?"

"I do. It's easier. I just carry the necessities and a few outfits with me. I ship the rest."

I hate bloating his ego, but he deserves the credit. "Smart." My shoes are pressed together and added back into the left compartment, but a bag for one pair falls behind the case so I stretch for it.

"You have a really great ass, Janie."

Sitting straight up, I tuck and clench. I have no idea why. "You shouldn't say things like that to me when I'm mad at you."

"Maybe you won't stay mad if I give you compliments."

"So you only said it hoping I don't stay mad at you?"

"No, I didn't say that. That would be a bonus. I told you that you have a great ass because you do. No hidden message there. You can take it for full face value. You have a great ass."

I giggle. "You're ridiculous. You know that?"

"I'm well aware. Did you know your tits are spectac—"

"I think we should play the quiet game."

"Nah, I suck at that game."

"I know, but maybe we can try." I see my white bikini and grab it."

He laughs and starts turning through the channels again. "Hint taken."

"I think I'll go for a swim." Luke starts to stand, but I put my hands out. "Alone. You, Mr. Chatterbox, can watch TV."

"You don't want any company?" He actually looks sad.

I don't want to hurt his feelings but I need to sort through mine and I can't do that with him in the same space. I follow the length of his body and remember him spooning me back in Austin before... This is exactly why I need a few minutes to myself. Because I love being spooned by him too much and it clouds my more sensible side. "I won't be gone long."

He acquiesces, sitting back down, and aiming the remote at the flat screen again. "Okay."

I pass through the lobby restaurant and order a bottle of wine, then head to the pool. The water's warm and I have the pool to myself. It's easy to think clearly with Luke not here. He clouds my judgment and makes me forgive too quickly. Yet when I see him, my insides still twist from his betrayals. Two to be precise. Can I really keep the past in the past and give him this third chance he's so insistently vying for? Do I owe him this third chance? If I give him another one, will he one day need a fourth or fifth? Am I being a fool for wanting to relinquish the bitterness I carry or should I be holding on to it even tighter?

So many questions. Too many that I'll need answers to before I even think about getting in that car with him again. It's time to know where I stand with him.

The solitude is nice, my emotions eventually drowned by the wine. I'm not sure how long I've been down here but my fingers and toes have pruned. I cross the pool back to where I left my towel and wine. I take three swigs, and turn around to set the bottle down again when I see him. I've had just enough wine to allow me to hold his stare. And more than enough to let my anger go for the night and enjoy the view... I mean company. Damn, he looks good. "Luke Anders. You always were quite the sight. You were the crowning glory of our senior class. Popular and smart. *Most* Handsome. *Most* Charming. *Most* Likely to Succeed. *Most* Likely to Move to Hollywood. Couple *Most* Likely..." I don't finish the last one.

"Couple Most Likely to Get Married. We accepted that one together."

I burst out laughing. It's not funny at all, but the irony still gets me. "Well we sure showed them."

"Jane Lewis. Salutatorian. Prom Queen. Voted *Most* Beautiful and *Most* Creative. *Most* Likely to Become Famous."

"I don't feel very *most* these days." I grab the bottle again and take another long drink.

"You're most everything to me."

"You do realize you dumped me for an attention-whoring actress, right?"

He kneels down next to the wine, keeping his eyes on me. "We should talk about that."

"Do we have to ruin a perfectly good night? Look up, Luke. The sky is clear. The stars are out. It's beautiful."

"So beautiful," he replies and when I look back to him his eyes are still on me.

"You know, you keep saying such nice things to me and I'm gonna feel really shitty if I don't forgive you."

"That's the plan."

"Oh, I bet it is." I swim a few feet away from the edge, away from him. Looping back to the topic I'd rather avoid, but need to discuss, I say, "You're right. We should talk. Am I going to need another bottle for this?"

"I think one might be enough. Having a hangover on the road will suck."

"Fuck it." I laugh. "Everything's gone to hell and here we are in the middle of nowhere trying to piece a distant life back together. That's what you're wanting, right?"

He nods, but doesn't say anything.

I swim closer and rest my arms on the cement edge. Looking straight up at him, I ask, "Why do you want that? Why do you want me?"

"Because I love you."

Anger rushes my body as I push off and push away the pain he's causing. I swim to the other side of the pool. "All I ever wanted was my *Most Likely* life back, but you didn't want me, Luke. You made that clear when you broke up with me in that stairwell. We were over. So what are you doing?"

"Janie—"

I lower, wanting to escape but I don't. I stay. I stay because we need to talk this out. "It breaks my heart hearing you call me that as if your love for me is something I can still call mine." My head lowers, the first tear lost to the turquoise water.

I'm pulled into strong arms, the same arms that used to protect me. Holding my head to his chest, he kisses the top of it and says, "You are all that matters to me."

CHAPTER 29

Luke

THE WATER IS warm, but Jane's body is cold as we stand in the pool. I jumped in the pool to save her, not from drowning, but from the pain that was starting to overtake her. My clothes are soaked, but it doesn't matter.

She is all that matters.

"If I'm all that matters to you, what happened to us?" she asks, shivering.

I wrap my arms even tighter to warm her. Leaning down, we sink into the water and I whisper, "Life happened, but I love you. I love you, Jane. I love you."

Her body begins to float and she holds on to me, her arms wrapping around my neck. With her cheek against mine, she says, "I loved you with my whole being. I love you still, even when I shouldn't." Tucking her head down, she rests on my shoulder, letting me hold her as I pull her to shallower waters.

I don't care that we haven't talked or that my heart is breaking listening to hers break before me. I kiss her. On the cheek. And then I kiss her again on the jaw. And again on the chin. Holding her face, our eyes meet and I kiss her on the mouth, doing anything I can to quiet her cries, stop her tears, and heal her heart.

Anything for her. All for her.

But then...

She kisses me back and gives my soul a reprieve.

Her legs come around my waist and a fire begins to burn between us. Friction alights the kindling that remains of our hearts. She pulls back and whispers, "Say it again."

I don't have to guess. I know what she wants to hear, what she needs to hear, and what I foolishly led her to believe wasn't real. "I love you. I will always love you."

"Why did you hurt me? How could you look me in the eyes and ever let me think otherwise?"

"I was..." I look away ashamed to tell her the truth, even if my objective was meant well. "I had the best intentions. I tried to protect *you* by giving *her* what she wanted."

"And she wanted you?"

"She wanted everything."

"I don't understand what everything includes."

"I fucked you over when I left her today."

Lowering her feet to the bottom of the pool, she releases me, but I hold on to her waist, needing for us to do this, to talk about it. She asks, "What did you do?"

"I made a deal I can't go back on."

"With her? You made a deal with her?" She's not yelling, which gives me hope. "What kind of deal causes you to intentionally hurt the person you say you love?"

"The worst kind."

Jane raises her voice out of frustration. "Give me something to work with here, Luke. I'm trying. Again. For us. To put us back together, but you have to tell me what is going on."

Unsure of what to say that won't fuck this situation up even more, I say, "I've screwed up, Jane, but I'll fix it."

"We'll fix it together." Children's laughter fills the entrance to the pool and we both turn to see a family coming for a swim. Jane swims to the side with the wine and her towel, gets out, and says, "We should go back to the room."

I drag myself out of the water and grab my wallet and phone from where it was left. I'm a soaking mess as I follow her back to the room. "Do you mind if I take a quick shower to get clean and warm up?"

"Go ahead. I'll take one after." I want to join her, but I'm not brave enough to ask just like I'm too weak to ask for help. There's nothing she can do but worry and if I can take some of that away, she's better off for it.

After I'm dry, I walk into the room to get clean boxers, but stop when I see her in my bed. She's curled on her side facing my direction, and says, "If I forgive you, can you forgive me?"

"I already have."

She sits up and the white tank top she's wearing is distracting as her nipples peak beneath the thin fabric. "I want to hate you for the pain you caused. I want to, but I'm struggling to hold on to it because I want to forgive you more." I remain quiet as she continues, "I've found it's easier when you're not around, but when you are, I remember the good times we've had. We had so many that it feels like a lifetime of them clouding my judgment."

I put my boxers on and climb under the covers to sit right next to her. "We've spent a lifetime together and I don't want to throw it away."

"Then don't." She speaks again, this time her voice quieter. "I became who I am because of who you are. We grew up together. We became adults together. Our lives are so entwined—the good and the bad—all together as one." She releases a sigh. "I know what my life looks like without you in it. I've lived with you and without you... and I hate you because even now, after how you've hurt me," she sniffles, "my life is better with you in it."

After eight and a half hours in the car together and over 575 miles and we're finally back to where were before Jessica flipped the script. "Jane? What can I do to make this better?"

"Tell me you want me in your life just as I want you in mine. Be completely honest with me, like I have with you, and tell me what you're protecting me from. I need to know. I have that right."

So much. So many things I held back, not wanting to lose her or hurt her, but that's all I've done in the process. "Jessica said she'd walk off the movie if I didn't agree to this charade with her."

Her mouth falls open and she closes her eyes. When she opens them again, she asks, "She blackmailed you into dating her?"

Jessica asked for more than dating. "I screwed up when I hooked up with her. It was just once, and I was drunk."

"I could say so much to that, Luke, but I won't."

"I think you should. I think you should say whatever you need to say because I should have to hear it."

"Okay. Well, firstly, you gave me away to be with a psychotic bitch. I'm not trying to sound mean, but you're reaping what you sowed." She slides down into the bed and looks up at me. I follow her lead so we're at eye level. She says, "When we were apart I was looking for anything or anyone that could make my soul feel whole again. But you were busy breaking yours apart piece by piece to give to anyone who wanted it. What does that say about us, about me, and you?"

"Is that what you think?"

"I think you opened your arms and bed to anyone who batted their eyelashes at you, and sadly, I think you've given away some of the best parts of you and are lost without them."

"The only part of me I ever gave away was my heart, the

second I saw you across the quad, and I haven't seen it since." The late hour makes me defensive. "If you don't like who I am, why are you in *my* bed?"

"Your bed?" She flips the covers from her legs, and goes to her bed. "At least I'm not a whore like all the women you sleep with."

"That's real nice, Jane. Punishing me by sleeping over there? Let me ask you something while we're on the topic of sleeping with other people. What was that initial attraction that Lawrence wooed you with? Was it is his big bank account, bigger ego, or the weekend mansion in Malibu?"

She's a flurry in motion, grabbing her robe. "Fuck you."

Fast reflexes land me a corner and I tug, flipping her back onto the bed. I jump and am over her before she's back on her feet. I don't yell, not when I'm this close to perfection. "No, Jane, fuck you." I also don't take her shit.

Her hands pound to my chest and she pushes up while gritting her teeth. "I will fucking scream if you don't let me up."

"Scream, 'cause it's not happening until we get this all out."

"Get what out? That I sold my soul for financial security and you sold yours for pussy? Is that what you want to hear? Fine! You've heard it. Now let me up."

"No." I grab her flailing arms and pin them on either side of her body. Leaning very close to her, I say, "You and I both know that's not what it was about, and those things aren't what *we* are about."

Exasperated, she stops fighting and asks, "What are we about then? Tell me."

"Can't you see? It was never about anyone else for us. There will *never be* anyone else but us. You said it yourself. We are who we are because of the other. We're only half ourselves on our own. So when you say I gave away pieces of who I am, you need to hear my truth. I never had one girlfriend, not one constant without you. You're the only one I will ever truly love." I sit to the side of her and take a deep breath. She stays still and watches me. "If you don't love me anymore, I won't hate you. I couldn't if I tried, Janie. If there's not one ounce of hope left for us in your heart, if you need to move on to find happiness with someone else, then I will open that door and support you." Her lips are parted, distractingly so, but she sits up and my heart drops. She doesn't say anything. "I will always love you, Jane Lewis, like I have my whole life, but I would rather you be happy than hurting. I never want to see you cry again, especially not over me."

Another minute ticks by before she says, "If this was a romance movie, or even a book, I'd kiss you for your confession. But it's not, and this isn't a fairy tale, Luke." Her voice is somber, not the one I recognize as hers, not the one I hear when I recall the love she once professed. "This is real life. This is our life, the only one we're guaranteed and we've lost the plot."

The last of my hope dissipates, the adrenaline draining from my body. I stand, but she reaches for me, taking me by the hand, and I stop. "We can still live a great story."

Looking down at the only woman I've ever felt passion for, the only one who made my days worth waking up for, the only woman I will ever spend the rest of my life with if given the chance, I whisper, "We already have. A lifetime of words, CHAPTERs, and stories written between us, about us, recording our love and lives."

"Our story's not over. It's just a new CHAPTER." She stands up and her hands slide up my neck until she's cradling my face. "*This* is the part when you turn the page and kiss me, because I do love you, Luke. I do and always will."

Fuck. Yes.

I kiss her, not missing this opportunity and not willing to ever take this woman for granted again.

CHAPTER 30

WINE.

Vino.

Sauvignon blanc.

Whatever name I want to call it, I blame it.

I also blame Luke's face—unshaven jaw, bedroom eyes, that bottom lip when he bites it, and that *too charming for his own good* smile. Why does he have to look so sexy, ruggedly so right now, even sleeping?

My body is melty, liquefied from our make-up sex last night. I peel my arm away, not wanting to move, but wanting to shower more. Slowly, I slip out of bed and tiptoe into the bathroom, shutting the door as quietly as I can so I don't wake him. I turn on the shower and turn back to look at myself in the mirror.

Oh good God!

Frantically patting my hair down, I forgot I went to bed with it wet... well, more than my hair was wet, but I digress.

I step into the shower, hoping to detangle my messy hair when the door clicks open. Luke peeks around the curtain and says, "Good morning." His voice is husky and pure sex.

Not that it isn't any other time, but damn. I turn around and give him a good look at my body while soaking my hair. "Join me."

"I intend to."

Shampoo bubbles cover my hair when he steps in looking rejuvenated and smelling minty fresh. He tries to kiss me, but I turn my mouth. "Morning breath."

"I just brushed."

"I didn't have that option."

"Don't worry about it. You've never had bad morning breath. Now let me kiss you." His hands roam over my slippery body convincing me. "You taste amazing."

I blush. And brace myself as he gets to his knees before me, and looks up. "Hold on, baby."

That look in his eyes easily makes my knees go weak, but my arms tighten, holding me steady. Lifting my leg up, he sets it on his shoulder and kisses a trail up my thigh. When his lips meet mine, he says, "You are so goddamn gorgeous, Jane." Then he kisses me there until an orgasm shivers through my limbs.

My willpower with this man is annihilated again when he turns me around. The front of his body presses against my back, and he reaches around and squeezes my breasts. Whispering in my ear, he warms me as his breath pebbles my skin, "Tell me how much you want me. Tell me how much you've missed the feel of my cock inside you, your soul submitting to mine in every way imaginable. Tell me where you want me. Here?" He slides his hand down my stomach and fingers my clit. His other hand glides over the curve of my waist to the middle of my back and lower where he dips just barely inside, teasing, my most forbidden place. "Or here?"

My breaths become gasps as I scramble to make sense of the erogenous vibrations he elicits from my body. "I've never—"

"You've never what, baby?" My heart races as he finishes my sentence. "You've never had anyone touch you like this? You've never had anyone take you here before?" The pressure mounts as the tip becomes more.

I don't pull away. I'm unmoving, so still, looking at the tiles for answers of what I've allowed this man to do that I would never allow anyone else.

"Janie? Are you all right?"

"I'm good." My pitch is uneven.

I can hear the amusement in his voice when he asks, "Are you sure?"

"I'm sure."

Kissing my neck, he keeps his voice low and his lips close to my ear. "You're doing so good, baby. Do you like that? Do you like me touching you there?"

Closing my eyes, the lines of my sexual desires blur, the pleasure of new sensations turning me on, or maybe it's just the man that's doing it. Dropping my head back, I murmur, "I like... that."

"So do I." He presses a little more, but the stretch is not painful. "I like making you feel good, excited." With his other hand still on my clit, he says, "Even without the water, your pussy is so slick, so wet. Is that for me? Are you wet for me, baby?"

His words are intoxicating, his voice a drug to my body, an addiction I can't break. "Only for you," I manage to reply.

I'm rewarded with faster, direct pressure between my legs and the slightest in the back. "I like owning you in ways that you didn't even know you wanted to be touched, to be *fucked*." He pauses. "Do you know much restraint I'm heeding? Do you know how much I want to fuck you right now? Fuck you until you're on your knees, begging for more and then collapsing into a heap of satisfaction at the bottom of this shower." Running his nose along the curve of my neck, he inhales. "But the time's not right. You're not ready for me and I don't have," he says carefully, "anything to help ease things in." Licking the nape of my neck, he makes sure to keep circling below.

My fingers splay against the tile, my orgasm building.

"Janie," he whispers again, my name becoming a melody on his tongue. "I want you to tell me what you want me to do. Tell me how I can please you."

"More."

"More of what?"

I never thought I'd want this. I never thought it would feel this way. "Both." My voice is decidedly clear.

"I'll go slow, but I'll make you feel so good. Just feel, baby."

My body joins the slow rhythm his talented fingers have set. Each time I move back, he moves forward just enough for me to feel the burn that accompanies a new stretch. It doesn't hurt. He makes me want more—faster and harder, but I don't press him, trusting his pace.

Just as he rubs my swollen clit, he fills me from behind and touches me in ways I didn't know could feel impossibly dirty and equally amazing. "Oh God. Luke." My head falls gently forward joining my hands on the tile as he surrounds me inside and out, filling my soul and body, ecstasy breaking me into a million little pieces. Universe shattering. Mind-blowing. Darkness filled with bright bursts. A strong arm holds me up while I fall apart.

My body stammers to life, reality coming back into focus, the rushing sound of water returning to my ears. Kisses are placed on the back of my shoulder with purpose.

A possession being owned.

A territory being marked.

A soul being reclaimed.

I release a breath and sigh in satisfaction just as he promised.

Turning around slowly I keep my body weighted against the tile for support, and look up at him. Luke with the dark lashes, hair just over his silvery-blue eyes. His body is one of a gentle giant, not threatening despite the well-defined muscles. Droplets of water run over his skin and the way he's looking at me... *Love.* That is what love looks like. That is what *my* love looks like.

Pushing off, I'm in his arms, his protective arms. It's easy to forget any pain and forgive any lies he told to shield me from whatever is out there trying to hurt me. We have time to talk. We have hours left on the road to figure out where to go from here. Our destiny mapped out long before we met, the journey leading us straight back to each other.

"I forgive you."

He chuckles. "It was that good, huh?"

"You were that good, but this isn't about sex."

"You sure?" he asks, tilting his head to the side. "Because you have this look in your eyes that makes me think you're just on a sex high."

I laugh. "It was good. Really good, but we can't speak of it again."

"Why?"

"Because it's embarrassing."

"Why is it embarrassing?" With his eyebrows scrunched together, he looks genuinely confused.

My eyes go wide and I frown. "You know. It was so... naughty." I immediately hide my face from his by tucking myself against him under the water. Thank goodness for endless hot water at hotels.

His arms wrap around me and he kisses my head. "We didn't do anything naughty or embarrassing. We did what felt good." Tilting my chin up to look at him, he says, "Don't ever be embarrassed about anything we do together. There's not a right or wrong, good or evil. Everything we do is based in love. It comes from somewhere perfect where no one and nothing else matters. Only us. Okay?"

I nod and return to hug him as tight as I can, letting him do the same to me.

WE REACH THE Arizona border an hour after leaving El Paso. The scenery is one we're used to at this stage in the road trip, but it's still a beautiful day. A healed heart allows you to see the hope on the horizon much more clearly.

With his eyes on the road, he says, "That was quite the orgasm you had back there."

Blood rushes to my cheeks and they heat, so I smack his arm. "I said do not speak of it again, Luke."

"I'm just saying, that was *quite* the orgasm."

"Oh my God. Are you gonna keep saying that?"

"I'm kind of proud."

"Kind of?"

Reaching over the console, he takes my hand in his, weaving his fingers with mine. He brings my hand to his mouth and kisses it several times, then says, "More than kind of. Like supremely, phenomenally proud. Not only did I give it to you, but I own it forever."

The back of my head hits the seat as I laugh. "Look, I'll give you that one—"

"And every one after," he interjects.

Surprised by this claim he's staked, I ask, "You want to own all of my... all of them?"

"*Them?* You can't say it, can you?"

"I can say it."

"Say it, Janie."

It doesn't escape me that he hasn't released my hand. The warmth of our connection is felt deep inside my belly. But with that word being thrown around so casually, I giggle nervously.

He kisses my hand again. "You're cute. I like that words like *orgasm* make you blush. What about anal?"

"Luke! No. Do not talk about this." Throwing my hoodie over my head, I pull the strings as tight as they can go and hide.

His laughter fills the car. "Fine. I won't talk about how incredibly sexy you were when I touched you *there* and then you squirmed when I touched you *elsewhere*. And that the, you know, was not only good for you, but amazing for me."

"Okay. Okay. You're being silly. You can say the words. I can say the words."

"Then say them," he pushes, challenging me.

I take the hoodie off to prove I'm braver than he thinks. "Anal. Pussy. Orgasm. Happy?"

"Wow, you don't hold back. You have a dirty mouth, Ms. Lewis."

I roll my eyes. "You're impossible."

"Impossible to resist."

"My eyes actually hurt from the epic rolling."

"I know of something else epic we can talk about."

"Pull over!"

"What?" Luke's face is frantic. "I wasn't serious."

"No. No. Not that. That," I say, pointing toward the yellow gas stop.

When he finally sees it up ahead, he asks, "You want to find out what *The Thing* is?"

Excitedly, I ask, "You mean you don't?"

With fake enthusiasm, he says, "Hell yeah, I do."

Laughing, I look at the rest stop museum. "You don't mind? For real?"

"I'm all for an adventure."

An hour later, we're back in the car. I look at him not sure what to think about that place. I'm still trying to process what we just saw when I say, "That was weirder than I expected."

"They accomplished their mission. I'm gonna have nightmares." He takes my hand and holds it, resting our bond on his thigh. I can tell he's going to be holding it for the long haul, and I couldn't be happier.

We've made many mistakes, but helping him escape Austin, *her*, and our past was not one of them. I was wrong to ever think we were a mistake when he's the best parts of my life. Lifting his hand up, I kiss it, and receive the best smile in the world in exchange.

That boy is so in love.

He's lucky because I am too.

CHAPTER 31

Luke

JANE'S BEEN ASLEEP for over an hour. We're somewhere between Tucson and Kingman, so more than halfway. Taking our late start into account, we won't make it back to LA before early morning. I haven't seen a pit stop since she fell asleep and I need to take a piss. Deciding I can't wait any longer, I pull off the road and take the path less traveled until the highway is in the distance and we're hidden to any cars driving by.

Maybe I'll get some winks in too. I cut the engine and take the keys, locking her protectively inside, and trek off. When I return to the car, the headlights are on and she's sitting on the hood. "I was looking for you."

"I had to piss."

When I come closer, she lies back. "Have you seen this?"

"What?" I ask, maneuvering between her legs while running my hands up and down her outer thighs.

"Look up."

I do. "The stars?"

"The universe, Luke. It's like we're the only two people in the universe. It's spectacular."

313

"We need to get out of the city more."

"Lie next to me."

Silently, I climb up on the hood and lie down. I take her hand and we stare up at the vast desert sky together. The silence doesn't last long because I ask, "Wanna have sex?"

"Sure do."

She can't see it right now, but my smile grows to mass proportions, matching other parts of my body.

Cool desert air.

Dark, star-filled night.

Headlights creating shadows of our union.

The most beautiful woman in the world.

The smooth, silver surface of her BMW.

My hard against her soft.

I have the best fucking life.

Thirty minutes later, we're tangled in the backseat. Her eyes are closed, her breathing even.

This.

This right here is perfection.

I want this all the time.

I want this woman in my arms forever. "Janie?" I whisper and rub her arm. "Jane?"

When she stirs, she yawns. "Hmm?"

"Marry me."

Her body goes rigid, and then pops up, pressing her palms to my chest. Looking down on me, she checks to make sure she heard me right. "What did you say?"

"I don't have a ring and I'm not down on one knee, but I want to marry you more than I've wanted anything in my life. Let's get married and live *A* forever together."

"You want *A* forever with me?" she asks, smiling.

Stroking her hair back and tucking some strands behind her

ear, I reply, "I do owe you one, after all." I sit up, readjusting her on my lap. Her arms are around my neck, and I lower mine to her hips. "Will you marry me?"

The moonlight shining in the back window reflects in her teary eyes. Reaching up, I run my thumbs gently under each, catching the tears before they streak her pretty face. "Don't cry, baby."

"They're happy tears."

"So that's a yes?"

Nodding, her smile grows wider, and she throws herself against me. "Yes, so much yes." Her head drops to my shoulder and her body shakes in my arms.

I kiss the back of her head. "I love you."

She lifts up and kisses me even harder. "I love you, too."

"I have always loved you and I always will. I promise I will never hurt you again and I will always fight for us." With her complete attention, I turn serious, needing her to understand the depth of my love for her. "I will never let you walk away again because I never want to be apart from you again."

"I'm sorry. I'm sorry I left. I'm sorry I didn't stay and fight for us. I'm sorry I was blind to what we had and..." She looks away, shame filling her features when she squeezes her eyes closed. "I'm sorry I was with someone else." I caress her cheek with her eyes on mine. She says, "And I'm sorry I let you sleep with half of LA."

When she smirks, I do too, and correct her, "I wouldn't say half."

"A good quarter?"

"Maybe one-eighth. It is a city of seven million. I'm good, but I don't think even my ego can make that claim."

A playful punch to my chests pushes me back. I lie down again. It's horribly uncomfortable back here, but being with her like this is so worth the seatbelt latch stabbing me in the back.

Jane shifts and moves on top of me. Lifting up, I kiss her cheek. "Love you."

With a knitted brow, she asks, "What about Jessica?"

"I've been thinking about that situation."

"Situation indeed."

I angle toward her. "Most likely she won't do any voiceover work or retakes since I took off. I need you to be prepared for the possibility of this movie never being finished."

"But there's a contract in place?"

"She knows the loopholes."

"She'll ruin the movie because she can't be with you? That's why you agreed to her deal, to make sure the movie is finished?"

I nod.

"You broke my heart to save my movie." The pieces fall into place and she rests her hand over my pounding heart. "You did it for me, didn't you?" The quiet stretches between us. "Tell me, Luke. Please."

"I know the contract you signed. If the movie doesn't get sold, you lose the backend payout. I can't sell a movie if it doesn't get made."

"Silly man. Why would you ever think I would rather have a paycheck than you?"

"It felt selfish to sacrifice money I know you need because I wanted to be with you."

"I want to be with you, Luke." She laughs lightly. "I just agreed to marry you. The money is meaningless without happiness."

Looking out the window, I confess, "You don't know how to ask for help. You lived in a motel for months. I don't know your current financial situation, but I can guess. So maybe I was being selfish, but I couldn't stand the thought of you not able to support yourself."

"Look at me, Luke." When I do, she says, "It was a hotel, not a motel. Secondly, I'd find a way. I always do. I have a second script in the hands of several directors and producers. Hell, I bought my own car. I'm not doing too shabby. So what you did, I want to be mad at you for doing that to us, but now I know. I know you did it for me and I just can't be mad at you for that." She kisses my temple. "Anyway, how can I be upset when we're together and getting married?"

"You can't." I waggle my eyebrows. "See how that works."

Her laughter fills the car. Best sound ever. "So the movie's gone is what you're saying?"

"I'm pretty sure she'll check herself into rehab to shelve the project."

"It's a beautiful film. It'll be sad that no one will see it. As much as Ian was annoying, he's a brilliant director with a great vision."

"I knew he'd do this movie justice."

"Is there anything we can do to finish it? I'll give back the money I've already been paid if that helps."

"You're not going to pay for it. I've already taken two hits on my paycheck for it. Ian even took a twenty K pay cut to help."

"Why did I not know about any of this?"

"Because it's my job to worry about, not yours. I still failed you though."

Her fingers run through my hair, her nails lightly scratching my scalp. I close my eyes not wanting her to see the guilt I carry.

"You did not fail me. Listen to me," she says. I open my eyes to see her determined ones locked on mine. "You did more than you should have. Ultimately we can't control if the movie is completed. We can only do our best. Jessica is going to do what Jessica wants to do like she always does. We'll do what we have to."

"When we get back, I'm going to make some calls. I'm not giving up yet. But I'm going to have to talk to her."

"How do you feel about talking to her as a married man? I want to seal this deal sooner than later."

"I could be tempted."

"Just us."

Just making sure she's thinking through everything thoroughly, I say, "You know our families will be upset. Our friends might be offended."

Her head goes to my chest and tilts down, all her energy escaping as she molds to me. "I'm willing to take the chance."

Jane

I WATCH THE sunrise from the back seat of my car wrapped in Luke's arms. It was the best sight I've ever seen. Both of them. I feel at peace for the first time in years. I'm finally on the right path again. I can feel it in my bones.

As I doodle on his chest, he smiles, his inner peace shining in his eyes when they open. "Good morning."

"The best morning."

He takes my left hand and kisses my ring finger. "We're engaged."

"Yes, we are," I reply happily.

"Let's get married in Vegas."

"No dress. No guests, No—"

"Nothing but us."

I kiss him on the lips. "Sounds divine."

"I don't think I can feel my legs."

Looking over his tall frame, I slide to the side and open the back door to get out. Luke works his way out and stretches toward the sky. "Remind me to get you an SUV. This car is a killer on the body."

"I didn't buy it thinking I'd be sleeping in it."

"True. I'll be back." I watch as he walks thirty yards or so, but turn and tend to my own business, hiding behind the car.

Meeting back at the car, I say, "I cannot wait to get to Vegas to shower. I feel gross." I take him by the front of the shirt and sway a little, flirting. "I can't wait to be back in yours as well."

Taking me by the waist, he says, "About my shower—"

Ten minutes later, I'm sitting behind the wheel of my car with Luke in the passenger's seat, and I'm completely flabbergasted. "You traded your house to get my movie made?"

"It wasn't a trade. It was collateral."

"I don't understand why you would do that."

"I felt confident in the movie, and because you always dreamed of having one of your scripts made into a film. It was a risk, but how could I not help make that dream come true?"

My heart patters, my feelings about to burst from my chest. He did everything for me. He was showing his love when I was too blind to see. I'm glad I know so I can spend my life showing him. I know inside that we would have found our way back to each other, but I still have to give him a hard time. He took a chance on something he shouldn't have. "There's a difference between a calculated risk and a gamble."

"I don't see it that way."

"You trading your dream for mine was a gamble and now you might lose your home."

"It's a house, not a home." Taking my hand in his, he says, "You're the only home I know and want. Owning that house was amazing, but there will be others. Your movie—I read the first page and knew that was the one. Your story is magic, the script captivating from the first page."

"I've never heard of someone putting their home up as collateral to get a movie made."

"I called in favors from friends. We needed the money. We had an investor pull out after production started. If we can get it through editing, I can sell it."

"You've done so much for me and for this film. How will I ever be able to repay you?"

"You don't have to repay me. We're getting married. That's my dream come true."

His hand warms my cheek, the feeling flooding my veins. "I can't have you lose your house because of me."

"It's not because of you. It's because of Jessica. So I'll pay her a visit after we get back and sort it out."

"You sound confident." I'm not happy about this situation he's in, especially because it all balances on the whim of an overly dramatic starlet. "What happens if she won't agree to finish the film?"

"You're worried, but I'm not. I have money saved. I'll make more. This will work out. I promise you, Jane."

"I believe you. I believe *in* you."

"I never thought I'd hear you say that again."

"You've more than earned my trust. I'm sorry I lost faith."

He kisses me gently. "This is where we are, so we'll deal with it, and homeless or not, we're together."

"That is way more important than any movie."

CHAPTER 32

Luke

11:46 A.M.

Jane bolts upright. "Today's the day."

She was sleeping one minute and the next she was wide-awake from her nap. My heart is racing, startled by her. "Today?"

"Today is our wedding day."

"It is. We'll be in Vegas soon."

She looks over at me and pokes me in the abs. Her smile brightening the morning like it does my life. "Hit the gas, Granny. I need time to shop."

"I thought you agreed to no dress?" I pretend pout. Naked sounded perfect to me.

"I'm a woman. I need a dress. The perfect dress, so stop wasting time. Giddy up, cowboy. Time to hit the trail."

She's too damn cute to resist. "I love you. You know that?"

Through a fit of giggles, she says, "I love you, Luke Anders. I always have and I always will. Today is our day."

"I owe you a ring."

"Make it big."

Bringing her hand to my hardening cock, I say, "I always do," not referring to jewelry at all.

"And just like that—you proved it's not just bigger in Texas, but in Arizona too."

Giving her my flirtiest wink, I ask, "How about we test it in Nevada?"

THE SUN IS setting. The garden is filled with blooming flowers. Nothing is natural in this oasis in the desert, but surrounded by the plants and being secluded, I almost forgot we're in Vegas.

Standing here, I'm not nervous.

I'm ready.

I'm pretty sure I've waited for this my whole life, despite the lapse in judgment I once showed.

Soft music begins to play and the most beautiful sight I've ever seen—Jane Lewis, my soon-to-be wife—walking straight to me. Her white dress flows gently behind her, her hair loose with a halo of pale pink flowers taming the top of her wild blond hair.

Twenty feet until contact...

Ethereal.

My sweet angel.

"You're a very lucky man, Mr. Anders."

Fifteen feet until contact...

The girl has become a woman and the only one I want to

spend my life with. "I am. The luckiest."

Contact...

When she reaches me, she smiles, but there's something more in her eyes—an inner peace that comes with comfort. "Hi."

"Hello, beautiful."

The Justice says something, but I can't seem to take my attention away from Jane to listen. Words of love linger around us and I watch as her eyes move from him to me. The lightest of pink colors her cheeks, and I smile. Mission accomplished.

She nudges me and I can tell she hates all the attention I'm giving her.

"Luke," the Justice says, "you may share your vows."

Taking Jane's hands in mine, I speak, my heart attaching to hers, to reside ever more. "It was always going to be us. You were my past, you are my present, you will be my future. Jane, you are light when life is dark. You are my smooth night when my day has been rough. You are the first girl I ever loved and the last woman I ever will. You are beauty to me always, and always I vow to be your light, your smooth, and your everything to make life beautiful. I will love you for the rest of my life and if we're granted more time together, I will love you longer."

I place the ring I gave her years earlier back on her hand.

The Justice looks to Jane and says, "Jane?"

She glances down, the moment seeming to overwhelm her. I squeeze her hand just enough to remind her she's not alone. Never alone again. Bringing her hand to my mouth, I kiss it, causing her to look into my eyes. A soft smile appears, and she says, "Your courage brought us together. Your strength kept our hearts bonded even when we were apart. Your faith believed when there seemed to be none. You, Luke Anders, were brave for us both. I'm honored to be here today, fortunate to be facing the only man I've ever loved, and grateful I get to wake up to you every day of forever. I love you, Luke. I always have and I always will."

"Well, let's not waste any time. By the state of Nevada, I now pronounce you husband and wife." The Justice nods his head toward Jane. "Go on, son. Kiss your wife."

With one hand on her lower back and one on her neck, I bring her closer and kiss her. I'd normally censor myself, but not today. Not ever with her. She deserves all my love and to feel every ounce of passion I have for her.

When our lips part, we both inhale, and then smile. Our foreheads are pressed together, and I whisper, "I love you."

"I love you, too."

"Come on, I want to go love on you in private."

She giggles as we walk back to the wedding office. The coordinator has us sign the certificate, and escorts us to the private elevators.

No gawkers.

Nobody intrudes on the first few minutes of our life together as husband and wife. I'd give her the world if I could, but even more, I'll spend every dollar I have to make her happy. Jane's eyes go wide and her smile grows when the doors open into the suite.

"Luke, it's beautiful. I can only imagine how much you spent."

"I may be homeless but I'm not broke. Anyway, I love your smile."

She lifts up and kisses me on the cheek. "You'll see it because I get to wake up to you every morning for the rest of our lives."

It's funny how things change... how we change as we reach different stages of our lives. The phrase "rest of our lives" scared me before. It sat unsettled in my stomach a few years back. But then I got a large dose of what life was without this gorgeous blonde standing in front of the windows overlooking the Las Vegas Strip and that scared me more.

She turns around. "You can see almost the entire strip from here." A look centers in her eyes and her lids grow heavy. Leaning against the glass, she licks her lips. "I want you to make love to me."

"Happily."

"Then I want to do dirty things against this window."

My smirk slides into place, and I chuckle. "Your request is my command, my beautiful wife." *Fuck, I love saying that.*

"LIE ON ME."

I chuckle, and move on top of her. "Tell me if I'm too heavy."

"I like your weight on me." She breathes out harder than I like, but I remain. "You comfort me."

Balancing some of my weight on my forearms so she doesn't notice, I kiss her.

"There's this line in the movie that speaks of being sex drunk. I understand what that means now."

"You wrote the lines," I point out. "You didn't understand it before?"

"Not like this."

"Tell me what it's like."

"It's deep, engrained in my muscles and bones. A feeling that encompasses so much happiness that it can't be explained in simpler terms."

"It's euphoric and enrapturing."

"Exhilarating and pure bliss. I never want to forget this feeling."

I kiss a line down the center of her chest and even lower. "I'll never let you." And then I go farther, my lips finding that special place that will turn euphoria into orgasmic.

I'M TEMPTED TO smoke, and I've never smoked. Sitting in the plush chair by the window, I have all of Vegas outside lighting up the night sky. But I can't keep my eyes off the sleeping beauty in front of me.

Jane's hair spans the pillow, covering it. The crown of pink flowers she wore to get married is off to the side. She debated sleeping with it on, loving it so much. I gravitate toward her bare skin under the scent of floral, unable to resist my bride.

She sleeps so soundly and I find pride in the fact that I've worn her out. I'm glad she's able to rest since I don't know what tomorrow holds. So much weighs on this meeting with Jessica. Looking at my angel sleeping I can easily admit that I don't want to lose this, this innocence that fills this suite, the trust that fills her smile when she looks at me.

I sit down, the bed dipping, but she doesn't stir. I touch her cheek and run the tip of my finger over her bottom lip. I nearly lost my heart, but now she's mine forever. "I will spend every day loving you," I whisper, then place one more kiss to her forehead before climbing in behind her and holding her to me.

CHAPTER 33

Luke

LOS ANGELES AFTER hours is not my favorite scene. Not anymore. It's funny how a place I've called home for so many years now seems foreign. I could say Austin changed my mind, but I'd be lying.

It's the woman.

Jane woke me up in the middle of the night and told me she'd spent enough time in hotel rooms. She was ready to go home. *Home.* We packed our stuff and drove home together. I pull into my drive and park. Jane yawns as we sit in the car a moment longer just shy of five a.m. She looks at me and I voice what I think we're both feeling. "We're going to be okay. Everything will work out how it's supposed to."

"It will," she replies, trying to sound convincing for me or herself, or maybe both.

"C'mon, let's go inside."

I grab her two suitcases and walk her to the door. After I unlock it, I push it open and let her go first. Watching as she walks in, I'm familiar with the setup after living here almost two years, but having her here, here as my wife energizes the air.

Although the moonlight is on the verge of disappearing for the day, it remains bright for us, flooding the living room in greeting.

This was never supposed to be a forever house for me. It was always just a place for a moment. But with Jane's aura, her soul filling the space, it feels more like a place I could call home permanently. I place the luggage just inside the door and go back for my bag and her boxes. When I return, she must not hear me because she's standing in the middle of the living room just where I left her. I take the opportunity to look at her, really look at her. She's too beautiful for the space, my stuff not fitting for her presence. I never committed to buying anything of quality after she left. Maybe my subconscious knew all along—life was always meant to be spent with her.

Setting the boxes down, I make a bigger production than necessary to give her the heads-up that I'm here. She turns, and says, "I'm not sure what to do, how to fit into your life. I've been here, but it feels foreign."

"We have a lifetime to figure out how to do this again." I shut the door and set the alarm. "Are you hungry? I can't imagine I have much since I've been gone for a month, but I might have something in the freezer I can cook for you or find some snacks in the pantry."

"I'm not hungry. Thank you."

It's too stiff in here, too formal. I try to break the ice. "I want to shower before bed. Wanna join me?"

"Yes."

Hoping the plan Danny helped me put together is in place, I lead her upstairs, and then stay back when she enters the bedroom. Jane's mouth drops open. A gasp. A hand covering her sweet lips. When she looks back at me, she asks, "How did you do this?"

"I have my ways of making magic happen when inspired, and

you have inspired me, Mrs. Anders."

I join her. She leans her back to my chest and tilts her head to the side while admiring the room reminiscent to the tree house I once wooed her in. "I love when you call me that."

I kiss her neck, taking full advantage of tasting the delicate skin and then whispering in her ear, "I love calling you Mrs. Anders. It's like calling you mine forever."

Blankets and pillows cover the area in front of the fire. Flowers fill vases all around. "Just like the tree house. How did you remember?"

"I never forgot." I walk from one candle to the next lighting them while Jane sits down on the pallet with awe in her eyes.

"You have candles this time."

"We're not sixteen anymore. No parents to hide from." My grin is evidence of something more to come.

"You're a sexy romantic, my sweet husband."

"You deserve romance and," I say, sitting down next to her and kissing her, "I want that picket fence and to have lots of babies with you."

Her breath staggers. "You do?"

"I do."

"Luke..." She drops her head down, and leans against my shoulder. "I never knew life could feel this good. I never thought I'd feel love so deeply. You've made my dreams come true."

"They're in the making, but we'll make them all come true." Lifting her chin up, I kiss her lips again. "And I feel the same for you."

DANNY POINTS AT the biggest diamond on the dark blue velvet tray. "You have to go for that one. It's princess cut, which women love. It's just over two carats. Great clarity. That's the one to seal the deal."

"The deal is already sealed."

He scoffs. "I can't believe you just blurted it out in the back seat of her car. That was the sex talking, my friend."

"It was morning... the sun was rising in the desert—Fine! It was the sex."

He laughs. "Great sex will do that to you. I know this firsthand." Patting me on the back, he adds, "I'm happy for you. This has been a long time coming, so buy the ring."

"Are you sure?"

"Yes, Jane was very specific in the text she sent me." He holds his phone up and shows me.

After glancing at the text, I ask the sales rep, "Do you giftwrap?"

"YOU GOT ME a present?" Jane asks.

"I did. Open it."

She pulls the tissue from the bag and pulls out the box. Her eyes meet mine and I know what she's thinking, my plan totally working. "Aren't you supposed to, oh I don't know, present it to me or something?"

"Open it, Janie."

She unwraps the little velvet box. Glancing back at me briefly, her smile is contagious. I watch in anticipation as she opens the hinged box. The surprise is seen in her expression, her eyebrows raised. Another quick glimpse to me before returning to the box and reading aloud, "Do you have plans this Friday?"

Her memory serves her as well as mine. Twelve years after the first time I asked her that question, I ask her again, hoping for the same outcome. "I'm free," she replies.

"Not for long."

I drop down on one knee with the ring between my fingers. "The first time I ever saw you, I stumbled into my locker. My best friend teased me endlessly. Five years later, he was tripping over himself to get you to date him before I had the chance. But you saw through him. You also saw through me and right into my heart." Taking her hand, I find joy in the expression in her eyes as she looks down at me. "Through all the years we've spent loving each other—whether we were together or not, we both knew it would always come back to us."

I slip the ring on her finger as she whispers, "Oh, Luke."

"I want to spend the rest of my life with you. If you give me your hand in marriage, Jane Anders, I will spend my life giving you *A* forever I owe you."

"You were the most handsome boy I had ever seen, cuter than any movie star and swoonier than any boy band. I saw you coming from twenty feet away, but my heart wasn't prepared for you. You stole it and my eternal love that day in eleventh grade. Now here you are stealing my breath away along with it." She pulls me to my feet. Looking up at me, she says, "You had your answer that day, but just in case, yes, Luke Anders. You didn't just steal my heart, you became it, so yes." Giggles fill the room. "So that's how you would have done it if you had a ring?"

"You deserved the full marriage proposal package. Did you like it?"

"I loved it just like this ring. It's gorgeous." She holds her hand up in the air and admires the ring on her finger. I spend the time admiring her instead.

I wake up before her in the morning, grab something from my closet that makes me laugh, and work my way to the spare bedroom. After adding to the box, I pull out one of many from our life before that I've stored in here. Setting it down on the coffee table in the living room, I push the black fabric and peek inside at the rest of the contents.

Before I have a chance to pull anything out, Jane comes down the stairs holding my phone. "Blaise keeps texting you."

"I'm sorry. Did it wake you?"

"It's okay. What are you doing up already?" She comes down the steps and sits next to me.

I take the phone and set it down next to the box. "I wanted to show you some of our stuff. I kept most of it."

"You did?" she asks surprised. Reaching inside she pulls out a CD. "Foo Fighters."

We chuckle. "That was your copy."

"I can't believe you kept it all these years."

"It's a great album."

"It is. Do you have a CD player?"

"I have it downloaded." I pick up the remote and turn on the sound system.

With a smile on her face, she digs in to find what else I've kept. Pulling out the black turtleneck, she laughs. "So I finally get my sweater back?"

"Yeah, I'm not going to need it anytime soon," I joke.

It comes flying and hits me in the face. "Keep it. It looked good on you."

My phone buzzes so I check the texts from Blaise, wondering why he's even awake at this hour much less texting me. When I open the text there's a link. I press it and am taken to an article on a gossip page.

Jessica Pyles Enters Rehab - Round Two.

"Shit!"

Jane sits back. "What is it?"

I grab the remote and turn on the TV. It's headline news on every major station—Jessica Pyles enters rehab.

I'm dressed and out the door in fifteen minutes. I leave Jane with the box of memories and rush to talk to Jessica about the stunt she just pulled.

Malibu Cliffs – Oceanside, is a retreat for the rich and famous under the guise of a rehabilitation center that will help them kick their substance addiction. I've never known anyone to come out of there and actually stop using his or her drug of choice though. But it's great at giving celebs time out of the camera's eye.

Jessica's games never cease to astonish me. I'm listed as a guest on her list at the facility. Of course I am. I'm let right in and directed to her room. I knock lightly to not disturb her neighbors though I'm curious who they might be.

When she answers I almost don't recognize her. Her face is clean of makeup and she's dressed in sweat pants and a baggy T-shirt. She looks younger than her twenty-five years and prettier without that mask she wears. "I've been expecting you."

She opens the door wide, but I take a step back. "Want to go for a walk outside?"

"Sure. I can use some fresh air." She reaches for a hand mirror, but stops herself before picking it up. Instead she grabs her room key and slips the chain over her head, wearing it as a necklace.

We walk side by side silently down the hall and through a living room. She leads me out a back door and past the pool, and then ten steps down to the beach. I say, "It's a nice day to be at the beach."

"I like this place better than my own home. That room in there has my stuff. My eight-thousand square foot house was decorated by a professional for looks, not for me."

"Redecorate."

"You make it sound so easy."

"You're in control of your life, Jessica."

"Am I? 'Cause I don't think I've been in control of my life in years... or maybe not ever." She bends and picks up a tiny seashell. When she stands up, she gives it to me. "This is hard for me, Luke. I know you won't believe anything I say, and you have that right, but I still need to say it."

Her vulnerabilities are what make her a great actress. I want to put down my guard, but I'm not sure I should yet. "I'm here. Let's talk."

"The night we met was one of the lowest of my life." We start walking again. "But there you were. You were funny and charming. You treated me like you cared." She doesn't wait for a response she knows is not coming. "I was disillusioned. My therapist reminded me that just because I want something does not mean I will always get it. You may have been one of those things." She peers over. "I got fired that day from a movie I fought to get for two years."

The anger I had for her starts to diffuse. It's hard to hate someone who has struggled so much. She's been used and abused by the Hollywood system and then is left alone to function as if it's wine and roses and awards every day. "Why?"

"I've had problems with pills. The night we met, I drank too much and I was on an anti-depressant. You made me feel something for the first time in a long time. I got attached. I hadn't had anyone treat me like a human in a long time."

"How do they treat you?"

"Like a cash cow or an ATM."

"I'm sorry."

She stops and smiles. "Stop being nice. I basically destroyed your life and you're apologizing to me? Don't do that. I owe you. I'm sorry for everything. I'm especially sorry about you and Jane. She was actually very nice."

"She is. Too nice when it comes to me."

"I know you've spent time with her. You made up I hope."

"We did."

She laughs and playfully nudges me. "I had no doubt you'd be able to talk your way back into her life."

"I should tell you that we have a long history together. I loved her before and I love her now."

Jessica looks surprised but smiles. "I should have picked up on that. You two had a connection I thought was unbreakable."

"You proved us wrong."

"I'm ashamed of my behavior. I felt desperate for someone to love me, and you were there, *again*, in my life, maybe in my path is a better word. I just thought if you could give me a chance, spend time with me, that we could reconnect and maybe be more than we were."

I'm about to speak, but she says, "Don't say it. Please don't say it. I know. I know our connection was only physical so I don't need to dissect it." She inhales deeply, then exhales with a sigh. "You were just so damn resistant all along, and then seeing how you treated Jane, how you looked at her... I don't know. It fueled me somehow to make you as miserable as me.

"Then we would be miserable together?"

"Something like that. It was hateful, not just to you but to Jane, and to myself. I would have rather had a few weeks with someone than come back here to no one. It's pathetic. I really am sorry." She stops talking and starts walking again. "You know, I caught Ryan cheating on me. He was never interested in me. Not really. Not how I wanted. Pain makes people do desperate things."

"It wasn't about you."

"When I found him having sex with a man, I kind of figured it wasn't. We made a great couple for tabloids though. It was hard to face the reality of losing your boyfriend and your fame at the same time. What do you call someone used to protect someone's sexuality?"

"A beard."

A burst of laughter escapes her. "I was his beard." She picks up another seashell but holds on to it this time. "How can I make amends, Luke?"

This almost seems too easy, but sincerity is heard and that's what makes this time different than before. "I need you to finish this movie."

"I can do that. I'm not a prisoner here. I just needed a timeout from my life, or more honesty, from the people in my life. So tell me where to be and I'll be there."

"Really?"

"Yep, and no strings attached. The movie is great. I'd like to see it through."

"Thank you." We turn around and start back. "I wasn't wrong in casting you, Jessica. You portrayed Jude exactly how I saw her. Jane felt that, even after everything we put her through."

"Thanks for saying that. I need to apologize to her personally. Does she like edible arrangements?"

I laugh. "She loves them, especially the ones with pineapple and chocolate." The laughter ends when I see the pain she carries written in her eyes just beyond the joy of the moment. "You have a heart, Jessica, so don't let managers and publicists, or the press define your character or write your ending. I know Hollywood sells our souls to the devil for a headline and a fee, but your life is more than one picture or sound bite."

"You're right. It wasn't just my life that was broken. It was my soul. I was sick of feeling used by everybody. I grasped on to something that wasn't real, but for brief moments, I didn't feel so alone."

"There are more movies in you and there are good people out there. Don't lose hope and don't give yourself away so easily. You deserve a good life. Make sure you allow yourself to have one."

"Thanks, Luke, and I really am sorry." We turn back.

This is the woman who won Hollywood over before she was ten. She can get back there, back to being healthy mentally, despite where she's currently residing. "Thanks." Walking up the steps, I say, "You deserve better than you think you do."

"You think?"

"I know." I stop her and hug her, surprising her again. Surprising myself. I would have never thought I would embrace her by choice, but here I am and it feels good to have things settled with her. Her arms hang at her sides for a few moments and then she hugs me back. I say, "This feels like the war between us might be over."

We step apart, but the comfort between us remains. "I genuinely hope so. I don't want to waste anymore time being upset, unhappy, or angry. I need peace for a while."

"I hope you find it. I really do."

"I appreciate that. I have more amends to make, but I'm a work in progress, so one day at a time."

"You never were the patient type."

"It's only been three days. Damn. Give a girl a chance." She laughs. Her smile is genuine. Her eyes are clear. It's good to see this side of her. "I'm working on that too." Once we reach the door, I stay and she steps inside. "Email me when you need me."

"I will. Thanks again."

"And good luck with Jane."

Just the mention of her name makes me smile. "I think it will work out."

EPILOGUE

Luke

IT ONLY SEEMED right to be back in Austin. The city has rolled out the red carpet and I watch as Jane walks ahead talking to the small press line, posing for photos, and beaming with pride.

She deserves this. All of it.

Early reviewers agree—the movie is a masterfully woven film with beautiful scenery and touching scenes. Jessica has become the darling of the indie film circuit and Ryan got offered the next superhero series. His fascination with Danny remains a secret, except to Danny, because yeah, I couldn't not tease Danny about the phone incident. Danny laughed. Nothing really fazes him anymore when it comes to people who like to ogle him.

With Ian, there was a forced greeting for the cameras when we arrived, but now he stands a few feet away from me. Sour grapes over Jane? *Douche.* He has four projects lined up. He should be happy. This film is getting great recognition and so is he. So I don't know why he seems to be holding a grudge, but he's keeping his distance. That's fine. The film is done and we both can move on. Luckily for me, I get to move on with Jane. I pop my imaginary collar.

Danny steps back from the carpet, and tucks his hands into his pockets. "You should be proud."

I don't know if he's referring to the movie or the woman at the center of attention, but I answer for the latter, "I am." Turning, I shake his hand. Jane looks back at us, and smiles. We owe Danny a lot. I don't know what he told Jane, but his words worked magic for both of us. I'm sure he told her something similar to what he told me—stop being an ass and fight for love—though I'm sure he didn't call her an ass like he did me. The best part of my best friend is he never judges, at least not harshly. I laugh. He just calls it like he sees it. "Thanks for being here."

"I didn't get invited to the wedding," he ribs. "So I figured this was the next best thing." He chuckles.

"No one was invited, except that beautiful woman right there."

While watching Jane, he says, "Remember that time you came over all crazy crying about the woman who got away?"

"I was not crying and did you fly out here just to tease me?"

"Fine. You were whining, and teasing you is always fun, but no."

"Whatever. What's your point?" I ask smiling.

"Look at you guys now." When I look at him, his smile is genuine, not joking at all on his face. He adds, "I had to come see how the story ends."

"You see us in LA all the time."

"Not you guys. I always knew you guys would make it." Nodding toward the theater, he says, "The movie."

"Spoiler alert: the good guy wins."

"As he should, my friend. As he should." He pats me on the back. "Are you going inside?"

"In a minute."

"You've always managed to avoid the red carpet." He says, "I don't think that's going to be possible anymore."

Jane waves me over, but before I go, I reply, "No, I don't think it will be." I join my wife, wrapping my arm around her waist. Leaning down, I kiss her on top of the head. "You're stunning, Mrs. Anders."

"You're charming, Mr. Lewis."

Watching the press call her name, vying for her attention, I say, "I believe it's you who's charming."

When we finally make it inside the theater, she pulls me off to the side. Embracing me wholeheartedly, she whispers, "We did it."

"We did. We make a good team."

"We make the best team."

"Speaking of, how do you feel about working on your next movie together?"

"Are we speaking hypothetically or it's a done deal already?"

Smiling, I look around the room before returning my gaze to her. "It's kind of a done deal already."

She returns a smile. "When do we start?"

"Right after we find a place to live."

"Your friend Robert is a real asshole for cashing in on the house as collateral. The movie was only one week late."

Cupping her jaw gently, I tilt her face to mine. "I never cared about that house anyway. It was only a place to sleep until I found my home again."

"And have you found it?"

"It wasn't lost. My home was right here all along." I kiss her, first with everyone else around us in mind. Then I kiss her how I want to, not caring one bit about an audience or public displays of affection offending anyone. "Now that I found you again, I'm never letting you go."

"Promise?"

"Promise. Things are settling down with the movie so we can

start looking for the house you always dreamed about."

"I'm rethinking things."

"Oh yeah?"

"Now I'm leaning toward a gated property to keep the girls out. I've seen the Instagram comments on your posts. You've developed quite the fan base in the last year."

"Ha! Rest assured, my dear Janie, I only have eyes for you."

"Only eyes? A few other things come to mind that you have."

"You know the way to my heart."

"It's not your heart I was referring to."

"How about skipping this premiere and heading back to the hotel early?"

"Come on. Let's go make our appearance so we can get back to fu... back to make love."

Jane still has trouble using the dirty words out of bed, *but in bed*, she's become quite the dirty talker.

But she did learn from the master. I squeeze her ass, and tease, "I can't wait to... *make love to you.*"

My lips capture hers and I kiss the sweet taste of the words away, swallowing them and each breath she gives me.

We met when we were kids. I fell in love with her when we were only sixteen. The woman in my arms is still that same girl, but so much more—she's my guiding compass and the other half of my forever. The two years we spent apart have become just blips in the scheme of eternity. As much as I wish I could erase them, we needed them to get to this point, to live our great story.

When we part, I open my eyes and look right into hers. A sweet smile, my favorite sight in the world appears, and she says, "Thank you for giving me *A* forever."

Following my heart paid off professionally and personally.

This movie brought us back together physically and cemented us together forever emotionally. We made a hit movie and I got the girl. "Best move I ever made."

The End

Keep reading for excerpts
from *Sweet Talk and The Resistance* by S. L. Scott.

Sweet TALK

S.L. SCOTT

DANNY WESTON

Height 6'3"

Waist 33.5"

Chest 41.5"

Suit 42 L

Inseam 34"

Shoes 13

Eyes Light Brown

Hair Medium Brown

Editorial Note: Most sought after male model in the industry. Hollywood calling. Best known for his body—underwear modeling, fitness, runway, print ads. Needs extra room in the inseam. Easy to work with.

Flirts. *A lot.*

Follows through. *Even more.*

CHAPTER 1

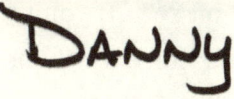

DANNY

"GOD, I WANT you, Danny," Simone whispers into my ear. She licks just below it before sliding down over my jaw and biting me.

My hold tightens around her hips, steadying her. I should have seen the bite coming. They all do it, assuming they have to do something extreme to be sexy, to get my attention. Like every other time it happens, I pull back and run my fingers into her hair at the nape of her neck, then tighten my grip.

She gasps and digs her nails into my shoulders while the innocence she's trying to portray in her eyes fails under the skepticism found in mine. Our bodies are pressed together and heated, the fan not strong enough to cool us down.

Tilting her head back, I kiss the divot at the bottom of her neck, then lick from base to chin, taking my sweet time. Simone's back arches, pushing her breasts against my chest and she moans in pleasure.

"That is so hot. Keep it up," a voice intrudes.

Simone sighs, irritated, and pulls away. I turn to the photographer's assistant standing at the edge of the set just as Simone reveals her frustration by leaning back and swinging her leg over me to stand up. Leisurely, my gaze slides up her lean legs. She's taller than most women and the heels she's wearing add another good five inches. Appreciating her physique, I smile and recline back with my hands behind my head while watching her adjust the strings at her hips. Her head snaps up and her eyes narrow on the assistant off set. "If you want us to *keep it up*, then shut up next time." She storms off, her shoes clacking loudly against the gray cement floor.

Knowing an angry model needs time, I sit up, and ask, "How much time do we have?"

Everyone is well aware that the mood has changed on the set. Worry creases the assistant's brow when he answers, "I think, umm... five or ten minutes."

The guy's anxiety rolls like waves crashing around me. Feeling bad for him, I reassure, "Don't worry about her. She'll be fine. Just give her a few minutes to cool down."

"Thanks." He smiles though it's weak. "Are you doing all right?"

I smile genuinely while standing up. "Yeah, I'm good. Thanks." When I start to walk, the knit boxer briefs I'm wearing for the shoot tighten uncomfortably, so I stop to adjust. They're a size too small, so I grab my cock and shift. "Actually, I could use a larger size. These are cutting off my blood circulation down here."

Before the assistant can respond, two women suddenly appear from the darkened side of the large loft. A cute, petite blonde offers, "Let me take a look. Maybe I can help." She's bold, not shy like I would have guessed from the librarian look she's chosen.

The other lady—taller with some gray strands running through her dark hair—seems new to the modeling world. She stands there staring below my waist, and by the way she's ogling me, I'm guessing she might be new to naked men in general. Maybe she's never worked on an underwear campaign before. She clears her throat and finds her voice. "They fit around the waist so I can add more material, if you'd like? But I'll need them to do that."

Bypassing the first offer, I accept the second. This is my job. I'm a pro, a model, and used to being naked in front of strangers, so I drop my drawers. I bend down to get them, and when I stand back up I'm greeted with two mouths hanging wide open. "Ladies, you're gonna make me feel shy," I tease. *I'm not shy at all.*

Lifting their chins until both their mouths are closed, I chuckle as they continue to stare unabashedly. The taller woman says, "Oh you have nothing to be shy about."

"Absolutely nothing," the blonde adds insistently.

"Thanks," I reply, my voice it's usual charm. I hand the boxers to the lady and walk off set to grab my robe. When I slip it on, Becs from wardrobe approaches and says, "I can add some room in there for you. I'll have them back in ten minutes."

"I already gave them to the seamstress."

"What seamstress?" she asks.

"The one over there." When I turn to the set, they've vanished. Scanning the loft from one side to the other, the two women are nowhere to be found. "She was just here with a blonde lady." Perplexed I scan again. "I have no idea where they went."

Becs rolls her eyes, shakes her head, and sighs loudly. "Good grief. Not again." Turning on her heels, she yells out, "Security. We've had another breach." With her eyes narrowed on my waist, she adds, "Tighten the belt. You don't want anyone selling a photo of your frank 'n beans to the highest bidder." Her mood lightening, she smiles and shrugs. "Or maybe you do. I'll get your next wardrobe change—"

I laugh but point to my privates. "Extra roomy."

Becs waves her hand in the air while walking off. "Yeah. Yeah. I got it."

I make my way to craft services where I find Simone eating what appears to be her third Snickers by the wrappers littering the table next to her. "Do they have fruit today?"

She speaks with a full mouth. "Down at the other end of the table."

The photographer's assistant announces, "Five minutes."

Eyeing her as she shoves the last of the candy bar into her mouth, then makes what I guess is the universal sign for vomiting with her finger, I try to hold my lecture for another time. When she disappears down the hall, I understand the stress she's under. The modeling world is competitive. One pound over the other girl and a model can lose the job. Simone desires to keep working, to stay on top of her game, but I've never found gaunt sexy. When the camera adds ten pounds, I get why they do it.

Grabbing an apple, I eat while walking back to the set. Becs is there and hands me a pair of customized black briefs, extra fabric finely sewn into the middle. "Let's get these on and see how they look."

I pull them on under my robe before untying the belt to let her take a closer look. She bends and eyes my dick, making me smile. When she stands up, she clasps her hands together. "Yep, looks good."

"Thanks," I reply smugly. *What?* I'm human. "You're not so bad yourself."

Becs's attempts at playing it cool are undermined when her cheeks pink. "I don't date models, Danny."

"Who said anything about dating?" I wink playfully.

"That's *exactly* why I don't date models," she replies, not able to hide the cute blush. Watching her walk away, I notice the pep in her step and hope I made her day a little more enjoyable.

After three-pointing the apple core into the wastebasket, I mentally celebrate scoring with a self-satisfied smile while returning to the bed and waiting.

When Simone returns, she sits next to me. Her body is tense, her hands have a slight shake, and she's paler than before. As makeup rushes over and starts touching her up, I whisper, "You okay?"

She stares down at the floor while they apply more powder. "Fine."

I've known Simone for a few years. Not quite twenty-four, her career is going strong, but sometimes she's moody. I think it's the constant lack of food, so I offer, "Wanna grab a bite after?"

The makeup lady leaves and Simone looks up. Touching my cheeks, she says, "You're always so sweet, but you know I don't really eat, much less out at restaurants in front of others."

"I was hoping you'd break your rule for me."

She smiles, and sounds hopeful. "I'll break mine if you break yours. Why won't you sleep with models?"

"I've slept with many models."

"Then why haven't we ever slept together?"

With a cocked eyebrow, I point out, "You were too young." Taking advantage of young girls isn't my thing. A lot of male models go through these girls with abandon, but by the time I hit my upper twenties, there was no appeal in dating a girl barely legal to drink just because she was hot. Now that I'm in my early thirties, I don't want a girl. I want a woman. "And as you pointed out, we're friends."

A gleam enters her eyes when she laughs, leaning back on the bed. "That's right. You were the first to ever turn me down. The only, in fact. Why are you so good, Danny Weston, when being bad is so much more fun?"

Memories flash through my mind like a spinning Rolodex. "I've done a lot of bad, and nothing worked out. Maybe a little good will suit me better."

Maneuvering her body, she wraps her legs around me, and drags her nails very lightly down my chest, careful to not leave a mark. Moving close enough to kiss, she whispers, "Well, if good doesn't work out for you, come find me."

The photographer shows up and without noticing the intimacy, starts filling us in on the angles he wants to complete the shoot. "We're not going to use the bra in this set. You two will be blurred in the background, but I want side breast and shadows. Covered nipples, but that's all I want hidden. Intimate, desire, like in pre-sex. Give me foreplay. I want kissing but no tongues showing. Simone, his scent is driving you wild and you can't keep your hands off him." He turns around and shouts, "Prepare for the close-up of the cologne bottle. Whoever has been spraying my studio with that shit is fired."

When he leaves, Simone's lips quirk into mischievousness, ignoring his rant. "Foreplay. Pre-sex." She reaches around, her breasts pushed out, and unclasps her bra. Bare before me, she directs her eyes on mine. "We can do that, right, Danny?"

Keeping my eyes on hers, I don't deviate lower. "I think I'll manage."

From the sidelines, the photographer instructs, "Touch her breasts." When I do, he adds, "So hot. Keep going."

Two hours later, Simone lies on the bed, her gaze is lowered, her body exposed without care. I try to stand, but she stops me by grabbing my waistband and tugging. "Maybe I'll see you again soon."

"Yeah, maybe we'll be booked together again. See you around, Simone."

"See you around."

Fifteen minutes later, I walk out pulling my T-shirt down over my head. "Hey, Becs, I'm late meeting the guys. Got anything I can snag from the shoot to wear?"

"I've spoiled you in the past, but you know you're not supposed to take anything. We have to turn in our expenses and return all of the clothes." She takes a navy blue button-down shirt from the rack and hands it to me. "So don't get caught. Wear it like you already own it."

I tug the shirt off and swiftly slip on the other. "Thanks." I kiss her on the cheek as I button up.

Good-humoredly, she shoves me away. "Go, handsome. Get out of here and have some fun."

Shining my million-dollar smile, I reply, "You're the best."

"Always the charmer, Danny."

"You know it."

"I think I see you on a shoot next week anyway, so go."

"If you miss me in the meantime, you've got my number." While heading for the door, I waggle my eyebrows.

"Oh, I have your number all right. Go, ya big flirt. Go find someone who will fall for that line."

"What about these abs and my sparkling personality?" I rub my abs to tease. "No love for these?"

With her hand on her hip, she continues to play along. "Those abs are easy to fall for."

"Ouch. Nothing for my personality?"

"Go!"

Laughing, I sneak out before I get caught with the shirt. "See you next week."

"See you then, playboy."

Checking the time, it's just gone ten. I jog to my Jeep, which is parked down the block. Dinner with the friends has long passed. I'll catch hell for missing it... like I always do. I rev the engine to life and take off so I can catch them for the second half of tonight's festivities.

Tempted to drive home instead, I turn on the radio to

mentally amp up for the night. I have a feeling tonight will be the same as Wednesday and the Sunday before that. I'm ready for something different, a change in scenery, a change in company, something or someone that makes me excited to go out.

Silver lining: every night is a new opportunity, every day, a second chance to make things right.

I arrive at the club and toss my keys to the valet, who gives me a welcoming nod. "Dan Man."

"When did you start working here, James?"

"Last week. The hotel canned me for taking a lady for a ride in a Ferrari."

"Did you at least score points with the lady?"

The valet smiles and purses his lips. "You know it."

"Way to go, but I imagine the owner of the Ferrari wasn't too happy."

"He was more upset about me borrowing his car than his wife blowing me. My boss didn't like that either."

Bursting out laughing, I fist bump him. "Oh shit. Well, take care of the Jeep. No joyrides."

"You got it, bro." Just before he hops in, he calls to me, "Good luck and have fun."

"I intend to."

The Resistance

S. L. SCOTT

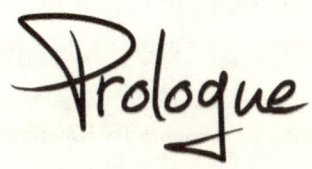

Prologue

I'M A FUCKING fool.

I'm not even sure how I got into this mess, but I know I need to get myself out of it. I look down at the hand on my thigh inching up higher and my stomach rolls. Squeezing out from between the tight confines of the third row in this van, a girl on each side wanting a piece of me, I fall over the seat into the cargo area and move away from their astonished stares. They're speaking German and I don't know what the fuck they're saying, but I've been in this type of situation enough to know how it will end, if I let it.

Everything has changed... or sometime around my last birthday I changed.

I didn't invite these chicks. Dex did. He'll fuck'em all before the night's through and the bad part is, they'll let him. Thinking they're special, that they'll be the one to tame him. They'll let him do what he wants just to be close to him.

Beyond this set up being predictable at this point, it's really fucking old or I am, probably both. I ignore their taps on my shoulder and them calling my name. I ignore everything to do with them and focus on my phone.

On the inside, I'm freaking the fuck out that I'm sitting in the cargo hold of a huge van in Germany with attractive girls willing to do anything I want them to, but I prefer to look at a photo of a little blonde with hazel eyes. Freaking the fuck out might be an understatement.

I'm a player or was, supposed to be, maybe still am. I don't keep score or anything like that, but I've slept with plenty of women, sometimes more than one at a time. I used to blame my lifestyle, but more recently, I realized I'm the common denominator in the bad relationships I've had.

The car comes to a stop and the driver rushes around to the back to let me out. I stumble while climbing out, and hurry inside away from the sound of my name being called. The girls will be upset when they realize I'm not staying to play, but Dex will be thrilled—more pussy for him.

Cory hops out from the front, and follows me. "Wait up," he says, jogging to catch up.

When we reach the elevators, we look back. Dex is helping the girls out of the vehicle one-by-one. With a cigarette hanging from the corner of his mouth, he's sloppy, already drunk. He never lacks for female companionship. By the way he acts, I don't see the appeal, but I don't think that's why they're hooking up with him anyway.

Cory looks at me and nods once. "What's up? What happened back there?"

The elevator doors open and we step in, pushing the button for our floor. "Over it. Over it all."

"The girl from Vegas?"

"She's not from Vegas, but yeah, I've kind of been thinking about her."

When the brass doors reopen, we walk down the hall to our rooms. Cory and I don't do small talk. We've been friends for years, best friends if I think about it.

"Maybe you should call her," he suggests as we open our doors.

"Maybe I will."

"Night."

"Night," I mumble and shut the door behind me.

1

Holliday Hughes

"Comfort zones are like women. You have to try a few before you find the one that feels right." ~*Johnny Outlaw*

THAT DAMN LIME and coconut song has been playing on a loop in my head, driving me nuts for hours. I make a mental note: Fire Tracy in the morning for subjecting me to that song twenty-thousand times yesterday. She called it inspirational. I call it torture after the first two times.

Rolling over, I look at the time. 4:36 a.m. I have four hours before I need to be on the road. This may be a business trip, but it will still be good to get away for a few days. I need a break. I've been in a bad mood lately. The spa and I have a date I'm really looking forward to. The thought alone relaxes me. I close my eyes and try to get a few more hours of sleep before I need to leave for Las Vegas.

I get two tops.

I tighten my robe at the neck. Just as I open my front door to get the paper, I hear a male voice say, "Hello?"

Peeking through the crack, I hold the door protectively in front of me just in case I need to close and lock it quickly. "Hi."

"I'm your new neighbor. I just moved in last week. I'm Danny."

Curious, I slowly stick my head out to get a better look at this Danny. Strands of my sandy blonde hair fall in front of my eyes, so I tuck it behind my ear and get an eyeful. To my surprise, he's quite handsome and has a big smile. "Oh, um," I say, dragging my hand down the back of my hair, hoping to tame the wild strands. "Hi. I'm Holli. Welcome to the neighborhood."

He nods toward the paper on the bottom of the shared Spanish tiled steps that lead to our townhomes. "I'll get your paper since you're not dressed."

"Thanks." I watch him. He looks like he just got back from a run or workout—a little sweaty, but not gross, in that sexy kind of way. Or maybe Danny's just sexy. He's well built with short, brown hair and when he bends over, I notice his strong legs and arms. Well-defined muscles lead to—*Oh my God!* Not just my face, but my entire body heats from embarrassment. Hoping he doesn't say anything about me checking him out, I turn away and start picking at a piece of peeling stucco near my house number. "Um, so are you settled in, liking your place?"

His chuckling confirms I was busted. But he's a gentleman, so he acts as if it didn't happen. "I like the neighborhood. The place is great," he says. "I like all the space, especially the patio. I'm thinking of having a party to break it in, maybe in a few weeks after I finish unpacking." He hands me the paper and takes two steps back. "You should stop by."

Nodding, I look into his eyes. I think they're brown, lighter than mine, more honey-colored. His offer is friendly, not a come on, which is good since we're neighbors now. "Thanks for the invitation."

Walking back to his door, he steals one more glimpse over his shoulder. "Have a great day. See you around, Holli."

"Yeah, see you around."

I shut the door, paper in hand, and fall against the wood with a smile on my face. One of my golden rules is not to date where I sleep, but I still appreciate that my new hottie neighbor is easy on the eyes. He might know it, but he doesn't seem arrogant.

I lock the door and get ready to leave.

Los Angeles is hot, smoggy, and grey at this hour and I have a feeling it won't be much different a few hours from now. I close the patio door and lock it, double checking for safety. After pulling the drapes closed, I take one last look around to make sure I'm not forgetting anything. I text Tracy and let her know I'm leaving. She doesn't reply, but I'm not surprised. Her boyfriend proposed last night after six years of dating. Being the kind boss and friend I am, I let her out of this trip, so she could spend the weekend with their families to celebrate the engagement.

There are selfish reasons as well for letting her off the hook. I really don't think I can handle hours of sitting in the car with her as she reads bridal magazines and plans every detail of her big day. After too many dud dates in the last couple of months, I'm not in the right frame of mind to plan her happily ever after.

With my garment bag in one hand and my suitcase in the other, I click the button, disarming my car's alarm as I walk to my parking space. I've lived here a couple of years. I wanted a place near the beach that also had space for my office, and I was fortunate enough to find both in this townhome.

A meme I created went viral three years ago this month. Who knew a snarky-mouthed fruit would be the way I make my fortune. I took it though and ran with the brand, building it into a small empire I named Limelight. The company is lean and I keep my costs under control. My fortune has grown by a few million in the last year alone.

I back out onto the street and take the scenic route, one block up to the beach. Driving slowly along with my windows down, I let the sound of the waves and the smell of the ocean center me. At the first stoplight, I take one deep salty air breath, roll the window back up, and leave for Vegas.

An hour into the trip, Tracy calls. I answer, but before I have a chance to speak, she asks, "Can I please tell you all about it again?" Happy laughter punctuates her question.

"Of course. Tell me everything." I'll indulge her wedding fantasies because that's what friends do... and because I have four hours to kill in the car. Listening to her takes my mind off the time and the miles stretching ahead of me as she relives every last detail of the proposal. Fortunately for me, she skims over the engagement sex.

Her excitement is contagious and because I've known her and her fiancé, Adam, for so many years, my happiness exudes. "Congratulations again."

"Thank you for letting me stay home this weekend. You'll be great and don't be nervous. It's just a rah-rah go get'em presentation and cocktail party. The rest of the time is all yours."

"You know how much I hate these kinds of events."

"You don't have to prove anything to anyone. Your company's success speaks for itself."

"Thanks. I'll try to remember that."

"Drive safely and squeeze in some fun."

I laugh. "You know I'll try. Bye." When we hang up, I turn on some music and let the miles drift behind me.

After a stop for gas half-way and a coffee later, I enter the glistening city in the desert. Pulling up to my hotel, I valet my car and take my own luggage to my room after checking in. I like this hotel because of the amenities, but the men aren't bad to look at either—a little edgy, a lot sexy—lucky for this single girl.

I spend a couple of hours checking emails and work on a proposal before I realize the time and need to get ready for the night. It's Vegas, so I mix business with some sexy. I pull on a black fitted skirt that hits mid-thigh, an emerald green silk camisole with spaghetti straps, and a short black jacket. I slip on my favorite new pair of stilettos and after one last check of my makeup and hair, I head out.

The meet and greet isn't long, but I slip out at one point to use the restroom. As I'm walking back toward the ballroom, I'm drawn to a man standing with a group of people nearby. His magnetism captures me. He might just be the best looking man I've ever seen—tall, dark hair, strong jaw leading me up to seductive eyes aimed at me. His head tilts and for a split second in time, everyone else disappears. I break the connection by looking away, everything feeling too intense in the moment. When he laughs, I add that to his ongoing list of great attributes.

When I pass, the feel of his gaze landing heavy on my backside warms my body. With my hand on the door, I pause, wanting to look back so badly. I resist the urge, open the door, and return to the party. The presentation portion of the evening is interesting. Despite that, my thoughts repeatedly drift back to the hot guy in the corridor—fitted jeans, black shirt, leather wristband. *Damn I'm weak to a leather wristband.*

I'm mentally brought back to the presentation when my company is recognized as one to watch. The acknowledgement is nice, and it feels good to be among my peers.

The dinner becomes more of a party as everyone wanders around instead of taking their seats. I'm not hungry and need to psych myself up to mingle. Tracy is awesome in these types of situations. Me, not so much.

The ballroom is dimly lit, I'm guessing to set the ambiance, but since this is business, I can do without the romance. I head straight for the bar just like everyone else—one big cattle call to the liquor to make the rest of the night a little more bearable.

"I usually hate these things," I hear from the guy behind me. When I look over my shoulder, he gives me a half-smile—half-friendly, half-creepy. "But they don't usually have attractive women either."

I roll my eyes while turning my back on him and his cheesy pick-up line.

"I'm sorry. That was bad. I know," he says with a weird nasally laugh.

His breath hits my neck and I jerk back. "Do you mind? Ever hear of personal space?"

"Sorry. You're just really pretty." He shrugs as if that makes everything better. "Your beauty is making me stupid."

"You think?" *Big mistake.*

He actually takes my sarcastic comment as a conversation opener. "Yes, I do. But I can't be the first to be dumbfounded by your beauty."

Standing on my tiptoes to see how many more people are in front of me, I exhale, disappointed by the long line. One person in line would have been too many at this point. "Excuse me," I say and slip out of line. I find the table with my name tag on it, set my purse down, and take off my jacket. This hotel ballroom is crowded and too warm.

Saved by a friendly face, I see Cara, a marketing strategist I know from L.A. Weaving between the tables, I sit down in a chair next to her. With her eyes focused on the paperwork in front of her, I ask, "Working during the party?"

She looks up, smiling when she sees me. Opening her arms, she leans in and hugs me. "Holli, it's so good to see you."

I went with a different company than hers for a campaign a while back and glad she's not holding it against me. "Good to see you again."

"Congratulations on your success. Well deserved."

"I'm not sure if a smartass lime deserves the success it's gotten, but I'll take it."

She taps my leg. "You deserve it. It's funny and quite catchy. Just take the accolades."

"Thanks."

Looking over my shoulder, she leans in and whispers, "I'm skipping out of here early, but I'm meeting a few people for dinner tomorrow. If you're still in Vegas, you should join us."

"I'd love that. Thanks."

She stands up and grabs the papers in front of her. "Fantastic. I'll text you the details tomorrow. I'm so glad we ran into each other."

"Me too. See you tomorrow."

I'm left sitting alone. When I look around the room, like Cara, I'm thinking that skipping out early might be the way to go. If I do, I know Tracy will kick my ass, so I decide to suffer and give this party one last chance. But I definitely need a drink and the line for the bar in here is still way too long.

I head for the doors to buy a drink in one of the many hotel bars—any bar without a line. Guy from the bar line jumps in front of me as I try to exit, startling me. "Hey, hey, hey. You're not leaving already, are you?"

Since my glare and earlier hints didn't work, I reply, "I'll be back, no need to worry yourself."

AVAILABLE BOOKS BY NEW YORK TIMES BESTSELLING AUTHOR

S.L. SCOTT

Talk to Me Series

Sweet Talk

Dirty Talk

Hard to Resist Series

The Resistance

The Reckoning

The Redemption

Welcome to Paradise Series

Good Vibrations

Good Intentions

Good Sensations

Happy Endings

Welcome to Paradise Series Set

From the Inside Out Series

Scorned

Jealousy

Dylan

Austin

From the Inside Out Compilation

Stand Alone Books

Until I Met You

Naturally, Charlie

A Prior Engagement

Lost in Translation

Sleeping with Mr. Sexy

Morning Glory

To keep up to date with her writing and more,
her website is www.slscottauthor.com or to receive her newsletter
with all of her publishing adventures and giveaways, sign up for
her newsletter: http://bit.ly/1pF049r

Join S.L.'s Facebook group here: http://bit.ly/2bq2Tfa

S.L. SCOTT

New York Times and *USA Today* Bestselling Author, S. L. Scott, was always interested in the arts. She grew up painting, writing poetry and short stories, and wiling her days away lost in a good book and the movies.

With a degree in Journalism, she continued her love of the written word by reading American authors like Salinger and Fitzgerald. She was intrigued by their flawed characters living in picture perfect worlds, but could still debate that the worlds those characters lived in were actually the flawed ones. This dynamic of leaving the reader invested in the words, inspired Scott to start writing journeys with emotion while injecting an underlying passion into her own stories.

Living in the capital of Texas with her family, Scott loves traveling and avocados, beaches, and cooking with her kids. She's obsessed with epic romances and loves a good plot twist. She dreams of seeing one of her own books made into a movie one day as well as returning to Europe. Her favorite color is blue, but she likens it more toward the sky than the emotion. Her home is filled with the welcoming symbol of the pineapple and finds surfing a challenge though she likes to think she's a pro.

To keep up to date with her writing and more, her website is www.slscottauthor.com or to receive her newsletter with all of her publishing adventures and giveaways, sign up for her newsletter: http://bit.ly/1pF049r